CW00862937

A special thanks to Charly.
My friend, editor, manager, graphic designer, top hype woman, rant
buddy, and top book recommender.

Thanks to you, my TBR is huge,
and this book is glowing.
Thank you so much.

UntilMyLast Breath

THE DEMONIC CONVERGENCE

BOOK 1

SUE ALLERTON

Second Edition

Edited by: Charlotte Brassington
@charlybooks (tiktok)
Cover art by: Sue Allerton

Layout by: Charlotte Brassington & Sue Allerton

For my mum, who gave me the confidence to keep going

NIAH

1

His plea to surrender fell on deaf ears.

The boy flew backwards, landing in a pitiful heap. She didn't bother hiding the wicked smirk that curled her lips as she straightened her spine.

Her training was paying off.

The boy looked up at her, flustered and panting; if he expected help getting to his feet, he would be sorely disappointed. Instead, she squared her shoulders, and stalked for the benches.

"The only time I see you smile is when you've knocked someone on their arse," Nolan muttered when he came to stand at her side. Niah shrugged, unwrapping the black training bandages from around her hands, not that she saw the point in them. There was something oddly satisfying about split knuckles after a day of hard training.

Her eyes slid to the boy, now on his feet talking with some boys in the group. They glanced at her, not bothering to hide their contempt, those looks had infuriated her to no end years ago, and she'd beaten them black and blue for it. But now? They weren't worth her time or effort.

Snorting, Niah turned away, slumping down on the bench to swill water around her mouth while Nolan paced in front of her, which he did when he was annoyed at her.

He was still the head trainer at the academy, as he was when she arrived eight years ago. She was a child then; compared to him, she still was. Yet, he looked barely older than twenty-five. It was a Shadow perk.

He stopped pacing and turned to her, his brow furrowed, lips set in a grimace. He said nothing. There was no need, she could already feel the annoyance rolling off of him in waves.

Niah clicked her tongue, "Are you going to lecture me?"

Jumping to her feet, she snatched up her bag. Nolan's piercing eyes bore into her; there was a time when that glare sent a shiver crawling up her spine. Not anymore. She no longer cared about the lectures, the punishments, the whispers in the corridors. It was beneath her.

When he said nothing, she huffed a sigh and turned to leave, stopping when he caught at her arm. Her skin prickled as she fought the urge to shove him away.

"Stop looking at everyone as if you want to kill them. We're here to train, not for you to beat everyone black and blue," Nolan muttered. He slowly released his grip and took a step back, ignoring the icy glare she gave him.

Her head tilted to the side, "It's not my fault they can't keep up." Niah flicked her eyes to the group of boys. They quickly averted their eyes when they met her gaze. They were all the same.

He let out an exasperated breath, "No, you were deliberately trying to hurt him. I know the difference. Anyway, where are you going? The session isn't over."

"Fine," she sighed, "who do you want me to beat up this time?" her bag thudded to the ground at her feet.

"You're no better than them." Nolan glowered, his lip curling in a snarl.

Niah scoffed, "I beg to differ."

For a moment, they stared off against each other. Nolan broke first, running a hand through his golden hair as he looked over at the trainees. Niah knelt to retrieve her bandages from her bag, but Nolan took them from her with a scowl. For once, she didn't argue.

"You four, in the ring." he barked. Niah watched the boys glancing at one another, "Today!" the boys hurried into the ring, ducking under the rubber barrier. Nolan met her gaze, daring her to say something in defiance. Instead, she merely offered him a sweet smile as she stalked into the ring.

She took up her position at the centre of the ring and flashed Nolan a smirk as the boys took their positions around her. Beads of sweat glistened against their brows as they checked their positions and tried to stop their hands from trembling.

The smirk faded from her lips.

With a deep, controlled breath, Niah closed her eyes. Barefooted, she flexed her toes, feeling the rough canvas beneath her feet, grounding herself. She ignored the murmurs surrounding the ring where the other students had gathered to watch, and focused on the boys around her—listening for the rise and fall of their ragged breaths.

Everything slowed.

Her heart steadied, her breathing levelled out as her mind quietened.

There was a slight tear in the air as one of the boys lunged for her. The thud of a step being taken vibrated through the mat, she ducked, feeling the air churn above her head where the boys' arm tore through it, missing her by inches. She delivered a swift punch to the ribs that had him staggering back a step, grunting his frustration.

Still with her eyes closed, Niah straightened her spine, flexing her fingers at her sides as she anticipated the next attack.

Adrenaline pulsed through her veins.

Two of them attacked at once. The heat of their bodies, the sounds of their steps and breath, the way the air tore as they moved told her everything she needed to know. She twirled away on the balls of her feet, throwing her hand out to grab one of their wrists.

Her eyes flashed open. The boy she had grabbed cursed through gritted teeth. With minimal effort, Niah flipped him over her shoulder. The boy cried out, but she didn't care. The boys had lost the match before it had even started.

The boys attacked repeatedly, and Niah let the match drag on, if only to prove a point. She didn't attack or do any fancy deflections; she only dodged. Twirling around them like a dance, enjoying the frustration rippling off of them.

The boys did exactly as she knew they would.

They got angry.

Anger made people desperate, that was Nolan's first lesson all those years ago. Because she knew it would rile them up further, she smirked.

The four boys came to a silent agreement and attacked as a single unit, coming at her from all sides. Niah ducked and let their momentum do the rest. At least one of them punched another.

After a few more minutes of toying with them, she decided she'd made her point. After a nose bent beneath her fist, a kick to a sternum, a punch to the groin, all boys were on their backs.

Niah stood over them, her lip curling in disgust as they writhed around on the mat.

One of them scrambled to his feet. Niah was impressed, he was gripping his stomach in pain, but his glare wasn't half bad. "Bitch!"

She cocked her head to one side, "Still not managed to come up with something more creative?"

The boys' cheeks flushed, his chest heaving with the effort of standing after the blow she'd delivered to his lower stomach. To his credit, he didn't shrink under her glare; until she took a step forward.

Niah was used to the fear in the other students' eyes. She was accustomed to the contempt and disgust in the way they sneered and shrank away from her. She could feel the eyes of all of them around her, burning into her. Whispers surrounded the ring.

She wasn't there to make friends.

Nolan stepped forward, arms folded across his chest, but there was a glimmer of pride lurking in the depths of his eyes. He dipped his chin as she turned away, ducking under the barrier of the ring. The crowd parted for her as if she were a feral beast.

The glorious adrenaline that had pulsed through her body only moments ago, quickly turned to ice in her veins. Her hands curled into fists at her sides. She barely registered the ache in her bruised knuckles as she scooped up her bag, and left the room without a glance back.

The steaming water did little to thaw the ice that had seeped deep in her bones. It was always the same. Those same looks found her no matter where she was in the academy. The whispers followed her through the corridors and chased her to her tiny room.

It was always the same.

She hoped, years ago, that one day the glares and murmurs would stop. That people would stop flinching away. She'd been a child then, desperate for affection. Her fingers drifted to the locket around her throat, warm from the water. Her hand curled around the necklace, squeezing until her bruised knuckles barked in protest, a heavy hollowness settled in her chest.

Niah shoved the thought away, buried the savage ache in her chest, and busied herself with scrubbing the grime from her skin.

She towel-dried her long, onyx hair and dressed in dark jeans with a long-sleeved t-shirt with her usual sturdy boots that laced up the front of her shins. Unable to stand being in her tiny box room any longer, she slung her bag over her shoulder and headed for the library, locking the door behind her.

The academy was huge. It was a remodelled castle situated at the top of a cliff overlooking the English coast. Yet, despite the sheer size of it, the building always felt too claustrophobic. The walls were dark red, decorated with paintings and tapestries, the windows covered with heavy drapes that blocked out the light when they were drawn.

The academy was a training facility for halflings: demon and human hybrids. Niah was born from a long line of decorated Shadow soldiers, she had been chosen to enrol when she was barely old enough to walk.

Shadows, despite being part demon themselves, were chosen to defend the human world from pure demons. It was their duty, they were proud to do it, even if Niah had a different motivation for wanting to be a Shadow.

Centuries ago, Nephilim – human and angel hybrids – and halflings battled each other for their masters. Both sides endured severe casualties when the war ended. Still, the Nephilim won over the halflings and offered them a place in their army to eradicate the demon infestation from the world. Since then, halflings became Shadows soldiers, and the Nephilim took leadership. Still, their numbers began to dwindle due to complications during birth as well as difficulties conceiving in the first place, whereas halflings had no such troubles.

As a result, Nephilim became almost extinct. Only a few remained.

With the number of halflings increasing, academies were established to train them. Children born from elite Shadow soldiers were chosen to attend, but only a handful showed enough promise to be picked for the tests. With even fewer who made it into the ranks of the Shadows.

Niah had been training since she was old enough to walk. Her parents taught her how to wield a blade and separate her emotions from her duty. They taught her what it meant to be a Shadow, as well as the honour that came with it.

She remembered her first visit to the academy. She'd been so excited, not that she let it show. She remembered the proud smile on her father's face when the headmistress had examined her and said she was a prime candidate, that she would go far. She remembered the way her mother had gripped her shoulder the way she did whenever she wanted Niah to know she had done something well.

Everything seemed so simple then.

But as all good things did, those simple, blissful years came to an end.

In a few short weeks, Niah would turn eighteen, and she would be tested to see whether she would be taken further in her training. Then, she would be plunged into a whole new world, after receiving her mark, a world full of violence and chaos.

Her heart thrummed at the thought.

Her hand went to the locket around her throat. The silver was intricately detailed, with a single blue topaz embedded in the front, inside was a picture of her parents.

The nightmares of that night still haunted her. There were still no answers as to why her parents were murdered or who wanted them dead. The headmistress had suggested that maybe it was a random attack with no real meaning, but Niah would never forget the hatred that rolled off of the attackers; she could practically taste it.

A random attack wouldn't have warranted the sheer *hatred* those men possessed.

There was no doubt in Niah's mind that someone sent them for a reason. *That* was why she wanted to become a Shadow. She didn't care about protecting the human race, or duty, or honour. Her only goal was finding the truth.

The truth of her parent's murder.

Finding out why her parents were killed, and whether they had intended for her to die too.

When she had the truth, when she had the person who had ordered her parents death, she would feel their life slip away between her fingers.

She would relish in every second of it.

The headmistress always told her she was safe. That no one would find her at the academy, even if they did, they wouldn't get past the patrols. That should have brought her *some* comfort, but her parents had taught her not to let her guard down. So she never did.

During those initial weeks at the academy, Niah barely slept. The smallest of noises had her clutching her dagger and her heart racing. Every creak of a floorboard or squeak of a door sent her hiding under her bed. She was only small, and she'd already learnt how little use she was in a fight.

Once she was brave enough to step out of her room, and once she had asked the headmistress all the questions she could, Niah turned to books. She didn't expect to find answers in them, but she hoped there might be a glimmer of an explanation.

There never was. But it was a distraction, if she went to sleep, she knew she would have those nightmares. So, she spent her nights surrounded by decade's worth of knowledge. She immersed herself in the history and culture of the various species. She learnt about fey, vampires, and werewolves; it reminded her of her parents' stories when she was going to sleep.

Stories she would never hear again.

She pushed the library doors open, the groaning of the heavy wooden doors alerting the woman behind the desk of her presence. The woman lounged with her feet propped up on the desk, she had piercing blue eyes, with hair the exact shade cut in a short pixie style, showing off the delicate points of her ears, a clear sign she was one of the fey. The delicate creature sighed and closed the book she had been reading.

Niah held her card out, but the woman waved her away.

"How long are you going to torture yourself for?"

The woman had been there since Niah arrived, always in the same spot. Her name was Mela; Niah had asked her where certain books were located when she first arrived. The library was massive, with multiple levels, it was all too easy to get lost in there.

"As long as I see fit," Niah huffed.

Mela sighed and pressed her lips together. Niah looked away, unable to stomach the sympathy in the fey's eyes, and stalked toward the furthest staircase to climb to the top floor.

The maze that was the library had books stacked to the ceiling. Many of them weren't labelled, but some had signs indicating what kind of books were in a row.

No one ever seemed to go to the top of the library; very few people came in at all. The top floor was covered with a thin layer of dust, long forgotten, and left to rot. Niah brushed off the dust and found those particular books were works of fiction. The day she found them was the first time Niah had smiled since before the attack.

She could have stayed in her room, she supposed, but the bustle of other students traipsing up and down all day grated on her. The dorms constantly thrummed with activity. But the top floor of the library, was a pocket of tranquillity.

Ever since that night, there was a lingering dread in the pit of her stomach, but surrounded by nothing but the written word, it was the one place in the entire building she felt safe.

When she wanted to devour something more factual, to learn about the different species and cultures, Niah soon found that many of the books were copies of one another with different covers. She couldn't fathom why, and had asked Mela about it once, but the woman only shrugged, stating that the books had been there long before she had.

What was the point?

Over the years, questions started piling up. The longer they went unanswered, the more the headmistress told her to be patient; her frustration and hunger for revenge grew more intense. Some nights, the anger burned so bright that not even her favourite book could calm her.

It was those nights, when she couldn't settle, that she would seek out Nolan. He was hesitant to train her so soon after her parent's death, but when he realised she would train whether he helped her or not, he decided it was better to make sure she did it the right way rather than pick up any bad habits.

Nolan soon became the person she ran to whenever she got too angry, too impatient with being too small to do anything useful. He told her to use the time to get stronger, so that one day, when she finally found her parent's killer, she would be ready. He told her he was proud of her, he would ruffle her hair when she'd done something good, and on the rare occasion they were allowed cake, he would sneak her an extra helping.

He pushed her, just like Niah had asked him to, she became the best through hard work and determination. For that reason, it infuriated her that he suddenly expected her to go easy on the other students. It wasn't her fault they couldn't beat her, and she refused to apologise for it.

Niah trailed her fingers along the shelf, making her way to the little nest she had made for herself. Blankets and pillows on the floor against the wall, snacks hidden in the shelves for when she didn't feel like eating in the bustling canteen.

It was her one place of safety and peace.

Just as she got comfortable, nestled between two stacks on the floor, her sensor began to buzz. She groaned and reached into her bag to fish out the small black object with a screen; the headmistress's seal flashed.

Knowing she couldn't keep the headmistress waiting, Niah hauled herself to her feet, snatching up her bag in the process, and stalked from the library.

From her little pocket of salvation.

The headmistress's office lay at the most northern point of the academy, overlooking the ocean. It was close to sunset, oranges, and golds dancing across the skies, reflected on the water stretching far into the horizon.

Sometimes, Niah would sneak onto the roof through the skylight in the library, just to gaze at the ocean.

The door was already open when she arrived, as it usually was. Niah closed the door behind her and stood in the small room, barely able to hear the clock's ticking over the pounding of her heart.

Behind the large oak desk, were two glass doors that led out onto a small balcony with a thick stone railing wrapping around it. To the left of the room was a large fireplace made of white marble, one side had an angel carved into it, the other side a demon. A large painting of the academy hung above the mantel.

Headmistress Karliah Springtower stood on the balcony, her hands clasped delicately behind her back as she gazed out over the horizon. She didn't turn when she heard Niah enter. She never did.

"Come here," the headmistress said in a low voice.

Niah wiped her clammy hands against her thighs and walked to stand beside the headmistress on the balcony. The gentle breeze carried salt on it, and Niah inhaled deeply, her eyes fluttering closed as she let the calming nature of the ocean soothe the knot in her stomach.

Something about the ocean called to her. It was as mysterious as it was terrifyingly beautiful. Who knew what lurked in the darkest depths.

Niah tore her eyes away, letting them fall on the headmistress. She had a stern face, all angles with narrow cheeks. Thin lips pressed into a hard line and narrow blue eyes. Her pale blonde hair was almost gold in the warm glow of the setting sun, pulled back harshly from her face, twisted into a neat bun at the back of her head. She wore a slate grey pantsuit tailored to fit her slight frame perfectly.

Despite the way she dressed, the headmistress, like Nolan, looked no older than her mid-twenties. The pair of them were two of the last remaining Nephilim left in the world, as well as siblings.

Halflings and Nephilim aged, albeit slower than humans, but they were still mortal. So, the Shadows created a mark to stop the aging of their soldiers as well as the Nephilim leaders.

Niah questioned why the headmistress *and* the head trainer were Nephilim when they were so endangered and said to be the leaders of the Shadow organisation. Still, she could never form the words to ask the headmistress, or Nolan.

"What do you think this is about?" the headmistress asked. Still, she did not look at Niah.

Niah took a steadying breath, "Would it have anything to do with the four boys I put in the infirmary?"

"No. But we will come back to that," Karliah said softly, "this is about your parents."

At that, Niah paused. Her heart started hammering, an icy chill crawling up her spine as her mouth fell open. She quickly closed it and turned back to the horizon, fighting the urge to wipe her hands down her jeans.

"I'm curious why you haven't come to ask me any more questions since the night you arrived." At last, she turned that glacial gaze on Niah. The gaze that was forever calculating, analysing, as if she could see the very thoughts swimming around in Niah's head.

She assumed Karliah knew nothing of why her parents were killed. She certainly never gave any answers to suggest otherwise. Karliah stared at her with those analysing eyes. A chill slithered up her spine.

"Do you know something?" Niah asked, masking her features into indifference. She'd learned long ago that to show her emotions was to show weakness. She never forgot those lessons, and around Karliah, she wouldn't let her mask falter.

Karliah squared her shoulders, "I know many things."

"Will you tell me?"

Her heart filled with a cloud of hope she hadn't felt in a long time.

"When you arrived here and told me your parents were murdered. I went to your house, but your parent's bodies weren't there. The bodies of the murderers were, but not your parents," Karliah's eyes narrowed, taking in every inch of Niah's face.

Her mind fell silent. She wasn't sure she was even breathing. All thoughts of keeping her emotions off her face were forgotten.

"What does that mean?" Her voice came out as a strangled whisper. She didn't care.

There was no reason why her parent's bodies wouldn't have been there. She'd *seen* them die, had felt her mother's body go limp beneath her touch. But then again, she was only young, and hadn't yet known how to take a pulse.

"It means either someone collected them, or they simply got up and walked out," Karliah's eyes glinted with the final rays of sunlight.

Niah stared at her blankly. *Got up and walked out.*

"You think they're alive?"

Karliah's lips quirked up on one side, her eyes dancing with something Niah couldn't read, "I don't know, I'm simply telling you what I discovered at the house. It seems more likely that their bodies were collected by someone else. Though for what purpose, I don't know."

Niah turned to the ocean, away from those calculating eyes. Had she been wrong? No, she had *seen* them both die. They were both stabbed in the chest. There was no way either of them could have survived it. Yet, she hoped with all her heart that somehow, they were alive. It didn't matter if they were held prisoner somewhere; she would find a way to get them out.

Her ears were ringing. So loud that she barely heard the sound of the office door opening and closing, accompanied by footsteps striding towards them.

"Niah, about earlier," Nolan began.

Niah didn't hear the rest of what he said. Instead, all sounds blurred together as if she heard it all underwater.

Her eyes slid to the headmistress. Karliah was looking at Nolan, a wicked grin across her lips. There was nothing friendly or warm in that smile. It was not a thing of beauty, but cruelty and coldness.

"Niah!" Nolan snapped her out of her reverie.

"What?" she snapped, her voice edged as sharp as a blade as she turned to him. He blinked, but quickly smoothed his features. His blue eyes, the same shade as Karliah's, hardened as he took her in.

"I was talking about earlier, in training."

"Oh, and?" she shrugged. Over the years, Niah had grown comfortable enough with Nolan that she often forgot he was her superior.

"You did well. Despite putting four of my best in the infirmary, I'm proud of you," he said with a small smile.

"They can't be your best."

"Don't get cocky. You still have a long way to go. Remember, the tests start next week," If she passed, she would receive her Shadow mark and would go to another facility where she would continue her training. Then, she would have access to better resources that might finally give her answers.

Niah nodded and turned to the woman, "Is that all, headmistress?" Karliah tilted her chin up as if she were examining a prized beast; Niah kept her eyes low, not looking the headmistress in the eye, but saw her turn away to the ocean.

"Yes, thank you. Make sure you get something to eat." Niah strode for the door, all the while feeling the burning gazes of the siblings on her back.

NIAH

2

Something wasn't right, it didn't make any sense.

If Karliah had been back to the house *eight* years ago, why hadn't she said anything sooner? A shiver rolled up Niah's spine at the dark thought, whilst her mind raced at the idea.

None of it made sense.

The way Karliah's eyes gleamed whilst she smirked at Nolan. It spoke to something deep inside her, something that whispered to her in the dead of night. A warning, perhaps?

It wasn't the first time she'd felt such a cold indifference from the headmistress.

She didn't have a logical explanation for it, but whenever she thought that perhaps the headmistress may have been involved, or at least knew why it happened, a sharp pain would radiate from her temple. As if it were a warning to stay away from those particular thoughts.

It only made her more curious.

On nights when sleep refused to claim her, Niah would lay in bed and gaze up at the ceiling, wondering whether someone would come for be Nolan. But that thought caused her throat to tighten.

If either of them were involved, it would make sense that they were in on it together. Even if Niah didn't want to believe it. She didn't want to believe it at all, and other than a gut feeling, she had no reason to believe the Springtower siblings had anything to do with her parents' death. And yet, there was no escaping that feeling of impending doom looming over her.

When she arrived eight years ago, Karliah had told Niah that she was safe more times than she cared to count. Her parents would say the same thing. Every night before she went to sleep, they would tell her she was safe, that they were watching over her.

But she wasn't safe.

Her fingers brushed the locket hanging around her neck. How long had she wished they were alive? There was still no certainty that they were; Karliah had only told her their bodies weren't at the house.

Once again, she was left with no answers, only more questions, with a lingering ember of hope in her chest.

The next few days dragged by unbearably slowly. Niah barely heard what her professors said during class, she'd lost the urge to fight in the training sessions.

She couldn't shake the fog that was clouding her mind.

Sleep didn't claim her for more than an hour or two at most. When they released her, she woke clutching at the dagger, soaked in sweat, struggling to breathe.

Her appetite hadn't returned, the food tasted like ash in her mouth, she couldn't bear to be around the hateful glares and whispers of the canteen.

Not even her favourite books could bring her comfort. Her mind was too loud, full of screaming theories that prevented her from concentrating on anything else.

"Niah," the gentle voice cut through the jumble of thoughts, and she jumped, tearing her eyes away from the ocean outside the window.

Talon stood over her desk, the history teacher. He looked no older than anyone else, perhaps even slightly younger. His ashen hair was swept back, the same shade as the beard that lined his jaw. Yet, the first thing Niah had noticed when she first met him, was the silver that ringed his brown eyes.

The ring that mirrored her own. Except where his iris was brown, hers were as black as night.

They were the only two in the whole academy with that silver ring. For that reason, she found herself drawn to him and found that she wanted to know more. Why did he have that silver ring that matched her own? Why just them?

His eyes watched her now, a flicker of concern lighting them, "You look tired."

It took a moment for her to realise the room was empty. She couldn't remember the last time she had been so lost in a daze that she hadn't known what was going on around her.

Niah gathered up her books and rose to her feet, "I'm fine."

"Hm," Talon hummed, pocketing his hands, "Is everything okay?"

No.

"Sure." She answered through her teeth, turning for the door. Talon stepped into her path, and she let the full force of her glare fall on him. "Move."

"You can tell me what's going on; you don't have to suffer alone."

Niah tilted her chin up, "When I want your opinion, I'll ask for it."

She stalked through the corridors, keeping her eyes forward; the students jumped out of her way. Shrinking away from her as the bitter tang of fear filled the stuffy halls. No one spoke a word until they thought she was out of earshot, but her hearing was far better than theirs, she always heard every word.

During the first few months after arriving at the academy, those whispers had been questions like "Why is she here?" "Why would they let her come here?" "She's a monster. A freak." Niah hadn't understood why, and still didn't.

The murmurs grew around her. Sometimes, it was all she could hear. They were deafening.

Niah closed herself in her room, gritting her teeth together as she focused on the roughness of the door where she pressed her forehead against it, taking deep breaths to leash her rising temper.

Since her parents' death, she had been consumed with burning rage. It only grew more insistent with each passing day, and sometimes, she didn't bother hiding it.

One day, it grew so unbearably hot, that she'd snapped during training. She was sparring with a boy, and he said something under his breath. Niah couldn't remember what he had said, but whatever it was, snapped the leash of control.

She couldn't remember who stopped them, nor whether she had to be dragged away from him. The only thing she could remember, was the intoxicating high that took over her body, the sting of her split knuckles, and the warmth of the blood that coated her skin.

The boy never returned.

Nolan had assured her he was alive, but after the *incident,* he would not return. Karliah was furious, and Niah was isolated for two weeks. When she returned, the whispers and fear remained, amplified even, but everyone avoided her—scared that she might snap again.

Niah decided that she didn't want to experience that numbing, all-consuming rage again, even if the whispers continued to slowly pick away at her control.

Nolan had told her not to concern herself with the fears of others. He told her she was better than them, different, and that's why they were scared of her. People fear what they don't understand. He never explained what he meant.

Needing to burn off her frustrations to clear her head, she changed quickly and headed to the gym.

It was dark and empty when she arrived. Exactly how she liked it. Her footsteps echoed through the room. The sparring ring was in the centre of the room, treadmills and various machinery methodically set up, running along the back wall was a considerable weights selection.

She glanced down at her hands and flexed her fingers, the bruises from the other day had already healed. Niah read that human's take days, even weeks to months, to recover from some injuries. It had never taken her more than a day to heal from even her worst injury when she received a savage punch that broke her nose. It bent at an angle and healed with the tip facing to the left with a bump in the bridge, the on-site healer had to re-break it to put it back into place.

Her usual routine of wrapping her hands and stretching soothed the chill that had set deep in her bones. In recent weeks, training had become somewhat therapeutic. Pummelling the punching bags took the edge off of her growing frustrations and, not that she would admit it, fear.

For years she wondered whether the murderers would find her. Almost prayed that they would try so that she could finally kill them herself. In those early years, the thought of killing someone seemed impossible. How did one muster the courage to take a life? But, as the years passed, that question became mute. She'd harnessed her anger and grief, honing her body into a weapon; the thought of killing wasn't quite so daunting anymore. It still made her heart race, but in a very different way.

After years of questions left unanswered, Niah had begun to grow restless. Impatient for a day that may or may not come. She only relaxed when surrounded by books in that little pocket of tranquillity at the top of the library.

Many nights, she didn't bother going back to her room. The nightmares didn't reach her quite so easily there—a slight reprieve after waking in cold sweats and retching for years on end.

After long days of poring through useless books, she found solace in fiction. Namely, fantasy written by humans. Their imagination and creativity were whimsical. The characters held a special place in her heart. Since arriving at the academy, no one had made an effort to befriend her, nor had she.

Growing attachments meant the difference between winning and losing. Attachments were a weakness, and caring made her vulnerable. So, she found friendship in the pages of books. Imagined going on all those adventures with them, living in other worlds.

A world in which she could be someone else.

An escape.

Shaking her head, Niah snorted at the thought. It was silly to dream, to imagine a different life. Though sometimes, she found herself wondering, if only for a break from the constant darkness brewing in the back of her mind, what life might be like, had that fateful night not happened.

Sometimes she thought she was getting used to it or learning to live with it. Then she would wake up drenched in sweat with her parents' death tattooed on her eyelids. It was those times, when she felt ready to crawl out of her skin, that she found comfort in split knuckles and a dead punching bag.

A loud bang echoed through the room as the door swung open, hitting the wall. Niah whirled to find a man striding toward her.

He had unruly, dark brown hair that glowed copper in the light, and carried himself with lazy confidence.

He was tall, at least a head taller than Niah. With broad shoulders and arms roped with lean muscle. He had a sharp jaw with a slight bump in the bridge of his otherwise perfect nose. She noticed his eyes, grey, with a shimmering silver ring surrounding the iris, twin to her own.

Seeing it made the breath hitch in her throat.

The stranger stopped a few feet away, his hands in his pockets, and looked her up and down. She glowered through her lashes, letting a warning growl slip through her teeth. No one had ever dared look at her like that.

The man cocked a brow, a coy smirk playing at one corner of his mouth as he tilted his head to the side. As if to annoy her, he said nothing.

"Can I help you?" Niah snapped.

His smirk only grew as he took a step forward. Her fingers inched toward the dagger hanging from her belt, those unusual eyes of his flicked to her hip, the amusement faded from them, and he raised his hands in surrender. Niah's hand gripped the handle of her blade. She would've remembered seeing someone like him around the academy.

"Easy," he muttered as if she were a startled horse.

He was a built guy, but all that muscle would make him slow, Niah was positive she'd have an advantage over him. It didn't look like there were any weapons on his person from where she stood, but that didn't mean they weren't there.

Niah's hand tightened around the dagger, "What do you want?" With him standing between her and the door, she'd need to fight her way out. Adrenaline surged through her veins as she shifted her feet into position.

"I was told I could find you here," he said, a wry smile tugging at the corners of his lips. He pocketed his hands once more, the picture of nonchalance.

Her voice dropped low in warning, "That doesn't answer my question."

"My name is Fin. You're Niah, right?" he offered with an easy smile. She said nothing. The man, Fin, observed her; he released a heavy breath and conceded a step, keeping his eyes on her face, searching for something.

"I'm a transfer from Australia. They sent me here to do my Shadow tests," he announced as if that explained everything. It did, however, explain his thick accent. But she'd never heard of transfers, not in all the time she'd been at the academy. Alarm bells were screaming now. Niah's heart thundered, her blood heating with the anticipation of a fight.

Something rustled in his pocket; he pulled out a piece of paper and held it out for her.

Niah's eyes narrowed, "Unfold it."

He sighed as he shook his head, that grin once again curving his lips whilst he unfolded the paper and held it out for her to read. Indeed, there was the academy logo which looked very much like an official document. She couldn't ignore the unease that had settled in the pit of her stomach. Niah thought it was time to leave.

"Well, Fin, as riveting as this conversation is, I better be going," she said, keeping her hand on her dagger as she stepped widely around him.

Fin raked a hand through his wild hair, "Sure, I'll see you around."

There was a promise in those words.

A promise she couldn't ignore.

Niah turned back to him, with one hand still around her dagger, she reached out with the other and grabbed a fistful of his shirt.

"Why are you here?" Niah demanded.

All humour vanished from his expression, he held his hands up, showing he wouldn't fight back, "I told you, I'm a transfer."

"Liar." The fabric of his shirt started to tear beneath her grip.

He cocked a brow, "Hm, you know, if you wanted to rip my clothes off, you could have just asked."

Niah shoved him away, not bothering to hide her disgust, and turned for the door, being sure to listen for any sound of movement behind her.

She ran through the darkened corridors toward Nolan's room but froze when the murmurs of hushed voices rippled down the hall. Niah pressed herself against the wall and peered around the corner, holding her dagger, now unsheathed, by her side.

Two people dressed in long, black coats with large hoods were striding up the corridor toward Karliah's office.

Her heart pounded in her ears.

Niah crept across the hall and turned another corner, jogging silently until she reached Nolan's room.

Strangers were inside the academy. Her mind was whirling. Had they finally come for her?

She knocked on the door, then again when Nolan didn't answer. Her breaths came fast and shallow, her palms growing slick as she knocked again. She tried the handle, but it was locked.

Niah focused on calming her erratic heart. People had come for her, just as she knew they would, she had trained for this very moment, she was ready. But in the cramped corridors, she was at a disadvantage.

If she went back to the gym, she would likely run into that cocky stranger, or the other two. It left her with only one option, get to an open space that she knew well and use it to her advantage.

With that in mind, she turned down the corridor. Niah needed to concentrate, if she didn't, she might end up dead.

Silence surrounded her, the only sound was the throb of her blood pulsing in her ears. Niah turned, raising her dagger at every slight creak.

The doors were locked at night, but there was a broken latch on one of the windows. She slipped through and let it fall shut behind her, then she was running.

Niah ran as fast as she could toward the edge of the cliff. She didn't bother trying to pick her way down the steep steps; instead, she jumped over the edge, and fell through the air.

A fifty-foot drop straight down. The ground rushed up to meet her, but she felt no fear. Niah rolled on landing as she had been shown, and sprang to her feet, panting and sweating.

Her nerve endings were tingling. Her lungs burned for air as she dropped to her knees in the cool, hard sand. The sun had set, replaced by the full moon. It shone brightly, cascading a pale glow over the world.

Niah sat on the beach for what must have been hours, holding her knees to her chest, listening to the waves lapping gently at the shore. No one came for her. Whether they were searching the academy grounds, or whether they had left, she didn't know. The longer she sat on the hard sand, the more she wondered whether they were attackers at all.

They were going to Karliah's office, maybe they were there to see her?

She sighed as she dragged a hand through her hair. For all her bravado and arrogance, the moment Niah laid eyes on those two figures dressed in black, she turned into that helpless little girl from all those years ago.

The girl that could do nothing to prevent her parents' death.

She'd been scared.

Something she had vowed never to be again. Niah had created many scenarios over the years, fantasied about what it would be like to fight back, to demand answers. The reality was somewhat different.

The wind turned bitter against her skin; tiny frozen needles pierced her face and arms. The uncomfortable feeling lasted only a few seconds as her body adjusted to the sudden temperature shift—a perk of being different.

Niah hauled herself from the sand and started back toward the academy, climbing the steep stairs up the side of the cliff.

She heard them before she saw them. Hushed voices with a sense of urgency, the glow of a dim yellow light shone above the stairs. Without a glance, she leapt to her right, catching hold of a slight ledge jutting out from the side of the cliff and hauled herself higher until she was crouched on top of it.

Niah climbed her way further into the shadow of the building looming above them. She willed her heart to calm so to hear what the strangers were saying. There were three sets of footsteps, three different voices. At first, she thought that maybe it was the two in coats, and the other one, Fin.

The top of their heads came into view as Niah pressed herself against the wall of rock. Two hoods, as she'd expected. The third, illuminated by the pale glow of the moon, had a head of golden hair.

Niah's stomach lurched.

"Just hurt her. Bad enough that she won't be able to take the tests," unmistakably Nolan's voice, though it was tired and strained.

"How do you expect us to do that? The training room is usually full," another voice protested, a female voice, one she didn't recognise.

"I never said it had to be in the training room," Nolan muttered, his voice turning cold and hard.

There was a pause before a strange male voice asked, "How much pain are we talking?"

"Enough to incapacitate her for a while. I must warn you; this won't be easy. She put four boys in the infirmary a few days ago; one of them still hasn't recovered," they were talking about Niah.

Niah swallowed through the thickness in her throat, barely able to breathe through the twisting of her gut.

"You'll need this. It will slow her healing," Nolan said, a pause where he must have handed something over. Taking deep breaths, Niah willed her heart to slow.

"That's why you called us," the female voice said with dark amusement, "we could kill her if you want, save you some trouble?" Niah couldn't see them clearly as they made their way down the steps. She could only see the top of Nolan's head and the torch he was holding. She ground her teeth, biting down on the growl rumbling through her chest, feeling the sting of her canines sliding free of her gums.

"No. She cannot be killed. Under any circumstances," he snapped. There was a moment where all she could hear was her heart pounding.

She wanted to rip his throat out for betraying her, but she needed to know why he was doing this.

"Who is this girl? Why are you asking this of us?" the woman asked, suddenly serious as she spoke in a low voice.

"I'm paying you to do a job. You needn't know more than who your target is and the level of harm to come to her," Nolan answered, venom seeping into his voice. They said nothing more, only continued down the steps to the beach.

Niah began climbing, slowly at first, then faster until she was almost sprinting up the side of the cliff, stopping only when she reached the top and stared at the large building that perched on the edge.

The building she had run to when she was a child. The people inside had taken her in, fed her, given her new clothes, books, weapons. They *trained* her. Why were they now trying to hurt her? They didn't want her to take the tests, possibly because they had something to do with her parents' murder, and knew that she would find out if she passed the tests.

Her breaths came fast and shallow, her hands clenching and relaxing at her sides. She retched, emptying her stomach.

Her parents told her she'd be safe at the academy. She may have never trusted Karliah, but Nolan had been there for her. He made everything a little more bearable, he never asked questions she didn't want to answer.

She ground her teeth together, looking up at the stars to fight the sting in her eyes as anger curled in her stomach.

The only thing Niah knew for sure, was that she needed to escape the academy.

NIAH

3

The halls were deathly silent.

After pulling herself together, Niah climbed back through the window. The two strangers speaking with Nolan may have left, but the third from the gym was unaccounted for.

Niah wished she didn't need to return to her rooms, but whilst creeping through the corridors, she concluded she needed a few belongings.

As she made her way through the halls, listening for a whisper of movement, she grasped at the hilt of her dagger, eyes darting wall to wall until she reached her rooms.

It was silent.

Eerily still, and almost unnatural.

She unlocked the door, swinging it open while she remained in the corridor, dagger raised.

Empty.

Stepping inside, Niah released an abated breath, but left the door open while she checked the bathroom. She only closed it when she was sure she was alone. Then, with a racing a heart, she grabbed a rucksack, hastily shoving clothes inside, and snatched up her lockpicking kit.

As she turned for the door, pausing briefly to listen for movement, a sharp *crunch* sounded outside the window.

Her heart stuttered.

Turning sharply towards the offending noise, Niah stared at the two cloaked figured blocking the moonlight. Shadows obscured their features, but Niah could just make out the devilish sneer that curved their lips.

She knew she wouldn't be able to fight them in close quarters. Fighting four boys in the gym was a walk in the park, they were weak and unmotivated. But these two? They were a mystery, paid mercenaries. As much as she hated to admit it, this was not the time to fight.

It was time to run.

So, she did just that.

The sound of shattering glass followed by the thundering of footsteps pushed her forward. They certainly weren't concerned with being discreet.

Niah didn't risk a glance back, but she could only hear one set of feet chasing her. The quickest route from her room to outside the academy was through the back door. Niah knew the door would be locked, but the broken window was just down the corridor.

It dawned on her that they had split up, which meant if she stopped running, she'd only have to fight one. But it still meant she'd be facing an opponent of unknown abilities.

Her canines snapped down as simmering anger and adrenaline slammed through her veins. She felt every breath in her lungs, the familiar leather grip of her dagger beneath her fingers, the wooden floorboards beneath her feet.

If she carried on running around, sooner or later, the other one would seize her. With her blood singing in her ears, she knew she was out of options.

Niah slammed her foot down and turned, thrusting her dagger forward into the open air. The attacker was right on her heels, and she should have caught them off guard, but instead, they stopped and went down on one knee.

The air tore apart, and Niah barely had a chance to duck before a vicious looking blade sailed by.

The second attacker had found her.

The first was already on their feet, advancing on her. Niah slashed up with her dagger and scrambled to her feet, sprinting down the corridor before they could grab her.

Why was no one waking up?

Why was no one coming to help her?

Niah pumped her arms and legs faster, feeling the burn in her lungs as she gasped for air, using the walls to propel herself around corners.

She was trapped.

Every door was locked, the broken window was in the other direction, even if she did reach it, the attackers were too close for her to be able to sneak out.

She hit the stairs running, taking them two at a time, knowing they were right on her heels. Niah hoped that the maze of corridors of the upper floor would put some distance between them.

As she sprinted down a corridor, a hand curled around her arm and yanked her through a door. Swinging her dagger in a savage arc, Niah was shoved into the wall. Struggling, she thrust her knee up, but it was blocked with a grunt.

"Will you stop?" a rough voice growled. Grey eyes fixed her in place. Then, beyond the door, footsteps thundered down the hall. Fin pressed a finger to his lips, and they both held their breath as enraged voices rippled through the corridors.

"Where the fuck did she go?" the female demanded.

"She must have taken the servant stairs. You go that way, I'll go this way." The male barked, followed by footsteps stalking in different directions.

For a moment, there was only the pounding of her heart, and the rasps of her breath. Her mind was whirring, it took her a second to realise Fin was still pressing her against the wall, standing close enough that their breath mixed between them.

She pushed him away.

"What are you doing here?" she hissed through her teeth.

Fin raised a brow, "I enjoy playing the hero."

"I didn't need your help."

One corner of his lips quirked up, "No, of course not. So you're just running for the exercise then?"

Niah paused, turning slightly to listen for any movement.

"Why are they after you?" his voice was suddenly serious, his eyes hard and cold. Like the first time Niah met him, there wasn't so much as a hint of hostility in his demeanour. But that didn't mean she was going to tell him a damned thing.

Rolling her eyes, Niah yanked the door open and stalked for one of the windows. Then, dropping to her knees, she fished for her lockpicking kit and jammed the lock open.

"Where are you going?" Fin questioned. Rising to full height while shrugging her rucksack onto her shoulders, she ignored him, hoisting herself onto the roof.

Her original plan of using the skylight to go to the library went out the window; Nolan would have definitely told her attackers where she would go.

Escaping the academy grounds wasn't an option either; the patrols in the surrounding forest would inevitably catch her and haul her back. She turned to the ocean, contemplating whether to swim for it, but she'd have to swim miles, so that wasn't an option.

Her hands curled into fists at her sides. She was trapped. Nowhere to run, surrounded by people that wanted to harm her, the only one who didn't, was a complete stranger.

Niah slumped on the roof tiles and let her head fall into her hands.

Nolan and Karliah had betrayed her.

A bubble of panic rippled through her.

Her throat tightened, but she choked it down, needing to focus. The attackers were going to Karliah's office when she saw them earlier, maybe there was something in the headmistress's office that could tell her who they were.

Niah rose to her feet, the bitter wind whipping around her as she made her way across the roof until she stood over the balcony of the headmistress's office. There was no light emanating from within, and though it was difficult to hear over the howling wind, she couldn't hear anyone inside.

Taking a steadying breath, Niah lowered herself onto the edge of the stone railing and peered into the office from the corner of the glass door. It was empty. She tried the door, found it was unlocked, and slipped inside.

Niah began searching the large desk. Papers were scattered over the surface, but they all appeared to be ordinary administration documents one would expect a woman in Karliah's position to oversee.

Her head swam, her vision blurring slightly as a sudden wave of nausea churned her stomach. Niah crouched behind the desk, taking a moment to breathe deeply.

Shaking the blur from her vision, she rooted through the drawers in the desk, checking for hidden compartments, whilst listening for any movement in the corridor. There was nothing of importance. Nothing that gave any indication of who those people were.

Knowing she didn't have much time, Niah turned for the filing cabinet in the corner. Inside were folders with the names of every student, except they were all empty, including her own.

What was the point?

Why go to the trouble of having a folder for every student with nothing inside them?

The folder with her name on it trembled in her grasp. Why would her mother tell her to come here? The answer was a simple one, they couldn't have known. After all those years, had she finally found the people behind her parents' murder?

There had to be *something* in the office that would tell her who the

Springtower siblings were, or who they worked for.

Niah scanned the room one more time, focusing lastly on the pictures hanging on the walls, the final picture caused her to stop.

The large landscape hanging above the mantel. Niah hooked a finger underneath and tugged gently, hoping to find a secret safe or key, but instead, a picture fluttered out.

A crinkled, black, and white picture that showed the Springtower siblings and Niah's parents. Her brow scrunched as she gazed down at it. She knew they were familiar with each other, but her parents were halflings, and the Springtower siblings were Nephilim. It was unheard of for the two species to work together so closely, but the thing that stood out the most was that they all wore white lab coats, they appeared to be standing in a medical facility.

Her parents were soldiers; they'd never stepped foot in a lab. Except clearly, they had. It didn't look like they were working for the siblings either. They were all smiling, Nolan's arm around her father's shoulders, her mother and Karliah holding each other's hands between them.

They were friends.

Her hand flitted to the locket around her neck.

Who were her parents?

Niah gazed at the picture a moment longer, trying to make sense of it, when she caught a glimpse of a woman in the background. A woman with hair as black as ebony, tumbling down her back in waves. She was standing side-on, talking with someone else not in the picture; her mouth was set in a frown, her brow furrowed.

Something about her was familiar. Something that tugged at the back of her mind and set her teeth on edge.

Niah's head snapped up at the sound of footsteps in the corridor. She folded the picture into her pocket and moved swiftly to the glass doors. She gently closed them, and leapt over the stone railing, landing quietly on the grass beneath.

The balcony doors opened above as she pressed herself to the wall beneath the balcony, holding her breath so whoever it was wouldn't hear her panting.

"Where the hell is she?" Karliah's voice demanded.

"She saw them and ran. It seemed she was prepared for an attack." Nolan answered sheepishly.

Karliah clicked her tongue, "She ran? I thought you said that no matter what, she would fight? That she wouldn't back down because of her arrogance?"

Niah's lungs constricted, making it hard to breathe as she swallowed the lump in her throat.

"She is not a trapped beast." Nolan snapped, "She's calculating. She would have known that her chances of winning were slim."

"Then you can damn well find her," Karliah hissed. There was a pause, "Come on, we have to check-in." the doors closed above, and Niah released a sharp breath.

She sagged against the wall, tipping her head back against it as she closed her eyes. Niah shoved away the thoughts of her parents and the picture; she could deal with that later. She buried the siblings' betrayal. Locked away the hurt and confusion. Attachments were a weakness, she had made the mistake of trusting Nolan.

Her heart slowed to a steady beat, the embers igniting in her stomach. Her skin tingled, heat spread through her veins, and she handed herself over to the anger she had tried to rein in.

If she were going to escape the academy, Niah would have to fight her way out.

NIAH

4

awn broke on the horizon.

D
Dense clouds rolled overhead, casting shadows for Niah to hide in. She kept to the roof, and the remainder of the night was uneventful. Still, that didn't stop her from investigating every little noise whilst pacing the rooftop.

Fighting her way out of the academy with only a dagger would be challenging.

She listened for the tell-tale signs that the academy had risen for breakfast; Niah couldn't believe that no one had heard the commotion last night, and not a single student had helped her.

Without her rooms to go back to, and not knowing whether the attackers were roaming the halls, Niah opted for her little pocket of silence. More than anything, she needed to rest and work through a plan before jumping into anything.

Popping open the skylight, Niah shimmied into the library, landing with a light thud. It was empty, as she had hoped, the large doors still shut.

From the top of the library, she could see who came and went. Niah lowered herself into her nest, leaning against the bookcase so she could watch the doors.

Her eyes stung, her lids growing heavy with each passing second, she shook her head to clear the drowsiness. Her mind was sluggish, unable to create rational thoughts; she could feel it seeping into her body, making her limbs heavy.

She was so tired.

So very tired.

Niah hadn't yet processed what she'd found in Karliah's office, if she were honest, she didn't want to deal with it at all, her mind wasn't clear, it was all too hazy.

Her lids grew heavier.

It was so quiet.

She knew she had to stay awake. She rubbed at her eyes and adjusted her position into a less comfortable one, hoping that would be enough to chase the tiredness away. Her body turned heavy, her mind swimming as her vision blurred at the edges.

A foot fell in front of her.

Her eyes snapped open, and she reached for her dagger, slashing out without seeing who it was.

"Jesus! What the hell?" a familiar voice shrieked, stumbling whilst staring at Niah with wide, blue eyes.

Niah's heart raced, "Mela..."

The fey got to her feet, as did Niah, and the two stared at each other for a long moment.

"You broke in again?" the librarian groaned, placing her hands on her narrow hips. Niah said nothing, nor did she sheathe her blade. If Nolan was capable of betraying her, then who could she trust?

Mela's brow furrowed, "Niah?" the fey took a step forward, her hand reaching out as if she meant to grip Niah's arm.

She raised the dagger in answer, keeping her narrowed eyes on the delicate creature.

Mela frowned, letting her hand fall to her side, "They found you." Niah blinked at that.

"You *knew*?"

The fey sighed, "We expected it."

"We?" Niah spat through her teeth.

"Come, let me explain," Mela said. When she realised Niah wasn't following, she stopped and turned to her, "If I wanted to harm you, I would have done so already."

Before Niah could answer, a knock at the door echoed through the library. Mela didn't bother waiting for a reply, as she went down to answer it whilst Niah watched from the railing, ready to run if it was the hooded assailants.

On the other side of the door stood Talon. He slipped inside, and the door clicked, locking behind him. The two looked up at her, Talon with his hands in his pockets.

She could still escape through the skylight, she didn't have to stay, but there was a nagging sensation in her gut that told her to listen. Mela had information that Niah needed.

She descended the stairs, sliding the dagger into its scabbard, but kept a hand firmly around the hilt.

"We're not trying to hurt you," Talon said when she stopped a safe distance away.

"Forgive me if I don't believe you," Niah growled.

Talon pressed his lips together, but it was Mela who said, "We can get you out of here."

Niah's eyes narrowed, "You can't believe I would trust you_"

"No, I know you don't trust us, but what other options do you have?" Talon questioned.

He was right.

Niah had limited options, she couldn't put her trust in someone else. Niah barely knew Talon, he'd only been a teacher for a month; but she knew Mela.

She turned her eyes on the fey, "Who are you?"

"We're from another academy. When I heard about your parents' death, I transferred here to make sure you were safe, and now we know you're not." Mela explained.

"Why not take me away eight years ago?"

"You were a child who had just lost her parents. They told you to come here, that you would be safe. Would you have come with us then?"

Niah shrugged and flicked her eyes to Talon, "And you?"

"Mela asked me to come. She felt that something wasn't right, and with the tests coming up, we decided it was best I came to get you out." He said, his brown eyes searching her face.

It didn't matter what they said. Niah didn't believe either of them. Either way, she was out of options. Going with Talon, while still risk, was better than facing it alone. It didn't have to be for long, she only had to stay with him until she was far enough away from the academy that the patrols wouldn't find her.

"Fine. Is there a plan?"

"Meet me at the front gates at midnight." He said.

Niah frowned, "And if the attackers are around?"

"Then get to the roof, and we'll go from there." Talon shrugged as he turned for the door, "I should get back."

She wanted to ask more, demand more details, but he was already gone. Mela slid the bolt across and stalked behind her desk, for a door Niah didn't remember seeing before, "I need to give you something."

Niah didn't follow her. The fey woman emerged after a few minutes, carrying a large, leather-bound book. It was covered in a layer of dust that rose into the air as it was brushed off. There was no writing on the front or side, a faded brass lock kept it sealed. Mela set the book on the desk and reached around the back of her neck to unclasp a silver chain with a small brass key dangling from it.

There was a small symbol on the cover, faded, and barely visible. But it was there, a small spiral. Niah trailed her fingers over the mark, feeling a tug at the depths of her memory. There was a faint itch at the back of her neck, the trail of thought vanished as she reached back to scratch it.

"What is this?" Niah questioned.

"Answers."

Niah's heart stilled, "You've had this all this time, and you're only *now* giving it to me?"

"You needed to grow up first, you needed to understand what it is inside this book. It was always the plan to give it to you the day you left here." Mela explained, her voice quiet and gentle.

Niah sighed and tugged a hand through her hair; she only wanted to know the truth.

"Why am I being targeted?"

Mela sighed, "It's because of what you are."

"And what, exactly, am I?"

The fey pressed her lips into a firm line. "I'm afraid I can't say."

Niah gazed at her; could she trust her? The thought of Mela betraying her caused her chest to tighten and her mouth to turn dry. Mela had let Niah into the library when she was young and roamed the corridors after waking from a nightmare. To distract her, Mela gave her hot chamomile tea with a fantasy book she'd never read before.

The thoughts turned bittersweet as she reminded herself that Nolan had also been there for her.

"Is there *anything* you can tell me?" Niah asked, her voice little more than a whisper.

Mela shook her head, "Afraid not. Merida wants to tell you everything herself. I know you're sceptical; you have every right to be. Meet her and decide for yourself."

There was no point in arguing with her or demanding more information. If what she said was true, then she'd have answers soon enough. But that didn't mean she liked the idea of meeting another stranger.

She nodded, and Mela reached a hand out, but quickly lowered it when Niah stepped away, her hand resting on the hilt of her dagger.

"I have to open the library, but you can shut yourself away in the back room_"

"It's fine," she interrupted, "I'll just go to the top floor."

Mela only dipped her chin and made her way to the doors as Niah scooped up the book and necklace before making her way up the stairs to the top floor. She closed it away inside her bag, the temptation to open it now almost too strong. But Mela was right, it would be better to wait until she was somewhere safe.

Niah could feel the weight pressing down on her chest, making it difficult to breathe. Knowing she couldn't sleep, and being too jumpy to settle into a book, Niah packed a few of her favourites into the bag, along with some of the snacks she'd hidden in the shelves.

She took the picture from her pocket and gazed down at it for a minute. How did her parents come to work with Nolan and Karliah?

She fastened the chain holding the brass key around her neck with her locket. The thoughts in her mind were too jumbled to think clearly about anything she had learnt in the last few days. There were so many questions that she couldn't focus on a single one. Her temple ached, all she wanted to do was sleep.

To keep herself occupied, she organised the books around her into alphabetical order. It was a perfectly mind-numbing activity, but by the time she had finished one case, night had fallen.

Niah peered over the railing to see Mela heading for the door, the fey paused and turned to her, offering a light smile with a wave before slipping out, locking the doors behind her.

The silence that followed was near deafening.

She usually loved the library for that very reason, but with her thoughts screaming at her, she'd give anything for some outside noise. If only so it took her mind off of everything else.

Whether she was walking into another trap or not, surely going with Talon was better than staying in the academy? But there was a part of her that wanted to stay. To fight. To do everything she had fantasised about doing for years.

Those thoughts had scared her once. It was frightening how dark her mind became when she thought about dragging every answer out of whoever she got her hands on first. She wanted to hear their screams, the way her parents had screamed that night. She wanted to see their blood, feel it between her fingers.

Those thoughts had scared her once. But not anymore. Not now she had delved into that pit of rage and vengeance. All those feelings of fear, hurt, and grief, evaporated against the flames that licked up her throat.

She relished in it.

It was freeing, in a strange sort of way, to not be shackled by fear. For years, she laid awake at night wondering whether someone would come for her, and now they had.

Part of her wanted to hunt for the attackers lurking inside the academy, but the forever analysing part of her mind stopped her, made her focus on the bigger picture. It wasn't *just* the attackers she would have to deal with, but the siblings, the guards patrolling the perimeter, and possibly the students. They may not have shown any interest in helping her, but Niah wouldn't put it past them to help if *she* was the target.

It would be wiser to get away from the academy, learn her way around the world, and come back, maybe with more people.

Even if she was going with Talon, he was just one man; she could fight her way free if she had to. Mela had mentioned that a woman named Merida wanted to explain things to her, that she had answers. Niah couldn't deny her curiosity. Though she couldn't shake the feeling that perhaps she would be trading one prison for another.

It would be in her best interest to get free of Talon before they arrived at the destination he'd planned for them.

The clock chimed midnight.

Niah had lost track of time as she re-organised another stack of books, now she was scrambling through the skylight onto the roof. The wind howled and pushed her as she steadied herself.

She hadn't heard any movement since the sun went down, but that didn't mean the attackers weren't skulking through the corridors waiting for her.

The roof was the safest option.

She scanned the darkness, looking toward the front gates for Talon. She couldn't see him, but he'd said he would be there. Knowing she had no other option, Niah jumped from the roof and sailed through the air, landing in a crouch on the lawn and sprinting toward the open gate.

Voices murmured behind the corner of the east wing; she crouched behind the stone pillar attached to the gate and peered around the edge.

Behind the wall, out of sight from the rest of the building, was a strange piece of machinery with lights and wheels; two figures stood beside it, one of them wore a smart suit. From where she crouched, Talon's voice reached her.

She crossed the grass to him, his head snapped up, and he guided her toward the machine.

"You're late," he snapped. Then, the other figure came into view, Fin.

"What is *he* doing here?"

"He's going to help you get away from here," Talon answered as he hurried her towards the machine.

"What is that? And I don't need help." she protested.

"The fact that you don't even know what a pickup truck is suggests you do need my help," Fin smirked as he opened the door for her. She bit down on the urge to punch him.

"Niah, you need to trust me," Talon said calmly as Fin walked to the other side of the truck.

She whirled on him, "People are trying to hurt me; how do I know you're not one of them?" his thoughtful gaze didn't falter.

"You don't. But there's no time for that; let me know you're safe when you reach your destination," he handed over a dark, thin block made of glass, "use this." he pushed her toward the truck. She didn't have time to respond as he slammed the door shut, then they were hurrying away, leaving Talon staring after them.

She turned as the truck hurtled down the gravel track until they reached a smooth road surrounded by trees on each side.

The truck roared along the road. It felt odd, almost wrong in some way. She gripped the edge of the seat hard enough that the material started to tear beneath her fingers. Then, without warning, the truck pulled to the left and stopped.

"Hey," the voice from next to her sounded. She had almost forgotten she wasn't alone. "Here, put your belt on," Fin reached across, but she smacked his hand away with an icy glare. He pulled his hand back to the stick in the centre but said nothing. His eyes gave nothing away either.

"I'm fine," she murmured, letting the warning seep into her voice. She turned away, though still felt his gaze linger.

Her head snapped to him, "What?"

"I'm here to help you. I was asked to come here by Talon." His voice dripped with authority, a tone she didn't often hear, "So I'd appreciate it if you didn't look at me as if you're planning my demise," his grey eyes glinted in the moonlight streaming into the cab. She took a steadying breath, not realising how hard her heart was pounding.

"Where are you taking me?" she asked quietly, refusing to meet his gaze.

"The Perth academy, in Australia," he answered, she stilled.

"*Australia?*" She glanced to the door handle, wondering how far she could get on her own.

"Yes. And we better hurry. We need to put as much distance between the academy and us before dawn," he said with a slow grin as the truck lurched into motion.

Niah said nothing; what else could she say?

She watched the scenery blur by, pressing her forehead to the window beside her; the brief cold was a reprieve against the throbbing in her head.

For better or worse, she was out of the academy.

Her fingers curled around the locket at her throat, accompanied by the brass key Mela had given her. A thick haze set into her mind, her body turning heavy, tired.

She was so very tired.

She blinked, looking down at tiny, blood-covered hands.

She was once again in the house. The house she had grown up in, the only place she knew in the world. They lived on a small farm and grew their own crops and vegetables. It was a private, simple life they lived.

That very life was destroyed that night.

No longer peaceful and happy.

But dark and cold.

She crept through the halls of the house, not sure if there were any more attackers.

Empty.

The whole place was deathly silent, almost completely void of colour. Lifeless.

A shiver crawled up her spine as she gripped the door handle. The door itself was intact, not a scratch on it. She gazed blankly at her hand around the handle. Her skin was crusted with scarlet, her mothers' blood.

Her stomach churned, and she doubled over, unable to get air into her lungs. Her eyes were watering, her throat sore and ragged from gasping. Her entire body trembled.

Her parents would be disappointed.

She dragged herself to her feet and staggered through the door. Not looking back at the home she was leaving. At the home she would never see again. The home that was now bathed in blood.

She shivered as she shoved open the barn doors. The horses nickered inquisitively. She didn't bother with a saddle, scrambling onto Storm's sturdy back, hugging his warm neck.

He launched into a gallop when she nudged his sides, gripping fistfuls of his thick mane, crouching low over his neck so he could stretch. Her hair whipped around her like an ebony ribbon as Storm weaved between trees.

Her father had taken her to the academy only two weeks ago. She remembered the way, but the further they travelled, the more everything started to blend together. The more the trees all started to look alike. Her heart was pounding in her ears over the thundering of Storms hooves beating the moss-covered ground. She clung to him with everything she had.

Dead.

Her parents were dead.

The air hitched in her throat as a strangled whimper escaped through her teeth.

Something leapt out from the underbrush, causing Storm to veer to the side, kicking up his heels. She was unseated and landed in a heap on the ground as Storm galloped away through the trees. Pain lanced through her ribs as she pushed herself into a sitting position.

"Storm! Come back here, you worthless beast!" her eyes stung, "Come back, don't leave me," her voice was a pathetic, strangled whisper as she hugged her arms around herself.

Her parents were dead.

They weren't coming back.

Taken from her just like that without warning.

She realised her dagger wasn't at her hip. Her heart was racing as she ran her hands over the ground in search of it, her eyes burning hotter until her hand grazed something sharp. A stinging pain shot through her finger. She didn't care. She clutched the dagger to her chest as tears rolled down her cheeks. She couldn't remember the last time she had cried.

She didn't know how long she sat there, clinging to the dagger and her locket as if her life depended on it.

Empty.

She felt utterly empty.

Her eyes fell on the dagger she held loosely. Never again. Never again would she allow herself to cry. Not over her parents' death, not over anything.

Her hands, coated with scarlet and black mixed together.

The first time she saw her blood was black and not red, she thought something was wrong with her. She thought she was a demon trapped in a human body. That was five years ago. Her parents had explained what she was. A halfling, half-demon and half-human. They told her she was special. That she was unique, that's why she had special eyes and blood as black as night. That the silver of her eyes symbolised she was born for great things. That she would kill many demons.

She had felt proud then.

It was ironic, really. Her parents had told her she was born for greatness, yet she could do nothing to stop them from being killed. She was powerless against those men and could do nothing as her mothers' life slipped away between her fingers.

She tilted her head, looking up at the grey sky through the branches. Thick clouds rolled overhead. She knew it was cold. She remembered seeing her mother wrapping shawls around herself on days like this, her teeth chattering and vapour leaving her mouth as she breathed. Yet Niah felt nothing. Always comfortable. Always adjusting immediately to whatever the weather threw at them. She asked her mother about it once, but received a sharp slap and a warning never to speak of such things again.

She picked herself up. Clutching her dagger in one hand, the other around the locket at her throat. Whatever challenges lay ahead, she would face them with her head held high. Because she was a Shadow. Because she was born for great things.

FIN

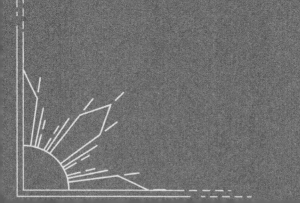

5

This wasn't exactly the way he expected this trip to go. When he received Talon's message, there was very little information to go on. All he knew was that he needed to get her out and keep her safe.

He knew she had a sheltered upbringing, that she had watched her parents die when she was young. Stupidly, Fin had expected a timid creature; he certainly wasn't expecting the angry, dark-haired beauty sitting beside him.

A shudder rippled through him.

There was a coldness within those walls. Something sinister lurked there. He'd never felt anything like it. It was no wonder the girl was the way she was. He glanced over at his travelling companion. She had fallen asleep against the window after a few minutes of staring at the scenery, gripping the seat whenever he hit a bump.

She'd fought the call of sleep until she couldn't any longer. He was surprised she held out as long as she did. Her skin was pale, her eyes ringed with dark smudges. It was no surprise, after he'd pulled her to safety the night before, he didn't expect anyone would be able to sleep.

Fin grabbed his phone from the armrest and dialled the familiar number; Merida answered on the first ring, "Do you have her?"

"I'm great, thanks for asking, awful weather here in England."

There was an exasperated sigh from the other end, "Fin."

"I have her," he glanced over at the girl, "You can expect us tomorrow."

"She's coming willingly?"

"Well, she didn't have much choice."

There was a pause, "What do you mean?"

"She was attacked. She's fine," he said before Merida could ask anything further, "They didn't get to her. We'll be home soon."

"Thank you, Fin. Be safe."

"Until my last breath." He muttered; the line went dead.

The moon lit up the cab, a pale glow illuminating her features. Her nose was slightly too long for her face, her bottom lip slightly too full to match the top. Her brows arched fiercely, to match her sharp jawline that made the hollows of her cheeks stand out.

The moonlight flickered over something around her throat—two separate chains. One held a silver locket with a precious stone on the front laid within intricate detailing, the other held a small key. He wondered what it unlocked.

She flinched and jerked as she slept, the odd whimper escaping her trembling lips as beads of sweat glistened against her brow as if she were having a nightmare. Fin thought about waking her, but he didn't want to startle her with that nasty looking dagger strapped to her hip. He already knew she wasn't afraid to use it, and he'd rather keep his organs inside his body.

Getting inside the academy was easier than he anticipated. After several weeks of surveillance, he knew multiple patrol units were monitoring the perimeter, yet when he met up with Talon, he didn't see a single one as they made their way to the back entrance. No one noticed him; they didn't even look twice in his direction. He knew why, but it was chilling all the same.

It was like he was nothing more than a ghost.

He made a mental note to ask Talon how he managed to find a safe route through the patrols when he returned. Talon would remain for another day or two to monitor whether anyone would be coming after her. After a few hours of driving, Fin had expected a phone call; but none came.

It wasn't like the Shadows to be careless enough to lose one of their assets. Fin hated that word. As he glanced over at the sleeping girl once more, he couldn't help but wonder why they wanted *her* of all creatures.

He supposed it would only be a matter of time before he found out.

Night melted into dawn as Fin pulled into the Services along the motorway. It was nothing special, a petrol station, a building with showers, and somewhere to get food. After not being able to wash for a few days since Talon shoved him into a room without a bathroom and not daring to use someone else's, he was in desperate need of a shower.

Perhaps Niah would want to freshen up too, and something to eat might put the colour back into her cheeks.

He parked the truck and considered nudging her awake, but wasn't entirely in the mood to be gutted.

"Oi, wake up."

She jerked awake, drawing her dagger, poised to do precisely what he feared she would. Her eyes were narrow, her canines lengthening as a warning growl escaped between her gritted teeth.

She reminded him of a trapped animal.

Fin held his hands up in surrender, showing he wasn't a threat. Her breaths came fast and shallow, her knuckles turning white where she gripped the hilt of her dagger.

"Easy," he said gently. For a moment, all he could hear was the rapid thump of her heart. Then she blinked, her canines sliding back into her gums. Slowly, she lowered the dagger, stowing it away once more.

"I'm not a horse," Niah grumbled.

He lowered his hands, "What?" She looked over at him. Her eyes were impossibly dark, the silver line around her iris shimmering in the early morning sunlight.

"The way you say 'easy', holding your hands out like that, it reminds me of trying to calm a horse," she clarified, sounding irritated that she even *had* to explain it. This was going to be a long trip.

"You've had much experience with horses?" he asked, if only to stop her looking at him like he was an idiot.

"Yes." was all she said before turning away, analysing her surroundings. She didn't meet his gaze as she asked, "Where are we?"

"Services, I've been driving all night, and I need a break. I figured you might be hungry," he shrugged, grabbing his wallet from the armrest, shoving it into his pocket as he opened the door. As if on cue her stomach rumbled, he resisted the urge to smirk as she shifted in her seat.

It was as though she thought being hungry was a weakness.

With a frown, he decided not to dwell on it, and got out of the truck. He glanced back to see she was still sitting inside, it occurred to him that maybe she didn't know how to open the door. So, he opened it for her, and she stepped out in almost a crouch, her fingers inching toward the dagger at her hip.

All humour and mocking left him.

Fin sighed, raking a hand through his hair, "No one will hurt you," she glanced at him with an arched brow before straightening her spine and squaring her shoulders, "You may also want to cover that," he gestured to the dagger strapped to her hip. Niah glanced down as she pulled her black, leather jacket around herself, zipping it at the front. The sheath still poked out the bottom, but it was good enough, and he didn't dare ask her to remove it completely.

They walked in silence toward the building. It was plain red brick with large thick windows. Nothing exciting. Inside, the smell of coffee and greasy food wafted through the air, a few people were sitting at the various eateries or perusing the magazines in WHSmith.

With his backpack slung over his shoulder, he walked toward one of the coffee shops, stopping when he realised Niah wasn't by his side. He turned to see her still standing at the entrance, staring at the automatic sliding doors as if they might attack her, her fingers inching closer to the dagger once again.

It might be a funny story one day, the girl who stabbed a door. But as he watched her, there was nothing funny about it. He stood opposite her, his hands in his pockets, a smirk on his lips.

"Scared?"

Annoyance flicked across her eyes, she scowled at him as she strode through the doors, being non too careful about bumping into him as she passed by. He chuckled under his breath. Any other time, he might have been disgruntled about being shoved, but at least she was through the door.

Now, onto the next challenge.

"This way," he told her and walked towards the coffee shop, choosing a booth tucked away in the corner. She followed him, her eyes darting around their surroundings, her hand gripping the strap of her rucksack over her shoulder so tight that he thought she might tear it.

She sat down at the booth, and still didn't meet his gaze as she located every exit. Fin wanted to tell her it was okay, that she was safe, but he had the feeling it would have the opposite of the desired effect.

"What do you want to eat?" he asked, glancing at the counter.

"Um...Fruit and eggs," she said absentmindedly.

"Sure, wait here. Don't go anywhere," he gave her a firm look. Niah met his gaze then, those cold eyes boring into him as if weighing him up. He didn't shift from her gaze, she was searching for something, and he'd let her see everything.

She must have been satisfied, because she turned to look out of the window and mumbled, "Fine."

Trusting her not to run, he turned for the counter, grabbing fruit and water from the chilled section before placing them by the till.

The pastries in the glass cabinet called to him, as the woman behind the counter looked up, she offered him a dazzling smile. She was pretty, with big brown eyes. He grinned as he asked for two pastries with two large coffees along with the fruit and water for Niah. The girl's smile faded when her eyes landed on Niah, and when she handed him the tray of items, the smile wasn't quite as dazzling.

When he returned, Niah was still gazing out of the window, but there was a smattering of crumbs on the table that hadn't been there before. He made no comment about it; he was just relieved she had eaten something.

He set the tray down on the table, sliding into the booth to sit opposite her as she eyed the various items with suspicion.

"What's that?" she asked, pointing at the pastry.

"It's a croissant; try it," he gestured as he picked up his own and took a bite. The soft, sweet taste filled his mouth as he savoured it.

She looked at it hesitantly before picking it up and picking off a small piece. Fin almost choked on his food when she sniffed it. Then, deciding it was safe, she popped it into her mouth, and he had the satisfaction of watching her eyes widen as she took another bite.

They ate in silence. Her eyes flicked to the mug of coffee on the tray, her nostrils expanding as she sniffed at it.

"It's coffee," he told her, lifting his own mug to his lips. Her eyes followed the cup until he lowered it back to the tray. Hesitantly, she picked up the mug, her lids fluttered at the first sip.

It was strangely rewarding watching her try new things. She caught him staring and scowled before quickly turning away once again. He sighed. A long trip indeed.

"I assume you've never had anything like this at the academy?" he asked, she shook her head as she drained the coffee.

"We're only allowed to drink water, and the meals are kept small and healthy," she shrugged as she peeled the banana on the tray and took a bite. He blinked. It was the first thing she had said without looking like she wanted to rip his head off.

"That's boring, sounds strict. I think you'll like Australia more," he answered as he glanced around, locating the washrooms. She said nothing as they finished their meal in silence.

"Do you want a shower?" he asked, he pointed in the direction of the restrooms when she narrowed her eyes, "Men and women have separate showers, though you're welcome to join me if you want."

Perhaps it was a mistake to separate, but he didn't want her to feel like he was holding her prisoner. It would give her time to sort through whatever was going on inside her head, as well as an opportunity to run.

Fin wanted to give her that option, to see what she would do. He'd go after her, if only to make sure she was safe, but he wouldn't force her to come with him.

He never forced anyone to come with him.

She rolled her eyes, "Fine, but I'll go alone."

NIAH

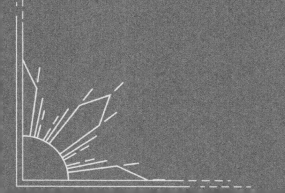

6

The nightmare lingered.

Niah hadn't meant to fall asleep beside Fin, but she couldn't fight the exhaustion any longer. As soon as her eyes closed, the nightmare descended. Sometimes she dreamt of blood filling her lungs, sometimes she was chasing her parents as they walked away from her, and sometimes, she dreamt of blue flames.

The flames and blood always stood out against the monotone greys of the dreams.

Fin's voice had brought her tumbling into consciousness once again; she only hoped that she hadn't cried out or screamed as she had done in previous dreams.

Despite sleeping, drowsiness tugged at her lids, her stomach grumbled angrily. That all ebbed away when she was faced with the uncertainty of the Services.

It was all so strange, like she'd arrived in a different world, she supposed she had. The smell of coffee and grease filled her nose, she picked up on every murmur from the humans, pinpointed every exit before she and Fin had made it to the table.

Even though she found herself in unfamiliar territory, her heart was calm. Her mind was quiet. For the first time in days, she didn't feel like crawling out of her skin.

The only thing on her mind was how hungry she was, and how much she still wanted to sleep.

When Fin mentioned a shower, her first thought hadn't been getting clean, but running. She'd done what she wanted to achieve and had escaped the academy, but she still had no idea where she was. It was better to stay with him a while longer, at least until they reached Australia.

The smell changed to a strong scent of bleach as they approached the restrooms. Niah had never showered in a communal area before. She frowned at the door with a symbol of a stick figure wearing a dress. She glanced at Fin, who had stopped outside what she assumed was the men's restroom.

"I'll meet you at the table we were just at. If I'm not there, just wait for me, I won't be long," he paused, a mischievous glint in his eye, "Unless you've changed your mind about joining me?"

Niah made a disgusted grunt and shouldered the door open, ignoring the chuckle that trailed after her. He was infuriating, and she found herself questioning whether staying with him was worth the aggravation.

Unfortunately, it was.

Beyond the door, the room was covered in white tiles. The showers were at the back of the room, with rows of stalls on each side. When she was safely locked inside a cubicle, she stripped out of her clothes and flicked on the water.

The warm water trickled down her body limply as she lathered soap from the dispenser into her hair and skin. It wasn't until she had finished that she realised there were no towels.

With a groan, she used her worn clothes to dab at her damp skin until she was mostly dry, then changed into clean clothes before standing at the sinks in front of a large mirror.

Some of the colour had returned to her cheeks, her under eyes not quite as dark as before. She gripped the edge of the sink hard enough for her knuckles to turn white, exhaustion rippling through her body as her mind swam.

She fished the picture from Karliah's office from her pocket. It made no sense. She'd spent her life looking for answers, now she finally had some, and she couldn't focus enough to know what any of it meant.

Mela said that answers were waiting for her, that a woman called Merida wanted to explain everything, whatever that was. The curious part of her mind wanted to know everything, wanted to follow Fin into the unknown and soak up every scrap of information she could.

But the other part of her, the cynical, calculating part, wanted to run. But, if this trip had shown her anything, it was that she had no hope of surviving in this world alone.

The word clanged through her.

Alone.

Yes, she was alone, wasn't she?

The heavy hollowness settled in her chest as her hand instinctively gripped her locket. No, she wasn't alone. No matter what, she had to believe her parents were watching over her. She had to believe there was a reason they had kept their pasts from her.

Her only fear was that when she found the truth, what would she have after that?

She shook her head in an attempt to rid her mind of those thoughts. It wasn't the time to feel sorry for herself.

It occurred to her that she was only leaving one academy for another. What if the Perth academy was no better? Would she find answers? Or more enemies?

Well, there was only one way to find out.

She gripped the sink tighter, jerking away when it crumbled beneath her grip. Niah stared down at the broken ceramic between her fingers.

Mela said she was being targeted because of what Niah was, but she couldn't tell her exactly *what* she was. It was no secret that she was different, but what mysteries lay within her blood that would make those she trusted turn on her?

Perhaps they were never on her side at all.

She had no proof whether the siblings had anything to do with her parents' death, but the more she thought about the day she arrived on their doorstep, the more she remembered the way Karliah had examined her. How the woman didn't appear surprised by the news.

Niah began to feel like she was nothing more than a fly caught in a spiders web.

She quickly gathered up her things and made her way out of the restroom before anyone saw her.

Fin wasn't in the coffee shop, so she decided to wait for him in the booth they had been sitting in before. Ignoring that it was exactly what he'd told her to do.

She gazed out of the window, watching the clouds rolling along the grey sky. It had started to rain, the gentle patter of water droplets against the glass was soothing, almost lulling her to sleep, or at least it would be, had her stomach not grumbled loudly.

Niah turned and looked toward the counter, spotting the pastries through a glass window. Hooking her bag over her shoulder, she decided now was as good a time as any to start learning about this strange new world.

The woman behind the counter looked up as she smiled when Niah approached. Niah had to remind herself to stop staring, having never met a human before.

"What can I get for you?" the woman asked with a bright smile.

"The...um, that," Niah said, pointing to the pastry in the window, "And a coffee," she added as an afterthought.

The woman nodded, "Large?"

"Uh...yes," the woman smiled and plated up a croissant and began making the coffee. She went to a machine at the front of the counter and tapped the screen a few times before turning to Niah, "That'll be four pounds and fifty-nine pence." Niah blinked, not understanding what the woman meant.

"Um...I don't_"

"Make that two of those, coffees and croissants," Fin said as he came up behind her, making her jump slightly. How had she not heard him? She didn't let him see the relief that he turned up when he had.

"Don't worry, it's confusing at first," he muttered without looking at her.

Her cheeks warmed as she shifted on her feet, suddenly finding the rain very interesting. Her stomach fluttered in a way that made her want to punch something, or Fin, she'd settle for either.

"Can I get these to go?" Fin added as the woman was about to pour the coffee into mugs. She smiled and replaced them with paper cups with lids and put the pastries into boxes.

"How much again?" Fin fished a leather item from his pocket.

"Nine Eighteen." The woman smiled. Fin pulled an orange piece of shiny paper from the leather object and handed it to her. Money, that's what the woman had meant.

"Keep the change," he winked; the woman's cheeks flushed as she took the money and hurried to hand him the items.

"Have a nice day," she called after them as they turned to walk away; Fin turned slightly and waved with what she supposed was a charming smile.

"Do women always fawn over you?"

He smirked, "Jealous?"

"Not even a little." She rolled her eyes. A low chuckle was his only response.

They sat in silence as Fin drove, occasionally sipping his coffee while Niah devoured her croissant. She kept her eyes on the scenery around them: rolling green meadows, large farmhouses, and fields of animals. Despite the darkness of the skies, Niah was mesmerized.

Something light dropped into her lap, the other box with the pastry inside. Niah lifted her eyes to Fin, but he was staring straight ahead.

"It's a shame to let it go to waste."

Niah opened the box, the sweet smell filling her nose, making her mouth water, "You don't want it?"

"No, go ahead." Fin said, his voice was so soft that she wasn't sure it was the same person.

But she couldn't deny she was still hungry, and the pastry was delicious enough that she didn't give it a second thought before stuffing it into her mouth.

"It's a lot to take in," Fin said after a while, "you'll get used to it," the reassuring smile annoyed her. She wasn't some delicate damsel in distress. Niah sighed heavily, biting back the urge to snap at him for being pedantic. Somehow, she didn't think that was how he meant it.

"Do you know what's going on?" she asked, looking at him. He stared straight ahead at the road, a muscle feathering in his jaw.

"It's complicated," he murmured.

She wanted to ask more, but knew it was pointless. Whatever she needed to know, she would find it when she arrived in Australia. Or perhaps it was just another trap she'd have to fight her way out of. Either way, whatever awaited her, she was ready.

FIN

7

A fter a few hours of driving, Fin turned the truck down a damp, dirt road. Fields stretched from either side of the winding road until finally, it came to an end at a small white cottage with a thatched roof and square, single-paned windows with flower boxes full of white and blue flowers.

He stopped the truck and told her to wait there. But, of course, she didn't listen. Niah stared at the house, her rucksack over her shoulder; surprisingly, she didn't reach for her dagger.

"Listen," he said, taking a step closer to her, "there's no reason to be nervous in there; Mirandra is going to get us back to Perth."

She raised a brow, "I can only hear one person inside. I'll gut both of you before you so much as lay a hand on me."

"I really should have you threaten me more often," he winked, if only because it gave her something else to focus on than searching for exits. Her lips pressed into a thin line, her grip tightening on her rucksack as she scowled and looked back at the house.

Teasing her was also a great form of entertainment.

Fin chuckled and retrieved his bag from the covered truck bed, before knocking on the green door. It was only when the door creaked open that Niah's fingers inched closer to her dagger, the green jewelled pommel glinting in the dim light.

Mirandra peered around the edge of the door. She was a slight woman with dark hair pinned up, contrasting against her pale skin and dandelion yellow eyes. She pushed the door open just enough for them to step inside, and quickly sealed it behind them.

"I was expecting you earlier," she mumbled. Niah kept her eyes on the woman at all times, occasionally sneaking glances around the house.

Fin frowned at the spell weaver, "If you're that scared the Coven will find you, why don't you join The Cross?"

Mirandra waved away his concern, "You say that as if the Coven are the only ones to watch out for."

"We'd protect you," he murmured.

Mirandra shook her head with a click of her tongue and turned for the wall lined with bookcases. A warm yellow light radiated from her fingertips, her eyes glowing with the use of her power.

Fin glanced at Niah; her eyes were wide as she watched the bookcase swing open, revealing a passage leading down to a curving staircase.

The house was a small cottage from the outside, but this was a spell weavers house, and they could manipulate physical spaces.

Mirandra descended the stairs, lighting the way with a yellow ball of light in the palm of her hand.

Niah reached for her dagger.

"It's okay, I'll go first," Fin offered. She narrowed her eyes at him, but the hand gripping her dagger relaxed a touch.

The bookcase closed behind them, he could practically *feel* the tension rolling off of her. Fin didn't dare look back at her, instead, he kept his eyes on the ball of light further down.

The smell of sulphur and ash grew strong, the air turning so thick that it made breathing difficult. It wasn't long before the stairs opened out into a large stone room, the walls lined with shelves upon shelves of bottles and jars of various powders and liquids. A small iron pot hanging above a fire pit blazing with unnatural yellow flames was at the centre of the room.

"This her?" Mirandra questioned, rolling up her sleeves.

Fin glanced at Niah; she was gazing at the shelves of jars, not noticing anyone had spoken. There was a softness in her face, delicate almost. When she looked back at him, her expression hardened, and that softness disappeared.

Interesting.

"It is," Fin answered as he picked up a jar of what looked like vampire fangs. He raised a brow at the yellow-eyed woman as he placed the pot back on the shelf.

"Don't ask, boy."

He held up his hands in mock surrender, he didn't want to know anyway.

"Back to Australia, I assume?" she asked, yellow sparks shooting from her fingertips.

"Yes," he answered coolly.

Mirandra waved her hand in the air as it glowed bright yellow until the shimmering, water-like surface of a portal rippled into existence.

Niah stared in awe; she couldn't have seen one before. Fin held his hand out for her to take, she glared at him.

"You don't know where we're going, it's for your safety," he said firmly, still holding his hand out. Niah glanced from his hand, to the portal, and back again before her glare softened into doubt.

"Trust me," he muttered softly. She stared at him, her eyes wide, searching, analysing. Then, with a slow exhale, she slapped her hand into his.

He couldn't help but smirk as they walked through the sparkling yellow surface. The portal exploded around them, a kaleidoscope of colours. They stepped forward once, the ground beneath them firmed as the colours faded away. He would never stop admiring the beauty of it, no matter how many times he had done it.

NIAH

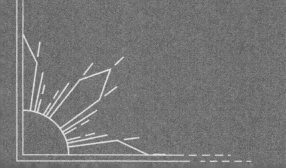

8

A million colours rushed past her.

There was a single second where she felt as though she were weightless, the colours dancing across her vision until she took a single step, and it all vanished.

The ground turned to soil beneath her feet, dry with a tint of red to it. It was the impossible heat that hit her first, stifling for that brief moment before her body adjusted. The brightness of the blazing sun overhead had her shielding her eyes.

They were standing near a beach, staring out over the glittering ocean. The sand was white and powdery, unlike the dark, hard sand in England scattered with rocks and pebbles. Here, the dunes rolled along the edge of the beach where the grass met the sand.

It was mostly quiet, apart from the odd one or two groups of people lying on towels, soaking in the sun's rays. People on boards in the water. Birds screeched overhead, and behind them, cars drove by.

Niah inhaled deeply, savouring the saltiness of the fresh sea air. It was so vastly different to the cold, suffocating academy. The warmth and scents chased away the lingering chill that had seeped into her bones.

Something inside her chest eased. A knot she hadn't realised was there loosened, and for the first time in years, there was no sense of fear or danger looming over her.

Niah turned to Fin, surprised to find he was already gazing at her. On closer inspection, with the sunlight shining in his eyes, she could see that they weren't grey at all, but silver, separated by a shade or two to the shimmering ring ringing his iris.

Fin cocked a brow at her, a smirk dancing at one corner of his mouth, as she realised, she was still holding his hand. Niah jerked away, ignoring the faint chuckle that rumbled through his chest.

"Come on," he said, turning toward a large building behind them.

This place, unlike England, was all angles; wood, steel, and glass in geometric shapes. There was an openness about it that was oddly inviting. Her feet moved on their own as if an invisible thread was tugging her.

As they approached, she felt a pull. The kind she got when they left the academy back in England. A cloaking barrier. Something they used to hide their existence from the human world. If humans wandered too close, they'd see nothing but a hollow shell of a building, or perhaps nothing at all. The magic would force them to turn around and leave.

Groups of people were sat around on the grass leading to the entrance. They were laughing, reading, drawing, or playing instruments. Some of them looked up and eyed her curiously before going back to whatever they were doing.

Her heart thrummed as her palms grew clammy.

The large front doors were a combination of wood and glass with a large metal handle; both were wide open, leading to the light and airy foyer. The floors were wood, the walls painted white, with a sweeping staircase on the left of the doors.

The building was so vast and airy that she thought it might feel empty, but somehow, she felt at ease. Only a few people meandered through the upper levels, peering over the railings into the foyer; none of them appeared to be concerned with her presence. One or two of them even waved, Fin waved back, and when his eyes met hers, they were calm.

Still, Niah was in unknown territory. As Fin led her up the stairs, she gripped the hilt of her dagger, noting every exit as they went.

They carried on down a long corridor with multiple doors on one side, a railing on the other where the floor fell away to look down onto the foyer. At the end of the corridor was a large set of wooden double doors.

Fin knocked, a gentle voice said to come in, and when he pushed the doors open, Niah took a moment to examine the room before taking that final step.

The office was bright, with a fresh breeze blowing in from the open window at the back behind a glass-topped desk. A leather couch sat on the right underneath another window overlooking the ocean.

Deciding it was safe enough, Niah stepped into the room.

Behind the desk sat a thin woman with long, mahogany hair that cascaded around her slim shoulders. She had a square-shaped face, but her delicate features softened the sharpness of her jaw. Her ocean-blue eyes ringed in silver raked over Niah, looking at her as if she were a miracle.

"Good trip?" the woman asked, her voice light and melodic.

"Apart from the weather," Fin answered.

The woman nodded once. Fin's tone and stance had changed, now standing with his back straightened, shoulders squared, and hands clasped behind his back. He looked at the woman but kept his eyes low out of respect.

So, she was the headmistress then.

"Thank you, Fin. You may go," she said; Fin dipped his chin and offered Niah a wink as he turned for the door.

For a moment, after the doors clicked shut, the only sound was the ticking of a clock. The sound set her teeth on edge.

"Niah," the woman smiled, rising from her chair, and making her way around the desk, "I'm glad we found you." her smile was warm, genuine. The woman sat on the couch and patted the cushion beside her; Niah remained standing.

"Found me? I don't understand. I thought Talon had arranged for me to come here?" The mention of his name reminded her of the small glass object he had given her. She fished it from her pocket and showed it to the woman.

"He did. He has been invaluable in helping us find others like you. My name is Merida. I am the leader here."

So this was the woman Mela spoke of. Niah noted the way she said *leader* as opposed to *headmistress*.

Merida took hold of the glass block and smashed it on the floor; Niah glared at her.

"Why did you do that?"

Merida blinked but smiled, "I guess Talon didn't tell you how it works, no matter; he's so forgetful."

"You said leader, surely you mean headmistress?" Niah questioned, letting her voice harden. Merida pondered that for a moment, a light smile brushing her lips as she slung her arm over the back of the sofa.

"No, I mean the leader. This isn't an academy. This is a training facility, an order, a guild, whatever you want to call it. More specifically, we are the Furies, the Fury Alliance," she said, her expression unreadable.

For a moment, Niah focused on slowing her thumping heart, taking slow, deliberate breaths as she forced her mind to focus.

"Talon lied." The words came out in a growl.

Her skin prickled as the ember smouldering in the pit of her stomach ignited. Her eyes flicked to the open window behind the desk; she could be out of it in less than a second.

"You had to think you were coming to do the tests; otherwise, you wouldn't have come. Would you?" Merida asked, the smile fading from her lips.

"No." Niah retorted.

A shiver slithered up her spine, her skin prickling as she angled herself toward the window.

Merida, as if sensing what she was going to do, got to her feet but kept a safe distance, "You have every right to be suspicious of me, here," the woman made a show of turning on the spot, letting Niah see that she wasn't armed. She listened carefully, not hearing anyone outside the doors, or below the windows.

"All I ask is that you listen to what I have to say. The only thing I want, is to tell you the truth. That's what you want, isn't it?" Merida went on when Niah remained silent.

She couldn't help but feel like they were using her hunger for answers to keep her there. But like Fin, Niah didn't sense a flicker of hostility on the woman.

"And if I don't like what you tell me?"

Merida lowered her hands to her sides, "Then you're free to leave."

"As simple as that, huh?"

"As simple as that."

Niah narrowed her eyes, searching the woman's face for the slightest tell that she was lying. There was nothing. Her voice was steady, as was the beat of her heart, she looked Niah in the eye when she spoke, and seemed completely at ease.

Then again, the Springtower siblings had appeared the same.

What did she have to lose by hearing the woman out? Niah lowered herself into one of the chairs in front of the desk, while Merida remained standing. Something softened in her face as she turned to gaze out of the window.

"You've been led to believe that you are a cross between demons and humans, but you're not," Merida turned back to her, "You *know* you're different, but you don't know why."

Niah's heart stumbled.

"So, what am I?"

The woman took a steadying breath and moved to the other side of the desk to take her seat, "You are a hybrid, part demon, part angel." Her gaze was steady, guarded almost.

"That's impossible," Niah growled.

She got to her feet, dragging her hands through her hair.

"Is it? How can you be so sure?"

"Angels and demons are mortal enemies; why would they breed?" Niah breathed, unable to fathom how that could be true.

Merida leaned forward in her chair, her fingers linking in front of her, "I can tell you, but I need you to have an open mind."

"I can't promise that."

"Fair enough," Merida sighed, "Thousands of years ago, there were only angels. Demons didn't exist, nor did hybrids, or fey, vampires, or any other species. It was only humans and angels. I assume you know the story of Lucifer's fall?"

Niah nodded, "He considered himself a God, and refused to bow to humans."

"Correct. After that, he was thrown to the earth, and the remaining angels realised there was a darkness in all of them, despite their benevolent nature. To prevent a similar incident, the angels found a way to split the darkness from themselves. That darkness became what we know as demons." Merida explained, leaning back in her chair as she watched Niah with unreadable eyes.

When Niah said nothing, Merida went on, "The demons were cast aside, and from their hatred, the demon realms were born. Thus, Lucifer, and six of his closest comrades became the seven Princes of Hell. No longer restricted by their angelic nature, the demons gained immense power beyond anyone's imagination. And the angels realised their mistake."

Niah found herself captivated by the story, but what if it was just that? A story?

"But surely that would just make reproduction even less likely?" she quizzed.

A light smile brushed across Merida's lips, "For every action, there are consequences. The angels may have cast their demonic halves out, but that didn't sever the bond between them. Angels disrupted the balance of nature, and in an attempt to right that wrong, the two halves were drawn to one another. Some people believe they didn't realise what was happening, but in any case, when the two halves joined, a child was born. A child able to wield both demonic and angelic powers."

Niah stared at the woman.

She was insane.

"And you believe I am a child of an angel and a demon?" she scoffed.

Merida's lips fell into a frown, "Not quite. Demons bred with many species, creating demon hybrids with fey, lycanthropes, even spell weavers. Angels would sense the essence of their demonic counter in that mix, and providing the crossbreed was female, the angel would lay with her, creating a hybrid with traits of the other species."

"Why would it matter whether the crossbreed was female?"

"Angels cannot carry children; only their demonic counters could do that. Since neither angels nor demons have specified genders, it didn't matter whether the pair appeared to be two women, males, or a mix of the two." Merida explained, pausing for breath as she watched for Niah's reaction.

She was silent for a moment, letting the words sink in.

"So, you're saying one of my parents was an angel, and one of them was a demon mixed with only Hell knows what?" she quipped, narrowing her eyes.

Merida nodded, "That's exactly what I'm saying."

"And what is it you think I am?" the words slipped through her gritted teeth, her fingers curling around the edge of the armrests.

"You are a hybrid, and a spell weaver."

The words swam through her head, until they faded into a meaningless haze in her mind. All this talk of angels and demons and spell weavers had a fire lighting in her stomach.

Unable to contemplate everything she had just heard, or conjure a logical thought or explanation, Niah started to laugh.

She laughed because there was nothing else to do. She couldn't cry, she couldn't scream or shout or cut it all out. She laughed because for so long, she had hungered for the truth, and now, with this story, she couldn't help but feel like there was some truth to it.

It was maddening.

But what if there was a chance it was all real?

Merida watched her silently, not moving an inch as Niah laughed, and laughed, and laughed.

She only stopped when she realised that if what Merida said was true, then it would mean...

"If my parents are an angel and a demon crossed with a spell weaver, then who did I spend the first nine years of my life with?"

Merida shifted in her seat uncomfortably, clearing her throat before she said, "They were your captors."

The breath left her lungs.

A red haze set in at the sides of her vision as roaring filled her head. Her canines slid free, stabbing into her lower lip.

"You're *lying*." She growled; never before had she heard her voice sound so feral.

"I'm not, Niah. I'm sorry, I know this can't be easy to_"

"Shut up!" she was on her feet then, slamming her hands down on the glass desk hard enough that a crack webbed across the surface, "I don't want to hear it."

Merida held her gaze; she didn't so much as flinch, "I told you I would tell you the truth, I'm sorry it isn't what you want to hear, but it *is* the truth."

Niah, blinded by rage, turned on her heel and stalked for the door.

"You said you would hear me out," Merida called after her. Niah stopped, whirling on the woman with bared, sharp teeth.

"I've heard enough. You said I could leave, or was that a lie too?"

The woman's lips pressed together as she rose slowly to her feet, "Of course, you're free to do as you wish. But please reconsider, take a few days to think it over before making any rash decisions."

Niah didn't bother to reply, she only stalked for the door and stormed down the corridor, ignoring Fin as he pushed away from the wall.

"Niah_"

"Go to Hell." She spat.

He made the mistake of taking hold of her arm, and she didn't think twice before swinging her fist and landing a solid blow to his jaw. His head snapped to the side, his hand falling from her arm, but when his eyes met hers, only understanding shone in their silvery depths.

"It's a lot to take in," he started, but before he could say anything else, she turned on her heel and prowled down the stairs toward the entrance. She'd heard enough.

Niah had no idea what she would do, she didn't care. She only knew she had to get away.

She ran straight out of the building, and then the barrier wrapped around it. She slowed to a walk, her lungs already heaving after the shock of Merida's words.

They couldn't be true.

They weren't true.

She gasped for breath, gulping down air as her mind raced. Her hand grasped the locket.

It couldn't be true.

Her chest cleaved apart, every doubt and theory bubbling to the surface. Her parents knew the siblings, they had *worked* together. So what else were they keeping from her? What if what Merida said was true?

What if they weren't her birth parents?

If that were the case, then who had she spent the last eight years mourning? Who had she vowed to get revenge for?

"Niah," a gentle voice said from behind her. She hadn't realised she was no longer walking, but rather stood facing the ocean.

She shook her head, "Go away."

"You wanted the truth, Merida is just giving you what you want." Fin murmured. Niah turned to face him, her brow scrunched as she fought the sting in her eyes.

"I can't believe it."

He nodded, pocketing his hands as he took a step forward, "I felt the same when I first arrived. It's insane, isn't it? But it *is* the truth."

Niah shook her head, turning to face the ocean once more, "No."

"Whether you want to believe it or not is your choice, but that won't stop it being any less true."

She huffed a humourless laugh, "I believed those at the academy, and look where that got me."

"We're not the Shadows." He said firmly, "Whatever you decide to do, we'll respect. But at least make sure you know everything before making a decision."

What did she have to lose?

She had nowhere to go, no idea about the world around her, and answers she didn't want to believe.

Niah inhaled deeply at the sea air, feeling her heart settle as she turned back to face him, "Fine. But the second anything feels wrong, I'm leaving."

A small smile tugged at the corners of his mouth, "I'd expect no less."

They walked through the corridors until Fin stopped outside a room and pushed the door open.

Inside, there was a double bed with slate grey sheets with an emerald blanket thrown over the top. Above the bed hung an abstract oil painting of greys, blacks, and greens.

At the far corner of the room was another door; she guessed it led to the bathroom. Opposite the bed was a large chest of white drawers with a flat, black screen on top and a narrow wardrobe next to it. A desk with a black object lying on top sat to the right of the door with a white swivel chair tucked neatly underneath.

Opposite the door was a sliding glass door leading onto a small balcony overlooking the ocean. It was open, the salty sea breeze pushing the gossamer curtains gently.

"Is this mine?" she asked, glancing around as she took a step inside. She turned to Fin, watching her; he nodded and leaned against the door frame, not stepping foot inside the room.

"What is this?" she asked, gesturing to the black object on the desk.

"Take a look," he said, remaining where he was.

Niah frowned and hooked a finger in the gap between the two halves, tugging gently until it opened; one half appeared to be a screen, while the other was covered with lettered keys.

"It's a laptop, I'll show you how to use it at some point," he said gently. Next to the strange object, was a thick, silvery book covered in worn velvet.

"What's this?"

"History, information on hybrids and other species." Fin shrugged, "It might be useful to read it rather than hear it."

Niah stood in the room, unsure what to make of it all. Her temple throbbed, her chest deflated with what she had already learnt.

How much more was there?

"Give it a few days, even if for nothing else other than preparing yourself for leaving," Fin said, cutting through her thoughts. She said nothing, only dipped her chin in acknowledgement. The door clicked shut behind him, and suddenly she was alone, with nothing but her wayward thoughts.

Niah took a moment to sit on the edge of the bed, taking deep breaths in an attempt to clear the fog from her mind. She glanced at the book on the desk, not sure whether she was ready to accept what any of it meant.

But before that, she wanted to check the room. Every drawer was empty; the door off to the side led to a bathroom with a shower that doubled as a bath. The wardrobe turned out not to be a wardrobe at all, but a weapons cupboard. It was fully stocked. Swords and daggers as black as night, a bow with a quiver full of arrows, and a pistol.

Either they forgot they left the weapons there or did it on purpose to make her feel at ease. As much as she hated to admit it, she felt more comfortable knowing they were there.

She stepped onto the balcony and peered over the railing, looking down at the ground. There were no patrols, no one keeping guard; she could leave if she wanted to, no one would stop her.

After hiding the weapons in strategic places around the room, she slumped in the desk chair and pulled the silver book toward her.

The words were alien, but somehow it all made sense. Loopholes within the Shadows stories were filled with the words on the page, explanations they couldn't give her written in that very book. Information on other species she hadn't known, pages upon pages of history and culture.

She hadn't even known magic was real before meeting that strange woman with yellow eyes in England. She knew of barriers and cloaks, but that was about it.

Niah may even be able to *use* magic if what Merida said was true. She glanced at her hands, never had there been a hint of power in her fingers, in her veins. If it was there, she had never felt it.

After a few hours of reading, she leaned back in the chair and dragged her hands down her face. Her eyes hurt, and her lids grew heavy, but she couldn't stop reading.

She wanted answers, these may not be the answers she imagined, and she wasn't entirely sure they were the truth, but it was more than she ever got at the academy.

There may still be more truth hidden in the pages of a book.

The one Mela had given her. She pulled it from her bag, unclasping the key from around her neck, to unlock the book.

Perhaps this book would ease her mind and explain why her parents knew the siblings.

The lock sprang free as she turned the key, and the book fell open. The pages were worn, the writing on them done by hand in black ink. Each page was dated at the top, diary entries, only the day and month, along with 'year one', and so on.

Throughout the book, between the pages were photographs of Niah through the years. But the photos seemed too *old*. Battered and black and white, the focus on them fuzzy as if taken with one of the first cameras.

Her heart launched into a gallop, her stomach twisting as she read the words.

It was a journal, a research journal.

Of her.

It kept a record of her progress over the years, her intellect, her combat abilities and so on.

They kept track of her throughout her childhood. Karliah must have grabbed it from the house, and Mela must have found it.

Niah's fingers trembled as she flicked through the old pages. They were testing her. It dawned on her that she was an experiment; they knew what she was and kept it from her.

They never once referred to her as their daughter, they didn't even use her name; they called her the subject.

Her heart wrenched.

Niah scanned the words with wide eyes.

May 19th, year nine

Subject is still far too attached.
She craves attention and doesn't care
whether it's positive or negative.
I fear that she will fall apart, but
perhaps that would not be the worst
thing.
The next phase will be starting in a
month. Only time will tell how
effective she will
be as a weapon.

She stopped reading the rest of the words.

A weapon.

They planned it all from the beginning. Raised her as their daughter, gave her a goal, a focus. Had her watch their murder and flee to the academy where she thought she would be *safe*. They knew she would want revenge for her parents' death. And they knew, they *knew*, with a select few words, that they could turn her hatred on whoever they damn well pleased.

Because she was thirsty for revenge.

Craved it.

Burned with it every single day.

Niah slammed the book closed and jumped to her feet, pacing the room as she gripped fistfuls of her hair. Her breaths came fast, her body trembling as sweat beaded on her brow. Her skin heated, her blood bubbling as she handed herself over to the simmering rage surging through her body.

She revelled in it.

FIN

9

Darkness fell around the facility.

He hadn't seen or heard anything of Niah since he'd talked her out of leaving. Fin had been expecting it. From the little time he'd spent with her, he would have been shocked had she *not* tried to leave. If that were what she wanted, he would have let her go; but he wanted her to hear the truth.

Even if she didn't believe it, surely it was better than living a lie.

He went to see Merida once he'd left her in the room. He knocked on the door; her voice was tired and strained when she said to enter. She was slumped at her desk, her head in her hands, when she looked up, her eyes were rimmed with red and silver.

"Is she...?" Merida trailed off, the air catching in her throat.

Fin sighed, pocketing his hands as he examined her, "She's still here."

A whimper escaped Merida's trembling lips, a single tear rolling down her cheek. He crossed the room to her then and folded her into his arms. She sobbed into his chest, and he let her. It was so rare that Merida cried, that he sometimes forgot she felt like everyone else. She kept everyone together so bravely, but who was there for her?

"I really thought she would leave," Merida croaked, pulling away to wipe her eyes.

"She was," he answered honestly, "but she wants to know the truth. It'll take time, M."

"I know," she sighed, "I expected too much."

"Are you okay?" Fin asked, seeing the paleness of her skin, and the dark smudges beneath her eyes.

Merida waved away his concern, "Of course."

"M, come on_"

"I'm fine, Fin, just tired."

He pressed his lips together, exhaling through his nose as she turned away and busied herself with some papers on the desk.

"Have you heard from Talon?"

Merida's hands stilled, "He was found."

Fin's heart stuttered.

"And Mela?"

"She was killed." Merida said, her hands trembling as they gripped the papers.

"Shit." Fin spat.

"We'll hold a memorial for her when Talon returns." The leader said weakly.

He nodded, feeling something in his chest deflate. He'd only met the fey a handful of times, but she was always kind and warm. He was saddened she had died at the hands of the Shadows.

"What do you need from me?" he asked.

Merida shook her head, "Nothing. You've done so much already, you brought her back to me."

He could usually cheer her up by making some sort of joke, but not when she was like this. Not when she spoke as though it was an effort just to breathe, not when her eyes held so much pain.

"Come on, you need to go to bed." He said, rising to his feet after kneeling by her chair.

She shook her head, but he spoke before she could, "I wasn't asking."

She let out a soft breath of laughter, "It's supposed to be me ordering you around."

"Only because I enjoy it."

She smacked him in the chest as she stood, but something in her expression had lifted. He guided her out of the office and down the corridor, but she paused and turned to face him.

"I'll be fine from here. Can you go and check on her?"

Fin sighed, "I doubt she'll want to speak to me."

"That's fine. I just want to know if she's okay."

He didn't bother asking any questions; he only nodded and kissed her on the cheek before she disappeared down the corridor.

He was halfway to Niah's room, when he heard a crash. Then he was running, ignoring the questioning glances as he barged down the halls and through the door into her room.

He barely had enough time to duck before a lamp sailed past his head and straight through the open door, over the railing to smash on the foyer floor.

It was an ugly lamp anyway.

Fin turned to her with a raised brow as he folded his arms over his chest. He might have made a joke, but as he saw the feral snarl across her face, the canines glinting in the moonlight, and the sword gripped in her hand; he decided it would be a bad idea.

"Get out." Her voice was little more than a growl, rumbling through her chest in warning.

"What happened?" he asked, keeping his voice low and calm. He stayed in the doorway, ignoring the questioning gazes burning into his back from bystanders lingering in the hall.

Fin refused to step inside, not into her space, not without permission.

She paced back and forth, her knuckles paling as she gripped the sword tighter. It had only been a couple of hours since he'd left her. His eyes flicked to the desk, at an open book beside the one he had left for her earlier.

"Niah," he murmured. Her eyes snapped to his, as if she had forgotten he was there.

"I said get out."

Fin bristled, but bit down on the retort forming on his tongue. He thought about doing what she said, but something told him not to leave her like this.

"What are you so angry about?" he asked.

Without warning, Niah reached and grabbed the remaining lamp, hurling it at him. It shattered against the wall as he dodged it.

Fine. A different method, then.

He raised a brow, letting a smirk curve his lips, "I'm not a fan of swordplay, but I might be able to get into it."

Her eyes narrowed, as hard and cold as onyx, "Get out before I throw something else at you, and this time, I won't miss."

He really should leave.

"Oh yeah? You've got nothing else to throw."

She snorted, her eyes trailing to the sword in her hand.

Oh.

Shit.

Fin was out the door before she released the weapon; the blade pierced straight through the door, stopping when the hilt hit the wood on the other side. Panting, he stood with wide eyes at the sword sticking out of the door.

Fin scratched the back of his head and gave a sheepish smile to those lingering in the hall, "Uh...new recruit?"

There was a series of Oh's before they carried on their way, much quicker than they had been previously. He lowered his hands to his hips, wondering how the hell they were going to fix the door if she wouldn't let anyone in.

"Whoa," a familiar voice muttered. Fin turned to see Sai and Gren coming up the stairs. Fin sighed, pinching the bridge of his nose.

"What happened?" Gren asked, eyeing the sword sticking out of the door.

"Not here, she's probably listening," he murmured and started down the corridor.

They walked until they came to the recreational room on the second floor. On the right were sofas and a tv with a games console, to the left was a pool table, and to the back were more sofas with some bookshelves. Fin slumped in one of the couches near the TV as Sai immediately started up the console and handed Gren a controller.

"That the girl?" Gren asked, his sandy hair slicked back as it always was. Sai and Gren were two of his closest friends. He'd known them both for decades, though Sai had been at the facility before Fin had arrived.

"Yeah," he sighed, leaning his head on his hand as he sagged against the arm of the sofa.

He didn't know how to help her.

"She'll come around, man," Sai said, offering a flash of a smile before turning to his game. Fin tipped his head back.

He didn't blame her. Most hybrids that arrived were angry, it took a while for them to settle. After years of not knowing what they were, and having nothing to focus on, it was expected that they would be a bit wild. But this was something else. She was a burning ball of raw emotion and rage.

"What was it like?" Gren questioned.

Fin looked at him, sighing as he leaned forward to rest his forearms against his thighs, "It was the worst place I've ever been."

Sai stiffened, "That bad?"

"It was just so...cold, sinister almost." Fin struggled to find the right words, unable to grasp how he felt.

"It's the Shadows, what do you expect?" Gren huffed.

Fin gave him a withering look, "Say what's on your mind."

"I don't trust her."

Fin shook his head, not at all surprised that his friend felt that way, "You don't know her."

Neither did he, not really, but that was beside the point.

"And you do?"

Fin sighed, dragging a hand through his head, "No."

"Then_"

"Gren," Sai groaned, "Give her a chance."

"She tried to kill him."

Sai scoffed, "Who hasn't tried to kill him?"

"She's from the Shadows." Gren bit out.

"And what were you doing before you came here?" Fin challenged. Gren held his gaze, but clicked his tongue and looked away, knowing he'd lose that particular argument.

"You know word has spread about a former Shadow being here?" Sai murmured after a long moment.

Fin groaned, "Great." He didn't need anyone else questioning Niah's presence, in the end, it was Merida's decision on who stayed in the facility.

"I'm guessing I have Dea to thank for that?" Fin questioned.

Sai waved a dismissive hand, "You know she can't help herself. She's not said anything negative about Niah."

That didn't matter, though. As soon as people learned she was from the Shadows, they would make their own assumptions, and after the sword through the door, rumours would spread like wildfire.

Fin huffed and got to his feet, Sai and Gren waving a quick goodbye without taking their eyes off their game. He wandered the corridors with his hands in his pockets. Only pausing outside Niah's room, the sword was now gone, leaving a narrow slit where it had once been. He carried on walking, not feeling like having anything else thrown at him.

Merida's voice carried through the door before he could even knock.

She was sitting at the desk in her room, looking over a stack of papers. Her eyes flicked to him briefly before offering a warm smile and turning back to the documents.

He sighed, folding his arms across his chest, "You're supposed to be resting."

"I just needed to check something." She muttered, not looking up from whatever she was reading.

"That can wait."

Merida's eyes lifted to his then, "Did something happen?"

"She threw a sword at me."

Her brows raised, a slight smile tugging at the corners of her mouth before she chuckled.

"Oh, well, I'm glad you find that so amusing," he sighed, leaning against the wall.

"I was just thinking how much she reminds me of you when you arrived."

He didn't care if she was laughing at him or not; it was just good to hear the sound from her mouth.

"Then we're all doomed," he grinned.

Merida exhaled slowly, leaning back in her chair, "I can imagine it's difficult for her."

"Hm, it's difficult for all of us."

The smile faded from her lips, "It's different for her_"

"I know," he sighed, "I know, M. You need to address this to the others. They're restless knowing there's a former Shadow under the same roof."

"Niah was never a Shadow."

"They don't know that," Fin breathed, "They won't know the difference, and after everything, they won't care."

Merida nodded, "Understood, thank you."

Sensing the conversation was over, he dropped a kiss on the top of her head and turned for the door.

With his hand on the knob, he paused, "Why do you want me to be the one to help her? Wouldn't you rather do it?"

Merida was quiet, thoughtful, before answering, "Because there are things you see in a person that not even I do."

Fin lowered his eyes, unsure of how to respond to that.

Merida went on, "And, I trust you above all others."

He tipped his head back, sighing loudly, "You know I can't resist when you say sappy crap like that."

"You asked." She shrugged.

"Fine, but if she throws another sword at me, I'm done," he chuckled.

"Just give her time. Be there for her," she frowned, a flicker of pain in her blue eyes.

"You know I will." he tried to give her a reassuring smile, but it didn't seem to reach her, he wasn't sure he felt it himself.

NIAH

10

The screams wove their way into her dream.

The colours bled away, leaving nothing but darkness. Something tugged at her slumbering mind, telling her to wake up. The screams came again, the darkness fell away, her mind sharpening into focus as her eyes flew wide, and she scrambled out of bed.

She grasped the dagger from the nightstand.

Banging, screams, and the clang of metal radiated through the thin walls. Niah wanted to clamp her hands over her ears to block it all out.

But that was her mothers' scream.

Her eyes fixed on the door handle, the dagger gripped tightly between both trembling hands. She had always been told never to open the door.

No matter what.

Every nerve in her small body shrieked at her to move. Footsteps thundered past her bedroom and into her parents' room, followed by shouts and more screams.

She willed her feet forward, clamping her teeth together as she reached out with a quivering hand for the doorknob. The door creaked open, and she stepped out into the hallway, holding the dagger as she had been shown.

Light streamed out against the wall opposite her parents' bedroom.

She crept along the hall, peering around the doorframe to see four big men attacking her parents.

Two of them held her mother's arms out to the sides, her once white nightgown now torn and bloody. The other two advanced on her father, his chest bare and heaving as he gripped his sword in both hands.

The air was thick with sweat and hatred.

The two men facing her father glanced at each other before they both attacked simultaneously.

She had to do something.

Adrenaline pumped through her veins, and she darted forward, plunging the dagger into the thigh of one of the men holding her mother. He roared, releasing her mother, and spun with his fist out, striking Niah in the jaw. Her teeth sang, jaw throbbing as she stumbled backwards, clutching at her face.

"Niah," her mother breathed.

With her arm now fee, she swung a punch at the other man holding her, he staggered back, and she lunged for him, but she was too slow. The man had pulled a dagger from his boot and drove it up into her gut. She stilled, blood trickling over her bottom lip.

A scream tore through Niah's throat.

Her mother took a shaky step back, the blade still buried in her stomach. She looked to her husband, who was staring right back at her as silver lined his eyes. The men facing him took advantage of his distraction, one of them plunging a sword through his chest. He cried out, clamping his eyes shut and gritting his teeth as he fell to one knee.

Tears rolled down Niah's cheeks.

Her father met her gaze. There was no pain in his eyes, no suffering. With blood trickling down his chin, he smiled.

No.

Please no.

In one last surge of strength, her parents' yanked the weapons protruding from their bodies and advanced on the men before them. Her mother slashed the throat of the man who had stabbed her, and quickly threw the blade; it sank into the forehead of the second attacker with a *sickening crunch.*

One of the men facing her father stumbled in front of the other, and her father took advantage, driving his sword as hard as he could straight through the both of them.

The men stilled; a final ragged breath escaped their lips as they fell to the floor in a heap. A still, lifeless heap.

Her mother fell.

Then her father.

Niah stared at the scene before her. Furniture broken and scattered across the floor, blood spattered up the walls. Bodies piled up around her.

A whimper escaped through her lips as her mothers' fingers twitched, and Niah ran to her, grasping her mothers' hand between hers.

Her stomach was roiling, bile rising in her throat as she tried to stifle her cries. She'd never felt the cold before, but she felt it deep in her bones now. Her Mother, barely conscious, only smiled and placed a bloodied hand on her daughter's cheek.

Her heart was pounding so loud in her ears she almost couldn't hear her. Her body quivered violently, a gaping hole had been punched straight through her chest.

"Don't cry. You must go to the academy...find Karliah," her mother instructed weakly, the ghost of a smile on her lips.

And then she was gone.

Her chest stopped moving.

The room was silent. She knew her father was dead too.

She didn't know how long she sat there, clutching her mother's lifeless hand. Her heart had slowed; the ringing in her ears grew silent as the tears stopped falling.

She picked up her dagger, glancing over her shoulder as she left the room, catching a final glimpse of her father's face, and then her mother's.

Five days. It had been five days since Niah arrived in Australia. Five days since she had stepped foot outside the room. Five days since she had eaten or slept. Five days, staring at those damn books. Five days of that same nightmare every time she closed her eyes.

She sighed, raking a hand through her tangled hair. Her eyes stung from lack of sleep, but she couldn't bring herself to close them.

Someone had knocked at her door a couple of times a day, leaving bags of food in the corridor. She ignored it. Hunger didn't call to her; the thought of eating anything made her want to throw up.

She sat now, gazing at the book on the desk, the same way she had every night since she first opened it. How many times had she read the words now? Enough that they were imprinted into her mind. Tattooed onto her eyelids, so that was all she saw when she closed them.

Niah suspected it was her mother, the woman who had raised her, who wrote the entries. The penmanship was consistent, they never referred to Niah as their daughter or even her name. And it never referred to them as 'we'; it was always 'I' or 'my'.

It broke her heart. She had loved them, and she was nothing to them.

A weapon, she reminded herself.

When she could no longer stand reading the bitter, cold words about herself, she turned to the book Merida had given her. Those words, at least, were easier to read. They didn't threaten to slice her heart into ribbons.

Hybrids. What a strange concept. A creature of both demon and angel. She read about their traits, the silver ring around the iris being the most prominent. Fast healing, great strength, speed, and stamina. They're immortal, whereas the Shadows had to have a mark to prevent their aging.

It wasn't just hybrids in the book, but all supernatural beings. Lycanthropes, spell weavers, vampires, and fey. However, there wasn't much information on halflings or Nephilim.

By the fifth day of doing nothing but reading those books, she felt hollow. At first, she had been full of anger. She vaguely remembered throwing a sword at Fin in a blind rage. He hadn't turned up since then. Good. She didn't want to see him.

After the first couple of days, when the anger had dulled, she hadn't wanted to believe any of it. She nearly left then. Not wanting to believe she meant so little to the people she thought loved her.

She tried sleeping that night. Only to wake up an hour later drenched in sweat and gasping for air before rushing to the toilet and vomiting until there was nothing left.

Her chest was heavy, her heart barely more than a led weight. There was nothing. No anger, no hurt, no pain; there was only a numbing silence.

Everything she grew up believing was a lie.

She wasn't born for great things, she wasn't special, she was simply a pawn—a tool to be used.

The Shadows would have used her anger and hatred to their advantage. They would have weaved some lie, and she would have believed it. Niah would have done anything for revenge, she'd dreamt about it enough, hungered for it more than air.

For a while, she tried to talk herself out of it, not wanting to believe any of it. There had to be some logical explanation; maybe it was a misunderstanding?

It didn't matter how much she wanted to believe it, not with all the evidence pointing to the contrary.

The numbing silence broke, scorched by the fire raging in her stomach. She got to her feet, pacing the space for something to take the edge off. It didn't. The fires choked the air from her lungs, blurring her vision and clouding her mind as she struggled to rein it in.

Why bother?

Her hand went to the locket hanging around her neck. Why had those people given it to her if they felt nothing for her? She didn't care.

Niah yanked the pendant from her throat and stalked to the sliding doors, stepping out onto the balcony as she raised her arm, preparing to throw the damned thing. But as she stood there, holding the locket in her hand, the breeze blowing her hair around her shoulders, something cracked in her chest.

It was real.

To Niah, it was all real.

The love she'd felt for them, the laughing, the books and horse riding through the meadows, the mourning and grief after. It was all real.

They must have felt *something*. They wouldn't have given her the necklace if they hadn't.

Maybe, in their way, they did care for her. What if they were forced to do it? What if they were pawns too?

There was so much Niah didn't know about the Shadows. After all she had witnessed, she wouldn't put it past them to sacrifice the very people that had raised her if it meant they would acquire a vengeful weapon.

Her knees buckled, and she found herself on the floor, gripping the necklace in her hand.

Were her parents' prisoners too?

Not her parents, she reminded herself. But they were, in the ways that mattered, they were. To her, at least.

She clasped the locket around her neck once more. Despite everything she had read, she wasn't ready to part with it.

Niah needed answers, and there was only one person she could turn to.

Niah made her way through the corridors, keeping her shoulders back and squared, her chin high as she had all those years in the academy. People passed by, but, to her surprise, no one flinched away. They didn't take a wide birth around her as if she were a dangerous creature. Some of them even smiled.

She didn't smile back.

Niah found the door, and knocked gently, and a tired sounding voice told her to come in. The door fell shut behind her, but Merida didn't look up until Niah moved closer to the desk. When she finally met Niah's gaze, her eyes widened.

The leader got to her feet, "Is everything okay? You look…"

Niah raised a brow, she hadn't bothered showering or even pulling a brush through her hair.

Merida cleared her throat when Niah said nothing, "I'm surprised you came to see me."

"I have questions." Niah shrugged. Something in Merida's graze brightened, and she sat in her chair, gesturing for Niah to take a seat opposite. She did so, noticing the crack in the glass-topped desk was gone.

"What did you want to know?" Merida asked.

A million questions were floating around in Niah's head; which ones should she start with?

"You said the academy was created to deceive me, but why would the Shadows go to the trouble?"

"You're a hybrid. If you don't have something to fixate on, a goal, for example, you'll grow hostile and, in some cases, feral. Giving you the tests to channel your energy into would have leashed your demonic impulses." Merida explained, her hands clasping together where they rested on the desk.

"And the other students?"

"They likely weren't students at all, just younger warriors in training."

"That seems like a lot of effort for the sake of conditioning one person," Niah muttered, her eyes narrowing as she searched Merida's eyes.

The leader loosed a slow breath, "Indeed. But you're not just one person, are you? Not only are you a hybrid, but you also have magic in your veins. There have only been two others with the same mix."

A weapon indeed.

If what the woman said was to be believed.

"You must be mistaking me with someone else," Niah sighed, "I've never been able to use magic."

"Were you ever shown how?" Niah shook her head, "Then how do you know it's not there?"

"Wouldn't I have felt it?" she retorted, her fingers curling around the arms of the chair.

Merida shrugged, "It's hard to say, not every spell weaver is the same." When Niah said nothing, Merida went on, "We could teach you how to use it, if that's what you want?"

One step at a time.

"Who *are* the Shadows? What is their role in all this?"

Merida leaned back in her chair, "They're an old organisation. They've been around for centuries, and truthfully, we don't know much about them. Their ambitions are a mystery, as are the leaders. The only thing we know for sure is that they've been hunting hybrids for hundreds of years, but that has stopped in the last two decades."

"I thought the Shadows were the protectors of the world. I was told they hunt demons, that they keep humanity safe. Is that not the case?" Niah questioned, her fingers relaxing.

Merida huffed a slight chuckle, "It would make our job a lot easier if it were. They *used* to protect the human race, but that stopped in the last one hundred years or so. The Fury Alliance stepped up in their place, and we have hunted demons ever since."

"So, the Shadows haven't really done anything?"

"Not entirely. They kidnap halflings, spell weavers, and other species when they see fit. It appears as though they've been building an army for centuries, but whenever we've sent warriors to find out why, they haven't returned." The woman explained, her tone turning grave as she looked down at her hands.

"Have the Shadows and the Furies ever come to blows?" Niah asked, getting to her feet to look at the books on the shelves.

"Only on a small scale."

"Why have you never retaliated?"

Merida sighed, "Our spies have never returned when they went looking. Whether they found where the Shadows are hiding or not, we don't know. I told you, we don't know much about them."

Niah trailed her fingers along the worn books, "And the Furies? What is it you want?"

"Freedom. The Alliance is more than warriors; we offer protection to those who seek it. Of course, there will always be those who choose to live independently of a guild or clan, but if they wish it, there will always be a safe place for them in the facilities." Merida said with a soft voice, a slight smile tugging at the corners of her mouth.

Niah turned back to the books, "Fighting for freedom sounds like a dream."

"It is, in many ways. The road is long and dangerous, but we fight for the freedom of all supernatural species, as well as the human race."

Niah dragged a hand through her knotted hair and sat down opposite Merida once again, "Why go to the bother of getting me out?"

Merida paused at the question, leaning forward to rest her forearms against the desk, "I knew your mother."

Niah's heart stumbled.

"Marina, a demon crossed with a spell weaver. I vowed I would protect you, I realise I failed, but I never stopped looking for you. I'm so sorry for everything you've been through." Merida's voice was barely more than a whisper, her ocean blue eyes glistening.

Niah wasn't ready to hear about her birth parents.

"So, what now?" she asked, hardening her features to give nothing away, "You have me. Do you want to use me like the Shadows did?"

Merida flinched at the sharpness in her voice, "No, of course not. I told you before, you're free to leave whenever you want; but I needed you to know the truth."

"How do I know any of this is the truth, huh? How do I know you're any better than the Shadows?" Niah accused, leaning forward in her chair.

Merida regarded her thoughtfully for a moment, "I suppose you will have to decide for yourself what you believe. I never expected you to trust me straight away. I'm surprised you stayed at all, but I'm glad you did."

Niah shrugged, "I have nowhere else to go."

"You and I both know that wouldn't stop you. As true as it may be, if you wanted to leave, you would have." Merida said, her eyes clear and comforting.

What was it about the woman that made Niah feel a little less on edge? Her very presence soothed something deep in her chest, and her mind opened to it, letting the warmth chase away the bitter chill.

It was that feeling of warmth and comfort flooding her bones, that she said, "I don't know what to do. I don't know what to believe."

Merida's face softened, her fingers twitching as though she wanted to reach across the desk and take Niah's hand in hers, "Your entire life has been based on a lie. Whether you choose to accept that or not is up to you. But you won't be able to move forward until you do."

Niah, not knowing what to say, rose to her feet and turned for the door. She needed to be alone with her thoughts, to process all she'd learnt over the last few days.

"Niah," Merida said when she reached the door, Niah paused with her hand on the handle, and turned her head slightly, "whether you decide to stay or not is up to you, but you can come to me for anything. Whether that be to ask questions, or because you need money or anything else to go your own way. You're always welcome, no matter what you choose."

She didn't know what to say, so she said nothing, and slipped out of the door, letting it click shut behind her.

Niah knew she had to make a decision, but it wasn't tonight.

NIAH

11

The facility was silent as she made her way through the halls. Another person was coming toward her, but she reached her door before they could cross paths. Niah went to close the door, but it thudded against something solid.

Her hand curled around her dagger as she peered around the edge of the door. Emerald eyes ringed with silver looked back at her, narrowed and icy with warning and contempt.

How many times had she seen that same look?

"Yes?" she said through her teeth when the strange man said nothing. She didn't open the door any wider, only held his glare with her own.

"I don't know what your intentions are here, but I won't let anyone get hurt. Merida and Fin might trust you, but I don't." the man growled, low enough so that anyone walking nearby wouldn't be able to hear.

She raised a brow, he wasn't supposed to be speaking to her.

"I'm sure you've thought of a great speech; consider me warned. Now, I suggest you move your foot."

He didn't.

"You've already tried to kill Fin once_"

"If I were trying to kill him, he'd be dead." Niah growled. The man's nostrils flared, his eyes narrowing a touch as his hands balled into fists at his sides.

"You're young and arrogant, and we have decades worth of experience and training on you. So I suggest you be careful."

Niah couldn't help but rise to the challenge, and shoved the door wide open, stepping close enough that she could scent the cologne on him.

"Well, don't just stand there making threats. Go ahead."

For a moment, she thought he would do just that, but the man clicked his tongue, leaning forward slightly.

"Hurt anyone in this facility, and I'll do just that." He snarled, and then turned on his heel, stalking down the corridor. Niah's heart was thrumming, adrenaline shooting through her veins as she closed and locked the door.

It had been too long since she had exercised, and that altercation made her realise how much energy and frustration she had to burn off. It would make for a good distraction too.

Niah went through her usual warm-up routine, minus the run, and began a workout routine. The burn in her muscles was welcome, as was the ache in her lungs. But, more than anything, it prevented her from having to think about what she needed to.

Another few days passed, and Niah was no closer to figuring out what she wanted to do. How was she supposed to accept everything she'd learnt?

It felt like a dream, or a nightmare; she wasn't sure which.

Being in the facility was turning into more of a comfort as the days went by. She ate the food left for her, slept for more than an hour or two, exercised in her room to stave off the boredom, and she'd been able to settle enough to read. She still jumped at every noise outside her door, but it was getting easier to ignore it.

After a shower and changing into a clean set of clothes that had been left for her, she stepped onto the balcony to gaze at the ocean stretching into the distance.

The moon and stars shone overhead; Niah could taste the salt of the sea breeze on her tongue, and closed her eyes as she inhaled deeply, allowing the warmth to thaw the ice in her heart.

The only thing she had been able to decide on over the last few days was that she wanted revenge, not for her parents, but herself. Whether Merida was telling the truth or not, she *knew* the siblings had tried to harm her, she'd seen proof that she was nothing more than a weapon.

It was enough to warrant her hatred.

Niah was perhaps the only person who could get close to them, and if she had to, she would use the Furies to do it. She had no loyalty to them, despite what they had done for her, but she couldn't allow herself to become complacent as she had in England.

No matter how at ease Merida made her feel, no matter how much safer she felt in the facility, she wouldn't be fooled again.

A knock at the door snapped her out of her reverie. Fin stood on the other side, a slight smile on his lips.

"Do you want to come for a walk?" he asked.

After being held up in her room for days on end, Niah was ready to crawl out of her skin. A walk might help clear her head, and she might get some information out of Fin in the process.

She nodded and stepped outside, locking the door behind her. Fin walked beside her, his hands in his pockets; he was unusually quiet.

Niah decided to break the silence, "How long have you been here?"

"Fifty-two years," he answered as they made their way out the back door of the facility and toward the beach.

Right, hybrids were immortal.

"How long did it take for you to trust the Alliance? And Merida?" she asked, being careful not to ask the wrong questions.

Fin glanced at her then, "A while."

"Define a while."

He shrugged, "A couple of months."

"Why stay if you didn't trust her?"

"Because it was better than the alternative." Fin answered, his voice edged.

"You've been fighting for the Alliance ever since?"

"There's nothing else to fight for," he grinned, "why the sudden interest?"

Niah shrugged, "I don't know whether to stay."

"Yes, you do, you just don't want to admit it," he said, turning his eyes to the sky.

"Don't act like you know anything about me," she said in warning.

Fin shrugged, "Don't act like you *want* to know anything about me." Niah narrowed her eyes, and he clarified, "Don't think I don't know you're just trying to gather information. I've been around a long time, I know when someone is genuine."

Niah clicked her tongue and turned away. Perhaps it was a mistake to stay.

They came to a stop on the path where the paving stones met the sand, and Niah just stared for a moment, letting the gentle lapping of the waves soothe her. She felt drawn to the ocean for some reason. Sometimes, she could have sworn it was calling to her.

"It's so...different," she murmured.

Fin chuckled under his breath, "Yeah, it is. You were unlucky; most of us grew up in the supernatural world. You were unfortunate, taught that you were no better than demons. It's cruel." His voice turned sharp toward the end, his eyes hardening.

"How do I know this is real? That it isn't just another lie?"

Fin didn't answer straight away, he stepped forward onto the sand, bending to take his shoes and socks off. Niah raised a brow at him, but he only smiled when he met her gaze.

"Have you ever walked barefoot in the sand?"

She shook her head, and glanced at his feet, his toes vanishing beneath the sand. Niah glanced around at her surroundings.

"No one will harm you," Fin said carefully, "This part of the beach is cloaked, and no one from the facility would do anything."

Except that there were people who didn't trust her, people who didn't want her in the facility. But Fin wasn't to know that.

With a sigh, she bent down and yanked off the trainers that had also been left for her. The powdery, cool sand shifted between her toes, but even that slight temperature change soon faded as her body adjusted.

"Do you feel like you're being lied to? What does your gut tell you?" Fin asked after a minute, going back to the question she had asked earlier.

She snorted, "How would I know? I was lied to for nearly eighteen years and didn't know."

"Then why would you believe me if I told you it was all true?" he quizzed, raising a brow. Well, he wasn't wrong.

Niah watched him for a moment, he was graceful, all angles, yet there was a softness to him. He walked with his hands in his pockets, his shoes dangling out by his legs held by their laces. His silvery eyes reflected the moonlight as it danced across the water.

She noticed he, too, carried a dagger at his side; instinctively, she laid a hand on the hilt of hers—more a habit than anything else.

"Do you trust me?" Niah asked. Fin sighed at that and dragged a hand through his hair.

"No. Merida does, but as you said, I don't know you. Trust is earned, and it goes both ways."

"There's a lot I need to figure out."

"That's to be expected. Take as much time as you need, but you have to understand that people here haven't had the best experiences when it comes to the Shadows. They're on edge, but they respect Merida's orders. Don't take that for granted, and maybe go easy on the sword throwing." He chuckled, an attempt to lighten the mood.

Niah shrugged, "I missed."

It was fair for Fin to ask her to be considerate of the others in the facility. She was a stranger from their enemy, she could even understand the threat from that guy, but Niah had never *tried* to be nice to anyone.

"I overheard that you put four boys in the infirmary in England," Fin smirked.

Niah raised a brow, "I was the best." Fin chuckled at that.

"*Was.*"

"I'd be happy to give you a demonstration," she scoffed, secretly hoping he'd meet her challenge, if only so she had someone to spar with.

Fin smirked, a glint in his eyes as he leaned a little closer, "Fine, but you've got to promise not to cry when I knock you on your ass."

Oh, she would enjoy making him suffer.

The Furies offered her something she never had before, choice. Merida claimed the Alliance fought for freedom, and so far, Niah had no reason to believe otherwise. No one forced her to stay.

She could choose to be someone else, not what someone wanted her to be. Her goal of revenge may be the same, but it was *her* choice. She hadn't ruled out that perhaps Merida wanted to use her, and if she tried, Niah would destroy the Furies as well.

Until she knew for sure what Merida's intentions were for her, she would keep at a distance, but there was a part of her that wanted to try. A part of her that wanted to smile and laugh and be just an ordinary girl. But what was ordinary in this strange world she found herself in?

Maybe, if she let herself, she could find out.

They walked a while in silence, Niah enjoying the soothing sounds of the rolling ocean, and the twinkling of the stars above.

"Fin!" a high voice called from behind them, they turned to see three figures striding toward them.

Fin reached out a hand and shook his head, she hadn't realised she had halfway drawn her dagger.

One of the people, a girl, sprinted straight for Fin. He smiled when she launched herself at him, wrapping her long legs around his waist, kissing him on the lips fiercely.

The girl was beautiful, as graceful as Fin was. She had long, snowy white hair that flew free as she jumped through the air. Her eyes were a bright sky blue with the same silver ring around the iris.

Niah turned away, feeling uncomfortable around such a public display of affection. The other two figures were boys, one tall with short, jet hair and light brown eyes with the silver ring. The other was a head shorter with slicked-back hair the colour of sand, his eyes were emerald green.

He was the one who had threatened her days ago.

The girl glanced at Niah and slid down Fin until she stood in the sand. She wore a pair of tight denim shorts and a top that showed off the flat lines of her stomach.

"Who's this?" she asked in a musically high voice, taking Fin's hand in hers.

"This is Niah, she's new," he said, glancing at Niah, "this is Dea, and that's Sai," he pointed to the taller, dark-haired boy. The name 'Dea' rolled off the tongue, pronounced 'Dayah'. "and that's Grenville." he gestured to the blonde.

"We've met," Niah said, her gaze lingering on the blonde. She felt Fin's questioning gaze, but didn't meet it.

"Oh?" Fin murmured. No one said a word, Niah could taste the tension on her tongue.

Sai cleared his throat and cracked a smile, "Ignore him, he's a sweetie when you get to know him."

A growl rumbled through Grenville's chest, but he said nothing, standing with his hands in his pockets, and a glare to rival her own.

Dea looked her up and down, Niah arched a brow and tilted her chin upward, squaring her shoulders. Dea's gaze drifted to her face, and she beamed a bright, dazzling smile, catching Niah off guard as she stepped forward and draped an arm around her shoulders.

Niah thought about shrugging the girl off, but something about her open friendliness stopped her. It was the first time anyone had been so casual with her.

"How do you like the building?" Dea asked, gesturing behind them toward the facility they had come from.

"It's...different," she said, not knowing how else to describe it. Dea was virtually bouncing along the sand as she walked, still with her arm around Niah's shoulders.

They all sat down in the sand, though Niah was dragged by Dea and hadn't had time to protest before she was sitting down.

The girl turned to her, still with her arm linked through Niah's, "We haven't seen you around, has everything been okay?"

Niah searched the girls' eyes, looking for any hint of distrust or contempt; there was nothing but kindness and genuine curiosity.

"It's been an adjustment."

Gren scoffed, and Niah turned her glare on him, ready to launch herself at him if he made another comment.

"Shut up, idiot," Sai groaned before turning his gaze on Niah, "Seriously, ignore him."

"With pleasure."

Dea giggled, "It's about time someone gave it back to him."

"Alright, enough, you bunch of children," Fin chuckled, shaking his head, "Gren, come and help me find some twigs or something." The blonde didn't hesitate before getting to his feet and following Fin down the beach, leaving Niah with Dea and Sai. She couldn't help but check and double-check her surroundings as the two chatted amongst themselves.

"Don't worry, he's harmless," Sai said after a minute, Niah tilted her head to one side. She didn't care whether Grenville was the nicest person in the world or the meanest, it wasn't as though she were planning to befriend him.

"It doesn't bother me." the words tasted like a lie.

A few minutes later, Fin and Gren returned with enough twigs to make a small fire. The crackling, warm glow was oddly relaxing, and Niah found herself a little more at ease. She leaned back on her hands, and gazed up at the stars, losing herself in the smells of the sea and fire.

She didn't hear what the others were saying, Niah was perfectly content to gaze at the night sky, listening to the sound of waves lapping onto the shore.

"You're from England, right?" Sai asked. She turned to look at him, his face was soft and boyish, but his jaw was sharp, his eyes angled in a way that could make him somewhat intimidating if he wasn't smiling. The warmth of the fire radiated his beautiful tawny skin, almost as though he were glowing from within.

"Yeah," she answered.

"I've always wanted to visit England," Dea sighed wistfully.

Niah couldn't hold back her snort. Eyes turned to her, but no one spoke. Well, that was one way to ruin the atmosphere. She opened her mouth to say something, but quickly closed it at the sympathy in Sai's eyes, and turned to gaze into the flames.

"The weather's awful anyway," Fin said, and just like that, it was as though nothing had happened. The three of them went back to talking, Grenville the quiet one of the three. Dea curled into the blonde's lap and started stroking his hair.

Niah flicked her eyes to Fin, if he was bothered, he didn't show it. Instead, he got to his feet and gestured for Niah to follow him.

"Well, I can't be sitting here watching this," Sai sighed as he got to his own feet.

"Join us if you want?" Dea suggested, the sound of her voice muffled by Grenville's lips.

"Nah, not tonight; I've got patrol." he smiled.

The three of them started back toward the facility.

"You said you're going on patrol?" Niah questioned, unable to hold it in any longer.

"Yeah, we usually get alerts of demonic activity, but we go on patrol just in case, it means we can get there faster if there's an attack." Sai explained.

"Does it happen often?"

"More so than we'd like, but we're always quick enough to stop any human casualties. It's why we're the best facility," Sai winked.

"Sai, like you, is very confident in his abilities," Fin mused.

"And there's every reason to be, right?" he teased, gently nudging Niah in the arm with his elbow, "Anyway, I've gotta run, it was nice to meet you, Niah." He loped away before she could say goodbye.

Fin and Niah started walking at a leisurely pace. Niah couldn't remember if she had ever strolled anywhere before, she usually just marched with a look of death on her face.

"Does that not bother you?" she asked, his brow furrowed, so she clarified, "Dea and Grenville?"

"Oh, no."

"Why not? Isn't she your girlfriend?" she asked. Niah had read about relationships in books; knew they were supposed to be between two people who were either boyfriends or girlfriends, or husbands and wives, or girlfriends and girlfriends and so on.

"No. We don't do that sort of thing; we're mostly polyamorous or non-monogamous. Monogamy was something humans came up with, it's only in the last couple hundred years or so that people started marrying for love. Before that, it was usually down to beneficial matches. Relationships and so on don't interest us. We just do what we want, when we want," he explained with a coy grin dancing on his lips.

"Don't you believe in love?" she asked.

He shrugged, "Love is a human concept, and we're not human. It's written in the book that we have a bond similar to how love is described, but it's something much deeper than that, a bigger connection. We call it 'the second half of my heart'" he told her, his expression unreadable, his voice void of any emotion.

"Do you?" he asked when she didn't reply. Niah turned to him, her brows pulled together, "Believe in love?" he clarified, arching a brow with a slight smirk on his lips.

"I've read about it."

"That wasn't what I asked," he chuckled.

She folded her arms over her chest, "No. I don't."

"I bet you've never even known friendship," he said, more as a statement than a question. Niah glared at him then, and he held his palms up in surrender. "I didn't mean it in a bad way. Just, it can't have been easy," a surge of annoyance washed through her veins at the sympathy in his voice.

"It was...whatever," she snapped and glared at the sand as she walked, shoving her hands into the pockets of her jeans, still holding the laces of her trainers as they bumped against her thigh.

"Snappy. You know, if you did want a friend, I guess I wouldn't mind."

"You *wouldn't mind*?" as if it were a favour.

Fin grinned, "Well, I am hilarious, and rather attractive, I could help you out learning about the world."

"Modest too, huh?"

"Ouch, sarcasm. I didn't know you could do that," he winked, teasing her. Niah scoffed and shoved him away. He stumbled, but quickly righted himself. To her amusement, it was the first ungraceful thing he'd done.

"Oh, is that how it is?" he crouched, and she cried out as he tackled her, knocking her flying. She cursed herself inwardly for not being more prepared. Though she tried to remember the last time she had laughed, or if she had ever laughed at all. The sound was so alien as it left her lips. And for that one moment, there was nothing else. There was no tormenting past. No books of experiments. There were no Shadows and no Furies. She was just a girl on a beach, with a boy she barely knew.

And maybe that was enough.

For a few minutes at least.

Niah didn't bother getting to her feet; instead, she lay on her back in the sand, gazing up at the moon and stars. The echoes of laughter rippled through her body as the smile lingered on her lips. She inhaled deeply, greedily at the fresh sea air, and closed her eyes. Savouring the sweet moment.

The sand shifted as Fin lay down beside her. She didn't open her eyes, didn't say anything for the longest of times. She just wanted to lay there, under the stars, and not fear anything. Even if it was temporary.

"I feel like I'm in a different world," she muttered when she opened her eyes. And just like that, the illusion shattered. Would it ever be easy? If she were immortal, surely there would come a time when she wouldn't be fighting. When she could be just a girl, with a boy, or a girl, she didn't know.

There were still a million questions in her head, but for right now, maybe this was enough.

The ghost of a smile brushed her lips.

"You are, in a sense. But, luckily, you have an amazing teacher, so 'ya know, you got that going for you," she could hear the smile in his voice, and huffed a short laugh. He rolled onto his side and propped himself up on his elbow, peering down at her with bright silver eyes.

"I know there's a whole heap of mess flying about in that head of yours, and we only just met, but, sword throwing aside, you could talk to me if you needed to." his voice was so painfully gentle. She sat up and let her arms dangle over her knees; Fin mimicked the movement.

"I've never spoken to anyone about anything. I still don't know if I'm going to stay, I don't know if I can trust any of you." Niah looked down at the sand between her feet. It was, perhaps, the most honest she had ever been with anyone.

"It's been what, ten days? These things take time. It's up to you when and how you tell anyone, if that happens to be me, then I'll listen, so will Merida." He held her gaze, his eyes gentle and understanding.

Niah had wanted to keep her distance, but at that moment, a door opened inside her. Could this be the different life she had dreamt of?

No.

It couldn't.

Because whether she wanted to admit it or not, her stay with the Furies *was* temporary. Whatever this was with Fin would inevitably end. It didn't matter whether Niah wanted a friend, or just *someone* to talk to, that wasn't her goal. But for the time being, she had to remind herself that the Furies were a means to an end. She would manipulate, lie, fight, do whatever she had to do to use their fighters.

Niah wasn't naïve enough to think she could take on the Shadows alone, but she had the best chance of getting close to them, and if she could earn Merida's trust enough to have her opinions valued, she might be able to acquire the Furies forces.

That was her best chance.

Maybe when it was all over, when the Shadows no longer stood, then she could think about friends.

Until then, she had to detach herself.

Fin walked her back to her room and leaned against the wall by the door, arms crossed, "Do you think you're ready to start training tomorrow?"

"I didn't realise you were so eager to be beaten senseless." Niah scoffed.

Fin chuckled, "We'll see how long you can keep that attitude up. I'll come to get you at five AM." With that, he turned and strode down the corridor.

Niah watched him go, reminding herself that he was a means to an end. He held sway with Merida, and if she could get Fin to trust her, then maybe it would be easier to convince Merida to do as she suggested.

He was a means to an end, nothing more.

Niah repeated those same words until sleep claimed her.

FIN

12

He felt her gaze burning into his back.

Fin didn't bother turning, just waited for the soft click of her door closing as he strode down the corridor.

He wanted to ask what she was thinking, why she suddenly felt the need to take a feigned interest in him. If he thought she would give him an honest answer, he might have asked her.

Something *had* shifted, though, even if he couldn't put his finger on what it was. Fin shrugged, he wasn't in the right frame of mind to think about what Niah was plotting.

He made his way to the recreational room, nodding to those who dipped their chins out of respect as he joined Gren and Dea by the TV with Char and Tyson. The guys were playing a fighting game, while the two girls chatted amongst themselves, Dea with a sketchbook on her knees, and Char scrolling through her phone.

Gren flicked his eyes to Fin as he sat down but turned back to the game just as Tyson's character delivered a devastating blow.

Fin was still annoyed with Gren. After hearing that he and Niah had already met, and from the way the tension soared, it wasn't a pleasant encounter. Fin had asked Gren about it while they went to get twigs, fully expecting Niah to have been the one to say something to upset

Gren, not the other way around. An unfair assumption, Fin supposed, but Gren had never been the type to start an altercation.

Dea glanced up from her sketchpad, "I like her."

"Who?" Char questioned, not tearing her eyes from her phone.

"Niah."

Char's head snapped up then, her brunette bob swaying with the movement, "You *met* her?" Dea's brow scrunched, and she shrugged.

"Why wouldn't I?"

"She's a Shadow," Char whispered.

"She isn't, nor has she ever been. Ignore the rumours." Fin said, casting a pointed glare at Dea. She offered an apologetic wince.

"They still raised her," Gren murmured, keeping his eyes on his game.

Fin gave him a withering look, "We can't help who we're raised by."

"Yeah, but none of us have been raised by our enemy. How do we know she isn't a spy or assassin or something?" Char questioned, putting her phone down against her thigh.

"Leave it, Char," Dea muttered.

Char turned to her, "But you're the one who said she might hurt someone."

"That was before I met her," Dea protested, "Honestly? She just seems lost." As much as Fin begrudged Dea for her big mouth, he admired how perceptive she was.

"Why don't we just give her a chance?" Tyson suggested, earning an accusatory glare from Char. The second half of my heart bond linked the two of them, a bond described as both a blessing and a curse. Fin had never cared enough to learn much about it, it wasn't something he wanted.

Fin kept quiet as the four of them bickered quietly amongst themselves. Dea defended Niah to no end, while Char and Gren argued that she could hurt someone or be working for the Shadows. They didn't know what he knew, they didn't see what she was like in that place.

He tried to ignore it, tried to justify it as ignorance, but they weren't even giving her a chance.

"Then why don't we just get Vinaxx to do a memory projection on her?" Char suggested. At that, Fin's teeth ground together. A memory projection allowed the caster to enter the victims' minds and play their memories for all to see like a movie. It was agony, and a procedure Merida didn't take lightly.

"That's enough." Fin growled, "Niah is here on Merida's orders. Unless you would like to take it up with her, I suggest you shut up."

Char blanched, and a low, warning growl rumbled from Tyson's chest at the tone Fin had taken with his soulmate.

"We're just concerned," Gren offered, sighing as he dragged his hands through his hair, "After everything the Shadows have done, surely you can understand why?"

"I do," Fin admitted, "But Niah is a victim as well." Not that she would admit that. Something in Gren's eyes softened at that.

"All I'm asking," Fin went on, "Is that you give her a chance." Gren held his gaze for a long moment, and eventually dipped his chin in agreement before turning back to the game.

Fin understood their apprehensions and concerns, he had his own when Merida told him about Niah and that she wanted him to bring her back to Perth. When Merida told him what Niah was to her, he understood and agreed without another argument.

His doubts remained, but when he laid eyes on her in that cruel place, they all ebbed away.

Fin had spent a few days in England before approaching her. There were very few officials around, only two or three that he could tell. He found the ones in charge, the two identical blondes.

He knew what they were the moment he smelt them. Fin had never met Nephilim before; their scent was almost *too* sweet, their skin a little too perfect to be human, and the way they carried themselves was full of arrogance and superiority. He kept out of sight but didn't think they would notice him even if he didn't.

The day Talon pointed Niah out to him, he was instantly intrigued. She walked the corridors with a glare, or her head in a book, and everyone avoided her. She slept at the top of the library under a thin blanket, with a book still in her hand.

What a miserable, lonely life.

She moved through those halls like a ghost. In the moments when she thought no one was looking, her face relaxed, softened even. Yet, even in those moments, her eyes were always hollow and distant.

Except for that night.

The night she overheard what Nolan had planned for her. Fin hid in the treeline, listening to it all. He saw it in Niah's eyes when she climbed up the cliff and dropped to her knees. He saw the hurt and betrayal burning in her eyes, and he'd wanted to go to her.

After all those years, he wasn't sure if Niah would be able to pull herself out of that vengeful mentality. Not that he blamed her. He wasn't sure he would have endured it any better.

But she had smiled.

She had *laughed*.

For a brief moment, there was a light in her eyes. Maybe she would never be able to trust them, not entirely, but that was okay, because at least she'd be safe.

Fin wanted to explain to the others so they would understand, but it wasn't his story to tell, and Niah would tell them when she was ready. But he didn't see that ever happening.

He couldn't apologise for snapping; as Merida's advisor, he outranked all of them, but that didn't mean it was easy. Unable to stand the tension any longer, Fin got to his feet, heading back to his rooms.

The guitar sat on the bed where he left it; he slumped down, dragging it into his lap and started plucking at the strings. The gentle, haunting melody filled him until there was nothing else.

He learned to play not long after he first arrived at the facility. It gave him something to take his mind off of the burning anger he felt back then. They were all the same when left to their own devices. Hybrids needed something to focus on, to harness all that energy and strength. Otherwise, they turned vicious.

They were once territorial creatures, little more than feral beasts. Hundreds of years ago, they lived in hordes, driven by their anger and hunger for the fight. Some of the territorial bullshit remained, but provided they had a focus, they were perfectly civil for the most part.

Niah had never learnt how to control those demonic impulses, she'd never learnt how to channel all that anger into other things. Hell, she didn't even know a single thing of the world in which she was a part of. Fin wanted to help her, but he knew she wasn't interested in that.

He'd seen it time and time again, hybrids that were so consumed by anger that they couldn't accept help. They tried using Merida's kindness, *his* kindness, and sometimes, no amount of help could stop them.

He saw that same intent in Niah's eyes. The will to manipulate them into helping her. He didn't need to know her story to know what she wanted to do, she'd been conditioned for revenge, and that was the only way she knew how to deal with her problems. She would use them to get what she wanted, and he knew that Merida would do whatever she asked.

It made him question whether he would stop her. Whether he would be the voice of reason and talk her out of whatever she had planned, or would he go along with it? Because Niah's enemy, and theirs, were and the same. Even with that thought, it felt too much like *they* were using *her*.

It didn't sit right with him.

Fin played into the night, allowing the music to soothe his tormented mind.

NIAH

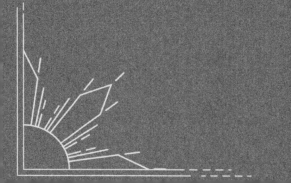

13

There was a knock at the door.

Niah opened her eyes, blinking the sleep from them as she glanced at the clock on the nightstand, five AM. She jumped out of bed and pulled on a pair of black leggings and a tank top before making her way to the door.

She could have sworn she set the alarm.

After yanking on her trainers and tying her hair up, she opened the door, unable to stifle her yawn.

"Jesus, that's a big mouth," Fin scoffed. Niah scowled at him and quickly closed her mouth.

"That's what you get for dragging me out of bed at five am."

He shrugged, "I can think of some exercises we can do *in* bed, if you'd prefer?" a smirk played at the corners of his lips. Not knowing what he meant, she tilted her head to the side and raised a brow.

"It was a joke." He clarified.

"Maybe you're just not funny?" she suggested.

"Now *that* is the funniest thing you've ever said." he grinned as they made their way out of the facility and onto the beach. Walking with trainers on the sand was harder than it had been barefoot. Sand slipped into her shoes, making it uncomfortable. She faintly missed the hard, unyielding sand back in England.

"Okay, we'll run to warm up," he said and began jogging.

Niah kept up with him, though barely. The sand constantly shifting under her feet meant she struggled to push off and get a good spring in her stride.

"You'll get used to it. If you can run on sand, you'll be even faster on solid ground," Fin called over the wind in her ears as she lengthened her stride, pushing herself faster.

"That's it," he encouraged, "Let's go." he spurted forward. Niah lengthened her stride but struggled to get a decent grip. She pumped her arms faster, the view around her blurring into colours as they sprinted down the long beach. Her lungs began to burn, as did her thighs, and she revelled in it.

The pounding of her heart cleared the fog from her mind; the air in her lungs shattered the ice encasing them. Finally, they came to a stop, both panting and sweating. The high of exercise was glorious, and Niah smiled as she tipped her face to the sky.

She didn't think she had ever run that fast before.

Niah glanced over her shoulder but was no longer able to see the facility. It didn't seem like they had run for that long. She kept walking in a circle, her hands on her hips as her lungs heaved for more air.

"Have you trained on sand before?" Fin asked through shallow breaths, she shook her head. The beach at the academy wasn't long enough to run on.

"We train this early because there are hardly any humans around, and even if there were, we'd spot them long before they saw us and slow to their pace." Fin explained, sweat glistening against his brow.

"I never knew I could run that fast," Niah muttered, mostly to herself.

There was a brief moment before Fin said, "There's a lot you never knew about yourself."

Those words were like a bucket of ice water being thrown over her. She turned her gaze to the rippling ocean. She supposed, in a way, she was like the sea. There was so much she hadn't known about herself, so many mysteries held within her blood. But like the ocean, what lay in her darkest depths?

"I'll race you back." Fin grinned, snapping her back to reality. Niah only dipped her chin and started running after him. She felt each breath in her lungs, the sting of the wind against her skin, the ache in her muscles, and the force of each stride in her toes. Sand flicked up behind them, and it wasn't long until they were neck and neck.

Everything else bled away into the void.

At that moment, she forgot everything else. It was freeing in a way she'd never experienced before. Exercise was always a means to an end, therapeutic in some ways, but this? It was euphoric.

They reached the facility, but her blood was singing, and she didn't want to stop. So she didn't. Niah kept running, and running, and running. Fin kept up, but hung back, letting her set the pace. Letting her decide how far she wanted to go.

Niah pushed for more speed, but as she did, a burning itch stung at the back of her neck, and her body weakened all at once. Her chest heaved, knocking the air from her lungs as one of her toes cracked from the pressure of her stride, and she stumbled.

Fin caught her arm and held her up while she regained her footing, "Everything okay?"

"Yeah," she panted, "my toe broke."

Fin pressed his lips together, "That shouldn't have happened."

Niah scratched at the back of her neck, "Well, it did."

"What else?" he questioned, his silver eyes darkening a touch.

Niah's brow scrunched, "I just suddenly felt weak, it's happened before." She waved away his irritating concern.

"When does it happen?"

Why all the questions?

She shrugged, "Usually when I push myself too hard."

"Can I have a look at the back of your neck?" he asked. Niah narrowed her eyes, "I just want to check something."

With a sigh, she turned her back on him and moved her ponytail to the side. She flinched at the touch of his fingers against her skin, trailing up her neck into her hairline.

Fin sucked in a sharp breath, "I should have known."

"Known what?" she questioned, turning back to him with her hand on the back of her neck.

"You're marked."

Niah's head fell silent.

"What?"

Fin sighed, dragging his hands down his face, "The Shadows have marks_"

"Yeah, I know, they make them stronger and prevent their aging."

"That's not all they do." he murmured, "There are different kinds of marks, but we've only seen two. A solid circle to control the victim, and a spiral for sealing strength and power. You have the latter."

Her hand flitted to the back of her neck once more.

"That's insane."

"It's true. That's why you suddenly felt weak, that's why your toe broke. From what we know of them, the sealing mark acts as a barrier in your mind; when you get too close to that barrier, the seal weakens you and forces you to back off." Fin explained, his voice grave.

"Wouldn't I *know* if I were marked?" she scoffed, unable to bring herself to believe a single word.

But after everything she knew of the Shadows and what they had done to her already, it should be no surprise that they kept her weak.

Fin shook his head, "It's probably been there since you were a baby; you wouldn't have remembered it being placed."

Niah turned away from him. There was nothing about a mark in the book, nothing about the Shadows weakening her. Though that didn't mean it wasn't true.

She turned back to him, "But just now_"

"I was holding back. I thought you were marked when you said you didn't know you could run so fast, but nothing happened, so I hoped I was wrong. And then you stumbled." He frowned.

Her mind was reeling.

"How much weaker am I?"

"It's easier if I show you."

"How?"

She barely got the word out before his fist was coming toward her at blinding speed. Niah barely had enough time to duck before she felt the air tear apart above her head. He was so *fast*. He immediately forced her onto her back foot, it was all she could do to evade the barrage of attacks.

Her eyes couldn't track his movements. He aimed low, she overbalanced, and he took advantage, delivering a swift uppercut to her jaw. She staggered back, her teeth singing as she clutched at her face. Her jaw had dislocated. Niah groaned through the pain and quickly pushed down and back, hearing a crack as her jaw snapped back into place. Pain lanced through her skull, but she clamped down on the whimper building in her throat.

"You see?" Fin said, barely out of breath, "With that mark on your neck, you're no match for me or any other hybrid."

Niah resisted the urge to rub her throbbing jaw. That's why the Shadows marked her; if she were as strong and as fast as Fin, none of the halflings would have stood a chance against her.

If she expected to be hurt or angry, she was mistaken. Instead, there was only a lingering disappointment in her stomach.

"Is there a way to remove it?" she asked.

Fin's eyes brightened a little, "There is, but it will be agony."

She didn't care.

"I want it gone."

He nodded, "Then come with me."

They walked down a long corridor of the ground floor, and through a set of double doors. The smell of sulphur stuffed itself up her nose as they ventured further in. Doors lined the hall, some of them looked to be classrooms, while others were labs growing herbs and various plants.

"What is this place?" she asked, gazing into a room with shelves of jars like the ones she'd seen at the spell weavers house.

"This is where the spell weavers and casters practise magic without risk of harming anyone else in the process. We don't have many weavers here, only a few dozen or so." Fin explained, pocketing his hands into his knee-length shorts.

Sure enough, she stopped outside a door to see what looked like a class in session. People with bright eyes of varying, unnatural colours took notes as one person at the front gestured to a plant Niah didn't recognise.

"Is this where I'll practise magic?" she whispered, tearing her gaze from the class to follow Fin down the corridor.

He shrugged, "Only if you want to."

Niah said nothing, it wasn't worth thinking about until the mark was off her neck. Was that why she'd never felt the magic Merida claimed was in her blood?

The thought fell silent as Fin led her through another door leading into a large, stone room. So unlike the bright, airy corridors they had just come from.

The room was lit by flame sconces fixed to the walls, the flames were white, not the usual orange and yellow. The air turned thick and stale, the smell of sulphur growing stronger the further they went. Shelves lined the walls, a hearth at the far side of the room with dancing white flames.

Standing over a desk was a tall, scrawny man with thick, white hair. When he turned to them, he was much younger than Niah expected. The lines of his face were flat and sharp, his cheekbones stuck out at an odd angle like they could slice through his skin at any moment. His eyes were a white flame, illuminating in the dimly lit room.

"Oh...oh my! I was not expecting visitors, I am unprepared, so unprepared...I apologise, I am never unprepared for anything," the man rambled in a high voice that spiked with tension as he fumbled with random jars on the desk.

Niah glanced around the room; the only way out was the way they came. Her fingers itched to go to her dagger.

"Vinaxx, it's okay. I disturbed you, I'm sorry," Fin soothed. The man, Vinaxx, turned slowly, his eyes wide.

"Oh...no, come now, it's not your fault, I should have known you were here...should have known, perhaps some tea might help," he said, scurrying over to another table with a bubbling pot of dark liquid. He grabbed the ladle, pouring the liquid into a handle-less mug and raised it to his lips for a greedy swallow.

Niah fought the urge to gag.

The man closed his eyes, exhaling slowly before placing the mug down, and with a clap of his hands, the room blazed with light as the torches brightened. He sauntered toward them, looking rather pleased with himself.

"Better?" Fin asked with a wry smile.

"Much. Now, what can old Vinaxx do you for?" he asked with a big toothy smile, most of which were stained with the black liquid. Niah's stomach churned.

"Niah is marked," Fin said, his voice suddenly serious. Vinaxx stopped in his tracks and turned to Niah as if he were seeing her for the first time. She met his gaze, wondering how powerful such a fragile-looking being could be.

"I see," he muttered, "my dear, if you please?" he gestured toward a plush armchair with a footrest in front of it.

"Hold on," Niah snapped, "I don't even know who you are," Fin sighed and took a step closer. She watched as Vinaxx shifted on his feet, fiddling with a button on his coat.

"Vinaxx is a very old and powerful spell weaver from The Cross; he's been with us a long time," Fin explained with a clipped voice. She remembered reading about The Cross. The guild in which spell weavers and casters belonged to, one of them at least. The Cross had allied themselves with the Furies during the last war. A war of which she did not know had happened until she read about it.

"Is that supposed to mean something to me?" Niah challenged. For a moment, she and Fin only glared at one another, until Vinaxx stepped forward and cleared his throat.

"M-my dear," he held his arm out to her, "take my wrist."

Niah pressed her lips together but did as he asked, taking his wrist in her hand, feeling his pulse thrumming beneath her grip.

"I swear I mean y-you no harm. I-I only want to remove the mark." He said. His pulse remained steady beneath her fingers. He was telling the truth, but the bitter scent of fear filled the air between them.

"Why are you scared?" she asked, letting her voice drop to a murmur.

Vinaxx tried to pull his arm back, but she held on, not tight enough to hurt, but enough to keep him in place so she could feel his pulse, "It will hurt...and I-I don't want to hurt you." his pulse was faster than previously, but maintained that beat as he answered.

"Niah," Fin muttered, stepping close once again, "it's your choice whether you have it removed or not."

She searched the weavers' colourless eyes but found nothing. Niah sighed and released his wrist, they had come to him after all.

She sat down in the chair, keeping her hand on her dagger. Vinaxx stood behind her, gently moving her hair aside as every muscle in her body tightened. His trembling fingers were cool against her skin as he ran them over the spot at the base of her skull.

"Is something wrong?" she asked through gritted teeth.

"This is no ordinary seal," Vinaxx breathed, "this is stronger, much stronger. Tell me, how long has this been on you?" he asked, all humour and jitter vanished from his voice. Instead, he was steady, concise even.

"I imagine since I was a baby," she answered, glancing at Fin, who was watching with his arms folded across his chest, his expression dark.

Vinaxx strode around the chair into her line of sight, "This will hurt...a lot."

"I can handle it." she bit out.

Vinaxx pressed his lips into a thin line, "Once I start, there's no_"

"I said I can handle it."

Vinaxx raised his eyes to Fin, but he only shrugged, "It's her choice."

"Very well," Vinaxx said, making his way to the back of the chair once more.

She felt a warmth on the back of her neck as a faint white light filled the room. The warmth turned to heat, and the white light blazed, bouncing off the walls as a dull ache gripped her muscles.

Fire spread through her body, searing her veins. The sensation was uncomfortable, growing to a blinding agony lancing through her skull. Her knuckles turned white as she gripped the armrests hard enough that the material tore beneath her grip.

She bit down on the scream building in her throat, gritting her teeth hard enough that they groaned. Niah wanted to tell him to stop, but the words wouldn't come. She thrashed in the chair, and ropes of white light snaked around her wrists, holding her in place.

"Vinaxx," she could barely hear Fin's voice over the pulsing in her head, "remove the_"

"If I do, and she moves, I'll have to start all over again."

Two lines of words or symbols in a language she didn't know appeared on her skin, one on each arm starting from the tips of her middle fingers, working their way up to the base of her skull.

The light blazed brighter. Just when she thought the pain couldn't get any worse, it did. Her entire body screamed, her back arching away from the chair as her nails tore against the arms of the chair.

The marks on her arms began receding. Her heart hammered so loud it was all she could hear, thundering along as if racing for its final beat. Black spots appeared in her vision. Niah thought she was dying.

"I have to use more power," Vinaxx shouted over the hum of power pulsing at the base of her skull.

"She's already in agony," Fin protested, desperation bled into his voice.

"If I don't, that mark will not come off," the weaver bellowed as the fire raged through her.

Someone moved into her vision, though she barely registered who it was until she heard the sound of his voice, "Squeeze my hand." It was involuntary, but she did as he'd said, and squeezed hard enough that she felt the bones grinding and cracking beneath her grip.

Fin didn't pull away.

The pounding in her ears melted into a single high-pitched whine as the colour drained from the world. Inwardly, she pleaded for it to be over.

A final burst of heat surged through her veins, and the marks vanished upward into her neck, where the heat concentrated for a brief moment. It was only then, when the pain was so intense, that she found her voice.

A shrieking scream escaped her lips and racked her body, burning as it tore through her throat.

Then nothing.

The light and pain vanished, the scream froze in her throat as she slumped back against the chair, her vision darkening at the edges until it consumed her completely.

Niah surrendered herself to it.

FIN

14

Her scream wrenched at something deep in his chest.

Fin barely registered the pain in his hand as Niah went limp, her eyes rolling into the back of her head. For a moment, he thought she had died. His stomach twisted, but before he uttered a word, her heart thumped and settled into a constant rhythm.

He loosed a breath, closing his eyes briefly as the ropes of white light evaporated from her wrists, and Vinaxx staggered to stay on his feet. Fin went to his side, guiding him into a chair as the weaver panted and gulped down air.

"Never...in all my years, have I witnessed a mark so strong," Vinaxx rasped. The colour bleached from his already pale complexion.

"How much power did that drain from you?" Fin asked.

Vinaxx slumped in the chair, "More than I care to admit, I will need a few days to rest."

"And Niah?" Fin glanced back at the unconscious hybrid.

Vinaxx followed his gaze, "She'll wake up later today, no doubt, but she will need to rest for at least a day or two."

Fin straightened, frowning down at the weaver, "Will you be okay?"

"Yes…yes, don't fuss over me." Vinaxx waved a dismissive hand.

"I'll get her out of here; you get some rest," Fin said as he scooped Niah into his arms, cradling her head against his chest. There was something unsettling about seeing her vulnerable.

Fin carried her through the corridors and up the stairs to her room; people frowned as they walked by. He paused outside her door, trying to unlock it while balancing her across his hip as he fumbled with the key.

"Here, let me," Merida said, taking the key from him as he put his arm back under her legs. The door opened, and he lay her down on the bed, taking her shoes off and placing them neatly on the floor. Merida stood with her hands on her hips, a look of worry and anger plain on her delicate features.

"Thank you, Fin," she breathed, taking a step closer. Her brows knitted together, and she reached out with a trembling hand as if to brush the strands from Niah's face; but she stopped, her hand falling to her side.

"You're worried."

Merida looked up at him through her lashes and sighed, "Of course, I am."

"She'll be fine. Vinaxx said she'll wake up later today," he said, rubbing her shoulder.

"That's a relief. Fin, you are my advisor. Tell me, do you think she will trust us?" she asked with a pleading look in her eye.

It pained him to see her under so much strain, and to see the worry creasing her brow.

It would take time for Niah to relax. She had been through so much, and been betrayed by people who should have protected her. She had spent her whole life believing one thing, and now all that had crumbled around her.

"I can't say, sometimes it seems she will, others it seems she is withdrawn. It'll take time," he advised; Merida gazed down at the girl. She sighed heavily and ran a hand through her thick, brunette hair.

"Stay with her, please?" she asked after a long moment and turned to walk away, pausing in the doorway as Gren, Sai, and Dea were passing in the hall. They stopped and bowed their heads to Merida.

"What's going on?" Dea asked, peering around Merida while standing on her tiptoes.

Merida stiffened, so Fin said, "Niah was marked, Vinaxx removed it." Gren's eyes snapped to his at that, but Fin shook his head, telling him not to open his mouth in front of Merida.

"Well, at least it's off now, right?" Sai smiled, clapping Gren on the shoulder. The blonde huffed a sigh, folding his arms over his chest.

"Is there a problem?" Merida asked, her voice edged.

Gren lowered his eyes, "No."

"I'm asking you all to give Niah a chance, include her in things, make her feel welcome. I trust you above all others, so please, do this for me?" Merida pleaded.

"Of course," Sai bowed his head, the others followed suit. Merida said goodnight and disappeared down the corridor, leaving him standing with the other three outside Niah's door.

"Is she okay?" Dea asked, poking her head around the door.

Fin dragged a hand through his hair, "She's fine; it just took a lot out of her."

"We'll come back when she wakes up," Sai said, nudging Gren in the ribs with an elbow. Gren nodded, shoving his hands into his pockets. Ordinarily, Fin might have made some kind of joke, but none came to him.

It wasn't funny.

"We'll leave you to it; text me if you need anything," Dea said, kissing him on the cheek before the three of them disappeared down the corridor.

Fin would be forever grateful for his friends. They were his rock the vast majority of the time; he only hoped they could be that for Niah as well.

He closed the door and turned to the bed. The harshness was gone from her features, sleep certainly became her. Even though she wasn't scowling at him, Fin wanted her to wake up. If only to see that she was okay.

"You might just be the death of me," he muttered to no one as he lowered himself down to sit on the floor, his back leaning against the wall as she slept.

NIAH

15

The nightmares never came...
Suspended in darkness, there was nothing but numbing silence surrounding her. Niah was weightless. It was more peaceful than her corner of the library, there was no grief nor joy.

There was nothing.

She thought she was dead at first. But the constant, steady rhythm of her heart was the only clue that she was alive. The numbness was blissful, but she would inevitably wake up.

As the darkness started to lift from her mind, she found herself clawing at it to stay. But the darkness left her and took that numbing bliss with it.

All the feelings came rushing back, and her chest cleaved apart with all she had learnt over the days. But as she lay there, struggling to keep everything contained, a tendril of something light and familiar brushed against her heart, chasing away the ache.

It vanished as soon as she opened her eyes, and her body screamed as if it had received a thousand beatings.

Her skin was grimy, and her bones felt like they had been shattered and moulded back together. Her hair was stuck to her skin, the bed sheets tangled around her midsection. She was too hot, too sticky. It shouldn't have been possible, but the heat was insufferable, suffocating almost.

Niah pushed herself up, instantly regretting it as a sharp pain lanced through her skull. Clamping a hand over her forehead, a hiss escaped through her teeth. Her muscles barked with the movement as she shoved the covers away.

Her head throbbed and pulsed as she lowered it into her hands, where she sat on the edge of the bed, trying to take steadying breaths.

Niah felt it then, a stir of something deep in her bones. Something *other*. Something that sang and soothed and welcomed her like an old friend. It thrummed through her veins, lighting them, easing the ache that dominated her body after having the mark stripped away.

She had been reborn in a strange way.

But there it was.

The hum of power in her veins, awoken, and restless.

Niah lifted her head from her hands and gazed down at them, wiggling her fingers as the ache ebbed away.

A tiny blue spark leapt from a fingertip. It was so fast that Niah thought she had imagined it, but her fingers warmed, and another spark emerged. It lingered, dancing across her skin.

The breath caught in her throat as she stared at the tiny spark. It was real. She had magic. Her heart raced, but in a way it hadn't before. The heaviness in her chest vanished, replaced by light and a surge of rejuvenation.

Niah smiled when more sparks of light bounced off her fingers, and that strange, unfamiliar power stroked against her heart. It *was* strange, to feel that power coursing through her body, but it also felt like home. It was comforting, light, and playful. It was the opposite of everything she was, but it didn't shy away; it only soothed and warmed her.

As the pulse in her head eased, she heard the shower in the bathroom running.

Ignoring the protest in her muscles, she jumped off the bed and fell as her legs gave way beneath her. Niah landed with a thud, cursing under her breath, though it came out as nothing more than a strangled whisper that burned her throat.

The water turned off in the bathroom, then the sound of scrambling before Fin burst through the door, his hair dripping wet as his fingers zipped up his jeans. His chest was bare, glistening with droplets of water.

Her mouth went dry.

Fin's body was undoubtedly a work of art, all solid muscle decorated with faint, silver scars. Twin to the ones that donned her hands from years of training with blades, and learning from her mistakes when she paid for it in blood.

As she gazed at his sculpted chest, tingles shot through her body, but she put it down to the magic now thrumming through her veins. It couldn't be anything else. He was beautiful, yes, but her eyes lingered on his scars, and she wondered how he had gotten them.

Fin made his way around the edge of the bed and knelt to help her up, but she smacked his hand away, using the bed for support as she dragged herself to her feet, despite her legs still unable to hold her weight.

"Well, if I knew you were going to fall for me that hard, I would have come out sooner," he grinned.

"Why are you here?" she panted.

He raised a brow, "I carried you here like the white knight I am." She only had to give him a withering look before he sighed and said, "Merida asked me to stay with you to make sure you were okay."

"Well, I'm fine," she snapped, clutching at the edge of the bed. There was something unsettling about Fin being in the same room while she was unconscious, but there was nothing she could do about it now.

"Clearly," he snorted.

"You can go now," Niah rasped, clutching at the bed to stop herself from swaying.

"I will if you can take a step without falling on your face." He challenged, straightening his spine as he folded his arms over his broad chest.

Niah pressed her lips together and took a step forward, her knee buckled beneath the weight, and she fell forward. Fin didn't catch her.

"I could get used to this," he smirked, kneeling beside her once more.

"Just get out," she ground out, hating that he was seeing her so weak.

"Let me help you," he offered, his voice gentle.

Niah shook her head, "I don't need help."

There was a moment of silence between them before Fin muttered, "Maybe if you let someone in, maybe if you let someone *help* you, you wouldn't be so alone."

Niah stiffened all over, "Get out."

"What are you so afraid of?" Fin challenged, "Accepting help every once in a while isn't going to make you any less capable. I'm not going to think you're weak just because you can't stand right now."

Niah had never asked for help before. But, she supposed he had already helped her in getting her away from the academy. It was different, but if she wanted him to trust her, to listen to what she told them when it came to the Shadows, she had to make an effort.

"Fine, can you help me into the bathroom?" She sighed, "I want a shower."

"If you can't stand, then a bath would be better." He got to his feet and disappeared into the bathroom, the sound of running water following before he came back into the room and held his hands out.

"May I?"

Niah pressed her lips into a firm line and nodded, expecting him to pull her to her feet; instead, he scooped her up into his arms and held her against his chest.

Her heart fluttered, her cheeks burning as he raised a brow at her; she quickly looked away. He was a means to an end. Nothing more. The flutter ebbed away, replaced by a hollowness she hadn't felt since England.

Fin set her down on the closed toilet and gazed down at her; there wasn't so much as a hint of mocking in his eyes, "Can you undress yourself?"

Niah might have scowled at him if it weren't for the gentleness of his voice. She'd already admitted to needing help, and all humour had left him. The tingling in her veins returned at the thought of Fin being present while she undressed.

She glanced down at her legs and leaned forward to yank off her socks. Every inch of her body screamed in protest, and by the time she gave up, she was sweating and panting. Her magic only helped ease the ache so much it seemed.

Niah met his gaze, despite his help and gentle tone, she wouldn't leave herself entirely vulnerable, "Can you get my dagger?"

"I'm not going to_"

"I'd feel safer with it." she admitted through her teeth, averting her eyes as her cheeks flamed.

Fin left the room without argument. When he returned, he offered her the dagger. She turned it over between her fingers, checking the blade before placing it on the edge of the bath without its scabbard. She steadied herself with a deep breath and reached down, yanking her top off, the muscles in her back groaning in protest. She held her shirt across her chest, covering her breasts as she held his gaze that didn't so much as wander south.

Her breath caught in her throat at what was to come next.

"I won't look," he promised. Niah pressed her lips together and nodded, her cheeks burning as Fin knelt before her and gently began rolling her leggings down.

"Can you lift your hips?" She couldn't, but she managed to angle herself so he could wriggle them out from under her.

He was so gentle. She watched as he rolled the material from each leg, being careful not to touch her skin. An unfamiliar warmth spread through her chest. True to his word, his eyes never once strayed to her private areas. Instead, he focused on his hands and tossed her leggings and underwear into the wash hamper. She used the shirt to cover herself as much as she could, her heart racing the entire time.

He moved as if he would pick her up again but paused, looking at her, asking for permission, she realised. When she nodded, he lifted her and placed her gently in the full bath with the shirt still clutched in her hands.

Fin remained by the bath, sitting on the floor with his back to her to give her some privacy.

"You don't have to stay in here with me," she mumbled, lathering soap into her skin.

"It's just in case you pass out," he said, though he didn't sound convinced by his own words, and Niah didn't have the energy to question it.

It wasn't the worst thing in the world to have him nearby, she supposed.

Every ounce of strength had abandoned her during the removal of the mark. Her muscles felt withered away, and her bones felt like they may break at any moment. But the longer she spent in the water, the more those knots loosened.

"How are you feeling?" he asked.

"Tired," she admitted.

"Understandable. Vinaxx said it was a strong mark, I can't say I'm surprised." His voice was edged, his shoulders tensing slightly.

"How many others have been marked?"

He loosed a slow breath, "Not many that we've seen, but who knows how many are marked."

"Do the Shadows usually mark random people?"

"No, not that I know of anyway. The information we have has come from centuries of spying. I've never seen one in person until I saw yours." Fin explained, his voice grave.

"How did Vinaxx know how to remove it?"

He shrugged, "Vinaxx is very old; I can't even begin to comprehend all the things he's seen."

It was strange to hear him so serious, with no humour in his voice. It made her realise there was more to him than jokes and bravado. Not that it mattered in the long run.

Niah scrubbed at her hair as Fin turned his head slightly, still not looking at her, and held up a cloth, "May I?"

"Go ahead," she muttered. Fin got to his knees and turned to her, keeping his eyes on his hand as he lathered circles into her back, massaging gently as he went, easing the knots in her muscles.

An involuntary moan escaped her lips, and she cleared her throat, shaking the drowsiness from her mind as he chuckled.

"Have you done this before?"

"What? Bathed someone? Sure," he shrugged, "it's not a big deal; it's just skin."

"Hmm." She hummed. Still, he didn't touch her bare skin.

"You're tense. Very tense."

"I've never been naked in front of anyone. Or even let anyone touch me for that matter," Niah murmured, turning back to the water, now cloudy from the soap.

His voice was soft as he repeated, "It's just skin."

"Isn't it a personal thing, though?"

"How so?" he muttered gently, almost absentmindedly.

"It's supposed to be private; I've always read that it's a big deal," she said. Fin's hand paused, and he moved along the edge of the bath until he was in her line of sight. His silver eyes held her own.

"It's up to you how you feel, how much of a big deal you want it to be. Our culture isn't...conservative. I imagine you picked that up watching Dea the other night. Just remember, all those books you read are written by humans, with very human views and lifestyles." he held her gaze, "We do what we want, when we want, we understand our bodies are just that, they're our weapons, just like the swords and guns we carry. Does this feel wrong to you?"

She looked down at the cloudy water, at the shirt still grasped between her fingers. It was strange, different, uncomfortable, but wrong? Nothing in her mind or body thought any part of it was wrong. She felt vulnerable in a way she hadn't before, but it wasn't necessarily a bad thing.

"No," Niah breathed, surprised at the honesty in the word.

She didn't feel awkward anymore, not tense, or self-conscious. Just as one person bathed another, there was nothing wrong with it. Nothing rude or any ulterior motive behind it. Fin had made that perfectly clear, and had been nothing but considerate and respectful.

Niah stiffened when a thought struck her. She could see herself becoming friends with him. In her attempt to get him to trust her, she found herself becoming...comfortable around him.

Her heart stumbled. That wasn't the plan. He was a means to an end, nothing more. Yet, that very thought tightened her chest, and caused an ache at the back of her throat.

"Good, bodies are just bodies, nothing rude about them. And besides, yours is *very* nice," Fin smirked.

Niah couldn't bring herself to even scowl at him, she was too distracted by the jumble of thoughts in her head. No matter what, she had to detach herself. She'd decided as much already, so why did it suddenly feel like a mistake?

"I think I can stand," she said.

Fin stood and held his hands out for her to balance on. She took hold of them and pushed herself up. Her legs trembled slightly but held her weight as she stepped out of the tub and reached for a towel. She wrapped it around herself, finally dropping the soaked shirt as Fin yanked on his own.

"What do you want to do?" he asked from the other side of the door as she dressed. She shrugged when she emerged, but her stomach rumbled loudly. He arched a brow and smirked.

"I'll go get some food."

"I can come," she said, wincing at the pain that rippled through her legs as she moved too quickly.

"No, you can't. You still need to rest. Just stay here; I need to let Merida know you're awake anyway," he said in a voice that left no room for argument.

The door clicked shut behind him, and Niah lowered herself onto the edge of the bed; the books on the desk caught her eye. Was she any different to the Shadows?

For years, they lied and manipulated, and now she was prepared to do the same thing to the Furies, to Fin. To the only people who had shown her genuine kindness. She thought she could detach herself, thought she could be as cold and as heartless as the Shadows.

But she didn't want to be them. They called her a weapon, made her resent her emotions, and she had snapped right back into that mentality after reading the book of her past.

Her choice to get revenge remained, but what if there was another way? What if she could do it without manipulating the Furies to get what she wanted?

Perhaps she was naïve, after all, she still had no idea what the Furies intentions were. Just because they were kind to her, didn't mean they wouldn't use her. Niah tried to remind herself of that, surely it was better to use them, rather than wait and be used *by* them?

The truth was that she didn't know who she was outside of the Shadows influence. The things she thought only days ago, plans of revenge and using the Furies for her own gain, all stemmed from years of conditioning.

Niah shook her head, shoving the thoughts aside. She couldn't second guess herself now, she'd come this far, and feeling guilty about using the Furies wasn't ideal.

For years, she had only anger and plans of revenge; without that, she had doubt and uncertainty. So, Niah shut away those thoughts and feelings, locked them away, with a promise that one day, she would let them out.

Perhaps her need for closeness overruled her ability to think logically. After finding out her parents weren't who they said they were, there was a void inside her that needed filling, and maybe she had latched onto Fin because he was the first person that had shown her true kindness.

There was no doubt in her mind that her future was bathed in blood. It's what she had been trained for, but it was *her* decision whose blood drenched her path. A dark thought, but that was the world she had been born into.

A weapon.

Knowing Fin would be back soon, she shoved the bitter thoughts from her mind and glanced at the screen sat atop the drawers, she'd learned it was called a TV, and there was an image of three women. One blonde, one dark-haired, and the other a brownish blonde. They were paused in various poses; the box next to the TV had *Friends* written across it.

She picked it up to examine it; simultaneously, the door opened as Fin and Merida walked in. Fin carrying a bag full of what she assumed was food.

"How are you feeling?" Merida asked as she glanced over her, her expression unreadable.

Niah shrugged, "I'm fine."

"Good, well, take a couple more days to rest, and then you can begin training," Merida said with a small, wary smile. Niah nodded, and Merida turned to leave the room, closing the door as she went.

"Let me guess, you have no idea what *Friends* is?" Fin smirked as he placed the bag down on the bed and reached over to pluck the box from her hand. He opened the box, pulled out a round, flat object, and swapped it for the other in the tray on the TV.

The two of them sat on the bed with a spread of food consisting of sandwiches, chocolate, fruit, and water. They sat together watching the show, Fin would pause it occasionally to explain something she didn't understand. She found herself relaxing around him, no matter how much she didn't want to.

That night she allowed him to stay in the bed; after all he'd done, she didn't think it fair to make him sleep on the floor, though they remained separated by a wall of pillows, her dagger unsheathed and gripped in her hand beneath her pillow.

Niah fought the urge to sleep for as long as she could, not wanting to leave herself vulnerable by sleeping beside him. But she already had, hadn't she?

She glanced over at him, his head resting against his arm, his long lashes fluttering against his cheeks, his lips parted slightly. There was an innocence about him as he slept, it made something wrench at her chest.

Her throat ached, and she turned away, not wanting to feel that weight in her stomach. She barely knew him. It wasn't a betrayal if she never earned his trust, was it?

The constant sound of his gentle breathing lulled her into a fitful sleep, and the nightmares descended.

NIAH

16

The front doors of the academy loomed over her.
They were so much taller than she was, and made of thick wood with heavy iron handles. She hadn't been able to find Storm in the woods, so she walked the rest of the way.

The academy rose from the mist like the dark castle in a fairy-tale. A wrought iron fence wrapped around the entire building, apart from the side where the ground fell away at the top of the cliff. Pointed towers reached up to the sky, the windows square with a diamond pattern across them.

She used the large iron knocker on the door, the boom of it echoing through the vast grounds, sending birds scattering from the rooftops and nearby trees.

The doors creaked open, and there stood a ghostly pale woman with light hair scraped back from her harsh face. Her eyes bore into her, almost as if she could see the horrors Niah had witnessed that night. She glared up at the woman until she stepped aside, gesturing for Niah to come in.

The woman narrowed her eyes at the child before her, but Niah didn't lower her gaze. The woman, Karliah, turned on her heel and strode down the corridor, the clack of her heels bouncing off the stone walls.

The woman led her through the building and across the grass at the centre. Crows squawked overhead, and Niah could feel the stares of the students boring into her. When she looked up, the windows were full of pale faces staring down at her.

She gripped her bloodied dagger tighter.

Karliah's office was large and felt as cold as the rest of the building. The headmistress took a seat behind the large desk and leaned back, gazing at the small girl before her with narrowed eyes.

"What happened?" she asked, her voice flat.

Niah didn't hesitate before she said, "My parents...are dead."

Karliah blinked, either from the statement or the hollow voice coming from such a small girl. A girl who should be at home with her parents. A girl who should be laughing and enjoying life.

Instead, she was standing in an office, clutching a dagger, her white nightgown covered in red and black blood, and dirt smeared across her face.

"Did you see who killed them?"

"Four men, they're all dead."

Karliah paused before asking, "Are you not upset?"

"I'm angry," she replied. Karliah nodded as if she were expecting that answer.

The light drained from the dream. Bleeding from it like her parents' blood had drained from their bodies. There was a loud dripping noise that cancelled out Karliah's voice as she spoke.

The way it always did.

Blood began pouring down the walls, thick and scarlet. Not black.

Her parents didn't have black blood.

But she did.

Karliah was screaming at her, but she heard only a muffled voice, as though she was underwater. Under an ocean of blood. It filled her ears, her nose, her throat. Choking on it, she staggered back, unable to breathe. Despite the blood pouring down the walls, it only reached her ankles.

She clawed at her throat, desperate to get air into her lungs.

Panic lashed through her.

She was drowning.

She needed air, and the only thing she could use was the dagger. So, she reached up, and drove the blade into her throat.

The dagger was still clutched in her clammy hand, aimed at her throat. The way it always was when she had that nightmare.

Niah was panting hard, sweat pouring down her body, her hair plastered to her skin. She held the dagger, gazing at the dim light reflected on the blade as she struggled to ground herself. She took trembling breaths to calm her pounding heart, but it would not yield.

That nightmare was always the worst.

Sometimes she woke to the dagger piercing her skin slightly. There was one time, she remembered vividly, when she nearly pushed it the rest of the way so that she would never have that nightmare again.

"Niah?" a horrified whisper sounded from the darkness beside her.

She started and lunged with the dagger. Her heart thundering as she tried to plunge it into the chest of whoever was there.

She didn't know who it was, and she didn't care.

"Niah...it's okay, it's okay," a soothing whisper.

She froze.

She knew that voice.

That calm, gentle voice.

The mist lifted from her eyes.

Niah was crouched over Fin, one hand clamped around his wrist, pressing it to the side of his head, and the dagger aimed at his heart. His free hand gripped the blade, black blood dribbling between his fingers and onto his chest.

He could have grabbed her wrist, but he knew she wouldn't want to be touched. He could have overpowered her, but he didn't.

His eyes were calm pools of liquid silver. There was no fear, no anger, just understanding.

"It's okay," he said again in barely more than a whisper.

The breath caught in her throat, "Fin?"

"Hey, Trouble," a faint smile brushed his lips.

Her body trembled, her breaths coming hard and fast as her brow furrowed. She sagged, her shoulders hunching. Her eyes burned as she stared down at him. A high-pitched ringing filled her head. And then she was running, hurling up the contents of her stomach into the toilet, the dagger still in her hand.

Fin was there in an instant, holding her hair out of the way and muttering soothing words of comfort and understanding.

She could have killed him.

Had his reflexes not been as good as they were, he would be dead.

"Fin I..." she started, her voice hoarse as she fell against the bath beside the toilet.

What could she say? She tried to kill him. Again. The man that had helped her, that had been trying to understand her, and she wanted to kill him.

Her stomach churned, her throat burning as she leaned over the toilet once again and retched violently.

He didn't touch her the entire time, only held her hair back. When she was finally finished, when her eyes burned with the tears she fought to keep back, he handed her a cloth. She wiped her face with trembling hands, unable to bring herself to look him in the eye.

"Here," he said, holding his hand out when she was done, he discarded it into the hamper and held a hand out to her, but she refused, using the edge of the bath to get to her feet.

The air hitched in her throat when she looked at his chest, his hand, both covered with black blood from the wound she'd given him. A strangled whimper escaped her throat, and a single tear slid down her cheek.

They stood for the longest time, her staring at his hand, him staring at her. Still, he made no move to reach for her. She was thankful.

She didn't dare look him in the eye, but held out her hands, "Can I?"

"Sure." He muttered.

Her hands were still shaking as she took his in hers and guided him to the sink. Niah turned the tap and waited for the water to warm before putting his hand under the stream and began washing the blood away.

The cut had mostly healed, leaving only an ugly pink line where the two sides were still stitching themselves back together. Fin silently let her wash his hand until the water ran clear.

"Come on," he murmured when she continued to run her quivering fingers over the wound, wanting to wait until it had fully healed.

Numbly, she put one foot in front of the other, her hands curling into fists and relaxing at her sides as she stood in the centre of the room, not sure what to do.

When Fin emerged from the bathroom seconds later, his shirt was gone, and his chest was damp where he had wiped the rest of the blood away.

Without meeting his gaze, she went back into the bathroom and retrieved the dagger she'd dropped by the toilet. She held it out for him, handle first, holding the blade between her fingers.

His eyes widened, "What are you doing?"

"Take it, hurt me, kill me, do whatever you feel is right," she ground out. How did someone make something like that right? She could have killed him. A simple apology wouldn't cut it, and she didn't know what else to do.

He sucked in a sharp breath and took the dagger from her. She braced herself for the blow, but it never came. Only a thud as he tossed it onto the nightstand. Fin pocketed his hands and remained standing before her, his chest rising and falling steadily.

"Look at me," he murmured; Niah shook her head, "*look*."

After a long moment, she lifted her eyes to his, her fists tight at her sides. There wasn't a flicker of anger in his eyes.

"Why did you offer me the dagger?" he asked, his voice a whisper.

"I hurt you."

"So?"

"So...that's how things go, I hurt you, and you hurt me back," she frowned; he cocked his head to one side.

"There are other ways to handle things. Not everything has to result in violence."

"But I *hurt* you."

"Yes. So what? You also threw a sword at my head, but you didn't feel guilty about that," the ghost of a smile brushed his lips.

Something in her chest guttered; guilt rippled through her, followed by anger. Anger at herself. That she had never bothered to deal with the trauma of her past. That she had simply shoved everything down and used it to fuel her need for revenge.

No one ever spoke to her about it.

No one told her she needed to deal with it.

So she hadn't.

Because it was easier than facing it.

"What are you feeling?" he murmured, Niah met his gaze then.

"Guilt."

"Good," he said, a smile tugging at the corners of his mouth, "It means you're feeling something other than anger," she could only stare.

She stared because he was right. For the first time in a long time, she didn't feel angry towards anyone or anything other than herself—only that roiling guilt in the pit of her stomach.

If she needed proof that he was her friend, that for the first time she had allowed herself to form an attachment with someone, that was it.

Yes, it would undoubtedly hurt if he was playing her.

But...she realised she couldn't play him either.

Niah took half a step toward him, their breath mingling. His eyes widened, his body stiffening, but he didn't shy away. She lowered her face and pressed her forehead to his chest. He was strong, a comfort, a friend. Her shoulders slumped. She hadn't realised how exhausted she had been from holding in all that anger. It was still there, just sleeping soundly, and she cherished this moment of calm.

Niah wanted to be close to him, to take comfort in his strength. She listened to the steady beat of his heart, savouring the quiet surrounding them. He didn't move, his heart jumped occasionally and sped up, but it soon relaxed into its usual rhythm.

It didn't matter what the gesture meant, whether Fin thought it was romantic, platonic...whatever it was, Niah didn't care.

Fin had coaxed emotions from her that she had long since buried, and she didn't mind whether he saw her that way.

"I'm sorry," she whispered. It was the first time she had ever uttered those words. Niah had never apologised for anything, not even when she had put other students in the infirmary.

The child within her wept.

The part of herself that craved affection more than air.

Niah had locked that part of her away, told herself she didn't need anyone. Because it was true, she didn't *need* anyone. But for the first time, she wanted someone to tell her everything would be okay. She wanted someone to rely on and someone to just be there for her.

The realisation made the backs of her eyes burn, and her breath tremble. Clenching her fists at her side, she bit down on the whimper forming in her throat.

Something had cracked inside her, and there was no closing it.

NIAH

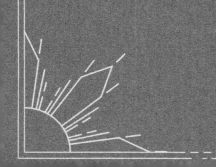

17

They spent the next day lounging in bed watching TV.
Niah would switch between watching and reading her books,
and Fin went out frequently to get food or something else to
watch.

It was strange, lounging in bed all day with nothing else to do. Niah
had tried doing sit-ups when Fin had fallen asleep, but he woke up
and scolded her, not to mention she severely paid for it when her body
burned all morning.

Just in case she had another nightmare and nearly killed him again,
he'd brought a foldable cot in and slept on that. It was far too small for
him, his long limbs dangled over the sides, but he didn't seem to mind.
During the day, he would join her on the bed, still keeping his distance,
and sometimes fell asleep.

Despite what had happened, and her realisation that she
didn't entirely hate Fin, she still snapped at him more than she
should; the only difference was that he was starting to snap back.
When they glared off against each other, they'd both end up smiling
and go back to whatever it was they were doing.

Easy and comfortable.

That's what things between them had become.

While he was getting lunch, a timid knock sounded at the door, and Dea came into the room. She wore a pretty green sundress with a sweetheart neckline and white flowers printed on it. Her snowy white hair falling in curls around her shoulders. She stood near the door, a smile curving her full lips.

"I heard you were feeling better and thought I'd come to see how you were," she smiled shyly. Niah only stared for the longest time. Someone wanted to check on her. Her heart ached. When Niah didn't answer, Dea shifted on her feet and picked up one of the books on the desk, a fiction about angels and demons.

"I've heard about this one, any good?" she asked, meeting Niah's curious gaze.

"It's one of my favourites," she managed to choke out once she had snapped herself out of her trance. Dea beamed and hurried to sit on the edge of the bed at Niah's feet, still with the book in her hands.

"What other books do you like?" she asked, her eyes bright. The girl almost *shone*. She was so bright and airy, her smile nothing but kind and trusting. No one had ever looked at her like that before. There were many things the people in the facility did that no one at the academy ever had.

"Anything fantasy, human imaginations are beautiful," she murmured, surprised by her honesty. Dea's brows pulled up in the middle slightly, her smile growing wistful.

"You have no idea," she said, her voice a gentle whisper. She blinked as if remembering herself and once again grinned. Niah might have questioned it, but Dea didn't seem to want to talk about it, not that Niah blamed her for that. There were things Niah didn't want to talk about either, or she wasn't sure she ever could.

"You can borrow it," she told the girl; Dea beamed and moved as if she meant to hug her but stopped when Niah flinched and tensed all over. Some things would take a while.

Dea leaned back, but the smile didn't leave her face, only a flash of sympathy in her eyes. Niah bit down on her annoyance. The snowy-haired girl was just friendly; no need to bite her head off.

"Thank you," Dea said, hugging the book to her chest as she got to her feet and walked toward the door, pausing a few steps away. "I'm sorry, for whatever happened to you. I know it's none of my business, and you might not want to, but if you ever want to talk about it, you can tell me," she offered with a warm, comforting smile—the kind of smile that made warmth bloom in Niah's chest.

She hated sympathy, hated people thinking she was weak. But when she looked into Dea's eyes, she didn't feel weakness, or annoyance, only light. Before she could answer, the door opened, and Fin strode in. His brows shot up in surprise as he glanced at the two of them.

"So it appears you only throw swords at me then," he smirked, cocking a brow at her.

"I like Dea more than you," she shot back, Dea's smile brightened, and she let out a soft giggle. Fin glanced between the two again, his features unreadable, only a slight smile tugging at the corners of his mouth.

"Anyway, if it's okay, there's a couple more who want to say hi?" he asked.

She was thoughtful for a moment. Little steps, they were only saying hi. She nodded, and the door opened. Sai strode in with a swagger, his arms behind his head like an anime character she had seen. Grenville followed closely behind, his hands in his pockets, but he didn't appear to be annoyed.

"How 'ya feelin'?" Sai asked. Fin moved to slide the balcony door open, and the gentle breeze blew the gossamer curtains into the room along with the fresh scent of the ocean. The smell instantly calmed her.

"Fine," she answered tightly; Fin glanced at her, giving her a reassuring nod. Her heart was beating faster, her palms growing slick. Maybe it was too many people all at once. Dea must have picked up her discomfort because she headed for the door.

"Thank you for the book. I'll come to visit you later?" she suggested. Niah was amazed the girl wanted to see her again, especially after the awkwardness of the beach. Suddenly, her heart was calm. Niah nodded, and Dea offered a bright, parting smile before leaving the room.

Sai and Grenville stayed a while; they talked about their games, patrol, their weapons, and the demons they regularly faced, though it was mainly Sai doing the talking.

Just the thought of being able to fight demons was exhilarating. A real fight. Something she hadn't had outside of sparring. It made her want to get stronger all that much faster.

After another day of rest, Niah felt strong enough to start training, despite Fin's protests that she should rest a day or two more. She'd had enough of lying in bed watching *Friends*, but she hadn't admitted to Fin that she secretly loved the show.

Dea, Sai, and Gren visited her, Dea twice a day, and Gren a little more begrudgingly than the others, but he came nonetheless. And after a while of being in the same room, he started to converse more easily with her, and she with him.

Everything became a little easier between them all, a little more comfortable.

They were standing in the training room now. The floors were slate tile, and the walls were painted white with one wall made of stone, a climbing wall, she realised. The ceiling was perhaps twice the height of that in England, beams lined the upper levels, and people jumped between them; some were sparring while balancing on impossibly thin, bendy poles up high, attacking each other with wooden swords or staffs.

Her blood thrummed in anticipation as she watched.

Machines and weights lined one wall, wooden training swords and staffs were racked up on the far end of the room, real weapons on the rack next to it. Next to them were targets with throwing knives, bows, arrows, and crossbows.

"Sparring?" Niah beamed, Fin shook his head.

"Treadmill and weights."

"Oh, come on."

He threw her a grin and started toward the treadmills, "Nope, I already don't approve of you being up and about, so we compromise; I assume you know the meaning of the word?"

"Could you *be* any more annoying?" she grumbled. Fin stopped and slowly turned to her, his brows raised.

"Was that...? Did you just...? You just quoted_"

"No, I didn't."

He gasped, his eyes widening, "You *do* like it! I knew it, what was the bet again? One thousand push-ups?" she cursed under her breath and rolled her eyes.

"Don't flatter yourself. That show is the first experience I've had with so-called humour."

"And my incredibly sharp wit," he reminded her as they reached the machines.

"Sharp?" she snorted, "Cute." She ignored the sidelong glance he gave her and started up the treadmill, turning it up to a jog that humans would consider a sprint.

"I may need to stop showing you TV shows," he frowned, turning the speed up on his treadmill to match hers.

"Are these going to go fast enough for us?" she asked, looking down at the dashboard.

"Weaver magic is a wonderful thing," he smirked, turning the speed up. Her blood spiked with adrenaline, and she turned hers up quicker. Competitiveness was in her nature, and she wasn't about to let him win. He met her challenge, but only turned his up to match her speed, not wanting to push her too hard too soon.

After a while, Dea, Sai, and Grenville turned up. Dea wearing skin-tight red leggings and a matching crop top, showing off the planes of her abs. Sai wasn't wearing a top at all, also showing off the solid ridges of his stomach. Grenville wore a black hoodie over a pair of knee-length shorts; his sandy hair scraped back.

Dea sauntered toward Fin and planted a kiss on his cheek as she perched herself atop the treadmill. "Want to spar?" she asked musically, crossing one leg over the other. Fin shook his head, a sheer layer of sweat glistening on his skin, he opened his mouth to say something, but Niah cut in.

"I will."

Fin was about to protest when Dea interrupted, "Come on then, beauty."

They walked over to a thin rubber mat spread out over the hard-tiled floor, Fin grumbling something under his breath, Sai sniggering at him as they crossed the room.

Dea and Niah took their stances, the two girls facing each other. There was no ego, no malice: just adrenaline and the urge to train.

Niah glanced at Fin, who watched them intently, his silvery eyes dark. Grenville, at his side, folded his arms, his emerald eyes analysing. Sai was practically vibrating with excitement.

As Niah's attention was on the boys, Dea leapt forward. Niah dodged her fist and lowered herself, shoving upward with her shoulder and elbow into Dea's ribs.

"I like this one," Dea panted, glancing at Fin.

The two exchanged blows, but Niah found she could read the other girls' movements a lot easier than she had been able to read Fin's while on the beach.

Strength soared in her body, the glorious ache of adrenaline surging through her veins as she felt every breath in her lungs, the way her muscles contracted.

Not only could she read Dea's movements, but she was faster too, so much faster that she stumbled and overbalanced. The other girl took advantage and delivered a swift punch to her ribs, but Niah barely felt the pain.

Outside the ring, Niah was vaguely aware of people coming to watch as music pumped through the gym. It matched the beat of her heart, and their blows came in time with the music. She'd never sparred like this before, had never enjoyed it quite so much.

There was so much to get used to when it came to her newfound strength and speed. Niah made mistakes, moved too quickly for the movement she was planning, dodged too early when she saw what Dea was going to do.

Nonetheless, Niah's blood sang, that power stroking against her veins, almost pleading to come out and play.

The music turned up louder. Dea laughed musically and spun on her toes in a neat circle before launching at Niah. The two blocked, attacked, dodged, attacked, deflected. Fists and feet flying at one another, sometimes connecting, sometimes not.

Dea threw a punch but lost her balance; Niah grabbed her wrist and arm and shoved her body into Dea's, flinging her effortlessly over her shoulder. The snowy-haired girl landed heavily on her back, the air leaving her lungs.

Niah locked her arm between her legs as she lay on the ground. Dea tried to move, but Niah's feet held her in place firmly. Then, much to Niah's surprise, Dea tapped out.

They both got to their feet, smiling, panting, and still, there was no anger, no resentment. Niah had never had an opponent like her, someone who could put up a decent fight. She was as fierce and unyielding as she was beautiful and kind.

The crowd clapped as Niah turned to Fin, also clapping, a slight grin on his lips. She held out her arms to the side to bow. He laughed. Dea came up behind her and wrapped her arms around her. Feeling Niah tense beneath her grip, she stepped away and draped an arm around Niah's shoulders.

"Nice fight," she praised.

"You too. I'm going to get some air," Niah breathed, striding for the doors without waiting for an answer.

She walked down the corridor, a smile on her lips, until she reached the airy foyer and tilted her head back.

A weight had lifted from her chest; she no longer felt a crushing pressure. The pressure that threatened to break her into tiny pieces, shattering everything that made her who she was. She had been suffocating, though never knowing it.

She flexed her fingers as she gazed at them; her strength was surging, suppressed for far too long. Even that power lurking in her veins thrummed from the thrill of the fight.

It dawned on her that she had forgotten all about revenge.

A realisation that was beautiful but brought it all rushing back. The embers curled in her gut once again, the anger that had walked by her side for years no longer slumbering. Maybe it would always be there, and maybe that was okay, if she had people around her to bring out this side of her.

The side that smiled and joked and didn't care about revenge. She still wanted it, but over the last couple of days, there were moments where she had forgotten all about it. In those moments, she felt lighter.

Giving up that goal would be easy, but what else would she do? If the Shadows were the Furies enemy, then sooner or later, there would be a war between the two.

More than anything, she wanted the Shadows to suffer; she wanted to know *why* they wanted her of all creatures.

Footsteps sounded down the corridor behind her, and when Niah turned, Dea was striding toward her, her expression grave. "Fin was going to come out, but I said I would instead," she said.

"Oh?" Niah arched a brow.

She thought the other girl was almost incapable of being earnest. Her eyes were large, usually full of laughter, but now full of despair. Her mouth pressed into a hard line. Her soft, delicate features had a sharpness to them that hadn't been there before.

The music down the corridor had stopped, deathly silence lying in its wake.

"We just got word. A facility has been attacked. We lost hundreds of warriors. There were survivors; most of them are on their way here."

Niah's blood turned to ice in her veins.

"Who did this?"

She already knew.

"The Shadows." Dea frowned, her eyes filling with tears.

"This is because of me," Niah breathed, her stomach twisting angrily. It was an effort to choke down the bile rising in her throat. Hundreds dead. That's what Dea had said. Hundreds of lives were gone in an instant, because they had lost their weapon.

Dea's eyes turned soft as she gripped Niah by the arms firmly, "No. This is because of the Shadows. *They* did this. Either way, you would have found out the truth. Either way, you would have turned on them."

It did nothing to ease the roiling guilt in the pit of her stomach.

"What does this mean?" her voice came out as a growl. Dea released her arms but took her hands in hers as she looked down at them locked together.

"It means that we all need to train harder, a lot harder, if we're to stand a chance."

"But we're not halflings, we're stronger and faster_"

"Yes. And we can't rely solely on that. The Shadows have always been a mystery, we don't know what weapons they have in their arsenal. Come," she said as she released Niah's hands and started toward the stairs for Merida's office. Fin, Sai, and Gren ran up behind them.

"Come in," Merida's voice sounded strained and tired through the door before they walked in. She sat behind her desk, her elbows leaning on the glass surface, chin resting on her clasped fingers. Niah's hand went to the locket around her throat instinctively.

She quickly lowered her hand.

"You've all heard the news," she said, her voice hard and cold, so different from the warm gentleness of the first time they met, "the survivors are on their way here, most of them at least. They killed over three hundred of our warriors. Four hundred managed to escape. They are being spread out across the other facilities. The barriers are being checked and strengthened as we speak."

Dea and Niah sat in the chairs at the desk, facing the leader of the facility. The boys remained standing.

"How did they find us?" Fin asked tersely.

"We don't know," she closed her eyes briefly, "it wasn't just hybrids they murdered, spell weavers, vampires, lycanthropes, and werewolves, anyone they could find. Including children..." she trailed off, unable to continue.

Niah's stomach churned. *Children*. Her fists trembled at her sides, her canines stabbing into her lip. Fin gripped her arm, but she shrugged him off.

Merida's eyes flicked between them, but she went on, "This is a sad day. Our warriors are not just cannon fodder to fight our wars, we're connected. All of us."

"What do we do now?" Dea asked, a tear rolling down her cheek. Sai seemed to be trembling as much as Niah was, his eyes burning with anger. Gren and Fin were more reserved, standing with their shoulders squared and hands clasped behind their backs, their eyes simmering.

"We expect they will strike again; I will be having a meeting with the other facility leaders later to decide how to proceed. In the meantime, we train harder than ever. It's going to be hard, but we must be ready if they strike again. We don't know how many soldiers they have, they could outnumber us one hundred to one." her voice was firm, unyielding, the voice of a leader. The voice of someone burning with despair, but knew she had to rally her warriors, knew she had a duty to uphold.

Niah couldn't bite her tongue any longer, "Why are we waiting? Why not launch an attack in retaliation?" Merida regarded her thoughtfully as she leaned back in her chair.

"Such decisions are not mine to make alone. Not when it will involve every warrior across the Alliance. We also don't know where they are."

Niah's eyes narrowed, "We know they're in England." Merida's lips pressed into a firm line.

"As far as we know, that's a training facility. Inexperienced and young Shadows. Just because they killed our children, doesn't mean we're inclined to do the same."

"But wouldn't starting at the academy or whatever it is be the logical choice?" Sai questioned.

"We've been calling it the compound." Merida said softly, "It's the first of the Shadows buildings we've been able to find, and that was by chance. Talon's last report said it was empty. That everyone fled after Niah's escape."

"Unfortunately, we have no idea where the Shadows are. The Alliance has been searching for centuries, but we've never found them." Fin added.

The embers in her stomach licked higher, burning brightly.

"I'm sorry, Niah," Merida's voice was so painfully gentle as it cracked slightly.

Her spine straightened, not wanting to hear the sympathy in the leaders' voice, not wanting to feel those empathetic gazes burning into her.

As if sensing her discomfort, Merida said, "You four are dismissed, Niah, please stay a moment," the others left the room, Fin lingering before closing the door.

"I would have told you sooner," Merida frowned, "but you had just received so much information in one go when you arrived."

Niah sighed and leaned back in her chair, "You did say you would answer any questions when I wrapped my head around things." A smile tugged at the corners of Merida's lips.

"I did. Do you have any questions?" for the first time, she didn't. Her mind was blank, silent, calm. The quiet before the storm. It pulsed in the pit of her stomach, a wave of anger so fierce that it rendered her completely quiet. The power in her veins stirred in answer, and a tiny blue spark danced around the tip of her middle finger.

"I want to learn how to use my magic, I...can feel it."

Merida nodded, "Of course. If you don't mind *my* asking, why haven't you asked about your mother? Your real_"

"I'm not ready." It was the truth. Finding out those people weren't her real parents' was enough for now. Merida's lips pressed together, but she said nothing else on the matter.

"I have another question for you." she murmured after a long moment, "You've only been here a short while, and as much as I would like to give you more time, unfortunately, we have run out. Can you trust us? I'm not asking if you *do* trust us. I understand it's too soon for that. But do you think, *truly* think, that you could?"

Niah held Merida's gaze, the blue of her eyes deep like the ocean. There hadn't been much interaction between them since they last spoke, but she'd seen enough around the facility. Fin had shown her enough. It was nothing like the academy. *The compound.* These people, despite the short time she'd been there, had wormed their way into her heart.

Against her better judgement, she realised she already trusted them. Perhaps it was stupid. Maybe it would end with a broken heart. But she didn't care. She wanted to trust. Wanted to be a part of something bigger, to fight for something *more* than revenge.

She'd get her revenge one day.

Niah rose from her seat and made her way around the desk, lowering herself to one knee, and bowed her head. She had never bowed to anyone, but she would bow to Merida. To the woman who carried the weight of all those deaths on her shoulders, in her eyes, and her heart.

"I already trust you. You may think me foolish for trusting so quickly, but I do. For the first time, I feel like myself. The moment I arrived here, a weight lifted from my shoulders, and I can't ignore that."

Merida whimpered, and her arms went around Niah in an instant. She tensed but didn't pull away. She had never been held like this, not with such fierceness as if Merida might break if she let go. The woman pulled back, holding her at arms-length by the shoulders.

"I have to tell you, I know you're not ready, and that's fine, but I was there not long after you were born. I was there when the Shadows descended on us and tore you from your mother. I barely escaped, and I curse myself every day for not fighting harder." she broke off as the air caught in her throat and tears rolled down her cheeks.

Niah was silent. She knew she had a real mother and father, but wasn't ready to face that part of her life, not yet. Someday, maybe, but not today.

Life with her adoptive parents' flashed through her mind; not once were they affectionate toward her, they scolded her more often than praised her. The only kindness they had ever shown was giving her the locket. Still, they moulded her partly into what she had become. She was strong because of the heartache it caused watching them die before her eyes.

"Thank you for telling me. You said she was taken. Do you know if she's alive?" she asked, Merida nodded, "Can we get her back?"

"We can try," Merida closed her eyes briefly. Niah nodded and rose to her feet.

"I better go," she said as she headed for the door.

"Niah," she paused and turned her head slightly, her hand resting on the handle, "Thank you."

She dipped her chin and left the office. She realised this was personal for Merida; it meant something to her to have gained Niah's trust. And now, feeling as though she had a purpose, it was time to become the weapon her former headmistress had always wanted her to be.

FIN

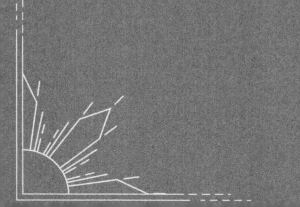

17

Fin was restless.

The news of the attack on the English facility had come as a shock, and he couldn't settle. After Niah had left the office, he and Merida had a conference call with several facility leaders, including Benjamin of the attacked facility.

Understandably, Benjamin was furious, but Fin couldn't help feeling like he was using it as an excuse to launch an attack in retaliation. It was no secret that Benjamin wanted nothing more than to eradicate the Shadows. Aside from Merida, he had put the most resources into finding them, but any leads they had always ran dry.

Following the news, patrols had been suspended so the facility residents could mourn the fallen warriors, though they would still be expected to answer any alerts.

The halls were ghostly silent as Fin made his way through them, if only to make sure everyone was okay. It was the early hours of the morning, night engulfed the facility, sounds of sleep drifted through the walls and doors.

As second in command, people came to him when they needed something. Merida was welcoming enough, but no one wanted to disturb her, knowing she would feel the weight of those deaths more than most.

So, they went to him.

After his years of experience, he didn't know what to tell them. There had never been an attack on a facility before. The Shadows had hunted hybrids for centuries, but they had never been brazen enough to attack the Alliance directly.

The warriors were angry, thirsting for vengeance. He wanted to give it to them, but neither he nor Merida knew where to start looking. Talon's report had come in mere hours before the news of the attack.

The compound was empty. That was their only hope of getting close to the Shadows, and now it was gone.

Fin dragged his hands down his face, rubbing at his heavy eyes as he made his way down the stairs and toward the gym. Except when he arrived, he wasn't alone.

Niah was pummelling a punching bag, her hands wrapped up, and her canines glinting in the light as she panted. He thought about leaving her to it, but something had changed between them over the last few days.

There was so much she had bottled up, Fin wanted to know more, wished she would open up about it even; but he couldn't ignore how far she had come in such a short space of time.

The door shut behind him, and her head snapped up. He strode toward her, hands in his pockets as she stretched out her arms.

"I wasn't expecting company," she breathed. He should have known she would come here if she were restless, after all, it was what she'd done in England.

"I was coming to blow off steam," he said.

Niah arched a brow, "No jokes?"

"Not tonight," he frowned.

She glanced over her shoulder at the sparring ring, "Spar with me?"

At that, he smiled. If anything, she was consistent. It was a good idea anyway, after watching her training with Dea earlier, he needed to go over getting the hang of her strength. Not that she didn't do well, but

Dea was holding back, giving Niah a chance to adjust to her new body.

Fin followed her into the ring, wrapping his own hands with the bandages he'd pulled from his pocket. He did a few warm-up exercises and faced Niah in the ring.

Both of them attacked at once. Niah had pushed off too hard and overshot her punch, Fin could have taken advantage, if he were in a better mood, maybe he would have. But he didn't want to use harsh lessons, not right now.

It was clear that Niah wouldn't go easy on him, but she was getting frustrated with the lack of control over her own body. Fin thought about giving her some advice, but before he did, she righted herself. She started catching herself when she overshot, she analysed, adjusted.

She didn't need his advice.

Those days he'd spent with her had been rewarding in many ways, she tried new things, learnt new things. She relaxed around him, she smiled, laughed, read, and slept peacefully. Never for long, but whenever she woke up, she'd retreat into herself for a while.

He never asked about it in fear she would close herself off. She was dealing with whatever was going on inside her head in her own way, and he wanted to give her space to do that. No matter how much he found himself wanting to know more.

That night she'd awoke from the nightmare and tried to stab him was the closest she'd come to opening up, and she had, in some way. Things shifted between them after that. Whether she felt it or not, he didn't know. But he did.

He had no idea what it meant, that feeling of warmth in his chest whenever he looked at her. He took notice of the way her lashes fluttered as she read a book, or the way she would cover her mouth with the neck of her shirt whenever she smiled while watching TV.

He noticed things he hadn't even been searching for, and he didn't know why. Hybrids didn't feel the way humans did. But he couldn't deny that there was *something* there.

Even if he had no idea what that something was.

Niah punched him in the jaw. He staggered back, cradling his jaw as he shook the fog from his mind.

That'll teach him to get distracted.

"I'm not that boring, am I?" Niah raised a brow, letting her arms fall to her sides as she stepped closer. Her eyes lingered on his jaw, checking for injuries, he realised.

"Boring isn't the word I'd use to describe you," he murmured, tasting blood in his mouth.

"What word would you use to describe me?" she quizzed, turning away to stretch her arms above her head.

Strong. Fierce. Smart. Beautiful.

None of them seemed enough to describe her.

So he said, "A pain in my ass."

"Jaw," she corrected.

"You seem in a good mood," he said.

Niah loosed a breath and turned to him, "I'm trying not to think about it."

"Same here. I thought you'd be pissed off."

"I am," she shrugged, "but there's nothing I can do right now."

"You could leave." He didn't mean it the way it sounded, he was simply pointing out that she hadn't yet left, when she had every opportunity and reason to.

Niah glanced down at her feet, "I know."

"Why haven't you?" he asked. Maybe if he pushed a little, she would tell him something honest, even if everything in his head screamed at him to leave it alone.

She met his gaze, her eyes impossibly dark and haunting, "Do you *want* me to leave?"

Yeah, he should have left it alone.

He shook his head, dragging a hand through his hair, "No, forget I said anything."

"What did you mean, Fin?" she pressed, her voice turning hard.

"Nothing."

"What, suddenly you have nothing to say? The guy who never shuts up?" she scoffed.

Maybe it was the pain of the day, maybe it was the tiredness and stress, but he said, "You're hardly one to talk."

Niah blinked, "I have told you_"

"Have you? *Have* you told me anything, really?"

Why was he saying this?

"I suppose none of this matters to you, does it. That we lost warriors today. You don't care. You're only here because you want to get to the Shadows, and we're the easiest way to get there. Well? Tell me I'm wrong."

He wished he could take it all back, it might all be true, but it didn't need to be voiced. Not like that. Not after everything.

Niah was silent for a long minute, her eyes never once leaving his as they glared at one another.

"You're right."

Something in his chest deflated.

"You're right, I didn't care. I was prepared to manipulate you, to *use* you and Merida to get what I wanted. I want revenge, I want it more than anything else, and I was ready to do whatever it took to get it." she walked toward him until there was barely a foot of distance between them.

His heart stuttered at being so close to her.

"But I don't want that anymore," she breathed, "I don't know why, and maybe I'm an idiot for it, it's only been a matter of weeks since I arrived, and yet, I can't deny this feeling." She placed a hand over her chest, "I trust you, Fin. You, Merida, the Alliance. I want to fight *with* you. But I won't apologise for my previous intentions."

He didn't expect her to.

Hearing those words from her lips struck a chord.

She trusted him, them.

Fin hadn't realised how much it meant to him, until he'd heard those words.

"Say it again," he muttered.

Niah's brow scrunched before her face softened, and she whispered, "I trust you."

The faintest of smiles brushed her lips, and he found himself leaning in slightly. Fin stopped himself. He realised how close they were standing. He didn't know what to do, and so desperately wanted to break that tension hanging between them.

Before he could say or do anything, the doors opened, and Merida strode in wearing workout clothes.

"Are you two sparring?" she asked when she came close.

"Yeah, do you want to join in?" Fin asked, stepping away from Niah.

Merida turned her eyes to Niah, "What do you think?"

"I wouldn't mind seeing how a leader fights," Niah smirked, striding into the centre of the ring.

His heart swelled as he watched them together. It was one thing seeing Niah smile, but seeing Merida like that, at ease, the weight of the world lifted from her shoulders, warmed him down to his bones.

Merida still needed to tell her, and she would when the time was right, he just hoped it would be sooner rather than later. None of that mattered at that moment.

Fin could have watched Niah and Merida all night, but, like all good things, it had to come to an end.

NIAH

18

The next few days were solemn.

The Furies of the Perth facility held a formal gathering to say farewell to those they lost in the attack on the English facility. The names of the fallen were written in a large, ancient book. The dusty pages were filled with the names of those who had died over the centuries.

Niah had taken a moment to let those names sink in as she flicked through the pages. So many names, dates, and causes of death. Merida explained that it was customary among the Alliance to keep detailed records like that. So many had died because of demon attacks, and many had been lost to the Shadows. The last four pages were all a result of the recent Shadows attack.

There was no word as to when the survivors would arrive, nor had the leaders of the other facilities decided on the next course of action. Merida and Fin had been in meetings that sometimes lasted from morning to evening with the other leaders. Both had emerged looking haggard and frustrated, having not achieved a plan, yet again.

More than half of the leaders wanted to wait, to dispatch spies to locate the whereabouts of the Shadows. The rest of them argued that they weren't likely to find them now after centuries of searching. Which led to the next point, if they couldn't find them, how were they supposed to launch an attack?

Fin explained to her, Dea, Sai, and Gren that someone had suggested searching the compound in England again, but Benjamin had already sent people to scout it when he learnt of its existence. The reports showed that it was empty, swept clean, not a single scrap of paper had been left.

Merida and Fin were growing weary of the back-and-forth arguments. And no one could agree on one particular plan. There were rumours of a Summit being held, whatever that was.

True to their word, everyone in the facility was training harder. They had to rotate, taking it in turns to use the gym. As big as it was, it was still far too small for the sheer number of warriors in the facility, and would be fuller still when the survivors arrived. When they weren't allowed to use the gym, they alternated between running along the beach, swimming in the ocean, or sparring within the cloak of the facility. Even running on the beach wasn't much of a workout unless they went before dawn, where there would be no humans to witness their speed.

With Fin being needed in the constant meetings, Niah trained with Dea, Sai, and Gren. The blonde had warmed up to her somewhat after a couple of sparring matches. To her surprise, he gave her advice on how to handle her new strength, as did Sai.

That morning, Dea and Sai had gone out on patrol, and it was just her and Gren. As Fin's friend, Gren was trusted to train the recruits in Fin's absence. He was blunt, straight to the point, but Niah preferred it that way. He talked her through various exercises and showed her some technique's she hadn't known.

It was an adjustment, to accept she needed advice. After years of being left to her own devices, she'd unintentionally picked up some bad habits, which Gren was all too quick to point out. But Niah found she didn't mind quite as much as she thought she would.

She was sitting on the bench drinking water when he came over, arms folded, and sat beside her, "Ready to go again?"

"In a minute," she panted. Sparring with the hybrids made her work up more of a sweat than she had been used to in England. They were amazing.

"Maybe we should stop for now," Gren murmured, smoothing his hair back.

Niah shook her head, getting to her feet, "I'm good, let's go."

"You know," Gren said, Niah paused and turned back to him, "I'm glad you decided to stay."

Well, she wasn't expecting *that*.

"Why? You made it clear you didn't trust me."

"Did being the operative word," he muttered, getting to his feet with his hands in his pockets, "it's been a long time since I've seen Merida so happy. I know it's because you're here. So, thank you, for that."

After Merida had hugged her, it was as if something had clicked inside her. Her chest grew warm, and all those doubts she'd felt ebbed away. She couldn't explain it, and she didn't understand why she trusted any of them so quickly, or at least, that's what she told herself.

"Merida saved me, so did Fin. I didn't know if I could trust any of you..." she trailed off, not knowing how to finish that sentence.

Gren nodded, as if understanding that fact, and said, "When I threatened you, it wasn't personal."

She held a silencing hand up, "You don't have to explain, I get it." a comfortable silence fell between them as they walked to the ring and took up their places opposite each other.

Nolan told her once that you could learn a lot through sparring with someone. Crossing fists and swords was like a dance. No words were necessary to communicate what one was feeling through the movements.

Niah had never understood it.

But she did now. She'd fought all of them, Fin, Merida, Dea, Sai, and Gren. She could read their movements, not just because her reflexes were sharper, but she *felt* a connection between them. A connection she'd never felt before.

When she and Gren were finished, she asked, "I can feel your intentions when we spar; why is that?"

"It's a hybrid thing. It's similar to the bond between wolves, except we feel it more deeply. Some say hybrids don't feel emotions, some say we feel more intensely than any other species, who's to say what's right? But when we achieve bonds of friendship and trust, we become a unit, that's why we work so well as warriors." Gren explained, a slight smile tugging at the corners of his lips, "So it means we're friends."

Niah didn't think it was a coincidence that she had achieved that bond with him and the others, they were the first people that had embraced her, accepted her. Even if Gren took a little longer than the others, in some ways, it was better, because they had overcome that and earned each other's trust.

Still, hearing those words from him made her chest swell with warmth.

Friends.

She had friends.

The void left by her parents' suddenly felt a little smaller.

That afternoon, Niah, Dea, Sai, and Gren sat in the canteen for lunch. Fin was in yet another meeting with Merida and the other leaders over the phone. Sai was leaning his head against his hand, a fork dangling from the other, his eyes drooping as he fought to stay awake.

"Anyone would think you don't sleep," Gren mused, pushing his empty plate away.

Sai jumped and gazed at him with wide eyes, "What?" Gren shook his head, taking a swig of water.

"We're all tired," Dea murmured.

Indeed, even the snowy-haired girls' shine had dulled since the attack in England. Niah felt a stab of guilt that there was nothing she could say to make it any better. There was nothing anyone could say to ease the sadness they felt.

It was strange. They hadn't known a great deal of those who had fallen, but the Furies loss was still felt across every facility over the world.

Sai draped an arm around Dea's shoulders, "It's okay, early night tonight."

Many of them had only been getting a few hours of sleep. Since the attack, patrols were set up around the facility and surrounding areas, in addition to the patrols in the cities for demons. No one was sleeping much, and the strain was beginning to take its toll.

Already, two fights had to be broken up in the gym that morning. Merida had excused herself from her meeting to give a motivational speech to the entire facility. It had worked and took the edge off the palpable tension. But for how long would it last?

They were playing a waiting game. With no idea where the Shadows were, their only option was to wait and be ready for when they inevitably attacked again.

If Niah's experience with the Shadows had taught her anything, it was that the Shadows would drag it out, savour the fear and anticipation rising throughout the facilities, wait until they were in turmoil with each other, and then attack.

That's what she would do.

Merida knew that better than most, which is why she tried to check in with everyone as often as she could—making appearances in the gym and other areas to bolster the efforts and raise the warriors' morale. She was doing all she could, but who was there to lift *her* spirits?

The five of them, including Fin, made a point to make sure Merida was eating and resting. Taking plates of food up to her office, or forcing her to take a break and go for a walk or train with them. Gren and Fin had even tucked her into bed one night when she was adamant she had missed something in the reports sent by Talon, who was with Benjamin and the other survivors.

Still, despite the weariness, they would endure.

Because losing was not an option.

For any of them.

That night, she lay in bed staring up at the ceiling, willing sleep to take her, but it never came. She had tossed and turned more times than she cared to count, unable to get comfortable, and unable to silence her overactive mind.

She'd done nothing but try to imagine what their next move might be. Her advantage was that Shadows had raised her. Whether they were pawns or not, they'd still taught her enough about how they thought, how they plotted.

But, try as she might, she couldn't think of what they might be planning. The attack in England was a shock, but Niah didn't think the Shadows had attacked the facility because they thought *she* was there.

No, they wouldn't be so violent if that were the case.

They did it because they wanted her to know they could find the facilities, that they knew she was with the Furies. It made her question how they could have that information. But, if the Furies were their biggest threat, then it would be a good guess that Niah was with them.

She hadn't been able to shake that uneasy feeling in the pit of her stomach that she was to blame for the attack. If she hadn't left with Fin, the Shadows wouldn't have attacked. Or maybe they would have. In truth, Niah had no idea what the Shadows were planning; perhaps they were going to attack the facility anyway.

But the timing was too coincidental.

And Niah didn't believe in coincidences.

She glanced at the clock on the nightstand, nine PM. She shoved the covers away and got to her feet, padding across the floor to the sliding door leading to the balcony.

The wind whipped her hair around her, but she relished in the fresh ocean scent. Niah gripped the railing hard enough that her knuckles paled. How was it possible that after centuries, the Furies had no clue where the Shadows were?

What would happen if she stayed?

How many more would perish because the Shadows had lost their weapon?

The word sliced at her chest, but she pushed it aside, determined not to let it hurt her as it once had. She wouldn't give the Shadows the satisfaction.

NIAH

19

A knock rapped at the door, snapping her out of her reverie. Fin leaned against the wall on the other side, wearing dark jeans and a button-up grey shirt; his hair looked different, tamed, as if he'd dragged a brush through it.

With him was Sai, wearing jeans and a black V-neck t-shirt. Gren wearing a black leather jacket, and Dea wearing an incredibly sparkly, short, red dress with high strappy heels, her hair falling around her shoulders like a sheet of snow. She was practically bouncing with excitement.

Words failed her as she stared at them, already regretting her decision to answer the door.

"Nope," she said, swinging the door closed, or she would have, if Fin's foot weren't in the way.

Niah stifled a groan as she opened it, dreading what was about to happen.

Dea turned to Fin with a grin, "Will you tell her already? The suspense is killing me." He rolled his eyes with a smile.

"Happy eighteenth birthday. Now get dressed; we're going out," she had completely forgotten about her birthday. Merida must have told them.

It wasn't something that had ever been celebrated before, it was always just a milestone to which she was tested to make sure she was progressing appropriately.

Niah took a deep breath, fiddling with a loose thread on her shirt, "Going out where?"

Dea pulled a white, sparkly feather bower from behind her back and wrapped it around Niah's neck, "We're going dancing."

"Is it even safe to go out? Given the attack," She frowned.

Fin met her gaze, the silver of them shimmering, "Merida has approved it. It's probably safer away from the facility, but I have my phone if we're needed. We're not going far, and we'd be back here in a matter of minutes."

Minutes would be all it took. As if reading that very thought, Fin added, "Vinaxx strengthened the barrier around the facility again this morning. We're ready. We're going armed." He gestured to Sai and Gren.

Niah chewed on her lip before asking, "Dea and I aren't?"

"Well, unless you know some magical way to hide knives in dresses?" Fin smirked. Unfortunately, she didn't. And judging by the look Dea was giving her, wearing jeans wouldn't be an option.

Still, it didn't stop the guilt creeping into her mind for all those who had lost their lives, and she was going to be out having fun. It didn't seem right.

Sai caught Dea's attention, the two of them fell into a conversation as Fin leaned in close and muttered, "Just for one night. We could all do with a break, and Dea has been excited about this for days."

"What if something happens?" Niah said through her teeth, gripping the hem of her shirt.

Fin loosed a breath, "If the Shadows decide to attack, they'll have to go through our patrols, the barrier, and the warriors ready inside the facility. They'd be stupid to attack right now while we're expecting them."

He wasn't wrong. But still...

"Don't you want to live a little?" his eyes glinted as a smirk danced at one corner of his lips.

Niah sighed, knowing none of them would give up, "Fine, but even so much as a whisper from the Shadows, and we come back."

He pulled back, his silver eyes understanding, but shining with triumph. Sure enough, Dea was practically glowing with excitement. Niah sighed, defeated.

If she were honest, it was nice that they wanted to celebrate her birthday, even if it did come at a terrible time.

"Come on, put something pretty on, tell me you have dresses," Dea beamed, gesturing to her own, incredibly short dress. Niah raised a brow.

"Do I look like I wear dresses?"

"That's a trick question, right?" Sai scoffed. She rolled her eyes, smacking him playfully in the arm.

Dea sighed, "Wow...you are useless."

"Wha_"

"Come on, let's see if I have anything for you," Dea gripped her hand and dragged her down the hall. She looked over her shoulder at the guys and mouthed 'help'. Fin just shrugged with a smile, Sai laughed, and Gren held up his thumb. Helpful.

Dea's room looked as if her drawers had exploded. Clothes were strewn over the floor and bed, she fluttered around the room, grabbing dresses whilst discarding them over her shoulder. Dea had dozens of dresses, yet there was something not quite right with each one.

Niah had lost track of how long she had been sitting at the desk used as a beauty table with a light-up mirror and trays of makeup.

"How are the guys going to keep weapons on them without being spotted by humans?" Niah questioned, admiring a shade of red nail polish.

"Oh, the weapons are made of *Ruclite*. A demon-killing metal. Humans can't see it, thankfully," Dea explained as she threw more dresses across the bed.

"So, why can't I keep a weapon on me?" Niah inquired, glancing at the various items of makeup on the cluttered desk.

"Because I said so, just because humans can't see the weapons, doesn't mean they can't see bumps in clothing that shouldn't be there or scabbards. The boys will just strap them to their backs, and nobody will be any the wiser. Now, stop with all this weapons talk," she ordered with a firm grin.

"But...I like weapons," Niah murmured to herself, knowing full well Dea wasn't listening, "Won't the scabbards be spotted, though?"

Dea let out a sigh, "They're made to look like elongated bags. We get questioning glances sometimes, but with the fashion these days being somewhat questionable, no one makes a fuss."

Niah didn't have a chance to respond before Dea shrieked, "This is it!" holding up a short, silky dress the colour of ebony.

"I hope that's a shirt," Niah muttered.

Dea whined, "Try it?"

With a sigh, Niah stripped down to her underwear, a lacy black set that Dea had gifted her when they arrived in her room. She'd gawped at it as if Dea had suggested shoving bamboo shoots under her fingernails.

The hopeful gleam in her friends' eyes had been enough for her to begrudgingly put them on. She'd only ever worn a sports bra, and when she questioned why her friend had gifted her lacy underwear for her birthday, Dea simply winked.

Niah's cheeks burned, and she thought about taking the garments off, but kept them on, secretly enjoying the feel of them against her skin.

The silky material of the dress slid down her body. The bust had an excess of material that hung down; Dea called it a cowl neck. The shiny material clung to her waist and hips in all the right places. Niah looked at herself in the mirror, having never noticed the shape of her body before, and felt exposed.

"You look incredible," Dea breathed as if she were about to cry. She dug around in a box under her bed and produced a pair of high heels with black, sparkly straps.

Deciding it was pointless to argue, Niah pulled them on and wobbled slightly when she stood. They made her look taller, her legs longer. She tried to tug the hem of the dress lower, feeling like it was entirely too much skin on show. After spending her whole life in athletic leggings and t-shirts or jeans, it was a big difference.

Dea frowned when she noticed Niah's gaze, "You can change if you want; I want you to be comfortable."

Niah searched her friends' eyes for any sign of disappointment; there wasn't so much as a flicker of anything other than understanding.

"It's fine," she breathed.

"You sure?" Niah nodded, "Beautiful, now sit," she did as she was told and let Dea run her hands through her raven hair, combing it and fluffing it up before curling it delicately.

Niah felt like a doll, and slumped in the chair, "Are we done yet?"

"Almost," Dea frowned, picking up small tubs with black powder inside; Niah stared, already shaking her head.

"It's makeup," Dea rolled her eyes.

"I'll remember this," Niah promised with a wicked smirk.

Dea grinned and went to work putting small, winged eyeliner on her lids, mascara on her lashes and a small amount of pinkish-nude matte lipstick on her lips. Niah gazed in the mirror; her cheeks were rosy, yet not unnaturally so, and her eyes appeared more upturned.

Dea smiled once she was finished, looking proud of her work, and opened the door as Niah got to her feet, just as the boys arrived. She caught Fin's eyes widen slightly before he looked away, a flush creeping across his cheeks.

"Damn, we're going to have our work cut out for us tonight," Sai grinned, offering her a wink as they stepped into the corridor. Gren nodded in appreciation and offered her a reassuring smile.

"You look great," he said.

"I feel a bit awkward," Niah admitted.

"Try to relax, if you feel uncomfortable, let me know." He pulled at the dark hoodie under his leather jacket that hadn't been there before, and her chest bloomed with warmth.

"Thank you." he only nodded and offered her a smile before walking ahead with Sai and Dea.

They were walking along the hallway when Merida strode toward them. Her eyes raked over Niah, and she clasped her hands over her mouth briefly.

"You look amazing, both of you," she breathed, turning her smile to Dea.

"Thank you," Niah said, feeling the heat rising in her cheeks.

"Have fun tonight. This may be the only chance you'll get in a while, and please be careful," Merida frowned before continuing down the hall.

Fin fell in step beside her, "How uncomfortable do you feel right now?"

"I feel like a new-born deer," she mumbled, glancing down at her feet in those strappy heels. Fin chuckled and leaned a little closer to her ear, his breath warm where it brushed her neck, sending tingles down her spine.

"Well, you look great."

"Are you feeling okay?" she asked.

"Yeah, why?"

"You complimented me," she smirked; he rolled his eyes, chuckling as he shook his head.

"For that, I won't catch you when you inevitably fall on your face in those ridiculous heels."

"I'm sure you'd just make some sort of joke about me falling for you," she snorted.

Fin gave her a sidelong glance, "Am I *that* predictable?"

"Yes," Sai said over his shoulder.

After a minute, Niah muttered, "I'd feel better with my dagger."

Fin grinned and handed her a small black bag with a silver chain long enough to cross her body. She popped it open to find her dagger inside. Her breath hitched in her throat as she smiled down at it, warmth spreading through her chest.

"Thank you," she breathed, looking up at him. His silver eyes were soft, and he only smiled in response.

NIAH

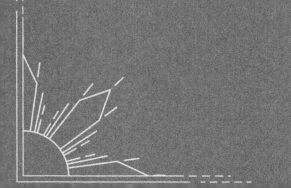

20

It was like a scene from a movie.

Bright lights, music pumping from bars and clubs, people bustling through the streets. The odd person stared at her as they passed, though their gazes never lingered long, not with the boys on either side of her and Dea. They were quite intimidating, she supposed.

Fin smirked down at her as if reading her mind. Even with the heels, he was an inch or two taller. Dea strutted down the street with her arm linked through Niah's, pointing out various clubs and bars she liked to go to. She said it was rare they got to go out, but when they did, they made the most of it.

They came to a bar that backed onto the beach, and found a table outside under a canopy of lights. Dea and Niah sat down as Fin, Sai, and Gren went inside to get drinks.

"Get tequila," Dea had shouted after them. She turned back to Niah and smiled brilliantly.

"I'm so happy," she sighed wistfully, virtually bouncing in her seat as two men walking past gave her a nod in appreciation, Dea offered them a wink and flipped her hair over her shoulder, her blood-red lips curled in a seductive smile.

"Why's that?" Niah asked, bringing Dea's attention back to her.

"I'm just glad you're here."

"There are plenty of other people at the facility."

"There are, and I get on with most of them, but I've never met someone like you," Dea said softly.

Niah tilted her head to the side, "What does that mean?" Dea giggled.

"It means, that despite everyone I know, I would rather spend my time with you. I know you didn't have friends in England, and I can see how much it means to you to have us now."

For a moment, Niah forgot how to breathe. How was Dea so perceptive?

"Why did you trust me?" Niah asked, leaning her forearms against the table.

Dea sighed wistfully, "I didn't. It's not every day someone formerly with the Shadows joins us. After seeing you that day on the beach, I decided to give you a chance."

Niah snorted, "That was awkward that night."

"Yeah," Dea chuckled, "It was. But it's not anymore." she reached across the table and took Niah's hand in hers. "I'm glad we're friends."

Niah shifted in her seat, but before she could say anything, Dea added, "You don't have to say anything, I just wanted you to know that. Now, enough serious talk, we're here to enjoy your birthday."

Niah's heart swelled. The void inside her shrank a little more as she smiled at the girl opposite, feeling warmer than she had done a moment ago.

Dea pulled her hand free and clapped when the boys returned with a tray full of glasses with varying-coloured liquids, straws, and tiny umbrellas.

Dea shifted over on the bench, and Fin sat opposite Niah, Sai to her right, and Gren on Dea's other side. The snowy-haired hybrid handed Niah a glass filled with white-yellow liquid, taking one for herself in the process as the boys did the same.

Niah watched as Dea tipped the whole thing back in one go, and, deciding she may as well go along with whatever Dea had planned, tipped her own glass back, swallowing it in one go.

She regretted it instantly.

It was bitter and warm. Very warm, very bitter.

Her face scrunched, a shudder rolling down her spine as she dropped the glass on the table. The others laughed. Fin handed her a glass of something pink with a tiny umbrella in it and a swirly straw. She ignored the straw and downed it completely. It was sweet, a slight bitterness as she reached the bottom.

"What was that?" she panted as she put the empty glass down.

"Tequila," Dea exclaimed; a few tables back, a group of men raised their glasses and cheered.

Niah couldn't help but laugh.

FIN

21

They left the girls outside while they headed into the bar to fetch the drinks. Fin had been almost unable to take his eyes off Niah during the entire walk. He didn't know what it was about her, maybe it was just because she was so naïve when it came to the human world. Maybe it was because, despite everything she'd been through, she kept fighting.

"Dea is so excited about tonight," Sai said, leaning his elbows against the bar.

Gren gestured to the bartender and snorted, "Dea's always excited about a night out."

"You think Niah will enjoy it?" Fin asked, glancing at Sai, who was smirking at him.

"She seems to be," Gren said over the noise in the bar as he turned to look over his shoulder; when he turned back, he was smiling. Not something Gren did often or lightly. The bartender came back with three bottles of Corona, two pink cocktails, and a small tray of seven tequila shots.

"You like her," Sai grinned.

Fin shrugged, "I like her more now she's not throwing swords at my head."

"Don't jinx it," Gren mused, taking a swig of his beer.

"Thank you both, for giving her a chance."

Sai clapped him on the shoulder, "Some of us took more convincing than others," a pointed glance at Gren.

The blonde rolled his eyes, "We've been over this."

"You owe me a twenty, Gren," Sai smirked. Gren groaned but fished the money from his wallet.

"Did I miss something?" Fin questioned, glancing between the two.

"I bet him that you'd get all sentimental tonight," Sai announced.

Fin chuckled, shaking his head as he grabbed the tray of drinks and started toward the table.

After Niah had downed the cocktail, it dawned on him that she probably wouldn't know it was alcohol. He took her hand when she reached for the second bright drink on the tray.

"As much as I would love to see you pull more faces, I bet you've never had alcohol before, so go steady."

Her cheeks flushed, her eyes flicking to his hand around hers. He let go, and she cleared her throat, "I feel fine."

"Drink anymore of those shots, and you won't be," Sai chuckled.

Niah scoffed, "I'm sure I can handle it."

Fin and Sai exchanged a knowing glance. If she wanted to drink, he wouldn't stop her. But he would most definitely laugh when she made a fool of herself.

Sure enough, after just one more cocktail, she was flushed and slurring her words, almost falling off her chair when she laughed, and gradually getting louder, as was Dea.

After their one beer, he and the guys stuck to water, just in case something *did* happen. Though he was starting to wonder how they would get the girls back quickly if the worst did happen. After a quick conversation, it was decided that Sai would stay with the girls while Gren and Fin rushed back to the facility.

With that in mind, it would probably be wise to replace the cocktails with juice.

Still, Fin couldn't deny that for the first time in what felt like an exceptionally long time, he was relaxed. He was laughing, and despite what might happen, he was able to push it to the back of his mind. Even if it did get harder, the more time went on.

Tonight was for Niah. It was the first time she'd ever celebrated a birthday, he couldn't ruin that.

"I want to dance," Dea beamed, slurring her words. Niah nodded eagerly.

This will be entertaining.

Sai banged his hands down on the table, "Let's go then."

Fin chuckled and shook his head as Dea stumbled around the table into Sai's awaiting arms, wobbling on those ridiculous heels.

Niah managed to stand on her own, but she tripped as soon as she took a step. Fin caught her, refraining from pulling her close to him, unsure whether she would flinch away. But, to his surprise, she clung onto him, smiling up at him with half-lidded, unfocused eyes.

"I like cocktails," she hummed.

"Can you be this lovely all the time?" he mused, guiding her out of the bar. Niah giggled in answer, and it was the most beautiful sound he'd ever heard.

They walked a block down the street to a well-known supernatural club. The bouncer was a lycanthrope, his eyes lingered a bit too long on the girls for comfort, and Fin gave him a warning growl. When the bouncer dragged his eyes to Fin and the boys, Gren quickly stepped in his path. The wolf quickly averted his eyes.

"We don't get many hybrids in here," the man murmured as they strode through the front doors, the people in the queue groaning and cursing at them.

"It's her birthday," Fin shrugged, gesturing to Niah, who was grinning. The man shook his head but nodded them through.

Being a hybrid had its perks. Not many species outside of the Alliance would get into a fight with them.

The music thumped through the doors. Bright, multicoloured lights filled the room as the bass vibrated through the floor. Thick smoke filled the dance floor like mist on the ground as bodies swayed in time with the music.

Niah glanced around, dark eyes full of wonder. A waitress hurried over to them. A tall blonde with large, green eyes and pale blue wings tucked in behind her, a drinks menu in hand.

Niah reached out as if she meant to touch the fairy's wings. The fey girl held her wing out in invitation; Niah smiled and reached out, her fingers gently grazing the thin membrane. The girl shuddered, stepping back and kissing Niah on the cheek.

"Special occasion?" the fey asked in Fin's ear.

"Her birthday," the fey pulled back and offered her hand to Niah. To Fin's surprise, she took it and allowed the fey to lead her to a small booth near the stage, the best seats in the club short of the VIP section. Fin thanked her and offered her money; she merely shook her head and smiled at Niah as she watched the lights shimmer against the girls' wings.

"Do you want any drinks?" the fey asked.

"Lots of water," Fin smiled; she glanced at the others, already sat down, and smiled before hurrying away.

He helped Niah into the booth. They sat for a while, still laughing. The waitress brought water, and the girls drank it greedily, not noticing it wasn't alcohol.

Niah pulled at his sleeve and leaned close to him, her lips grazing his ear as she whispered, sending sparks of electricity through his body.

"I want to dance."

"Well, it would be rude to decline the birthday girl her wish."

He helped her to her feet; the others followed, wandering onto the dance floor. Niah and Dea danced together for a while, laughing as they bounced in time with the thumping music.

Fin checked his phone, relieved to find no notifications. Knowing he wouldn't hear it in his pocket, he kept it to hand and put it on vibrate.

He watched as Niah threw her head back, laughing. Watched as she raised her hands to the ceiling when bubbles poured down around them. Watched as she moved her hips, rather distractingly, to the music.

She took his breath away.

Niah stumbled, and he caught her, spinning her into the circle of his arms as the music slowed to a heavy, swaying beat. She looked up at him through her long lashes, dark eyes unfocused, yet wide and alive, the silver of them impossibly bright.

They moved together to the beat of the music as she ran her hands over his shoulders, and down his chest. He closed his eyes, savouring the touch, running his hands over the bare skin of her back and thin straps of the dress. He hadn't noticed how low the back of the dress hung before. She raised her arms into the air, his hands falling to her hips as she moved them gracefully from side to side.

The sensation sent pulses through his body, straight to his groin. It was wrong. Niah was intoxicated. He quickly pushed the thoughts away, calming himself. It wasn't easy, but he wouldn't be *that* guy. He looked down at her to find she was gazing up at him, her lips slightly parted. She placed a hand on each side of his face and reached up.

His heart stumbled, and he spun her away, catching her hand to pull her back to him, so her back was pressed against his chest. Probably the wrong choice as her backside pressed into him in certain areas. He cursed under his breath, barely able to stop himself from reacting.

Getting turned on in the middle of a supernatural club where everyone could smell *everything*, wasn't exactly how he saw the night going.

Though as he thought about it, the scent of lust was stifling from all corners of the room.

He noticed a man with dark hair and black eyeliner leering at Niah as he made his way through the crowd. Fin stiffened, realising Niah had twirled free of his grip, and unknowingly, straight into the path of that man.

A savage growl tore through his throat, his canines sliding free as the mans' hands went around Niah's waist. Her eyes widened, and she jumped back, but the man held onto her.

Fin grabbed the guy's wrist and twisted, tightening his hold enough that he felt the bones groaning and cracking under his grip.

"Touch her again, and I'll break it off," Fin growled, flashing his sharpened teeth. The man, who possessed the scent of a werewolf, jerked his hand back and cradled it to his chest before hurrying through the crowd.

His heart was pounding.

He'd never done anything like that before, but for Niah, he hadn't thought twice, hadn't thought at all.

Fin turned, relieved to see Sai with his arms around Niah, and Gren with Dea, both looking to him for confirmation that all was okay.

He glanced around, noticing many pairs of eyes now on them, and the werewolf talking with a group of men by the bar, pointing in their direction.

"Time to go," Fin said to Sai and Gren as Niah returned to his side. His arm snaked around her, holding her close while Gren kept hold of Dea, and Sai watched their backs.

Fin didn't know whether the men belonged to one of the rogue clans, or whether they were lone supernatural's. If they were part of a rogue group, then he didn't want to risk a fight. Not when relations between them were already strained where the Alliance was concerned.

Thankfully, the men didn't follow them out of the club, only to the door. Though it did little to ease the tension now rolling off all three of them, the girls were none the wiser about what had happened. Good.

At least their night wasn't ruined.

The walk back took twice as long as it had on their way out. The girls were laughing and dancing despite the lack of music and fell over themselves. Fin just chuckled as they took their shoes off and walked barefoot back to the facility.

When they finally returned, Gren and Sai took Dea off to bed, leaving Fin with Niah.

She stumbled through the door, giggling quietly. He revelled in the sound of it. He wouldn't imagine the next time he would see her like this, carefree and laughing. All her walls were gone.

A part of him didn't want it to end, but at the same time, he wanted to see her like this when she *wasn't* inebriated.

She spun around in the room as she tried to get out of her dress, showing off her black lacy underwear.

It was torture.

Well, it wasn't.

But it was, because as much as he wanted to, he wouldn't touch her. Not in that state. Especially when she hadn't even been able to fend off another man in the club.

Fin looked away as she got stuck and stood with the dress covering her face. Fin grinned and helped her out of it, folding it neatly on the desk. She peaked up at him, standing in her underwear.

He wanted to kiss her, wanted to feel her lips beneath his, the warmth of her skin.

Not like this.

"You don't like looking at me like this?" she asked as he handed her a baggy t-shirt. He looked back at her as she pulled it over her head, thankfully covering herself.

"Believe me, that isn't it," he said in a gravelly voice, he helped her over to the bed, pulling the covers back for her to get in.

"So, what is it?" she inquired in a high voice. Fin went to the bathroom, filled a glass of water, and placed it on the nightstand.

"Oh, so many things," he said mockingly. She pouted and cocked her head to one side. She opened her mouth to say something, but he held up a silencing hand, turning back to the desk to retrieve the package he'd placed there earlier.

He held out a chocolate cupcake with a candle sticking out the top, and lit it.

"Make a wish," he breathed when he knelt by the bed and held the cake between them.

Niah smiled, "What do you mean?"

"Well, usually, on birthdays, there's a cake with a candle, you make a wish and blow it out, and it's supposed to come true." He explained, his voice a gentle whisper.

Something deflated in his chest. Everyone should know what a real birthday was.

"What do I wish for?" she asked, frowning at the candle.

"Whatever you want, what does your heart want?"

She raised her eyes to his then, "Would you kiss me?"

His heart swelled and broke at the same time.

Her first birthday wish, and she wanted to kiss him. But he couldn't.

"You have to blow the candle out, or it won't come true," he muttered. She did just that, and he leaned forward, pressing a kiss to her forehead.

Niah sighed lightly, "That's not what I meant."

"I know, but not tonight," he said. She made a face, leaning back against the pillows.

"Why not?"

He sat on the edge of the bed, tucking a strand of hair behind her ear, "Because, when I do kiss you, I want to kiss the real you. Not this drunken version, no matter how charming you are," at that, she smiled. He thought she would say something else, but she fell asleep, her chest rising and falling steadily.

"You really will be the death of me," he murmured into the darkness. He rose from the bed and left the room, closing the door as he leaned against it for a moment, tipping his head back and closing his eyes to take deep, steadying breaths.

"Is she okay?" a familiar voice asked, Merida; she must have been waiting up for them.

"She's fine, drunk, but fine. Sorry if we woke you," he whispered, pushing himself away from the door to gaze at her. She looked tired, dark circles lined her eyes. She shook her head, taking a step closer.

"Did you all have fun?"

Fin nodded, a smile spreading over his face at the memories of the night. Merida gazed at him thoughtfully for a moment, she reached up and brushed a quick kiss against his cheek.

"I'm glad, you deserve it," she smiled, glancing at the door, a quizzical expression flashing across her features. "You care for her."

He shrugged, "We're friends."

"There's something else," she shook her head as if struggling to put her finger on it.

"We're hybrids, Merida. We don't feel things like that; you know that better than anyone," he muttered, not unkindly. She regarded him thoughtfully before smiling and nodding once, walking the other way down the hall.

He repeated those words in his head as he made his way back to his room.

Hybrids didn't feel love.

Whatever he felt for her, he needed to work it out in his head before he did anything. Before he acted on anything.

Niah wasn't like most people he knew. There was trauma, pain, hatred lurking beneath that beautiful surface. If he wasn't careful, he'd only confuse her, and he didn't want to add to the hurt that already shone in her eyes whenever she thought no one was looking.

Hybrids didn't feel love.

NIAH

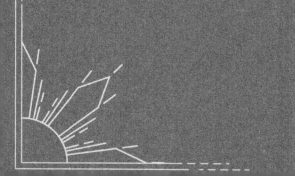

22

Niah was never drinking again.

She'd woken hours ago, but hadn't dared get out of bed until the room stopped spinning. Her mouth was dry and tasted weird, her head throbbed and swirled, and her stomach churned with each step when she finally managed to drag herself out of bed.

No, she was never drinking again.

Cocktails were deceiving.

Before Niah could bring herself to leave her rooms, she drank as much water as she could manage, which was another terrible mistake.

How could those fruity drinks make her feel so bad?

There was a cupcake with a candle sticking out the top on the nightstand, she had no idea how it got there, or what the candle was for. But she was hungry enough to eat it without question, and it was delicious, if not a little dry.

By the time she made it downstairs, the training room was packed. Her head was still pounding, but at least the room had stopped spinning.

Niah didn't remember much of the night, but the bits she did remember were full of laughing and dancing with her friends. She didn't know how she got back to her room, let alone changed and tucked into bed. But at least she wasn't on the floor.

Which was beginning to look very appealing.

Everyone turned to her when the doors slammed shut behind her. Fin, Dea, Sai, and Gren stood at the front of a large group, Sai struggling to stifle his laugh, Dea looked as rough as Niah felt, and no doubt looked just as bad. Fin shook his head with a slight smile and pulled the attention back to himself to continue explaining the plan for the day.

Her cheeks flamed when she watched him address the recruits. Something tugged at her memory of the night before, but it was too hazy to get a clear image. The breath hitched in her throat; what if she'd done something embarrassing?

The doors opened behind her; Niah turned to see Merida ease the door closed, and stride toward her.

"I won't comment on what you look like right now, but I guess you had fun?" Merida mused, a wicked smile dancing at the edges of her mouth.

Somehow, just being near the woman soothed Niah's heart, a sense of comfort washing over her.

"How kind of you," Niah offered a sweet smile, "I think so? It's all a little blurry."

"I wasn't expecting you to drink," Merida said, turning her attention to Fin and the others.

Niah shrugged, "I didn't realise what it was until it was too late."

"Well, no matter, but don't think you'll get off easy just because of a hangover," Merida smirked, clasping her hands behind her back.

Niah thought she looked a little more pale than usual, her eyes ringed with purple, and her lips dry.

"Are you okay?" she asked, turning fully to the leader.

Merida cleared her throat and turned for the door, "Of course. Oh, if you feel up to it, I'll arrange for you to start learning magic."

"Thank you," Niah answered, watching as Merida nodded and left the room. It was the first time since meeting her, that Niah felt a sense of unease.

Fin took a large portion of the group running on the beach, throwing her a wink on his way out. Dea took a group to go through fighting styles and techniques. Sai taught sword fighting with the wooden training swords. And Gren had taken his group up into the beams in the ceiling.

Niah wandered over to the wooden swords and slowly sipped at her water, having learnt not to gulp it the hard way. Sai stretched like a cat and popped his knuckles, a loud crack echoing through the room; dark circles were smudged beneath his eyes.

The tension in the room was palpable, nerves and adrenaline spiking, bringing her crashing back to the harsh reality of what they were facing.

She glanced around the room, these people were not like those at the compound; they were warriors. Yet, the same rage she noticed in herself was reflected in the eyes of everyone around her.

"What's up?" Sai asked as he stretched an arm over his chest.

"I can't help feeling like I'm responsible for this," she sighed and placed her hands on her hips, stretching from side to side.

The thought that the English facility wouldn't have been attacked if she had stayed in England still haunted her in quiet moments. She hadn't let herself think about it in the last few days but seeing the anger in the eyes of everyone around her, made those thoughts impossible to ignore.

"The Shadows would have attacked eventually anyway. It's just unlucky that they chose now," he shrugged, dismissing her grave tone.

Niah frowned, he sighed and placed his hands on his narrow hips, "The Shadows don't like losing. It was going to happen sooner or later. So, the question is, what are you going to do about it? Sit here and sulk, or get to work?" a small smile tugged at the edges of his mouth, a challenge glinting in his eyes. "Or are you feeling the effects of last night?"

"Aren't you?" she inquired.

Sai smirked, "Us guys weren't drinking, remember?" she *didn't* remember, but it made sense if they thought they might have to rush back at any moment. More guilt, she would have only been a hindrance if something *had* happened.

"Stop." He said sharply; Niah blinked and met his gaze, "You're allowed to have fun once in a while."

"What if something had happened?"

He sighed and gave her a level stare, "Then we would have dealt with it. Not having you and Dea fighting wouldn't have made a difference, no offence."

"There was no trouble last night, was there?" she asked, glancing around the room. He paused, "Was there?" she pressed, holding his gaze.

"Nothing worth mentioning, the night was cut short, that's all. Judging by the state of you, that's not a bad thing," he grinned, ruffling her already tangled hair. She batted his hand away and sighed.

"I didn't do anything embarrassing, did I?"

Sai shrugged, "Not really, you showed your complete lack of rhythm on the dance floor, but that's about it. Although what happened when you and Fin got back to your room, I don't know, might have been embarrassing," he wiggled his brows.

"Fin took me back?" her heart fluttered uneasily.

"Yeah, ouch, you don't remember? Poor guy," he said with a click of his tongue as he turned away. She scowled at his back.

Did he leave the cupcake?

Her entire body grew warm; what if something had happened between them and she didn't remember? A strange tingle swept up her spine and coated her face and neck, her stomach feeling like a led weight. Niah pushed the thoughts away, she'd deal with *that* later.

No one in the facility was a beginner by any means. They moved with the controlled speed and grace of those who had been training for decades, maybe even centuries.

Sai trained with her, a short stick in each hand, about the length of his forearm. They went over techniques that she had never heard of, not that she let him know that. He caught her off guard multiple times, knocking her to the ground. She'd have to get used to no longer being the best, it seemed.

"Come on. You can do better," Sai challenged as Niah lay on her back, glaring up at the ceiling.

She got to her feet, annoyed that she was fighting like a complete novice. Sai grinned wickedly and crouched, Niah readied herself, watching his feet when he launched. She caught the shift of his weight when he thrust forward, and caught the blow on her wooden sword.

"Bit more serious now, are 'ya?" he flicked up a brow and went on the offensive, more so than he was before. He forced her onto her back foot, but she was beginning to give as good as she got, and her blood sang with adrenaline.

Niah landed a blow to his gut, Sai groaned, stumbling back a step, his eyes gleaming. She attacked low and swept his feet from under him, he landed with a thud, and she crouched over him, one of her sticks aimed at his throat. He peaked up at her through his lashes.

He tapped the inside of her thigh with his wooden sword, "Better, but not quite good enough." She rolled her eyes and helped him up, biting down on the retort on her tongue.

There was a curse from above, followed by the sound of air tearing apart. She looked up to see a young woman plummeting through the air. Niah went to catch her, but Sai gave her a warning look. The girl righted herself, landing lightly on her feet.

The girl was taller, dainty like Dea, with narrow hips and shoulders. Her eyes were dark chocolate with the shimmering silver outer ring. Her hair was short and blonde, showing off the delicate points of her ears. Across her shoulders was a light pattern of what looked like pink and green scales.

The girl only flashed a toothy smile before leaping to catch the beam she had just fallen from.

"Fey blood?" Niah guessed; Sai nodded, following her gaze.

"Yeah, I'm surprised you know that, it took me months," Sai said, bending down to retrieve a set of wooden swords.

"Merida told me a while ago, to explain how I'm a hybrid with magic," she answered before swilling her mouth out with water.

"It's rare, you know?"

"What? Hybrids crossed with spell weavers? Yeah, Merida said there were only two others."

"That we know of," he added.

"You think there are more?"

Sai shrugged, "Who knows? There are millions of supernatural beings roaming the Earth. We can't exactly keep a record of each one."

"So, halflings are originally made by demons mating with humans_"

"Usually by tricking humans into sleeping with them, but yeah."

"Right, so does that mean Nephilim are made the same way?" Niah asked, helping Sai re-rack more of the training swords.

"As far as we know, angels don't mate with humans since humanity is considered sacred to them. We don't know much about Nephilim seeing as they're almost extinct, but we do know they were used to fight in the Angelic War nearly three thousand years ago."

Niah had read about the Angelic War, the first of the three great Wars in their history. Wars Niah hadn't known even happened before she arrived in Perth.

"What about halflings?"

Sai loosed a breath, leaning against the rack, "We don't know much about them either. As far as we know, halflings have been used in the Shadows army. I've never met one in person, and if there are any out there, we haven't heard of them."

"It sounds like there's an awful lot the Furies don't know," Niah muttered.

"Well, we only know what's been passed down through the ages."

"Who passes it down?"

Sai ran a hand through his hair, "The Elders. The Alliance is made up of five groups, the hybrids, spell weavers, lycanthropes, fey, and vampires. Each order has a leader, apart from the hybrids, we have two," he shrugged, "those leaders are the Elders. They pass everything down to us."

"It's all so confusing."

Sai chuckled, "It is, but when you're learning an entirely new culture, it's going to get a bit muddled."

Niah chewed on her lip, willing her racing mind to settle. "Come with me," Sai said.

Niah followed him out of the gym and down a corridor lined with doors until he came to a set of open double doors leading into a library with long tables and sofas around a cold hearth. It was perhaps half the size of the one in England, but Niah was captivated all the same.

"In here is everything you could ever need to know. Learn at your own pace. Agatha will help you find anything you need," he said, gesturing to a red-haired woman behind the front desk.

Niah didn't notice him leave, she was gazing at the rows upon rows of bookshelves. She lost herself pages of history and culture, learning the ways of the various species. She poured through weaver books on herbs and talismans.

She read about the three wars that defined the Alliance and all that led up to its forming. She learnt about their legends, that all species stemmed from the creation of one particular being. A supernatural anomaly said to possess traits of all creatures. It was just a myth, she'd read, but she found herself wondering; how strong might that creature have been? A creature capable of birthing the entire supernatural world.

A chill slithered up Niah's spine, and that power that thrummed through her veins turned to ice, as if shrinking away from the very thought.

NIAH

23

The world was nothing but smoke and ash.

Buildings were burnt to the ground; the sun blotted out by the dark sky. She was lying on the ground, ash falling like snow around her. The only sound was the gentle crackling of a nearby fire.

Winged demons circled the sky, a hole had opened in the clouds, a vortex of violent, swirling clouds, darker than the rest, with flashes of black lightning forking through it.

Niah stared up at it, feeling the electricity in the air as it made her hairs stand on end. Her heart launched into a gallop as she stared at those demons swirling overhead.

It was just a nightmare, it had to be.

But unlike all the others, this dream was full of colour, and she could feel everything.

The sky turned angry and dark, the falling ash turned to smouldering embers, bathing the world in lightning and flame.

The demons above screeched as she staggered to her feet. The demons were the only other thing alive, everything else already dead or dying.

She swallowed past the thickness in her throat, coughing on the ash filling her lungs as she staggered along what she realised was the beach.

Niah turned to the ocean, the once sparkling, clear water, now black and roiling, writhing with demons as they charged for land.

She'd never seen a demon face to face before. Never had she seen the rows upon rows of razor-sharp teeth, the beady red eyes, the ink-black, leathery hide. Now that she had, something in her blood stirred, and she longed to feel the grip of a sword in her hand.

She had nothing, not even her dagger.

And the demons were getting uncomfortably close.

Niah spun to find the facility behind her, and froze.

The building was burnt and crumpled in a pile of smouldering rubble. Bodies of her comrades lay strewn across the ash-covered ground. Ice gripped her lungs.

She dropped to her knees.

They were all dead.

A mountain of burning corpses.

Their faces all twisted in agony and terror.

Who could have done such a thing?

Ash filled her lungs; no matter how much she tried to cough it up, it stuffed itself down her throat—choking her.

A voice cut through her racing thoughts.

It was little more than a whisper, and she wasn't sure whether she had imagined.

As if in answer, the voice came again, louder, insistent.

"Niah", the voice crooned.

There was no one around. Everyone was dead.

Then it was screaming, shouting her name over and over. Niah clamped her hands over her ears and squeezed her eyes shut.

But there was no blocking out a voice in your own head.

She woke with a start, tangled up in the sheets. Breathing hard, Niah flung herself out of bed and dove for the sliding door, shoving it open to gulp down the fresh, night air. Her heart thundered in her ears, drowning out the sound of the gently lapping waves on the shore.

That nightmare was new.

And different.

So very different.

It felt so *real*.

Her eyes tracked the skies. Nothing but the moon and stars shined brightly overhead. No clouds, no vortex of fire and lightning, no demons circling. More importantly, there wasn't a mountain of bodies.

Was it guilt?

Guilt for leaving the compound and the Shadows attacking the English facility? Shame for all those that had lost their lives?

Maybe it was, or maybe it was a warning of things to come—an omen.

A shudder rippled through her body at the thought. Could things get worse? Niah gripped the balcony railing. But, of course, things could get worse.

The attack on the English facility was likely only a message. Whether they were coming for her, or starting a war with the Alliance, Niah didn't know; all she knew was that the Shadows were done being silent.

Niah forced her mind to settle, to focus.

The Shadows had attacked a facility close to the academy, which meant they wanted Niah to know that the siblings had orchestrated it. They wanted the Furies to know that while they had been searching for the Shadows, that they knew exactly where the facilities were.

They intended to strike fear into the hearts of all those in the Fury Alliance, and maybe sow discord from within. It was merely a tactic, nothing more.

That's what Niah would have done.

The Shadows had won the first battle, but how many more would

follow?

Only time would tell.

Niah jumped at the sound of a gentle knock at the door. She opened it to find Gren on the other side, his hands in his pockets, and his usually slicked back hair hanging down by his ears. He looked younger, somehow.

"What's wrong?" Niah asked, opening the door in invitation.

Gren stepped into the room, "Cassia asked to see you. It's about the lessons Merida was arranging."

Magic lessons.

"Now?" Niah baulked, glancing over at the clock, midnight.

"Something to do with drawing from the moon's power," he waved a dismissive hand.

Niah sighed and went into the bathroom to change, leaving Gren in the room. Magic wasn't what she had imagined for the night, but perhaps it would be a welcome distraction from nightmares and the Shadows schemes.

When she emerged, Gren was flicking through the stack of books on the desk. Books on various species, history, abilities, and archives on previous Shadow attacks.

"This isn't exactly light reading," Gren murmured, lifting a brow at her when she peered over his shoulder.

"I wanted to know who we're dealing with."

"They raised you, surely you know who we're dealing with?"

Niah ran a hand through her hair, "I believed a charade, I don't believe I ever got to see the *real* Shadows, not like this." She flicked to a particularly gruesome story of an assassin that devastated an entire shipping yard to catch a group of black-market owners that had stolen a shipment of weapons from the Shadows while in transit.

Gren glanced down at the pages, "And what have you found?"

"I think they're trying to scare us," Niah shrugged, "they're hoping we turn on each other."

"Tell me what you're not saying." His voice was firm, but his emerald eyes were gentle, reassuring even.

Niah exhaled slowly, "They're hoping you'll all turn on me."

"I think so too," he agreed, placing a hand on her shoulder, "don't worry, we're in your corner, especially Merida. Her warriors follow her without question."

"I don't want to get by on Merida's good graces alone," she frowned.

That sliver of truth shook her. She thought it was just Fin and their small group of friends she cared about, but somewhere along the way, she started to care about everyone else in the facility.

She wanted their trust.

Wanted to earn it, the way they had earned hers.

"You're going the right way about it, just keep doing what you're doing." He said, his hand falling from her shoulder.

Niah dipped her chin, unsure of how to respond to that, and Gren led her from the room.

"Will you tell me what happened to you?" he asked, breaking the comfortable silence.

Niah was silent for a moment before saying, "I will if you will."

"That's fair, but not tonight."

"There's no rush." The thought of talking about her past with anyone had her heart racing, and her palms growing slick.

Gren said nothing else on the matter, only led her down the stairs and into that wing of the facility that belonged to the spell weavers and casters.

The smell of sulphur and herbs filled her nose, growing stronger the further they ventured down the corridor. Lights were on in some of the rooms, and inside, people were practising magic, grinding herbs, or brewing strange liquids.

The power in Niah's veins stirred in answer.

Gren stopped outside a door to a room with a glass ceiling, two cushions on the floor, with a small table standing only inches off the floor in the middle. On one cushion sat a woman, cross-legged with her hands resting on her knees, her eyes closed.

The moonlight bleached some of the radiance from her bronze skin. But Niah was gazing at her closed eyes, at the pink glow radiating from beneath her lids. When the woman opened them, the breath hitched in Niah's throat.

She'd never seen anything so beautiful.

The woman's eyes glowed pink from within, bright as fuchsia that lit up the small room. Her dark hair, streaked with golds, curled around her head like a halo. The woman rose to her feet, the bracelets around her wrists jingling with the movement. Her dress hung to her ankles, sinched at the waist to show off her voluptuous figure.

The woman strode toward her, moving with the immortal grace Niah had yet to master, her hips swaying with the movement until she reached out and took Niah's hand in hers.

"It's a pleasure to meet you; my name is Cassia Church," the woman smiled, her voice was thick, but as sweet as honey.

"I'm_"

"Oh, my dear, I know who you are," Cassia grinned, "you've been the talk amongst us weavers for quite some time."

Niah cocked her head to the side in question, and Cassia clarified, "It's not every day we get to witness a hybrid with spell weaver blood."

"Have fun," Gren said from the door, when Niah turned to say goodbye, he offered her a soft smile and disappeared down the corridor, closing the door behind him.

"Merida said you wanted to learn magic, I'm here to teach you, but we can stop any time you want," Cassia said, guiding her to the cushions on the floor. They sat down opposite one another, and with a wave of her hand, a pot of tea with two cups appeared on the low table, along with a pocket mirror.

Niah couldn't help but smile. One day, she'd be able to do that too.

"I want to learn everything," Niah breathed.

Cassia chuckled, "Not even I know everything, but we'll do our best."

"Why do we do this at night?" Niah asked, lifting the cup to her lips.

The brew was sweet and revitalising, sending sparks of energy through her veins.

"It's easier to draw from the moon's power when we're first learning to summon magic. After a while, you'll need nothing but the power in your veins." Cassia explained, her eyes glowing brightly as if for emphasis.

"So, how do we start?" Niah asked, setting the cup down.

Cassia smiled, "Eager, I like it. When you felt your power for the first time, what did it feel like?"

Niah glanced down at her fingers, feeling the familiar warmth flood through her body, "It feels like an old friend."

"Very good. Our magic is as much a part of us as our personalities, it *is* us. It has its own identity; no two powers are the same. You can feel it now, can't you?" Niah nodded, "Good, let it come to the surface, close your eyes and clear your mind, let your power show itself to you."

Niah closed her eyes, "How do I call on it?"

"You simply think it."

She did as instructed, clearing her mind as much as possible until it was only darkness. The power in her veins pulsed and swam, eager to come to the surface. Colour exploded in her mind, bright and electric blue, flickering and dancing like a flame.

Her chest flooded with warmth.

"Good," Cassia breathed, "open your eyes."

She did as she was told, only to find Cassia holding out the pocket mirror to her. Niah scrunched her brow, but took it from her and peered into it.

She almost dropped it.

Her eyes were glowing with the same velocity blue she'd seen in her mind, the same colour of the sparks that leapt from her fingers.

"We all have different colours?" Niah asked, watching her eyes in the mirror. The silver ring was still in place, almost containing the blue as if it would run wild.

"Magic has its own identity, just as we do." Cassia smiled. Niah set the mirror down, unable to stop herself from smiling.

"There are many lessons we have to go over, but for now, let us focus on finding your element."

"What do you mean?"

"To begin with, we start with the element closest to ourselves. For example, I started with water, but eventually, you will master all of the elements, as well as much more."

"How do I know which element suits me?" Niah questioned, glancing at her hands.

"Close your eyes," Niah did, "now, your power will pick up the moon's energy, let that light soak into your skin, your bones, let your magic play with it."

As soon as she thought about it, her magic soared, reaching for that energy of light and power from the heavens. It flooded her, and for a moment, Niah thought she might burst with the amount of energy surging through her body.

She felt strong.

So much stronger than she ever had before.

Her power purred in her veins, stroking, soothing, dancing with the power of the moon.

"Wow," Niah breathed, unable to contain her ecstasy.

"Euphoric, isn't it?" Cassia murmured, a hint of a smile in her voice.

Niah opened her eyes, "Is it like this every time?"

"It only gets better from here," Cassia smiled, "eyes closed." she did as she was told once again.

"Now, focus on concentrating that energy in the palm of your hand, in one singular point."

Niah did just that, concentrating on her power moving toward her hand. Having a colour associated with her magic, knowing what it looked like, helped visualise it.

Tingles shot through her body, travelling down her neck, shoulder, arm, until it arrived at her palm. Warmth spread through her entire body, sliding down her spine, her hips, down her thighs and calves until it reached her toes.

The tips of her fingers tingled, the sensation growing more intense the more that power concentrated in her palm until it was a gentle, vibrating hum.

"Good," Cassia encouraged, "open your eyes."

Niah did so, the air catching in her throat as she gazed down at the tiny blue sparks leaping from her fingers.

"It would appear that your element is fire."

Niah's heart stumbled slightly.

Dreams of black and white, and blue flames flashed into her mind. A message, perhaps?

"But this is only sparks," Niah murmured, gazing at her fingers.

Cassia chuckled, "It's always the smallest things that tell us our true nature."

"Is it a bad thing?" Niah asked, meeting the weavers' gaze. Blue mixed with pink, the room glowing with a faint purple light.

"No, of course not. Do you want to continue?" Cassia asked. Niah only nodded.

"Very well. Close your eyes, and feel the heat in your palm, will it to ignite, your power will obey."

Niah did just that, focusing on that spot in the centre of her palm. Heat built in the centre of her hand, every nerve ending came alive as the power swirled in her hand. Niah willed the magic to ignite, and the heat grew hotter, yet not uncomfortably so.

Niah opened her eyes. And there, at the centre of her palm, was a tiny, dancing blue flame.

She smiled to herself, feeling her heart racing, her fingers trembling as she kept that flame flickering.

All these years, it was there, in her blood. A power so beautiful, and it had been locked away. It was wrong. But it would never be locked away again.

It was hers. It was a part of her.

"Good girl," Cassia breathed, "It will take time and patience, but one day, you'll be able to summon a wave of fire, water, whatever your heart desires, with only half a thought."

The thought was thrilling.

"Thank you," Niah smiled, the flame vanishing as she lost

concentration.

"I'll see you tomorrow night," Cassia said, rising to her feet as Niah followed suit.

Her body cooled as if it were doused with ice water, the power returning to its peaceful slumber. The room was in darkness, letting her know the light had faded from her eyes, but Cassia's remained glowing.

"Spell weavers can't turn our magic off like you can, it dulls, but they remain like this," Cassia said, waving a hand across her eyes.

"Does that make it difficult to go out in public?" Niah questioned as the two left the room.

"No, we have spells to hide it; you'll learn them one day."

Niah left it at that; her mind was whirling, but in the best possible way. She had magic in her veins, and fire in her fingertips, and that was only the start.

The facility was still and quiet. Niah could only hear faint laughter from the beach; the few vampires living in the underground rooms would be out enjoying the moonlight. Yet, as she walked the corridors, she couldn't take her eyes off her hands.

Her heart soared.

It was real.

It was all real.

She shook her head, but was unable to shake the smile that tugged at her lips.

Niah opened the door to her rooms and stilled. A dark figure was lying on her bed. Her hand curled around the training staff next to the door, and without making a sound, she brought it down hard.

The figure quickly reached out a hand and caught the staff. She tried to jerk it free of their grip, but a low chuckle told her exactly who it was.

Fin sat up on the bed and flicked on the replaced lamp after she threw the last one at his head.

"Need to be quicker than that," Fin smirked.

Niah dumped the staff in the corner and kicked off her shoes, "How did you get in here?"

"You left the door unlocked," he shrugged, flopping onto his back, interlocking his fingers across his stomach.

She huffed a sigh and pulled her hair free, letting it fall down her back, "And to what do I owe the pleasure?"

"No reason, I just wanted some company," he said, gazing up at the ceiling. She might have questioned it, but he'd done that a few times since the attack. He never stayed, but she got the feeling he wanted to.

A thought that unnerved her enough not to ask.

Niah changed out of her leggings and into shorts and a clean tank top for bed before climbing under the covers after yanking them free.

"You made my bed?"

He sighed, "Yes, you're very messy."

"I couldn't sleep, then Gren came and got me for training," she shrugged as she plumped the pillow behind her and leaned back, relishing in the softness.

"Oh? Why couldn't you sleep?" he asked, rolling onto his side to face her, propping his head upon his hand.

"I could ask you the same thing."

He gave her a wry grin, "I never said I couldn't sleep."

Niah raised a brow, "So why are you not sleeping?"

He rolled his eyes and flung himself back, his arms supporting his head, "Fine...I couldn't sleep. The survivors are arriving tomorrow, well, today. Benjamin hasn't been making it easy."

There wasn't so much as a hint of humour in his voice. Over the last few days, Niah had learnt how authoritative he could be. Yet, when addressing the warriors, he gave away nothing of the humorous, easy-going guy he was.

The first time he'd used that voice around her when telling a group of warriors what to do, it had heated something in her lower stomach. Something she'd never felt before.

"I've been thinking about the same thing," she muttered, "I had a nightmare; I saw the facility burnt to rubble, the world was grey, ash falling, demons in the sky circling a vortex. I can't help but feel like it's a warning of some kind."

Fin contemplated that for a moment, "Have you ever had dreams like that before?" Niah shook her head.

"Never. It felt so *real*, like I was there." a shudder crawled up her spine at the memory.

"I wonder if Merida or Vinaxx will know something."

Niah sighed, "I doubt it; it was just a nightmare."

Fin was silent, and, not wanting to ruin the elation of her training session, she sat up and said, "I want to show you something."

"Strip show?" he quirked a brow, chuckling when she smacked him in the chest.

"Shut up, idiot." But, try as she might, she couldn't hide her smile even if she wanted to.

Fin sat up when Niah pushed the blankets away and sat cross-legged to face him. She held out the palm of her hand and closed her eyes. The image of swirling blues came quicker this time, eager to come out and play once again. The familiar, tingling warmth spread through her body, and concentrated in one spot in the centre of her palm. She smiled as her blood sang and willed the power to ignite.

When she opened her eyes, there was a small, velocity blue flame dancing in her palm. Smaller than the one she had produced with Cassia, but it was still there, flickering gently.

Her chest swelled with warmth, her body tingling as she gazed down at what she'd accomplished.

"It's not much, but it's something."

"Is this your first attempt?" Fin asked, still gazing at the dancing flame.

"Technically second, but tonight is the first time," she said as the blue light illuminated the room. He looked up at her then, his eyes widening slightly.

"Your eyes."

"The colour of my power," she smiled. The flame extinguished itself, the only light in the room was the glow from her eyes.

They were so close, his eyes wide as they took her in, his lips parted slightly.

She'd never been looked at that way before, like she was...his world. She cleared her throat, fighting the urge to look away from his gaze while her cheeks heated.

He reached up slowly, cupping her cheek, his eyes searching hers, the blue of her own reflected in the silver of his. Their breath mingled between them, coming fast and shallow as her heart thundered.

But so was his.

Niah had never been kissed before, nor had she ever wanted to. Until now. Until Fin.

She didn't know who leaned in first, and she didn't care. Not when his lips met hers, and her world shattered around her. Her entire body came alive with flame and tingling, electricity sparking across her skin where he touched her.

His lips were warm beneath hers, moving slowly, letting her decide how far or fast she wanted to go. She was descending too quickly. She wanted to be closer, *needed* to be closer.

And then his hands were in her hair, pulling her closer, holding her to him as if he were frightened she would blow away on the wind.

But she wanted that closeness too, and her hands curled around his arms, brushing over his shoulders before resting on his gloriously sculpted chest. She parted her lips, inviting him in the way she'd seen in those programs he'd shown her, and he groaned low in his throat, his fingers tightening in her hair.

Heat bloomed in her chest and pooled in her lower stomach, the kiss sending sparks surging through her.

She'd never been kissed before, and now that she had, she didn't want it to end.

They broke apart after a long moment, both breathing hard. His thumb stroked along her cheekbone as the fire in her eyes hardened to onyx. For a moment, they just sat there, breathing hard with their foreheads pressed together.

Niah breathed him in, the scent of spices and sandalwood washing over her.

"What was that for?" she breathed.

"I just needed to do that," he murmured.

They stayed like that a few more minutes, before a frightening thought rattled through her, and she pulled away, letting her hands fall to the bed between them.

"Did it…mean anything?"

Fin gazed at her thoughtfully as if searching for the right answer. She didn't want what was *right*—just the truth.

He sat up then and took her hand in his, "Hybrids are unable to love the way humans do. The bond I told you about, the second half of our hearts? It's considered both a blessing and a curse. I've never wanted to feel it myself. But this? With you, it *does* mean something. I don't exactly know what that something is, but I've never felt this way before. I don't…I mean, does it, did it mean anything to *you*?" he asked gently, a flicker of something uneasy flashed across his eyes.

So much had changed over the weeks; *she* had changed so much. There was much of herself she was still finding out. And try as she might, there was no pushing away that lingering ice in her bones, the fire in her stomach, or her need for revenge.

It was still there.

It was *always* there.

Sometimes it was harder to ignore than others; sometimes, it screamed and thrashed until she was forced to acknowledge it. It was those quiet moments when she was alone, when the silence started roaring and threatened to break her apart, that it demanded to be felt.

And it was those times, that she would sit down and read through that hurtful book of herself. A reminder, she decided, of who the enemy was. A reminder of what she wanted to achieve, and who would be on the receiving end of all that wrath bubbling inside her.

Was there room for anything else?

Her dream of wanting to be something other hadn't included romance. It wasn't something she ever wanted for herself. Even when she read those books and the main character fell in love, she never understood or envisioned for herself. But with Fin, it had been different. There was no awkwardness, no ulterior motives, just comfortable easiness.

And maybe that was the problem. Because if Niah thought about it, if she looked deep enough. It was there—a steady thrum in her chest.

She *did* have feelings for Fin. But if she let herself admit it, let herself run with that feeling, he could be used against her. Love was a weakness. That lesson had been hammered into her since she was old enough to understand what it meant. Despite hating those who raised her, and the Nephilim siblings, they were right.

Her path wouldn't be an easy one. It would be full of fighting and blood, and death. Niah was prepared to walk that path alone, because she did feel for him, and Dea, Sai, Gren, Merida, everyone in the facility.

She'd walk the path alone if it meant they were safe. But to do that, she couldn't admit what she felt, couldn't say it aloud.

For the first time in so long, Niah had people she wanted to protect. But she couldn't do that if the Shadows found out what they all meant to her.

There was no way to have it all. She couldn't have Fin and chase her goal. It was one or the other. If that meant she lost him forever, to keep him and the others safe, then she would do it.

So, she took that smouldering feeling in her chest, gripped it with trembling hands, and shoved it down. So very deep down.

"No," she breathed.

His eyes guttered, but the smile didn't leave his lips. That part of her she'd just shoved down, wept.

"I'm_"

"There's nothing to be sorry for." The light returned to his eyes, though only slightly, " With so much going on, so much unrest and uncertainty, it was wrong of me to put that on you. *I'm* sorry."

Good, understanding, wonderful Fin.

It made the ache in her chest burn so much hotter. She forced a smile. He'd already told her hybrids didn't love the way humans did, so her telling him that their kiss didn't mean anything would likely be expected, but she couldn't shake the way his eyes had dulled.

"You're hurt."

He snorted, "It's not the first time I've been shot down." A lie. "We're not monogamous creatures, but…" he paused, as if deciding whether to say what he was planning to, "I'm sure that if love worked the same way for us as it does for humans, I would love you."

Those words, as much as she enjoyed hearing them, shattered her heart. And there was no stopping herself from brushing her lips against his as she fought back the tears stinging the backs of her eyes.

It was cruel.

So very cruel to turn him down and then kiss him. But he didn't pull away, his palm went to her cheek, and he deepened the kiss. Her entire body felt like it was alight with flames, at the same time as her chest tightened and her throat closed up.

Snapping herself out of the moment, she pulled away, once again breathing hard; his hand didn't fall from her face, his silver eyes only held hers, "I shouldn't have…that was cruel."

He smiled gently and pressed his forehead to hers, "Just because it didn't mean anything serious, doesn't mean it didn't mean *anything*. I know all too well how hard it is for our species to feel, so, whatever you want to give me, whatever you feel for me, I'll take it."

But it wasn't right. She couldn't do that to him. Not when she knew she couldn't allow herself to feel anything more for him.

"I just don't want anything, with anyone." To her surprise, he smiled.

"Then that's fine. Do what you have to do; no one expects anything of you, or will force you to do anything, least of all me." Before Niah could say anything else, he flopped onto his back, "Come on, get some sleep."

Unable to think of anything to say, she nestled down in the pillows and closed her eyes. Waiting for his breathing to deepen until she went to the desk and flipped through those hateful words.

Reminding herself that she was a weapon.

With one purpose.

FIN

24

Niah was gone by the time he woke.

It wasn't a surprise. If anything, he wondered why she hadn't walked out of the room after he'd kissed her. It was wrong to put all that on her shoulders, and he didn't blame her for wanting to leave. He just wished things were different.

But that was just a fantasy.

He woke up during the night and found her sitting at the desk, her head bent over a leather-bound book. Her shoulders were trembling, her hands balled into fists. He should have gone to her, asked what was wrong, but he knew that if it was something she did while he was asleep, then it was something she wanted to keep to herself.

Fin didn't know what he was expecting when he told her how he felt. He'd known, deep down, that she felt nothing for him. There was so much of the world she didn't know, and was still figuring out where she belonged in it. He shouldn't have said anything.

Yet, a part of him was relieved. He had the answer he'd been longing for, even if it wasn't what he'd hoped.

He meant what he said though, that he would take anything she wanted to offer him. Whether it was kisses that meant nothing, or something more serious, he'd take all of it. It wasn't love, he knew that, but it was something more than he'd ever felt. But even then, if she did give nothing, as she was entitled to, he'd accept it, because it wasn't his choice.

Her whole life had been decided for her, and Fin wouldn't influence *any* of her choices.

He got up and made her bed before heading for the door, pausing at the desk when the book Niah had been reading caught his eye. He grazed his fingers over the worn leather, a shiver crawling up his spine as he gazed at the swirling mark.

The same mark that had been on the back of Niah's neck.

He wondered what was inside. What could be written on the pages to make her tremble? He wouldn't ask. He'd already asked too much of her.

"Seriously? Come on, you can do better," Fin growled as the girl launched herself at him.

The warriors were getting better by the day, though they were still a long way off being ready. The young girl before him had only been with them a month, but for her age, she should be much more advanced than she was. But, he supposed, they couldn't help it if they had never had any training beforehand.

The girl snarled and attacked, but changed direction mid-step and kicked out at his legs; he almost didn't get out of the way in time.

"Good!" he encouraged. She was getting desperate and making silly mistakes, and Fin found he didn't have the patience to spoon-feed her advice when he had a full gym to oversee.

"Okay, stop," he said and glanced around the training room, spotting Niah with Sai; he called her over, and her dark eyes met his across the room.

She tossed the wooden sword to Sai and strode toward him, her spine ramrod straight and shoulders squared. Unlike the night before, her eyes were hard and cold, guarded even.

He could still feel the warmth of her lips on his, the way she ran her hands over his arms and chest. Heat surged through his body, and he had to shove the thoughts away to save himself from getting embarrassed in the middle of the gym.

He strode to meet her halfway, keeping his voice low so no one else could hear, "You took off early this morning."

"I went for a run on the beach to..." the unspoken words hung between them, thick and heavy.

The air grew dense around them, and he cleared his throat, slapping on a smile that he didn't feel committed to, "Would you mind going through the basics with Caroline over there?" he gestured to the copper-haired girl behind him.

Niah blinked, "You're trusting me to train someone?"

"Why wouldn't I?"

"I'm not as experienced as the others," she muttered, glancing over her shoulder at Sai.

Fin dragged a hand through his hair, "I can ask one of the seniors to train her if you don't want to." Niah was quiet as she considered that.

"It's fine," she offered a weak smile.

"Thank you," he turned to the girl, "Niah is going to go through the steps with you."

He watched the two of them walk over to the sparring mat at the centre of the room. To his surprise, Niah glanced back at him and offered a slightly brighter smile.

Perhaps what happened the night before wouldn't affect things between them as much as he thought. He wasn't sure how he felt about that. Relieved, disappointed?

Fin sighed and scratched at the back of his head as he made his way back over to the group he'd been neglecting.

That morning, half of the survivors from England had arrived, the others scattered throughout the other facilities. So many arrived in Perth because, compared to the other facilities, theirs was the least populated. And with over half of his warriors stationed here, Benjamin, their leader, came too.

When he left Merida's office that morning, they were already at each other's throats. Already, Benjamin's advisor, Helena, was trying to overrule Fin's judgements in the gym. He'd told her, not entirely kindly, that she could either shut up and watch or leave. After that, she took up a place leaning against a wall, watching him like a hawk.

"Okay, guys, I want you to spar together, remember what I've told you. I'll be watching," he said as Gren approached, his hands in his pockets.

"You look tired."

"Patrols," Gren grumbled.

"Anything new?" Fin watched as one boy punched his opponent square in the jaw, sending him stumbling backwards.

Gren grimaced, "*Messenger* demons along the border."

The borders separated the territory between the facilities. Australia was so big that it had nine facilities, though countless more were spread across the world.

"Which border?"

"Eastern, near Nullarbor."

Messenger demons were exactly that; messengers for their masters. The sealed doorways only stopped high-ranking demons from coming through, there were tears in the fabric between realms, and the demon Lords didn't hesitate to take advantage of that. They sent their minions through the cracks as their eyes and ears, and to wreak havoc.

"Do we know who's they are?" Fin folded his arms over his chest. *Messenger* demons usually bore some distinct feature or mark that labelled which Lord or Prince they belonged to.

"Nope, never seen their marks before," Gren shrugged, clearly annoyed he hadn't been able to gather more information, "I can tell you one thing though, they didn't feel like normal *Messengers*. Something's off, but I can't put my finger on it. I don't think it will be long before the Shadows attack again."

Fin looked at him now; the moodiness vanished from his features, replaced with concern.

"You think the Shadows control demons now?" as absurd as it sounded, it couldn't be ruled out. Only Hell knew what kind of weapons the Shadows possessed.

Gren sighed, "I hope not, but how are we supposed to know?"

It was a theory he was all too familiar with. Some older leaders within the Alliance speculated that the Shadows had found a way to tear through the barriers between realms, and used demons to thin out the Furies numbers, knowing they would hunt the beasts and kill them.

But that's all it was, a theory. There was no proof to back it up with, and without evidence, there was little they could do. Even if they couldn't find the Shadows, at least knowing what kind of weapons they possessed would be helpful.

If the Shadows *were* able to control demons...

It was a thought he'd rather not entertain.

One of the boys punched his opponent, the other boy fell, and the first sprang on top of him, raining down blow after blow. The boy on the floor went limp, his face bloody.

"Hey!" Fin bellowed, he and Gren darting over to grab the boy crouching over the one on the floor. Gren grabbed him by the shoulders while Fin knelt by the other, he was unconscious, bleeding from his mouth and cuts to his brow and cheek. He scooped the boy into his arms and started for the door, shouting orders for the senior members to keep everyone training.

"Fin!" he whirled at the desperation in Gren's voice to see the boy had somehow gotten free of his grip, and was sprinting toward Fin with such ferocity in his eyes. Gren chased him, but the boy was much too fast, and with the unconscious boy in Fin's arms, he could not defend himself.

He planted his feet wide, angling himself to block the boy in his arms from the impact, but the enraged youngster never reached him.

There was a blur, and the boy was thrown backwards, crashing into the far wall with bone-cracking force.

Fin turned to see Niah, her arm still outstretched, hand balled into a fist. Her chin was low, her eyes dark with fury. She straightened her spine, glowering at the boy crumpled on the floor. For a moment, he thought she was going to kill him, but she blinked and took a step back, glancing around until her eyes rested on Fin.

All eyes in the room were on them.

It was nothing that any one of them couldn't do, but Niah had never known her true strength. Her eyes were wide and wild. For the first time, he saw a flash of fear in her eyes, fear of herself. She was realising what she could do, and it scared her.

"Come on," he said to her, "Gren, can you make sure that one's okay? Keep everyone training, harder." he snapped as he glanced around the room; everyone hurried back to what they were doing.

The infirmary was large and white like a human hospital ward. Beds lined each side, all of which were empty apart from the one Fin lay the boy, Mason, on. He was already healing, though the energy it took to recover would mean longer for him to wake up.

Fin sighed; he should have been watching more closely.

"I'm sorry," Niah breathed. Her eyes were wide as she stared down at the boy.

"Why the hell are *you* sorry?"

She looked at him, her brows knitted together, "What I did to that boy, I didn't...I didn't mean to do that."

He wanted to take her in his arms, but he knew her well enough to know she didn't need that kind of comfort, not right now.

"I know, don't forget, you're still getting used to your strength." Fin frowned, thinking of how bloodthirsty the other boy had been, the rage in his eyes, he was ready to kill.

Just then, Gren hauled the other boy in by the back of his shirt. At least he was awake and walking, even if barely, with his nose bent at an odd angle.

He glanced in their direction before quickly averting his eyes as Gren

shoved him, not gently, towards one of the beds. Fin stalked toward the boy, Niah a step behind.

"You want to explain what that was?" Fin growled, low and rumbling in his chest. As much as he hated to use the voice that dripped with authority, now was the time to use it. The boy flinched at the bite in his words.

"I...I'm sorry, I didn't...I don't know what came over me," he stammered. The boy was tall, the same height as Mason, same dark hair, except shaggier, his eyes were dark green like moss, though the ring around his iris was dull, more grey than shimmering silver.

"Logan? Right?" Fin sighed, the boy nodded. Fin reached down and pulled Logan's face up to look at him, searching his dull eyes.

His heart stuttered.

There was something *wrong* with the boy. Something that spoke in caution to the darkest depths of his mind.

"Where did you come from?" he asked; the boy only blinked.

"I...I don't know, where am I?" his voice trembled.

Fin straightened his spine and turned to Gren, "Fetch Cassia or Vinaxx." Gren didn't hesitate before turning on his heel and running from the infirmary.

"What is it?" Niah asked, stepping around Fin to examine the boy.

"His eyes."

Niah tugged the boy's chin gently to get a better look at his eyes. Logan tried to look anywhere except her, but a firm tug on his chin had his eyes snapping to hers.

"What are you?" Niah muttered.

Logan's brow scrunched, "I...I don't understand."

Niah released his chin and took a step back, her eyes wide, her skin pale as if she'd seen a ghost.

"What is it?" Fin asked, folding his arms over his chest.

"His energy, his smell, it's like a halfling, but there's something else... something sweeter."

"He has the silver ring; he's not a halfling."

"Then what is he?"

Before Fin could answer, the infirmary doors swung open, and in strode Gren with Cassia at his side.

"What happened?" Cassia asked, her hands already glowing with pink light as she waved them over Logan's busted nose. There was a sharp crack as his nose snapped into the correct position, his eyes watered as he clutched at his face, groaning and whimpering.

"Niah punched him," Gren shrugged. Cassia looked to Niah with raised brows; no one uttered a word.

"Cassia, do you notice anything different? Specifically, in his eyes?" Fin murmured; Cassia eyed him suspiciously before turning to Logan. She tilted his chin back, gazing at his eyes. She blinked and pressed a glowing hand to the boys' chest. Logan winced, biting down on a whimper as the light from Cassia's hand blazed brighter until it dulled and fell from his chest.

"He's not a hybrid," she muttered. The boy flinched, but remained sitting, his eyes wide and full of terror, "He has been engineered. A halfling injected with Nephilim blood."

Fin's stomach twisted.

Niah was right.

He glanced at her, but the colour had bleached from her skin, her breaths shallow.

"The Shadows," she breathed, the words rattled through him.

"You're sure?"

"Who else would have access to halflings *and* Nephilim blood?" she said in barely more than a whisper.

"But he's just a child," Cassia whimpered.

"We all know they're not above harming children." Gren growled, his hands balling into fists at his side as he spared a glance at Niah.

Niah stepped close to the boy once more, and placed a hand on his shoulder, "Do you know who did this to you?" tears rolled down Logan's cheeks, his hands quivering in his lap.

"All I know...is that the Commander will return."

Before any of them could ask what he meant, Logan doubled over, letting out a cry as he vomited scarlet blood over the white floor. Niah went to his side, rubbing his back.

Fin turned to Cassia, "What's happening?"

She pressed her hands to each side of his head, "He's dying."

"How?" Fin ground out through his teeth, unable to do *anything* to help.

Niah and Cassia exchanged a knowing look, and Niah moved Logan's hair away from the back of his neck. And there, hidden in his hairline, at the base of his skull, was a black circle.

Fin's chest deflated.

The boy was marked.

A mark for controlling, not for suppression.

"Fuck," Gren growled, turning away as he dragged his hands down his face. Fin didn't know what to say, or what to do.

"Fin," Cassia's voice was hard, "the Shadows are killing him."

He knelt in front of the trembling, whimpering boy, and placed a gentle hand on his shoulder, "Do you know *anything?*"

Logan shook his head, retching again before he could get a word out, the pool of scarlet spreading beneath him.

"Why would they do this?" Fin bit out, barely able to contain his surging rage.

"They wanted a spy." Niah answered, her voice flat and empty, "They planted him in with the survivors at the English facility during the attack."

"How do you know that?" Gren asked, coming to stand over them.

Niah met his gaze, her eyes cold, "Because I would have done the same thing."

For a moment, it was all he could do to stare at her. She never spoke of her time with the Shadows, and he didn't know what her time with them meant. But in those few words, she'd told them plenty.

A thought struck him, "Where's Vinaxx? He can remove it."

"He's not here," Cassia answered.

"Where the hell is he?" Gren demanded. Cassia opened her mouth, but she was already shaking her head, her eyes welling with tears.

"Well, can you do it?" Fin pressed.

She placed her hand over the mark, her fingers glowing before jerking back and clutching at her hand.

"I'm not strong enough," she whimpered, shaking her head slowly, her eyes wide and tearful. Logan retched again.

"Is there *anything* we can do?" Fin growled, more to himself than anyone else.

"Please...please...I don't want to die..." Logan wept, tears of blood streaming down his face, falling into the pool beneath him.

Fin's chest contracted.

He should kill him. End his suffering.

Fin's throat closed up. There suddenly wasn't enough air in the room. They all stood as the boy whimpered and pleaded for his life. Fin's mind was racing, surely there was something they could do?

He whirled on Cassia, "Couldn't Morena do it?"

"You know we cannot call on her. She is an Elder, Fin. His organs are failing; he is dying," she murmured, "he is suffering right now."

As if on cue, Logan cried out, gripping his stomach and chest. Red tears stained his cheeks. He would die. And there was nothing any of them could do because of that damned mark on his neck.

Fin's hands balled into fists as he bit down on his lip, closing his eyes briefly, steeling himself for what he had to do.

Before he could move, Niah wrapped her arms around Logan; he rested his head on her shoulder, sobbing. She rocked him, and he clung onto her, his nails digging into her arms, drawing black blood. Fin started forward, but Gren caught at his arm. When he looked back at his brother, he only shook his head.

Fin turned his eyes to Niah and the boy, as her hands moved, one on each side of Logan's head.

"*Vale Frater,*" she whispered. Then, with one swift movement, she jerked his head to the side, and his neck snapped. His hands went limp at his sides. She lay him down on the cold floor and got to her feet.

Niah gazed down at the boy for a moment, no longer in pain or pleading; he looked at peace.

Without a word or glance at any of them, Niah left the room. The three of them watched her go, unable to speak, unable to breathe. Fin turned to the boy on the floor.

"Gren, could you start making arrangements, please?"

It should have been him.

Fin should have been the one to end the boys' suffering.

But he couldn't.

He was the advisor, second in command, and it should have been him to do it.

Gren nodded and scooped the boy up into his arms, carrying him out of the room. Fin picked up a cloth from the table next to the bed and knelt to clean the blood up. A hand gripped his shoulder, and he looked up to see Cassia standing over him.

"It's not your fault."

Fin shook his head, "I should have done something."

"It's never easy to take a life, even if it is a mercy," Cassia said, kneeling beside him.

"Niah did without hesitation." She knew what had to be done, and she'd done it, because it was the right thing to do. While Fin had stood there helplessly.

"Go to her. I will take care of this," Cassia said, her voice firm yet soft at the same time.

Fin didn't argue, and left the infirmary, his heart pounding. There was only one place she would have gone.

NIAH

25

The waves lapped gently onto the shore.

Seagulls squawked above; a gentle breeze carried salt with it, blowing strands of her hair across her face. Niah watched the gently rippling ocean, and the light clouds rolling overhead as pinks and golds danced across the sky.

She sat with her knees pulled into her chest, burying her toes in the cool sand. If she were a painter, she'd like to try to capture the serenity of the moment.

But her hands were not meant for such delicate things.

Niah glanced down at those very hands, stained with red blood once again. Memories of that night with her mothers' blood dried and crusted on her skin scorched her mind.

For better or worse, she had taken her first life.

It wasn't what she thought it would be like. Logan wasn't the person she wanted to kill. He was just like her, another experiment. Another weapon to be used as the Shadows saw fit.

The snap of his neck echoed through her. It was a mercy, she knew that, but it didn't make the burden any easier to bear.

Would she have the same feeling when she watched the light fade from Nolan or Karliah's eyes? She'd have to find out, she supposed. Either way, there was no going back, not after what she'd just witnessed.

Logan had told them a message, a warning, no doubt from the Shadows, if they were able to control him through the mark on his neck. *The Commander will return.* Niah had read that the Shadows army was commanded by one person, but there was no telling how true that was, not with the Furies limited knowledge.

A shudder rippled down her spine at the thought of coming face to face with the Commander.

The lengths the Shadows were willing to go were terrifying, and she knew, deep in her heart, that if she wanted to get to them, she too would have to do unspeakable things.

She would have to become a monster.

Because only a monstrous weapon.

Can kill the beast.

As she knew he would, Fin found her and sat beside her. He said nothing, just watched the sunset until the colours drained from the sky, and darkness draped around them.

Niah couldn't bring herself to look him in the eye; if it wasn't for what had happened in the infirmary, then it was because of the night before. His touch lingered on her skin, warm where he'd held her. No matter how hard she tried, whenever she looked at him, her eyes drifted to his lips.

She wanted to feel them now more than ever.

"I understand if you're angry at me, I shouldn't have been the one to do that," Niah muttered after a long while.

Despite the heaviness in her heart, she was glad she had done it. That she spared the others, spared *Fin*, from having to do it. She'd seen the colour drain from his face, the brightness fade from his eyes, and knew that it would devastate him to do it. To take an innocent life.

"Angry? You think I'm angry?" she turned to look at him, his silver eyes wide, his jaw tense, "No, I'm not angry. I'm disappointed," he pulled his hand through his hair, "In myself."

She didn't ask why; there was no need.

"No one should have had to have made that choice."

"You did."

For a moment, only the gentle waves filled the silence.

Fin had been there for her time and time again, and now, when he needed comfort, she couldn't bring herself to reach for him.

"I'm different," Niah muttered, she felt his gaze on her then, but still, she could not look him in the eye. "I was trained for death; I've dreamt about it for years. Granted, it wasn't the death I imagined, but perhaps I was more prepared."

She had never tried to comfort anyone before, and when she finally met his gaze, she knew she had failed.

"I should have been the one to do it, but I couldn't. I knew his pain needed to end, but I couldn't take the life of one of our own," he murmured, lowering his eyes to gaze at the sand. She knew how to deal with humorous, joking Fin; she could deal with angry Fin even, but this version? This defeated, shameful version…was a stranger.

"He wasn't one of our own. He was an experiment. The Shadows did this," she said through gritted teeth, her hands balling into fists, blue sparks shot from them as if in answer to the roaring in her veins.

It wasn't fair for Fin to feel like he was to blame, it wasn't fair that he'd even had to consider killing that poor boy. It wasn't fair that Logan got caught in the middle of a war and used as a pawn because the Shadows considered him expendable.

None of it was fair.

Fin was silent for a moment before muttering, "I've informed Merida, we need to act, not sit here waiting on a decision to be made by all the leaders."

"I hope they make a choice soon," her hand clasped the locket around her throat.

"I think after this, they'll be much more inclined to make a decision sooner rather than later," Fin ran his hands through his hair, his shoulders hunched where a line of tension ran through him.

Niah took a deep breath. Wanting to distract both of them from what happened, she asked, "Where did you come from?"

He blinked, but some of the light returned to his eyes. Even in the darkness, they shimmered. She never thought it was possible that another being could take her breath away quite like him. Was it okay? To think those things and not be able to act on them?

No.

It would only make it harder.

Niah turned away, looking down at her fingers fiddling with a loose thread on her shirt.

"Merida found me fifty-odd years ago. I wasn't very old and took my anger out on anyone I could find. I wasn't a good person. I didn't know how to control my strength; I'd go from bar to bar getting into fights." he said, his voice full of shame.

"Supernatural bars?"

"Sometimes," he shrugged, "or I'd wander into a lycanthrope pack or a vampire den; they were all the same to me. That's what happens when hybrids aren't given a focus, we have nothing to channel our energy into, and we become feral."

"Didn't you know this existed?" she gestured to the large building behind them.

"No. I don't remember the first few years of my life. A pack of lycanthropes found me and took me in when I was an infant, but I was still an outsider. Merida found me years later and taught me how to channel my anger; she gave me a purpose and a responsibility. I owe her my life," a small smile tugged at the corners of his mouth. He always seemed so sure of himself; Niah would never have guessed he was a lost boy with nowhere to call home.

Fin asked, "Did they always train you?"

"As long as I can remember, yeah. I was told being a Shadow was the highest honour I could ever receive, so I trained every day to achieve that goal." Her voice turned bitter.

"Clever, they gave you a purpose, something to aim for as early as possible. Tempering your demonic impulses."

Oh, they did much more than that.

"What did it mean?" he questioned, his brow furrowing.

"What?"

"*Vale Frater*. You said it to Logan before..." he trailed off, the words hanging between them.

"It's Latin; it means, goodbye brother," she answered, gazing down at the sand between her toes. She remembered the blood tears streaming down his face, the pool of scarlet beneath him, the pleading because he didn't want to die as he choked on his own blood. He was young, and underserving of the ending he had.

"I want to show you something," she said when he didn't reply.

Her heart pounded the entire walk back to her room. If she couldn't give herself to him, or her heart, she would give him the next best thing—a little piece of her past. An explanation, even if he didn't realise it.

The door clicked shut behind them, and she flicked on the light. He watched her unclasp the key from around her neck and unlock the book. Fin said nothing as she pushed it toward him, his eyes scanned the words, and he flicked through the pages, his brows pulling together. His eyes widened when he realised what he was reading.

"This is you," he murmured, still flicking through the pages, only stopping when he found a picture shoved between the pages. Her when she was young, the one taken just before her parents were killed. She was all arms and legs, positioned to strike, a sword gripped in her small hands.

He turned the picture over, 'Year 9' was written on the back. However, the picture looked much older than nine years, black and white and grainy as if taken on one of the first cameras.

He sucked in a sharp breath, "How does this make you feel when you look at it?"

"Like I was just like Logan, an experiment. That's all I was to them, my parents...the people who raised me. I was a weapon." His fingers twitched as he gazed at her, but he didn't reach for her.

Saying the words aloud stung, but not as much as she thought they would. Niah held his gaze, despite the pity shining in them, then he circled her in his arms, and she didn't pull away. Instead, she sagged against him, holding him close, letting his strength seep into her.

They stayed like that for the longest of times, neither one wanting to let the other go.

NIAH

26

Fin was called away to yet another meeting.

Not wanting to be alone, Niah went to Dea's room to find her and Sai inside, the latter sprawled across the bed while Dea stood in front of an easel.

A knot had eased in her chest after showing Fin that little piece of herself. It wasn't much, but it was a start. Maybe it was how she could start to heal, but that remained to be seen.

"Hello, Gorgeous, how's my favourite angry hybrid?" Sai grinned, opening his arm in invitation. Niah sat on the bed, taking a deep breath as she let Sai's arm flop to the bed around her. He seemed to understand her unfamiliarity with being touched without her needing to say a word about it.

He threw her a wink as if in confirmation of that very thought, and she couldn't stop herself from smiling.

"It's just not looking how I want it to," Dea pouted as she threw the paintbrush at the canvas.

Niah peered around the girl at the painting of a white expanse with a sky of swirling colours, and black, fluffy rocks on the ground.

"What, exactly, are you trying to paint?"

Dea huffed a sigh, "I'm trying to capture my dream from last night. The Northern Lights on a field of ice, black crows on the ground."

"*They're* crows?" Sai gawped, "I thought they were rocks."

Dea grabbed the paintbrush and flung it at him, but he caught it before it could touch him, or the bedding.

"Well, that wasn't nice," he mocked, setting the paintbrush on the nightstand.

"They're just not looking how I want them to look," Dea frowned, turning back to the painting.

Niah and Sai exchanged a knowing glance, and Niah went to her friend to get a better look at the painting.

"The sky is stunning," it was the truth; the snowdrifts and lights were captured beautifully.

Dea turned to her then, her bright, sky-blue eyes shimmering with unshed tears.

"I heard about Logan," Niah stiffened at the words, but Dea only wrapped her arms around her, squeezing tightly.

"How are you?" Sai asked, whilst getting to his feet.

Niah shrugged, "I don't know." Another truth. She didn't know how to feel about it. How was someone supposed to feel after taking a life? Remorse? Relief? She didn't know, despite having been conditioned for death, no one ever told her what to do *after* it was done.

The one thing she knew for sure, was that she wanted to be around her friends.

"Well, you know we're here if you need to talk about it," Sai said, his voice gentle and warm as he gripped her shoulder. Her throat suddenly felt thick, her chest swelling. She dipped her chin in thanks, unsure of what to say.

"This is going to get worse," Dea muttered. Niah and Sai turned to the snowy-haired girl; a single tear slipped down her cheek. Sai folded her into his arms, while Niah gripped her hand, squeezing gently.

"It will get as bad as it gets; we just need to be prepared," Sai said, dropping a kiss on the top of her head and stepping away, holding her shoulders at arm's length.

"I think we could all use a laugh, movie?" he suggested, glancing from Dea, to Niah, and back again. A movie with her friends was exactly what she needed.

Just as they got comfortable on the bed, the door swung open, and Fin and Gren stormed in, both wearing dark clothes with swords strapped across their backs.

Niah's heart skipped a beat.

Patrolling clothes.

"What's going on?" Dea asked as they all leapt off the bed.

"Demonic activity not far from here," Gren panted.

"Shit," Sai growled and darted from the room, no doubt to get changed and armed.

Dea was already changing when Fin took Niah by the arm and pulled her to the side of the room, "You don't have to come_"

"I want to." She interjected, pulling her arm from his grasp before sprinting down the corridor to her rooms.

Her weapons cupboard had been stocked with her preference, twin short swords that strapped across her back with an ordinary-looking rucksack for them to slide into.

The patrolling gear they wore were ordinary jeans and jackets, as humans might question if they wore their armour in public. Niah questioned why they would have it at all, to which Merida had told her it was in case of emergencies.

She was lacing her boots up her shins when Fin stalked into the room.

"Are you sure you're up for this?"

"Are you?"

He paused, "What do you mean?"

"You think I'm not up to it because of what happened with Logan. I'm only asking how *you're* doing." she straightened up and fixed the rucksack to her back, the straps crossing over her chest to keep the swords secured.

"I don't even know," he sighed.

"There was nothing more we could have done." The words burned like acid on her tongue, but it was the truth, "If this is a demon attack, then I'm going to need to learn what it's like sooner or later, right?" Fin nodded, "So, I'm coming."

"I should have known better than to argue with you. Fine, but don't cry when you break a nail." He smirked. Something eased in her chest at the humour in his voice, at the spark in his eyes.

"Just try to keep up," Niah grinned, feeling her blood humming with the anticipation of a fight.

"I could go all night," he murmured close to her ear as she brushed by him. Tingles shot down her spine, heat pooling in her stomach as she turned away, hiding the flush across her cheeks.

Thankfully, the others were hurrying toward them. Dea wearing a long, leather trench coat with her spear strapped to her thigh; apparently, it lengthened whenever she pressed a specific button.

"Stay close," Dea muttered as the boys descended into a conversation of weather conditions and traffic reports. "We fight as a team, and we watch each other's backs, no going rogue."

"I know," Niah said, and meant it.

"Just remember," Dea whispered, "They're demons. They have no feelings, no emotions, they're evil, and they'd kill you or anyone else without a second thought."

Niah held her gaze, understanding why she had said it.

As they ran through the building to the underground garage, Niah noticed more and more squads piling into cars and speeding onto the street. How many alarms had gone off?

They piled into one of the Jeeps, and Sai put his foot down. Despite being faster than most vehicles, they couldn't get away with running that fast without being spotted by humans. So the facilities had invested in cars for emergencies such as this.

Fin programmed the sat nav to where the activity was coming from, at the heart of the city. The vehicles were blacked out, specifically to run red lights and not be caught by cameras, but if police officers saw them, their only option was to flee. With hybrids heightened reflexes, it made high-speed driving easy, even in cramped city streets.

Sai had bragged once or twice about some impressive evasive manoeuvres to escape from the police.

When they couldn't get any closer to the location by driving, Sai parked the Jeep, and they all climbed out. Lights and bustling humans filled the streets. Luckily, humans couldn't see the assortment of weapons on their person, not with the holsters designed to look like bags.

"That way," Fin said, wrinkling his nose.

"He reminds me of a bloodhound when he does that," Sai muttered as they trailed after Fin.

They crossed a busy street and entered an alley. Dumpsters lined the walls along with loose trash bags, some split open, sending a foul smell into the air.

Niah's heart thumped rapidly as she and the others drew their weapons, the blades black and gleaming in the dim light.

"They're close," Fin murmured.

Niah breathed steadily, slowing her heart to force her mind to focus. Her senses sharpened as adrenaline spiked in her veins. Without even looking at them, she knew where each of her friends were. She could *feel* their breath, their anticipation, their lethal calm as they analysed their surroundings.

It was so different from anything she'd ever felt.

Her power stirred in her veins, and there was no stopping it shining through her eyes as she crept through the alley, guarding Fin's back while the others flanked her. Blue sparks leapt from her fingertips where she gripped her swords, her canines sliding free as an instinct she hadn't known was there reared its head.

Hybrids were born to fight, and as her blood sang, she knew why.

Dea nudged her with an elbow, her eyes shining with excitement, and offered Niah a reassuring nod.

This would be her first taste of battle. She couldn't wait for it to start.

Niah heard them before she saw them.

Gilmara demons poured down from the rooftops on either side of the alley. Ghastly, bubbling things with rows upon rows of razor-sharp teeth set into wide, gaping mouths. They had long legs sticking out in all directions like giant spiders, and six eyes atop large antennas along their backs.

Niah had studied demons for years, the reality of them might have been terrifying, but she didn't feel terror, or even a hint of fear. Instead, she only felt the glorious high of adrenaline hammering through her veins.

A demon landed directly on Fin's shoulders, catching him off guard and knocking him to the ground. Before anyone else could move, Niah was there, severing the demon in half with a scissoring action of her blades. Ichor sprayed over her jacket, sizzling slightly on contact.

Fin scrambled to his feet, his canines glinting in the light of the nearby street lights, and angrily swung at another demon launching itself at him.

"Little bastard," he cursed over the dying shriek of the demon he'd sunk his blade into.

A faint scuttle sounded behind her, and she turned with a swing of her swords, the blades sinking into the demon's side. It squealed and hit the wall, letting out a hiss as it tried to escape.

She drew a dagger from her hip and threw it, hitting the demon in the head; it bubbled into a pile of stinking goop before disintegrating into ash.

There were too many to count, and they kept coming from the rooftops. She and Dea locked eyes, a silent message passing between them. Then they were moving, scaling up each side of the alley, her nails cracking as she hauled herself onto the roof.

There was a hole straight through the centre of the building, disappearing deep down into blackness. Demons poured from the cracks, only their glowing red eyes visible through the darkness below. A rift, a chasm, whatever it was, Niah had no idea how to close it.

There was no end to them.

They kept coming.

The boys remained in the alley, dispatching the beasts that slipped through hers and Dea's blades. Niah's insides clenched, if they couldn't find a way to close the rift, and the demons kept coming, they wouldn't be able to hold the monsters off for long.

The building started to tremble beneath her, the ground groaning as the rift began to close up, the ground stitching itself back together as if it were never there, crushing demons as it vanished.

There was no time to question what the hell just happened, not when there were still so many demons to kill.

Her lungs ached for more air, but her body was electric with energy. The high of battle was exhilarating, and she found herself smiling with each kill. For those few moments, it was just her and her blades as they sang through the air before finding their mark. The sounds of dying beasts was a melody of death that she relished. It was a dance, one she didn't want to end.

She could feel the others around her, their hearts and breathing synchronised to read each other better.

It was euphoric.

Niah glanced across at Dea, dispatching the remaining demons on her side, she hadn't noticed one of them creeping behind her, but Niah had. Without a second thought, she threw one of her swords across the distance, satisfied when she heard the screech as the demon disintegrated into ash.

Dea looked up, glancing from the demon, to Niah, and smiled, dipping her chin in thanks before twirling away, sinking the blade of her spear into the final demon.

The two leapt over the edge of the buildings, which still had a gaping hole through the middle, and landed lightly in the alley before Dea handed Niah her sword.

"Nice throw," the snowy-haired hybrid winked.

"We've got each other's backs, right?" Niah said a little breathlessly.

It stank a lot worse than it had when they arrived; so much so that Fin had to cover his hypersensitive nose. They all paused when he froze, eyes widening. He tilted his chin back, sniffing the air. It was the next moment that Niah smelt it too. Smoke.

FIN

27

Something was burning.

The stench of fire, ash, and flesh was heavy on the air. His gut quivered as a bitter chill slithered up his spine.

"We have to get back," Fin muttered.

They were moving before he'd even finished speaking, running back to the car as quick as they could without drawing attention to themselves. They piled into the Jeep, and Sai slammed it into gear before performing an illegal U-turn, ignoring the blaring horns of other road users as the jeep roared down the road.

The scenery blurred by around them as the steering wheel groaned beneath Sai's iron grip.

"Sai," Fin warned. He ignored him, a muscle feathering in his jaw. Fin pressed his lips together and turned back to the road.

In the distance, a cloud of smoke rose from where the facility should be. His blood turned to ice in his veins.

"Shit," Sai ground out, putting his foot down, pushing the car faster, expertly weaving in and out of traffic. There was no point in telling him to slow down, Fin wanted to get back as much as he did.

As they grew near, the stench of burning flesh grew potent. Sai didn't bother parking in the garage, only drove up the curb and over the grass surrounding the facility, leaving the engine running as he dove out, abandoning it.

They froze when their eyes rested on the scene before them.

Right in front of the facility, was a large pile of burning bodies. Their faces contorted in pain and piled one on top of the other. How many had they lost in one attack?

Warriors gathered around the pile, some with tears in their eyes, some covering their mouths in horror, some stared blankly, others in shock. As they stood, more and more hybrids came through the cloak.

Fin choked down the bile that rose in his throat as his stomach churned. His shoulders slumped; they were too late.

"Oh my god," Dea whimpered, tears rolling down her pale cheeks. Gren pulled her to his side, unable to tear his eyes away from the devastation before them.

For the longest time, all he could hear was the sobs around them, and the crackling of flames.

Fin turned to Niah, but she was staring at the bodies, her swords held limply at her sides, her eyes wide and helpless, almost as if she'd seen it all before.

Because she had.

She'd had a nightmare of demons and a mountain of corpses outside the facility. She met his gaze; the look in her eyes said it all. She had no idea how it was possible. But it was.

Fin's chest rose and fell with shallow breaths as he glared at the scene, his grip tightening around the sword in his hand.

"Where were you?" he demanded of the group who had just come through the cloak beside them.

"There was a demon attack," one of them answered; Fin turned to his right, where another group was watching them.

"And you?"

"Same," the girl in front muttered.

Somehow, it was all orchestrated.

Now they knew for certain that the Shadows were able to control demons. He shuddered at the possibilities of what they could do with such a power.

He staggered forward, letting his sword fall to the ground as he dropped to his knees, defeated. The weight in his chest was suffocating.

There was nothing but a high-pitched wail in his ears as he surveyed the scene. More warriors were coming through the cloak, their faces a mask of horror and disgust when they saw the massacre before them.

He should be giving orders, he should be the voice of reason, but he couldn't find the strength to stand. He couldn't bear to see the grief in the eyes of so many as he tried to tell them it would all be okay.

He didn't know what to do.

Then there was a pair of soft, trembling hands on either side of his face, tugging so he would look at whoever was there. Slowly, his eyes met those of ocean blue and full of tears.

Merida knelt before him, soot and ash covering her skin and clothes, faint burns decorated her hands where she must have tried to pull bodies from the still-raging fire. Neither said a word, but their arms went around each other.

More than anything, he was relieved she was okay.

But how many had lost their lives?

"The attacks were a distraction; how many of us were here?" Fin asked when she finally pulled away, her eyes wide and puffy.

"Just over a hundred, all too young and inexperienced," she choked out.

He staggered to his feet, "How many dead?"

"None," she breathed; he stared at her incredulously.

"These are not our people. Nor are they from any other facility. I've had word from them all, and they have all had the same thing. This was not an attack. It was a message."

He stared at the pile of bodies, "Then who are they?"

Merida shook her head, "I don't know."

"How did they get through the barriers? How did you not *see* this?" he didn't bother to check his tone.

She dragged her hands through her hair, "The barrier was down. I don't know how; Vinaxx is investigating it now. The cloak remained up, but not the barrier. I...I was asleep." She was shaking her head as tears slipped down her cheeks. Fin's blood cooled. Merida hadn't been sleeping much and was in desperate need of it. He couldn't blame her for finally giving in.

"What about the others? Did no one else see it?" he questioned, his voice softer.

A shake of her head, "It happened so quickly. A portal opened in the sky, and the bodies poured out, already burning." His stomach churned. Dumped. All those people *dumped* on their doorstep as if they were nothing more than rubbish.

"Merida, we can't keep waiting around for them to attack," he said tersely, her eyes hardened.

Merida turned to the blaze, "I'm well aware of that."

People had begun throwing buckets of water at the fire as Cassia, and the other spell weavers used water magic to douse the flames. It seemed the more they tried to extinguish the fire, the more it spread. Then, slowly, the flames guttered and extinguished themselves.

Once the fire was out, everyone moved the bodies and lay them on the ground. Fin had been going through them, looking at the back of their necks; every single one was marked with the same controlling mark that was on Logan.

He caught Merida's eye, and she gestured for him to follow. The two of them, accompanied by Benjamin and Helena, walked up to her office, closed the door, and stood around her desk as she dialled a known number to the leaders of the facilities. So many of the voices were tired, exasperated even.

"We have to hold a Summit," Merida said over the rabble of voices; many of the leaders had begun arguing. At that, they fell silent.

"I agree," one said; many more echoed their agreement.

"We leave as soon as we can, clear the facilities out. We cannot leave anyone behind. There is enough room in the bunker," a male voice said tersely.

"Leave the facilities unguarded? But they could be destroyed," a woman protested.

"So could our warriors. The facilities can be rebuilt, but death is slightly more permanent." Merida growled. The line was silent before a unanimous vote of agreement, and the line went dead.

"We will start the evacuation," Benjamin said; Helena followed after him and closed the door on their way out.

Merida let her head fall into her hands, her shoulders shaking as she sobbed. Fin knelt beside her and pulled her into his arms. He said nothing; what was there to say?

When she finally pulled away, she wiped her eyes and muttered, "We will hold a memorial for the fallen before we leave; tell everyone to take only the essentials."

It didn't matter whether those lying dead outside were their people or not, the Furies would honour them as if they *were* their own. Though he knew not every facility would be quite so honourable.

"I'll go and let Vinaxx know," he said, getting to his feet. Merida was silent, and she barely looked up when he left the room.

When he arrived outside, most of the bodies had been laid out, but Benjamin was ordering the spell weavers to set them alight and be done with it.

Fin ground his teeth and stalked to the leader, "They're to be honoured before they're burned."

Benjamin turned to him with as much interest as he'd show an insect, and scoffed, "They're nothing more than Shadow dogs; they deserve nothing."

A low, rumbling growl tore through Fin's throat as his canines lengthened. Helena stepped between him and her leader, but Benjamin's eyes gleamed with wicked delight.

"They will be honoured, and that's final."

At that, the smirk faded from Benjamin's face, "You dare to give *me* orders, boy?"

"As second in command of *this* facility, I am authorised by Merida to do as she deems appropriate. If that means giving you orders, then so be it."

Benjamin's nostrils flared, but before he could get another word out, some of his warriors beckoned him, and Sai grabbed Fin's arm, tugging him away.

"Not today, brother," he muttered.

Fin glanced around at the faces watching him, anxious that he and Benjamin would brawl. Oh, how he wanted to.

"It's a waste of time, you know? We should have just left them to burn." Benjamin shouted over his shoulder. Everything in Fin's head screamed at him not to give in, but his blood was boiling, and as he whirled to do exactly what he knew he shouldn't, he was met with cautious, dark eyes.

Niah stood before him, a hand on his chest, keeping him in place.

"Let it go," her voice was calm, but laced with something dangerous. Of course, he hadn't thought of how this might have affected her.

His heart slowed as he held her gaze, but he saw the way she pressed her lips together, biting her tongue to stop herself from doing what Fin was about to do.

Knowing it was the right thing to do, Fin turned away from Benjamin, draping an arm around Niah's shoulders as they walked back to where the others were standing while Vinaxx said the rite of farewell.

"What did Merida say?" Sai asked.

"We need to go to the bunker as soon as possible," Fin sighed. The bunker was a massive underground facility situated beneath the Appalachian Mountains, easily capable of holding everyone in every facility with rooms to spare. It was built decades ago and was only to be used in cases of dire emergencies. It was the only place the Elders would venture when they were called for a Summit.

There hadn't been a need for such a formality, until now.

"We'd better go pack then," Dea said, taking Niah's hand before walking back inside with Sai on their heels. Gren stood, staring at the bleak scene before him.

"The bunker, eh?" he muttered after a long moment, not meeting Fin's gaze.

"A Summit has been called," Fin answered quietly. He watched as

Vinaxx finished the rite of farewell, the spell weavers raised their hands, and the bodies burst into multicoloured flames. Smoke rose into the air; the bodies turned to glittering ash and floated up into the sky, carried away by the gentle breeze.

"Until my last breath," Fin muttered as he gazed into the night sky.

"Until my last breath," Gren repeated; the two of them stood in silence for a while, watching the ashes float away. It didn't matter whether they had been experiments; they died at the hands of the Shadows. How many hundreds of thousands had to die to leave a pile on the doorstep of *every* facility across the world?

Gren clamped a hand on Fin's shoulder; he hadn't realised he's been staring off into space, his hands balled into fists at his sides. Gren eyed him with comforting eyes.

"They won't get away with this," he murmured; Fin could only nod.

It was no coincidence that the Shadows had finally made their move after Niah had escaped from the compound. Yet, even with everything that had happened, he didn't regret bringing her to Perth. He didn't regret getting her away from that place.

His only regret, was the deaths that lay heavy on his shoulders.

NIAH

28

Dea had finally stopped crying.

Niah didn't mind comforting her friend, but after a while, she ran out of reassuring words to say.

Dea wiped her face, "Sorry, I bet you think I'm weak."

"No," Niah shook her head, "None of that was easy to witness." Sure enough, Niah still felt chilled to the bone after returning to a nightmare. What was worse, was that she'd seen it before. She and Fin never had the chance to go to Merida about the dream, and she wasn't sure she wanted to bring it up now. Even if she knew she should.

Was there something she could have done?

"It won't do anyone any good to linger on what might have been," Dea murmured, getting up from the bed to grab a bag from the wardrobe. Niah said nothing; Dea was right. She could sit and stew over how she might have done things differently for weeks, and it wouldn't change what had happened.

If anything, it only made her more determined to find the Shadows.

The people they had dumped on the Furies doorstep were all marked; they were like Logan, like *her*. Nothing more than puppets to be used as the Shadows saw fit. But, she couldn't help but wonder why they hadn't placed a controlling mark on her?

Why would they only want to suppress her strength? Maybe one day she'd get her answer; the book certainly didn't have any insights.

Niah sighed, shoving the thoughts from her mind, and gazed at the painting Dea had been working on earlier.

"I didn't know you liked to paint," Niah said as she gazed around the room, noticing several canvases full of colour stacked against a wall.

"I had a much different upbringing than most hybrids," Dea replied gently, folding away clothes into the bag.

Niah scooted to the edge of the unmade bed, "How so?"

"Well, like most of us, we're all abandoned at birth. Angels can't carry children, but demons can, and so we usually get left because, let's face it, they have no idea what to do with a baby." She shook her head, "In my case, I got left at a human orphanage, which I suppose you could say isn't the worst place," she smiled to herself, "I was adopted by humans."

"Didn't they notice your silver ring? Or your strength?" Niah questioned.

"They thought the ring was unique. As for my strength, they never said anything. I always wondered whether they *thought* I was different, but if they did, they chose to ignore it. They were so desperate for a child but couldn't conceive on their own. I think maybe they overlooked things because they were just happy to have a child to love." Dea smiled, not looking up from her task.

"How was it?" Niah asked, "To have a human family, I mean."

"They were good people. They said everyone should know an art form, so I started painting. It kept them happy, and some paintings even made them proud. It wasn't like it was the worst thing to do, so I kept doing it. It gave me something to focus on," she shrugged, "it got to the point where I was supposed to be going to college; that's when Sai found me. Having to leave them was hard; they wouldn't have understood, so I faked my death. Easier for them to mourn me rather than finding out about hybrids."

Dea didn't meet Niah's gaze as she shoved more clothes into the bag.

Everyone had wounds that hadn't quite healed. Everyone had demons. The ones they'd fought earlier were easier to slay than whatever ate away at someone from the inside.

Niah didn't press the matter further. The once so bubbly, energetic girl, was now stoic, making slow and controlled movements as she packed her bag. But no one was themselves after what they had returned to.

The simmering rage in Fin's silver eyes had shaken something inside her. All she wanted to do was hold him close, but with so many watching them, she couldn't. It was all she could do not to rip Benjamin's head off herself for what he'd said.

It wasn't merely a reaction of her anger that made her want to tear his throat out, but she *wanted* his life. It didn't matter that he was a leader of the Fury Alliance; Niah wanted to feel his life slip away between her fingers.

It had rattled her, but she couldn't bring herself to care.

She was what she was, even if sometimes it was harder to accept than others.

Dea hoisted the bag over her shoulder without a word, and the two of them walked the corridor. Everyone was rushing around with bags to get through a portal as quickly as possible. She didn't blame them. Seeing so many bodies had turned her blood to ice.

Dea nudged her; they'd arrived outside her room and stood in the corridor while Niah stared into space. She unlocked the door and started shoving clothes into a bag along with a few weapons.

The door opened, and Fin came in, dragging his hands down his face. He eyed the two of them and gestured for them to follow. They did so, her hand going to the locket around her throat. A habit. She still wasn't ready to take it off.

In the courtyard, spell weavers held open shimmering portals as people disappeared into the void. They met Gren and Sai near a sparkling, pink portal held open by Cassia.

"It's a sombre day," the weaver shook her head, her brows pulled up in the middle.

Niah took a moment to survey those around them. Children clutching their bags to their chests, some holding hands with one another, the older youngsters were talking amongst themselves; none of them had any idea what was going on.

Half of the warriors had stayed back while the other half went first to make sure it was safe for the youngsters to come through. Many of them were trying to keep quiet, not wanting the children to hear how dire the situation was.

All around were murmurs of revenge and war. The warriors wanted blood, and Niah was inclined to agree. The power in her veins prickled against her skin in anticipation, longing for the high of battle once again.

She could taste the hatred filling the air. The smoke and ash stuffed itself down her throat, clutching at her lungs like a bitter embrace. A reminder.

The faces of those who had been killed were tattooed on the inside of her eyelids. She committed the gruesome images to her mind, not wanting to forget them. She would fight to avenge them, she'd fight to put a stop to innocents like them from having to go through the same thing.

As much as she wanted her own revenge, there were bigger things to fight for.

Niah wasn't sure what she was expecting when she stepped through the portal, but the bunker was exactly that. The room they'd stepped into was a vast, concrete box with screens dotted around on the walls and speakers playing comforting melodies.

A chill sank into her bones.

It was like a prison.

"Come on," Fin murmured into her ear, taking her arm as he led her out of the room. They were given room numbers on their way out, and thankfully, they were all together.

Harsh, fluorescent lights lined the ceilings, and smaller lights marked the walkways. Despite the sheer size of the room they'd just left, the corridors were cramped, with doors coming off each side into large, communal sleeping quarters with rows of bunk beds.

Only advisors and leaders got their own rooms, so Niah would have to share with Dea, Sai, and Gren, which she was silently thankful for. She wasn't sure she wanted to be alone.

They descended a spiralling staircase and came out into a long corridor, each side lined with metal doors. Gren shoved open the metal door to their room, but Fin gestured for her to follow him into another room opposite, next door to Merida's.

Inside was a double bed with a rusting metal frame, a sink in one corner, and next to that, a toilet.

Fin dropped his bag in the corner, leaning over the desk as he let his head droop slightly. Niah had never seen him so defeated, but they all were. Her lids drooped, but she didn't feel like sleeping, not with everything she'd seen that night.

She slumped down on the edge of the bed, and it squeaked beneath her weight. Niah sighed, tipping her head back to gaze at the grey ceiling. Fin pushed himself away from the desk and sat next to her, taking her hand casually in his. She let him, ignoring the voice in the back of her mind telling her not to lead him on.

Fin needed comfort, and she realised that he took comfort in touch, whereas she took comfort in actions.

"What are you thinking?" he asked, his thumb idly stroking circles on the back of her hand, as if *she* were the one who needed comforting.

Honestly, Niah wasn't sure how she felt. Angry didn't seem enough, nor did upset. There was simply a numbing coldness in the pit of her stomach.

"What are *you* thinking?"

Fin searched her eyes, "How I should have known better."

"The Shadows are no ordinary enemy," she muttered, holding his gaze, "there's so much we don't know about them, but they seem to know an awful lot about us."

For a moment, he just stared at her, before he swallowed and muttered, "That's the first time you've said *us*, as if you're a Fury."

A smile tugged at the corners of her mouth, "Aren't I?"

"In all the ways that matter, yes." He squeezed her hand, and she found herself wanting to lean into him, to feel his lips beneath hers.

Niah cleared her throat and looked away, pulling her hand free of his as she got to her feet and strode around the room.

"You know," she said, "I sometimes wonder what might have happened if I stayed in England."

Fin's voice was icy when he said, "You'd be hurt, or worse."

"Hurt, yes, but if they were going to kill me, they would have done so when I was a baby. They wanted me for something; had I stayed, I might have found out what it was." she chose her words carefully, he wasn't going to like what she was about to suggest, but after what had happened, it might be their only option.

The Shadows had only started attacking after Niah's escape; if there were a way she could stop it, she would. If there were a way to keep Fin, Merida, and the others safe, she would do it.

Her hand curled around the locket, and she turned back to him, seeing the caution in his eyes as he too got to his feet, and came to stand close enough that she could feel his breath on her skin.

"I hope you're not suggesting what I think you are."

Niah held his gaze, "And if I were?"

FIN

29

It was madness.

"No." Fin growled without giving her a chance to explain. He'd pieced together enough from her choice of words to know what she was thinking, and it was insane. It was suicide.

"It's not your decision," she hissed, folding her arms over her chest. Fin turned away, dragging his hands through his hair before turning back to her.

"Maybe not, but my input matters." He wanted Niah to make her own decisions, but this? It was too much.

Her eyes flared with blue flame, but the blackness of her iris quickly swallowed it.

"This only started when I left_"

"We don't know that's the reason why." Despite having already thought it multiple times.

Niah scoffed, "Oh yeah? Then tell me why they would start attacking almost straight after I fled?"

"I said no." he ground out through his teeth, struggling to keep his canines contained. Niah showed no such restraint.

"What's the life of one hybrid when all of this could stop?"

It made sense. His duty demanded him to be rational, to be logical. But losing Niah, after she'd already escaped once, he couldn't do it. He knew it might save hundreds, thousands even, and still, he couldn't send her back there.

He didn't care if she hated him for making her stay, but at least she'd be safe. If he were honest, Fin knew that she would find her way to the Shadows if she were determined enough.

"No."

"It's not your_"

"I said no." for a moment, they only glared at each other.

"You said I had a choice," Niah growled through her teeth, "you and Merida said I could leave whenever I want. You've always told me I had a choice, Fin, don't go back on that now."

She was right.

He just couldn't do it.

Not this time.

"What do you think would happen?" he murmured, "If you went back to them, huh? What lies were you planning on spinning?"

Her spine straightened, "That the Furies kidnapped me, and I finally managed to escape."

"And you think they'd believe that? After you'd already fled from their hired thugs?"

"I'd tell whatever lies I'd need to do it."

She meant every word, but he knew there was much more she refused to say aloud, that maybe she hadn't even admitted to herself.

Niah would do whatever it took to end the death, because she knew there was no other way. After all, she knew the Shadows wouldn't stop until she was back in their grasp. Which only begged the question, *why* did they want Niah so desperately?

"We'll find another way." The words tasted like a lie.

Niah snorted a bitter laugh, "I'm all ears. If you can tell me one half-decent plan, I'll stay." When he said nothing, she shook her head, "This is our only option."

"I can't."

At that, her face softened, "They won't kill me, Fin. Whatever they have planned for me, I'll endure_"

"No." he said again, shaking his head.

"If I go back to them, all of this ends."

"You don't know that!"

"Maybe not, but I know that if I sit here and do nothing, that I may as well be killing you all myself."

Fin felt the words like a sledgehammer to the chest. He searched her eyes. Too much. It was too much of a burden to place on one person's shoulders.

Words failed him, unable to speak through the tightness in his throat, he turned for the door, and left her alone. He had no idea where he was going; he only knew he had to get away from her before he said something he'd regret.

This was what the Shadows wanted. Everything they'd done had been a taunt to coax Niah from the Alliance and back into their hands. After what they'd already done, he could only imagine it would get much worse.

And still, he couldn't risk her life for the sake of everyone else, no matter what that said about him in his responsibilities. His stomach twisted at the thought of how many more would perish before this was all over.

For the first time in his life, Fin was torn between his personal feelings, and his duty.

What was the right answer? *Was* there even a right answer? No matter what he chose, he'd be sacrificing either one person, or thousands. Of course, it wasn't his choice to make alone, but he couldn't imagine Merida would give Niah up either. But the other leaders? If they knew about Niah's connection with the Shadows, they wouldn't hesitate to send her back.

Without taking notice of where he was going, Fin found himself in the canteen. Few people were dotted around at the various tables, but his eyes fell on Sai sat on his own, a steaming mug between his hands as he stared down at it.

"Why are you up here all alone?" Fin grumbled, slumping down on one of the stools at the round table.

Sai eyed him for a moment, raising his mug to his lips, "I could ask you the same thing."

"I asked first," Fin sighed, resting his forearms against the table.

"I'm wondering how long we're going to have to wait before we have a real fight," he said in a low, haunting voice. Sai was always relatively cheerful, aside from Dea, who seemed to bounce off the walls half the time; he was the happiest person Fin knew. So, seeing him like this, serious, murderous even, readying himself for battle, shook Fin to his core.

"After tonight, I don't think it will be long," he murmured, running his hands down his face. His gut twisted as the images of all those burnt, terrified faces flashed into his mind. Part of him wondered how long it would take to stop seeing them, but another part didn't want to stop. He wanted to remember them.

Sai eyed him over the rim of his mug, "What's up with you?"

"Niah wants to go to the Shadows."

Sai blinked, his brow furrowing as he put his mug down, "She doesn't want to stand with us?" hurt and betrayal laced his voice.

"No, no, nothing like that. She wants to pretend that we kidnapped her so that they stop attacking."

"It's risky..." Sai trailed off, gazing down at his mug between his hands.

Fin bristled, "Why does it sound like you think it's a good idea?"

"It's not the *worst* idea. Look, Niah wants to do what's right like everyone else here. She's not afraid. If any of us could do something that could help, we would. Niah is the only one we could get into the Shadows, and more than that, she could tear them apart from the inside."

If the Shadows were smart, they'd lock her away in a cell as soon as she returned. Niah would know that, and she was willing to go anyway. A chill crawled up his spine at the thought of what other experiments they'd subject her to. Or would they simply slap a controlling mark on her and use her like Logan?

He swallowed the lump in his throat.

"What if they kill her?"

"What if they kill every single one of us? We're warriors, Fin. This is what we do; we take risks, we live, we die. If I could, I would be the one offering to go. Wouldn't you?" he met Fin's gaze with determination. He was right. If he had the chance to do what Niah suggested, he would go if it meant saving everyone else. But there was no guarantee it would. Even if the Shadows *did* get Niah back, there was no guarantee they would stop the attacks.

"I know you don't want to see her go," Sai muttered, "neither do I, neither would any one of us, but we have a duty, not just to each other, but to the human race. Those piles of bodies could have easily been Fury warriors. So what happens if we all die? Who would protect the humans?"

"They'll use her against us." Fin bit out. "The Shadows will see straight through whatever lies she tells, and they'll control her; what would you do if we had to face Niah on the battlefield?"

At that, Sai was silent.

Fin shook his head, "It doesn't matter_"

"Except that it does," Sai sighed, "it *does* matter. I don't want Niah to go back to them, I don't want any of this, but if this is our only option to save our people..."

The unspoken words hung between them, choking the air from Fin's lungs. He knew he was being selfish, and maybe Sai was right. That's what he was afraid of.

"Come on," Fin sighed, getting to his feet, "we should get some sleep."

The two made their way through the corridors until they heard voices coming from an open door with pink and blue lights shining through the narrow gap.

"Good girl, but you can do more than that," Cassia's voice rang like a melody into the concrete corridor. Fin and Sai stopped outside and peered around the doorframe, hearing the faint crackle of flame inside.

Cassia and Niah sat opposite each other on the floor. Niah's eyes were ablaze with electric blue encircled by the shimmering silver ring. A ball of blue fire danced in her palm, much bigger than the flicker he'd seen when she showed him.

Her mouth pressed into a hard line, a bead of sweat sliding down her temple as she concentrated, her fingers trembling slightly. The flame sputtered before dying to a low ember. Niah gasped, clutching her hand to her chest. Fin almost burst through the door, but Sai caught at his arm, holding him in place.

"Is that all you've got?" Cassia challenged.

Niah's eyes flashed, her mouth twisting into a snarl as she held out her hand again. Her whole arm trembled as she gritted her teeth. Her fingers sparked before a considerable eruption of flame burst from the palm of her hand, vibrant blues of varying shades licked high, scorching the concrete ceiling.

"Excellent," Cassia crooned, "enough now."

Niah didn't stop.

The flame roared hotter, higher, engulfing the ceiling.

"Niah! Enough!" Cassia bellowed.

The flame sputtered and died as Niah's eyes rolled into her head, and she fell to the floor, sweat glistening against her skin.

Sai and Fin rushed into the room, and he scooped her into his arms, shaking her in an attempt to wake her.

"Don't, she'll be fine," Cassia breathed.

"Did you need to push her so hard?" Sai demanded. Cassia looked up slowly, brushing off her brown skirts as she got to her feet, pulling her shawl tighter around her shoulders, her gold bracelets jingling as she moved.

"She asked me to push her. Let her sleep. The more she practises, the more magic she will be able to use before this happens."

Fin got to his feet with Niah in his arms, cradling her against his chest. Just like the last time he'd had her in his arms like that, it was no less unsettling.

Sai kept his eyes on Niah, "Did she say why she wanted you to push her?"

Cassia shrugged, "Just that she needs to be stronger."

Fin and Sai exchanged a glance; there was no mistaking why Niah would want to suddenly be pushed so hard.

He carried her through the corridors, Sai at his side while Cassia went in the opposite direction to her room. Sai opened the door for him when they reached the room shared by the others, but Fin turned to his room and waited for Sai to open the door.

He lay her on the bed, careful not to jostle her, and removed her boots. It took him a minute to realise Sai was leaning against the doorframe.

"It's a good look on you."

Fin snorted, "What is?"

Sai said nothing, only flicked up a brow and closed the door behind him. Fin didn't have the energy to go after him and ask what he meant, and deep down, he already knew.

Fin removed Niah's dagger from her hip and lay it on the nightstand beside her before covering her over with the blanket. Before he turned away, he brushed a loose strand of hair across her face.

"You'll be the death of me," something in his chest ached, and he took a moment to sit on the edge of the bed to make sure she was okay. In reality, he didn't want to leave her alone, but he didn't think she'd want to see him when she woke up.

He watched the way her lips parted, and her lashes fluttered as she dreamt, and he knew, that he would do anything to keep her with them. Whether that meant thousands would die or not, he would do it.

Even if there was a part of him, that hated him for it.

FIN

30

He hated the bunker.

There was no sunlight. No breeze. It constantly felt as though the air could run out at any moment. It was a tomb.

Outside the door, people were beginning to move around.

Fin pushed himself into a sitting position on the creaking, rusted bed and swung his legs over the side, cringing at the coldness of the concrete floor beneath his bare feet.

He hadn't slept much, as well as worrying about Niah; he was concerned about the facility. It had become his home over the years, and the thought that the Shadows could be destroying it twisted his stomach.

He knew Merida wouldn't be faring much better.

After he left Niah in his room, he asked Dea to stay with her. Maybe he was being too overbearing, but he didn't care.

His muscles ached, bones cracking as he stretched before dressing, readying himself for the day, knowing it was going to be very long, and very stressful.

The leaders of the facilities were having a meeting to discuss their findings and try to formulate a plan. If the phone calls between Merida and the other facility leaders were anything to go by, they wouldn't decide for several days. Providing the Elders didn't step in.

Fin hoped they would.

Now more than ever, they needed the guidance of their Elders. There hadn't been a Summit in Fin's lifetime; the last time they were called upon was over a century ago when they discussed what to do about the assassin hunting hybrids across the world.

On his way out the door, Merida was standing outside his room, the door open a crack. She jumped when he tapped her on the shoulder and gestured for her to move aside as he carefully opened the door, trying not to wake the occupants.

Dea was reading one of Niah's books as the dark-haired hybrid slept soundly. Dea looked up as Merida stepped into the room and lowered her head respectfully, not that Merida had ever enforced such formalities.

"What happened?" Merida asked, standing with her hands behind her back. Almost as though she were stopping herself from tucking Niah's hair behind her ear or checking for fever.

"She was practising magic with Cassia and exhausted herself," Dea explained as she got to her feet and stood next to Merida. Dea chewed on her lip, her brow furrowed, and Merida reached out to place a tender hand on her shoulder; Dea met her gaze with dry eyes.

"We will be okay," Merida muttered.

She had always taught him that there was no point in sugar-coating things. Phrases like 'everything will be fine', 'it will all work out', had no room in the Furies. They never knew what the future would hold. Some may die, his heart clenched at the thought, but it was the reality of fighting a never-ending war. They had been fighting this battle for centuries, and would battle it for centuries more.

If something didn't change.

Something *could* change, if only he could put his personal feelings aside.

He and Merida left the room, making their way down the corridor toward the Summit chamber.

"We can get through this," Fin muttered.

"We always do."

"We should get some breakfast first," he said as they reached the canteen.

Merida shook her head, "I've lost my appetite."

"Merida," he warned, giving her a disapproving glare.

"I'm fine. You worry too much."

"Someone has to."

"Stop being such a mother hen," Merida snorted, forcing a smile.

"You're not fine, though." He said through his teeth. Sure enough, her skin was sickly pale, her lips dry and cracked, and dark circles ringed her eyes.

"I'll see Vinaxx when we get back to Perth." She said in a tone that suggested the conversation was over. He raked a hand through his hair, hating that she refused help when she so clearly needed it.

When they arrived, the Summit chamber was packed; everyone was at their assigned seats with a plaque of their name and which facility they were from.

Merida winced, the wind hissing through her teeth as she sat down, her hand instinctively going to her head. Fin frowned, but he knew better than to make a fuss around the other leaders.

Her visits with Vinaxx were becoming more frequent; Fin feared that she didn't have much time left. A thought that was hard to swallow, and harder still to accept.

The meeting room was huge and round, with a circular table in the middle. A globe map hung on one wall; a shining yellow light signalled where each facility was. The opposite wall was filled with screens showing surveillance from each facility. Thankfully, none of them had been attacked.

A thick tension hung in the air as the remaining facility leaders took their seats with their advisors next to them.

At the far wall, above the head table, hung a banner of a longsword, golden and brilliant with angel wings stretched out from behind it and demonic horns curving from the guard. Below, the table curved upward to a low platform with two onyx chairs, swirling decoration around the top, angel wings tucked in at the sides, and demon horns sticking out from where the occupiers' shoulders would be.

They were more like thrones.

Guardians strode in first, each carrying a shining, silver shield with swirling patterns and a spear in their other hand. Their origin and race were a mystery; it was one of few secrets the Elders kept to themselves. The Guardians were closely followed by the Elders.

At their centre, walked the Overseer and the Ambassador, their robes whispering across the floor as they went. A singular Guardian walked forward gracefully and banged his spear on the ground once; everyone rose to their feet and bowed at the hip.

Neither of them so much as glanced at the faces in the room. Lady Overseer's eyes remained forward, golden and pupilless, ringed in silver that marked her as a hybrid. She wore robes of ebony, lined with grey, her hands clasped delicately in front of her.

She took up her spot in her chair, the harsh lights almost bleaching the colour from her radiant, bronze skin. It was only then, that she let her eyes fall on the faces around her.

It was the first time Fin had seen the Elders in person; now that he had, he wanted nothing more than to leave. There was something about the Overseer, in the harshness of her face and her piercing eyes, that spoke to him in caution.

Merida brushed her fingers against his, a reassuring gesture. She'd told him beforehand what to expect of the Elders, but the reality was far beyond his expectations.

Then there was the Lord Ambassador, Ragnar. He was no less intimidating, with icy blue eyes and sandy hair pulled back in a single braid to show off the shaven sides and lines of tattoos that trailed down his neck and disappeared beneath his slate robes.

The stories he'd read of the Elders didn't do them justice, they were undisputed warriors who fought in the last great War. They were voted to lead the hybrids once the War was won, and they had remained in that position of wisdom and power ever since.

Being in their presence was...overwhelming.

"You may sit," Amarah said, her voice sharp as it echoed through the room. Everyone did as instructed as the Elders were handed a small pile of documents.

The only sound was the flick of paper as the Elders scanned the documents. After an unbearably long moment, Amarah sat the papers aside, as did Ragnar, the latter looking considerably more indifferent.

"This is terrible news," Amarah's said, her voice so low that it was barely more than a whisper, "How many casualties?"

"Three hundred and fifty-six," Benjamin said. Amarah's brows arched at the information, and she leaned to mutter something to Ragnar. The icy eyed Ambassador nodded and exhaled slowly, letting the full intensity of his gaze fall on the English leader.

"And we have come into hiding; why?"

"Lord Ambassador, this is merely a temporary measure to re-group and come up with a strategy," Silas said, leader of the American Facility in Savannah.

"I see we still have no reports as to where the Shadows may be hiding?" Ragnar asked, his eyes flicking to a document on the desk.

"No, Lord Ambassador," many voices answered.

"The floor is open; please, put your suggestions forward." Amarah crooned.

Merida rose to her feet, "We're used to attacks, but the Shadows are attacking children, youngsters who have no training, and therefore don't know how to defend themselves. We want to keep them safe, and I would like to propose that the children and youngsters stay here within the bunker to continue their training while the rest of us go back to our facilities and take our stand."

Ragnar's eyes softened a touch as he regarded her thoughtfully.

"Very well, all who agree, please raise your hand," he answered with a nod; many of the other leaders raised their hands, some didn't. "Those who did not agree, explain your reasoning." on the other side of the table, Benjamin rose to his feet.

"Seeing as we were the only facility that was attacked, I have seen the destruction caused by the Shadows. I believe our youngsters are as much a part of this fight as we are and should be treated as such," he announced, "bring them back with us and treat them as the warriors they will be." murmurs ran through the room, some in agreement, most against.

"What use would they be? They would be more a liability than an asset at this moment with little to no training," Merida protested.

"Then, at the least, they will keep the Shadows busy while our warriors cut them down," he snapped, his beady dark eyes glowering at Merida across the table.

"You mean to use them as sacrificial pawns," Merida growled, not a question. Benjamin tilted his chin up in defiance.

"They will have to learn one way or another," he murmured venomously. He and Merida glared at each other across the room. At the sound of Ragnar's fist striking the desk, Merida turned away, bowing her head to the Ambassador.

"The majority vote has it; the children and youngsters will remain safely in the bunker," he announced, a slight smirk playing at the corners of his lips. Benjamin was still on his feet, looking as if he wanted to protest; Ragnar fixed him with an icy glare, and he sat down. No one defied the Elders.

Fin wiped his clammy hands against his thighs as Merida took her seat beside him once again.

"We need to be united. One mind, one army, one heart. Not only do we protect the human world from demonic activity and rogue clans, but we are also stopping the Shadows from taking over. Their army may be halflings, but their leadership is Nephilim; they are the true enemy here," Amarah spoke coldly, glancing at Benjamin for a second.

Benjamin was a well-renowned leader, and had earned his position around the same time as Merida. Since then, both had achieved a tremendous amount of respect from the other leaders. Looking around the room now, Fin could see a clear divide.

"And how, exactly, do you propose we beat them?" Benjamin questioned. Amarah fixed him with a level stare.

"You seem to have an idea of what we should do; please, share it."

Benjamin glanced around the room before rising to his feet, holding his shoulders back and chest puffed out.

"I suggest we launch an attack on the compound. It is the only place we know the Shadows have been." His eyes flicked to Merida; a knowing look lingered in his eyes. Merida kept her expression neutral, giving nothing away, but Fin's heart was pounding.

Did Benjamin know about Niah's connection with the Shadows?

"The reports say the compound is empty. Your scouts reported that." Fin snapped. Benjamin ignored him; as an advisor, Fin didn't hold much sway within the council.

"I have to agree with him," a leader from the Pune facility spoke up, "Why would you have us march on an abandoned compound?"

"Maybe we missed something." Benjamin drawled with a cavalier shrug of his shoulders.

Amarah tilted her head to the side, "Do you have proof?"

"No, Lady Overseer." He said through his teeth.

"Then I see no reason to waste our time on such a pointless endeavour." Amarah dismissed, Benjamin shrank back into his seat, his cheeks turning a bright shade of red. "Does anyone else have any ideas?"

The arguments continued for several hours. In the end, it was decided that everyone would return to their respective facilities, leaving the children in the bunker, and prepare for another wave of attacks. More scouts would be dispatched in an attempt to find the Shadows, but it seemed like a pointless mission.

The Elders advised that a small number of Guardians would be appointed to each facility to boost numbers in case of another attack. Fin didn't see how it would help, but they needed any advantage they could get.

Their once proud Alliance, was reduced to nothing more than sitting ducks.

NIAH

31

Her dreams were of screaming and blue flames.

She woke to sweat glistening on her skin, and the thin sheets tangled around her. Niah was alone in the room and pushed herself up into a sitting position. Her mouth was dry, her throat burning; she snatched the glass of water from the nightstand and drained it.

It took her a moment to realise she wasn't in the shared room with the others, but in Fin's private room. Her stomach twisted as she remembered their argument, and then she'd hunted down Cassia, needing *something* to take her mind off of everything.

Still parched, and needing to get out of the room, Niah left in search of the canteen. It took her far longer than she'd like to find it, but when she did, she grabbed a full pitcher and drank straight from it, ignoring the questioning stares in her direction.

She slumped down in a chair and stared blankly at the pitcher as if it would magically refill itself.

Her mind was a jumble with schemes and lies she could tell to get back to the Shadows. Niah knew they wouldn't believe a single word she said. She knew they would lock her away, experiment on her, maybe even control her. She knew what she'd be walking into, and it didn't matter. If it stopped the attacks, if people stopped dying because of her, she would do it.

The thought startled her at first, how she was willing to risk her free will, maybe even die to protect people she'd only known a couple of short months, but that thought quickly ebbed away, replaced by a warmth that made her heart swell.

Niah knew what she'd be giving up. Her dream of revenge, for the people who had saved her in more ways than she cared to count, she would do it.

She would do it without giving up.

The Shadows wanted her to return to them, so she would, but she would make them regret it before they put that controlling mark on her.

It wasn't a selfless decision; she chose it as much for herself as she did for the others. If she wanted to get to the Shadows, she wouldn't be able to do it if she were with the Furies.

Something wrenched inside her, Fin was so happy when she referred to the Furies as *us*. She finally started to think of her and the Alliance as one and the same, but now, she'd have to separate herself from them.

Niah knew that Fin and Merida would fight to keep her with them, and she had to be prepared to say and do whatever it took to get them to let her go, or force her way out.

The difference between the Furies and the Shadows, was that she didn't *want* to leave them.

"I wondered where you were," a familiar voice sounded above her, snapping her back to reality. Niah looked up to find Talon standing over her with a smile on his lips. He looked different, no longer sporting a three-piece suit, but rather a short-sleeved black t-shirt and blue jeans, his hands in his pockets, and his hair in disarray.

"Funnily enough, I wondered the same thing," she mumbled.

Talon sat down beside her, "I hear you had your first run-in with demons," he said, more of a statement than a question. She nodded, still looking at her hands. "And?"

"And what?"

"How do you feel about it?" he asked, she turned to him then. Why did he care?

"They're demons," she shrugged, "I didn't feel anything." It was the truth. Killing demons was easy, but people? That was a different matter. Logan's lifeless eyes flashed into her mind.

Talon narrowed his eyes, "What is it?"

"How did you manage to infiltrate the compound?" she questioned, meeting his gaze.

"The same way Fin did, no one noticed."

Niah scoffed, "That's it?"

He shrugged, "It was easy enough to slip past the guards." After years of monitoring those very patrols, she knew it wasn't easy to sneak past them. And Fin was only able to get inside because Talon had succeeded first.

"So, what took you so long to get back?"

"I stayed to scout the place and monitored what happened after you left. They caught me that first day, and I managed to escape. But after that, I had to be discreet. Everyone cleared out," he frowned.

"Why didn't you follow them?"

"Because Jeremiah and Katarina showed up, and I wanted to know why they were there." she froze.

Roaring filled her head.

Her voice was little more than a growl, her canines stabbing into her lip, "*How* do you know those names?"

He tilted his head to one side, "They're the ones who raised you, aren't they?"

"They're also dead."

"I assure you, they're not. I'm surprised Merida didn't tell you; I sent her the information in my last report."

She banged her fist against the table; it shuddered before a loud crack snapped the whole thing in two halves.

She stood abruptly, her stool flying out from beneath her as she stalked from the room. Hundreds of eyes watched her as she left.

Niah heard nothing over the pounding in her head, the thundering of her heart as she stalked through the corridor. A hand curled around her arm, and she didn't hesitate to whirl, slamming whoever it was into the wall with her hand fisted in the collar of their shirt.

Talon's eyes were wide, his heart beating loud enough that she could hear it, "Don't *ever* touch me." she snarled, snapping her canines mere inches from his face.

"Niah," he murmured, raising his hands in surrender. Before he could get another word out, she shoved away from him, turning down the corridor.

People parted for her as she moved through the hallways, all staring as she passed by. She didn't care.

It was like a prison in the bunker. Like the walls were closing in on her. Her muscles quivered, sparks flying off her fingers as she struggled to rein in the power that sang with the embers soaring through her body.

Niah stopped taking notice of where she was going. A set of large double doors opened, and a group of smartly dressed men poured from the room holding shields and spears, followed by two figures in thick robes. A man and woman, the woman was beautiful and fierce, the man stern and icy. They glanced at her, the woman's eyes lingering for a moment before she stopped.

"You there," she said, "What are you doing in this part of the bunker?" she asked in a voice that demanded respect; Niah didn't avert her eyes or bow her head; only looked the woman in the eye.

"I got lost," she shrugged. The woman blinked as if she was expecting much more of an answer. Her eyes narrowed into slits beneath the thick black eyeliner surrounding them, but Niah was in no mood to feign respect, so she tilted her chin up, meeting the woman's glare with her own.

"You're either very brave, or very stupid." She murmured.

"Show respect to your Overseer," the man growled.

The Elders.

Niah barely noticed the man had spoken, she was still staring at the woman, at her pupil-less, golden eyes. Something niggled at the back of her mind, something she couldn't quite grasp.

"Apologies," Niah forced, lowering her eyes with a dip of her chin.

The man huffed, but continued down the corridor, while the woman watched Niah for another second before following, escorted by the guards.

Other people filed out of the room, none of them taking much notice of Niah, until Benjamin emerged, his beady eyes raking over her in a way that made her skin crawl.

"You seem familiar," he said, placing a hand on her shoulder; Niah looked up at him with narrowed eyes, her mouth pressed into a firm line.

"I suggest you remove your hand; unless you would like me to break it off?" she growled. A chuckle sounded from behind Benjamin; Fin and Merida appeared in the doorway. Fin with a grin spread across his face.

The leader held his hands up in surrender, a wicked gleam in his eye, "Feisty, I like it."

"Is that really how you regard women who don't want to be touched?" Niah turned on him, tilting her chin up despite the height advantage he had over her. The man's gaze darkened, a chuckle rumbling through his chest before he continued down the hall, the woman at his side hurrying to keep up.

"Did you have to do that?" Merida hissed.

"Did he have to touch me?" Niah retorted; Merida sighed, dragging a hand through her hair as they started down the corridor.

"He is a facility leader_"

"Does that mean I should let him get away with acting like an ass?" Niah inquired.

"No. He did, however, suffer a great loss, maybe be nicer to people?" Merida suggested.

"Yes, well, maybe I'll be nicer when people don't keep things from me." her voice was low, dangerous. Merida paused at that, turning her questioning gaze on her.

"I saw Talon," Niah clarified.

Merida glanced around before taking Niah by the arm and steering her into a room at the end of a long corridor, out of earshot of other people. The room was a small office, a splintering wooden desk with a few chairs and a rusted filing cabinet in one corner.

"I was going to tell you_"

"When?"

She dragged a hand through her hair, "As soon as things settled down."

"We have no idea when that will be," Niah hissed, "they're *alive*."

"Who's alive?" Fin questioned, glancing nervously between the two, angling himself as if he meant to jump between them.

"The people who raised me." she ground out through gritted teeth, barely feeling the sting of her canines slicing into her lower lip.

Fin turned on Merida, "I didn't know_"

"Talon's report came in yesterday afternoon. I was *going* to tell you when you got back from the alert, but...well, you know what happened." Indeed. They returned to a living nightmare.

Niah's chest tightened.

They were alive.

Jeremiah and Katarina, the people she spent *eight* years mourning. The people she had wanted to avenge. And they were alive.

"You should have told me regardless." She spat.

"Niah," Fin warned.

She turned her icy gaze on him, "No. I'm fed up with lies, of being kept in the dark. I am *sick* of people deciding things for me." he flinched as if she had struck him. Merida's eyes glanced between the two.

"What do you mean?"

"I suggested I go back into the Shadows, since we have no other options. Fin said no, as if I had no decision over my own life."

She didn't mean it, not entirely. But she didn't care. Her mind was reeling, and she wasn't thinking rationally.

Merida quietly considered that, "Well, regardless, it's ultimately mine and Fin's decision, and perhaps the remainder of the council."

"What about *my* decision?" Niah glowered, "You promised that I could leave at any time I wished." Merida pinched the bridge of her nose.

"How are you even planning on finding them?"

Niah shrugged, "If they want me that badly, they'll find me, as they already have."

"We don't know_"

"We *do* know that!" Niah seethed, "Look around, Merida, they *know* where I am. The Shadows are toying with us. Tell me my life is worth more than everyone else in this damned bunker."

Merida's eyes were thoughtful, "Niah, whatever the Shadows are planning, we can find a way without sending you back there."

Niah laughed a humourless, bitter laugh.

Her pulse was racing, the fire in her stomach licking higher as smoke curled on her tongue.

"You might be willing to sacrifice everyone else's lives, but I'm not."

At that, Merida flinched.

"When are you going to wake up and realise that *I'm* the reason any of this is happening?" the words kept coming, "When are you going to see that I was better off staying with *them?*"

"Niah," Fin warned.

She ignored him, "I *have* to go. Now more than ever. I need to know the truth, I need to see their faces for myself. I need to know who the hell I've been mourning for years!"

Fin stepped between her and Merida, his eyes as cold and as hard as steel, "Calm. Down." His eyes flicked to her fists at her sides; she followed his gaze to find they were both engulfed in flames. Niah sucked in a sharp breath and staggered back a step; the flames vanished in an instant.

She couldn't stop trembling.

Merida stepped around Fin, but didn't reach for her, "I promise I was going to tell you. I'm sorry I didn't, but there was so much going on, and I couldn't add to everything else." She took a shuddering breath, "I made a vow to protect you. So, yes, as much as my duty demands I do the right thing by the Alliance, if that means sacrificing you, then I refuse."

"Then you're killing everyone here." the words rattled through her.

Merida didn't so much as blink, "Then so be it." Niah couldn't believe what she was hearing. She didn't understand why Merida considered her life more valuable than hundreds of thousands, maybe even millions.

It all could be over, if only they agreed to send her to the Shadows.

"So, that's it?" she muttered, "I'm now *your* prisoner?"

"If that's how you want to look at it," she shrugged, "then fine. You can hate me all you want, but as long as you're safe while doing it, I can live with that."

"Why? Why risk so much for me? What don't I know?"

A shadow crossed Merida's features, "This is what the Shadows want. You know them better than anyone else, you know how they think. Tell me this isn't *exactly* what they want?"

The backs of her eyes stung, how many would die before Merida realised there was no other option?

"You said you trusted me," Merida whispered, Niah met her pleading gaze, "trust me now. Let me keep you safe, let me figure this out and keep everyone else safe too. You want to go because you don't see another option, let me come up with one before we entertain sending you back there, please?"

Niah searched Merida's eyes and saw nothing but agonised worry. She knew what she was risking, but she would do anything to keep *everyone* safe. Niah only feared that it wouldn't be enough. More than that, she wanted to give the leader a chance to prove she could do it. Niah didn't want to leave the Furies, if Merida said she could do it, then didn't she owe her that chance?

She couldn't form an answer, so she turned for the door, and left.

It was too much.

All the lies that had built over the years, the ones she'd finally broken free of, all came crashing down around her. Merida wasn't the Shadows, Niah knew that, but it did nothing to ease the pressure in her chest.

Her anger wasn't for Merida, not really. She understood why she hadn't told her when she received the news. It was the fact that they were alive. That they had *faked* their deaths in front of a nine-year-old girl. She gripped the locket around her throat, and very nearly yanked it off, but even in her rage, she couldn't bring herself to do it.

Pathetic.

Utterly pathetic.

The backs of her eyes burned as anger dissolved into despair and betrayal, and grief. She swallowed past the lump in her throat and willed her heart to harden as she made her way through the corridors.

Niah thought that the Shadows had sacrificed her parents' to ignite her hatred, but it seemed her parents were playing her too. That was, perhaps, the hardest thing to accept.

As she walked the halls, everyone was hurrying around, lugging bags over their shoulders, ushering youngsters to the top floor.

"What's going on?" she asked as she caught Dea rushing from her room with her bag slung over her shoulder.

"We're going back to the facility; the youngsters are staying here," she said before hurrying down the hall.

Niah sat on the edge of the bed, breathing hard. Her head throbbed; there was too much noise. Too many thoughts battling each other.

Her life had always been based on revenge and finding out who killed her parents. That had all changed. She pushed the heels of her hands into her temples, willing the thoughts to quiet.

It was too much.

Too damned much.

The door squealed open, and Gren came into the room, his emerald eyes wary. He sighed as he took her in, and crossed the room to her, sitting on the edge of the bed while being sure to keep a distance between them.

Niah didn't have the energy to tell him to leave her alone, and she found she didn't want him to.

"I heard about your idea," he murmured.

"Are you going to tell me it's a suicide mission as well?"

"No. I understand why you want to do it, I think it's a bad idea, but I understand why."

"So, why did you come?" she asked, glancing up at him.

"We had a deal, remember?" he smiled. Niah cocked her head to one side, remembering their conversation before taking her to train with Cassia. They had agreed to tell each other their stories. Maybe it wasn't the best timing, but she couldn't deny her curiosity to know where he came from.

"Who goes first?"

Gren didn't hesitate, "I don't know who found me when I was a baby; I don't know who raised me for those first couple of years. My first memory is of jewelled forests and fey.

They found me at some point and took care of me, trained me, fed, and clothed me. When I hit my teenage years, I didn't have a goal. I lashed out at them so often, but they withstood it. It wasn't like fey don't have their own short tempers. One day, I was so angry that I attacked them all. I don't remember it, I only remember waking up covered in blood."

He took a trembling breath, turning his eyes to his hands in his lap, "They abandoned me. Not that I blamed them. I felt so guilty for what I did that I went around looking for trouble. I wanted to feel the pain they must have felt. I found other fey villages and attacked; they were much quicker to beat the crap out of me. I thought I was going to die one day, hoped for it even. A vampire was about to snap my neck when Fin stopped it. He took me to the facility in Perth, helped me, and gave me something to focus on, killing demons. He trained me, as did Sai and Merida, even Talon. After that, I had a home and a family, I was luckier than most," he explained, his voice gentle, full of haunting sadness.

"Thank you," she whispered.

He offered her a slight smile, "Your turn."

"I grew up with parents. They trained me from the time I was old enough to walk. Taught me to hunt, how to kill, taught me to hide my emotions and that attachments were for the weak. I was so excited when they told me I was going to start at the academy. And a few weeks before I was due to leave, they were killed.

I went to the academy with nowhere else to go. Promised myself I wouldn't trust a single person again, that I wouldn't get close to anyone because I couldn't bear the pain of losing them like I had my parents'. The night Fin approached me, I heard Nolan talking to someone about harming me, but he didn't want me killed."

A knot loosened in her chest.

"You know the rest."

"I saw Talon earlier, he told me your parents are still alive," Niah stiffened at that, "how do you feel about it?"

She shook her head, "I don't want to talk about it."

"Fair enough, but you could, if you wanted to." he got up from the bed and gazed down at her, "If going to the Shadows is something that must be done, just know that you won't be going alone."

Her voice broke, "Gren..."

He held up a silencing hand, "No more. You're not that lonely girl anymore, you have people that care about you. If you're that determined to go to the Shadows, I won't stop you, but I won't let you go on your own either."

"You'd be defying orders."

"No one said *I* couldn't go to the Shadows." He said without a hint of humour in his voice. Niah didn't know what to say, her chest bloomed with warmth and a blissful ache. There was nothing left to say, and Gren left the room, leaving her to gather her thoughts.

It was good to be back above ground.

Niah inhaled the night air greedily, relishing that some of the tension had left her body. She gazed up at the stars above, the gentle breeze moving her hair from her face, and walked along the beach.

They were alive.

It still didn't seem real. Niah wondered if they found it easy, to raise her for nine years and fake their deaths, leaving her alone, though after reading the book, she already knew she didn't mean anything to them.

She removed the locket from around her throat and held it in her hand, the moonlight glinting off the precious stone. It was the one thing they had given her. The only thing she had left of them besides the book sitting on her desk.

She turned to the ocean, considering whether to throw it into the depths. She decided against it, her fingers curling around the metal. As much as she hated them, as much as she wanted to make them suffer for what they had done; their teachings, their deaths, had made her strong.

The book was her reminder of who she wanted to kill, of what she was. What she had been to Jeremiah and Katarina. A weapon. But the locket? It reminded her that despite everything, despite the hatred lingering beneath her skin, she had made it. She had survived. That she had gotten away from the Shadows, from the poison they tried to feed her.

She was free.

It may not be for long, and in some ways, she was still a prisoner, bound by her hunger for revenge. But it was her choice. It was for herself in which she wanted to end their lives. So, she clasped the locket around her neck and headed back to the facility. To the future she wanted.

And she did not look back.

FIN

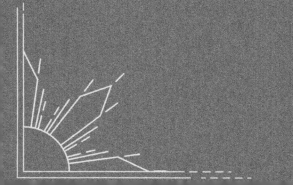

32

The door slamming was like a slap in the face.

He understood why Niah was angry, he'd known Talon had sent a report, but Merida had yet to show him. Was that why? Because she was afraid Fin would tell her? It didn't seem like something Merida would do, and yet, she hadn't told him.

Still, there were other things Merida had yet to tell Niah.

"Why didn't you tell her?" Fin demanded once he was sure Niah was out of earshot.

Merida stared at the door as if she could still see Niah through it, "I will, but right now, we have bigger problems."

Fin didn't want to press the matter, not when Merida looked so frail, but it couldn't be ignored any longer.

"You were stressing about getting her to trust you; how long do you expect that will last if you continue to keep things from her?"

Merida slammed her hand down on the desk, "Damnit, Fin. Don't you think I know that?" her voice broke, "I *know* I need to tell her; I *know* she has the right to know, but..." a tear rolled down her cheek, "just let me enjoy having her with us a little while longer."

"You realise no one would be able to stop her from leaving if she wanted to," he warned. He'd seen the look in her eye, the determination. He'd seen her preparing to fight her way out of somewhere before, that same gleam was in her eyes once again, and he hated that she was preparing to flee from them, but he didn't blame her.

"Do you think she will?"

Fin shrugged, "We're not giving her many reasons to stay."

"Just give me time to find some answers," Merida muttered, her voice strained.

He pressed his lips together, "How do you expect to do that?"

"I don't know, Fin. I don't know how to handle any of this. I don't...we don't even know who the leader of the Shadows is. We don't know where they are, what they're planning, we don't know *anything*. Centuries of searching and we've found nothing, how is that even possible? Most scouts we send to get answers either don't return or come back empty-handed." Tears rolled down her cheeks, Fin crossed the room to her then and took her in his arms. Merida was so strong for everyone else, that she rarely let herself cry.

"We'll figure it out," he sighed, resting his chin on her head.

Her hands tightened at his back, "I don't know what to do."

"I know," he muttered, "I know."

Neither did he.

He was Merida's advisor, and he had no advice to give.

The plan that had been reached in the meeting was hardly a plan at all. *No one* knew what to do.

"Maybe what Niah said isn't such a bad idea," she murmured. Fin pulled away, resisting the growl building in his chest.

"Not that we would send Niah in," she went on, "Not alone anyway."

"Go on," he said, perching himself on the edge of the desk.

Merida dragged a hand through her hair, "Niah was right that the Shadows would find her if she left, all we'd have to do is follow her, and then follow when they came for her."

Everything in Fin's body clenched, but he had to admit, it was the best idea anyone had come up with.

"Anyway," Merida went on, "I can't help feeling like it would be too much like using her."

"All we can do is explain the plan and see what she says, if she doesn't want to do it, then we look for another way."

She was quiet for a long moment, "Benjamin knows something about her, but I don't know what."

"I noticed that too," Fin sighed, "but what could he possibly know? The warriors at the facility know where she came from, but they don't know her story."

Merida shrugged, "Keep an eye on him when we get back_" her eyes rolled into the back of her head, and she fell forward; Fin caught her and lay her across the desk.

"Damnit," he hissed through his teeth as he undid his belt and shoved it between her teeth as she started convulsing. He pulled his phone from his pocket and dialled the familiar number, while pressing her to the desk with his free hand.

"It's happening," he yelled down the phone and snapped it shut. Only magically imbued phones could be used in the bunker, since it was so far below ground.

Merida's spine arched away from the desk, her heart hammering beneath his palm as she jerked and spasmed.

No. Not here. Not now.

No.

Her canines elongated, and her eyes turned black.

No.

Please no.

"Merida," he pleaded, "Focus, come on, stay with me. Come back."

The door banged open, and Vinaxx swept in, his hands already glowing with white light as he pressed them to her chest while Fin held her down.

Her long, claw-like nails dug into the surface of the desk as a feral snarl tore through her throat.

"Fight it, Merida." Vinaxx ground out through his teeth, beads of sweat already glistening on his brow.

Fin knelt beside her head, brushing her hair back from her face as he gripped her hand, "Come on, come back."

Merida's eyes rolled back into her head once again, and her body went limp, her heart slowing to a steady beat. It was only when her pulse returned to normal, that he released the breath he'd been holding, and straightened up to guide Vinaxx into a chair.

"Are you okay?" Fin asked quietly, Vinaxx narrowed his eyes at Merida.

"It's getting harder to suppress it."

"How long?"

"I fear not long enough," Vinaxx frowned.

Fin watched his friend for a moment, worried that if he looked away, she might slip away in her sleep. He couldn't lose her. Fin knew it wouldn't be long, and with everything else going on, that was the scariest realisation of all.

NIAH

33

That night, the facility was near silent.
Even with the extra warriors, no one seemed to want to speak too loudly as if they were worried they would be overheard. No one strayed beyond the barrier, and the patrols were only to go out if there was an alert.

Niah sat in the recreation room with Dea, Sai, and Gren. Fin hadn't yet returned with Merida, not that Niah knew what to say to either of them even if they were back.

Sai and Gren were playing a game on a console, while Dea sat with a sketchpad on her knees, but hadn't touched pencil to paper since they'd sat down. Niah knew how she felt, she'd read the same sentence in her book sixteen times, and still hadn't taken it in.

She gave up, tossing the book on the coffee table, and folded her arms as she slumped back in the chair.

"Well, this looks thrilling," an unfamiliar voice said as two people came to sit with them.

"I don't think anyone is in the laughing mood," Gren murmured.

"Niah, this is Char and Tyson, guys, this is Niah." Dea introduced them. The woman, Char, did a double-take, the colour draining from her face as she dipped her chin, while Tyson offered her a broad smile and draped his arm around Char's shoulders.

"Nice to meet you," was all Niah could muster.

The group fell into an easy, somewhat uncomfortable conversation that Niah didn't feel like paying much attention to. So, she said goodnight to Dea and the others, and went back to her room.

Unable to settle, and with nothing else to do, Niah practised magic. If her argument in the bunker had shown her anything, it was that she needed to work on controlling her power, especially when she was angry.

A blue flame flickered in the palm of her hand, and she focused on changing its size, expanding it into a ball, and letting it shrink to nothing more than an ember. By the time she'd repeated the sequence a dozen times, she was sweating, her heart hammering with the effort.

After that, sleep claimed her.

A blissful, dreamless sleep.

The scream sliced through the dream like a sword.

Niah thought she was trapped in a nightmare. Images of that night flashed through her mind. But the room she found herself in wasn't a small bedroom on a private farm. It was the facility.

Her heart thundered as she pushed herself out of bed, grabbing her dagger from the nightstand as she ran for the door, throwing herself into a sprint as more screams followed.

Not again. Please not again.

She met Dea and Sai along the way. They stormed downstairs; other people had emerged from their rooms and were racing toward the screams, most with weapons drawn.

They followed the screams to the gym. Standing at the centre was a girl with short, espresso coloured hair; she had her hands clasped around her mouth and was staring up, a pool of black blood lay at her feet.

Char.

Niah followed her gaze up to see a body lifelessly hanging from their feet, their arms dangling. Their throat had been sliced, and blood covered his face.

"Shit," Sai cursed.

Tears streaked down Char's face, and she dropped to her knees in the pool of black blood; her breath caught in her throat as silent sobs racked through her body.

Niah stared with wide eyes. It wasn't like hybrids to lose themselves to such emotion. She was once again that little girl clutching her dagger, staring helplessly, surrounded by death and blood.

"Oh...Char no," Dea murmured, kneeling beside the girl, wrapping her arms around her. Char clawed at her chest, leaving long, ugly black lines across her skin, like she was trying to claw her heart out. Was this the bond Fin was talking about?

"Let's get him down," Sai said in a low, dangerous voice.

He leapt up into the rafters and cut the rope; another hybrid caught him as he fell through the air and lay him gently on the ground.

"He was her other half..." Gren said, Niah hadn't even noticed him come to stand next to her. He was gazing at Char, kneeling in the pool of blood next to her, partner? Lover? She had always read in books about girlfriends and boyfriends, spouses, and soulmates, but somehow, none of those terms seemed enough for what she was witnessing.

Char had gouged deep gashes into her chest until Dea and Sai restrained her. Niah wanted to go to her, but her feet remained stuck in place. Just watching felt like a part of her soul was being ripped out. If this were what it was like to lose the person you were meant to be with, then she hoped she would never find it.

"Move," a loud voice boomed, the crowd parted as Merida, Fin, and Vinaxx burst into the room. They pushed their way to the front, their mouths falling open as they gazed at the scene. Merida went to Char, who was still sobbing and screaming while Dea held onto her, trying to get her to stop clawing at her chest.

"Give us some room, everyone; no one else needs to be here." Fin addressed the rest of the room, and slowly, they made their way out, leaving Niah and her small group.

The room fell silent as Vinaxx pulled his dulling hand away from Char's chest. The only way to get her to stop clawing at herself, was to render her unconscious. Niah couldn't tear her eyes away when Dea and Merida carried the hybrid out of the gym.

Vinaxx knelt over Tyson's body, his hands glowing as he worked them over his chest.

There was a piece of paper poking out from Tyson's pocket, and Niah knelt to retrieve it.

Her heart slammed to a halt.

It was a picture of five figures, black-clad with weapons drawn, fighting a pack of *Gilmara* demons. It was them, Niah and the others during the demonic attack.

She flipped the picture over to find a sentence scrawled across the back in swirling letters.

In mortem, nos manere in fide.

In death, we remain in faith.

She read the words over and over until they lost all meaning. Her heart was pounding so loud that she hadn't heard Fin saying her name. The gentle touch of his hand on her shoulder brought her crashing back to the gym.

He took the picture from her and read the words, his brow furrowing. Her stomach churned bitterly, her breathing shallow.

"In death, we remain in faith," she told him, barely able to project the words past the lump in her throat. The breath hitched in his throat, his fingers tightening around the picture. Niah didn't meet his gaze, she couldn't.

Another life lost because she hadn't done as the Shadows wanted.

"This doesn't mean_"

"Enough," Niah pleaded, her voice wavering as she turned away, unable to stomach the weight on her shoulders.

"I can't concentrate in here, too bright. Please, bring him to my study," Vinaxx said quietly; Sai and Gren carried Tyson away, leaving behind the large pool of black blood on the floor.

Niah's stomach twisted, the air turning bitter as she stalked to the edge of the room to grab towels, and went back to clean up the mess. She dropped to her knees and started soaking up the blood with the towels, but no matter how much she scrubbed, a stain remained.

Fin knelt beside her with a bucket of water and cleaning supplies; she didn't even know he'd left. His hand went around her shoulder, tugging gently, but she shrugged him off.

"Niah...Niah, stop for a second," he begged, pulling her back to look at him. She couldn't meet his gaze, only looked down at the blood soaking the towels and her hands.

His fingers tugged at her chin, and she finally met his gaze, "Please don't hate me for not letting you go." His eyes were shimmering silver pools, wide and pleading. She never hated him, she didn't blame him or Merida, she blamed herself.

Niah knew what she had to do, and because she didn't want to leave him or Merida or the others, she let them talk her out of leaving. She let them talk her out of doing the right thing.

"I could never hate you," she whispered. Some of the light returned to his eyes, and he encircled her in his arms. She let him. Niah let herself take comfort in his strength, let it chase away the chill that lingered in her bones.

She pulled away.

Hurt flickered in his eyes, but she wouldn't allow herself to take comfort in his embrace. Not when there was another death hanging over her head, not when, once again, the Shadows had won.

They were slowly, meticulously, wearing the Furies down. Wearing *her* down.

The Shadows could have killed every person in the facility that night. But they didn't. They chose to kill one. A person with that all-consuming bond in place. A bond that made the other try to claw their own heart out.

"You should go and find out what Vinaxx thinks," Niah muttered.

"I don't want to leave you_"

"I'm fine," she breathed, "I'll clean this up and then I'll come to find you."

Fin hesitated, but got to his feet with a sigh, and left the gym. Niah was thankful to be on her own. She finished cleaning, all the while, her skin prickled and heated as her power grew hotter and hotter.

As she knelt on the floor, the bloodied towels gripped in her hands, she couldn't hold the leash any longer.

The towels disintegrated to ash, engulfed in blue flames.

FIN

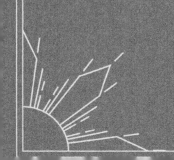

34

He felt numb from the inside out.

His legs were more like led weights as he made his way through the corridors to Vinaxx's office. Gren came to stand beside him when he closed the door and leaned against it, unable to go any further.

He just needed a moment.

Tyson was their friend. He was one of the first to approach Fin when he first arrived, the same for Gren and Sai. Just like that, he was gone, and Char was left behind. Fin hated to think what she might do when she regained consciousness.

"What is it?" Sai asked as he watched Vinaxx waving his hands across Tysons' body where he lay on a stone table.

Vinaxx pulled his dulling hands away, his brow furrowing as he went over to a workstation filled with jars and pots.

"It doesn't feel right...no... not at all," Vinaxx chattered absentmindedly. Fin usually didn't mind the random ramblings that came out of the weaver's mouth, but he was in no mood today.

"What do you mean?" Sai asked, his voice edged. Vinaxx glanced up at him briefly before gazing down at Tyson's blood-covered face.

It was wrong, seeing such a pained, lifeless expression on his face.

Tyson was always laughing, cracking jokes, and doing things others would call crazy, running down the street naked for all to see, jumping from rooftops and scaling buildings, swimming in shark-infested waters. He took advantage of his immortality but was determined to live each day like it was his last.

The memories didn't bother him quite as much as there were no signs of a struggle. No claw marks, no slashes from a blade other than the one across his throat, no bruises, or ripped clothes.

It was as if he hadn't even seen them coming, which he would have. His hearing was a lot sharper than most hybrids, his sense of smell too. No one ever snuck up on him.

Vinaxx shook his head and pressed his fingers to his temples, "I can't...it just doesn't, it isn't right..."

"Just spit it out, please?" Fin sighed, dragging his hands down his face.

"I can't sense anything human on him," Vinaxx mumbled, Gren moved away from the wall to stand over Tyson.

"So?" he muttered; Vinaxx sighed and sat down.

"Tell me, if you're so smart, what are the Shadows? Their species, to be specific."

"They're Nephilim, angel-human hybrids," Sai shrugged.

"Very good, now what species do their armies comprise of?" Vinaxx said with narrowed eyes.

"Halflings, demon-human hybrids..." Sai trailed off.

Fin's heart started to race.

"Very good, now please explain why not sensing human on this body would be odd," Vinaxx muttered. The room fell silent. Not sensing human energy on the body would mean that neither Nephilim nor a halfling killed Tyson.

"So, what is it? Lycanthrope? Fey? What species killed him?" Sai questioned; with so much uncertainty behind the Shadows, there was no ruling out that they *only* had halflings in their army.

Vinaxx's eyes slid to Fin, "Hybrid."

"You think they have hybrids in their army now?" Gren asked, his tone sharper than Fin had heard it in months.

"It's possible, they recruited that new one, Niah, into their ranks when she was just a baby…yes, very possible indeed," he replied, stroking his hairless chin.

"She was also the first we managed to get out of their grasp," Sai murmured.

If it was a hybrid, then maybe it was…

"They could have hundreds, even thousands more hybrids that we don't know about," Gren said.

"If that was the case, then why would they be *killing* lone hybrids across the world rather than abducting them to fight in their army?" Sai murmured.

Fin's mind was reeling.

It couldn't be true.

"More importantly," Gren muttered, turning his icy gaze on Vinaxx once again, "How did they get through the barrier?"

"They didn't."

"What?" Sai baulked. At that, everything else in Fin's mind fell silent. He hadn't even thought about the barrier.

Vinaxx sighed and sat down at the table, "The barriers have been intact. That's why there was no alarm."

"There was no alarm when a pile of bodies were dumped outside either," Gren growled.

"The barrier was taken down by an outside force that night."

"You're in charge of the barriers, Vinaxx; how is this happening?" Fin cut in. Vinaxx slid his eyes to meet his own.

"What, exactly, are you insinuating?"

"We're just trying to figure out how they managed to get through our defences, not once, but *twice*, in the space of two days." Sai sighed, an attempt to calm the rising tension.

Vinaxx stalked over to a desk with multiple screens sat on top, and began tapping at the keyboard, mumbling to himself about stupid hybrids, "Here." he snapped, pointing to one of the screens. The three of them stepped closer and gazed at the numbers and video feed from two days ago. Indeed, Vinaxx wasn't even in the facility when the barriers were taken down.

"So, whoever did this tonight was already inside the facility?" Sai breathed.

"We have to go," Fin muttered. The three of them sprinted to Merida's office, not bothering to knock as they barged through the door. Merida was sat at her desk, Niah sat opposite her. Both were on their feet in an instant, waiting to hear the news.

"They're still here." Fin rasped.

"How." Merida's voice sliced through the room like whiplash.

"Whoever dumped the bodies took the barrier down, they could have snuck in then," Gren said breathlessly.

Merida shook her head, "No one saw anyone though."

"Their attention would have been on the bodies at the front of the facility, there are multiple ways in." Fin reasoned.

"What did Vinaxx say?" Merida's voice was so low that it was barely audible.

"He said there was no human energy on Tyson's body, it was a hybrid," Sai said; Merida stared at him blankly for a moment.

"Is he sure?"

"You're welcome to ask him yourself, but that's what he said. He's positive," Sai replied. Her fist came down hard on the surface of the desk, a long crack running along the glass pane. He didn't miss the way the skin rippled on the back of her hand, as if claws lurked beneath, fighting to come out.

"There's something else," Fin muttered; Merida's gaze was icy when she looked up, "there were no signs of a struggle."

Her eyes narrowed, "They could have caught him by surprise..." her voice trailed off as she realised it was next to impossible.

"He wasn't expecting the blow," Niah murmured, turning her eyes on Merida.

"Char," Merida breathed, "Char was already in the room when everyone arrived. If he didn't fight back, then it's because he wasn't expecting it. It was Char...it must be," she explained as she got to her feet and began pacing around the room.

"Where is she now?" Merida growled.

"Weren't you with her?" Sai asked.

"She's with Dea," she murmured. A chill crawled up his spine; none of them hesitated before storming through the facility. They didn't bother even to take the stairs, just threw themselves over the railing to the foyer below.

"Niah, Fin, search the facility, if it isn't Char, then the killer is still here. Be discreet, don't spook them." Merida ordered.

Fin's heart slammed against his ribs, but she was right, the killer could have been anyone.

FIN

35

There was only ringing in his ears.

Fin and Niah searched the entire ground floor of the facility and found no one. Only after checking the necks of those they came across, did they explain what was happening, and recruited them into helping them search.

By the time they'd searched the entire facility, everyone had been checked for marks, which ruled out any of them being controlled to kill Tyson, but they hadn't found an intruder either.

Which left Char.

"Find Merida," Niah panted when they stopped in the foyer, "I'm going to take a group and scout the surrounding area in case they heard us and fled."

"Good idea," he took hold of her arm before she could turn away, her eyes met his own, and for a moment, he took comfort in their darkness, "Be careful."

Her hand splayed across his chest, sparks zapped through him at the touch. It was an effort not to pull her against him, but she said; "You too." And then she was gone, shouting orders to other warriors as she went.

He hadn't expected them to listen at first, but the tone she used left no room for argument. The tone of not an advisor or leader, but a commander. His chest swelled with pride before he snapped himself back to reality and went in search of Merida and the others.

Except what he found in the infirmary, wasn't at all what he expected.

Char was standing, tears streaming down her cheeks, her entire body quivering as she held a dagger, poised for anyone that came near.

Gren and Sai stood between Dea and Merida, and Char, ready to grab her, but Fin didn't want to frighten her any more than need be.

"What happened?" he asked, striding toward Dea when he noticed black blood trickling down her arm.

"She disarmed me when she heard you all think she killed Tyson," Dea explained, letting Fin examine her arm. It took longer to heal, but the blade she'd been cut with was *Ruclite*, a demon-killing metal.

Fin turned to Char, stepping around Gren and Sai as he crept toward the frightened hybrid. Char held the blade up, her face scrunched as she continued to sob.

"Tell me it's not true," she pleaded.

Fin's heart wrenched, "It's not your fault." He held his hands up and gestured to the blade, "No one is going to hurt you, I promise."

Char's eyes flicked to Gren and Sai behind him, "They would."

"They won't," he said, his voice firmer, "You know me, you know I wouldn't break a promise."

After a moment, the blade clattered to the floor, and Char sagged, dropping to her knees. Fin went to her, kicking the dagger across the floor as he pulled her against him. Merida was beside them then, brushing Char's hair away from the back of her neck.

A solid, black circle was at the base of her skull, hidden by her thick hair. It was short enough that she couldn't pull it up entirely, so when she did tie her hair back, there would be enough left down to keep it hidden. Tyson wouldn't have noticed either, even now, as they were looking for it, through the darkness and thickness of her hair, it was difficult to see.

It was the same mark that had been on Logan, and like him, it didn't appear to affect him all the time. It was as if the Shadows could turn it on and off like a switch.

Char stiffened, her nails digging into Fin's arms as a scream tore through her body. She scratched at the back of her neck, at the mark that now had black lines spreading down her neck and arms.

"What the Hell is this?" Merida breathed.

The air caught in Fin's throat, "The Shadows are killing her."

"But that didn't happen to Logan," Gren said, coming to stand over them.

"Logan wasn't a hybrid, he was a halfling injected with Nephilim blood; maybe it affects each species differently," Fin reasoned.

Char screamed again, "I'll go and get Cassia and Vinaxx," Sai said, running for the door.

"Help me get her onto the bed," Fin said through his teeth as he struggled to keep Char from clawing her skin away. Gren helped him get her onto a bed and held her down. Merida tried to soothe the poor girl as much as possible, but Char wouldn't stop screaming.

"It hurts," she whimpered, "it *hurts.*"

"I know, I know, Sweetheart, it's okay, I'm here, I'm here," Merida crooned, holding Char's hand, stroking her hair away from her face.

A minute later, the doors swung open, and in swept Cassia and Vinaxx, Sai leading them to the bed.

"She's marked, the Shadows are killing her," Fin filled them in as their hands glowed and went to Char's head and chest. The weavers' were silent, and exchanged a knowing, mournful glance between them.

"Vinaxx, remove it," Fin said through his teeth.

The weaver instantly placed his hand over the back of Char's neck; white light blazed before Vinaxx jerked back as if he'd been burned, "I don't have the power."

"What?" Fin barked, "But you removed Niah's."

"Yes, but they were different marks. Niah's was far older. And this is stronger than any other mark I've witnessed." All his jittering was gone, replaced by a sharp focus Fin rarely saw.

"What if we combined our power?" Cassia suggested. Vinaxx held her gaze and nodded.

Fin and Gren flipped Char onto her front and held her down as Vinaxx and Cassia pressed their hands to the back of her neck. They gripped each other's shoulders, pink and white light flared. A bead of sweat trickled down Vinaxx's temple, and they both pulled away, panting. Vinaxx met Fin's questioning gaze, an apology shining in his colourless eyes.

"If it's more power you need, why not grab some more spell weavers?" Sai asked through his teeth. Fin and Gren struggled to hold Char down as she screamed and thrashed.

Cassia and Vinaxx glanced at each other, a knowing look, before Cassia turned to them and muttered, "There are no more here."

"What?" Merida growled.

"After the Summit, Morena called all spell weavers back to The Cross, leaving only the ones in charge of healing and barriers," Cassia explained, her voice solemn.

"Why was I not informed?" Merida's voice rose, a flash of teeth in the harsh lights of the infirmary. Fin willed her not to lose control. Vinaxx gave her a wary glance, feeling it too.

"I...I don't know," Cassia's breath caught in her throat as a tear slid down her cheek, not because Merida was angry, but because there was nothing they could do to save Char.

"Shit. *Shit.*" Merida growled, turning around. It was rare she ever cursed or lost her temper. Fin gestured to Sai to take over his place, and went to her side to take her arm; if she lost control, there was no going back.

"If you have questions for her, ask now," Cassia breathed, sweat beading on her forehead. There was no point. Char wouldn't know anything, just as Logan hadn't.

Sai asked, "Do you remember anything, anything at all about how you got that mark?" his eyes told Fin that even he thought it was pointless to ask, but he would try anyway. Char jerked, her eyes watery as they met his.

"I...no...there was a patrol weeks ago...I," another scream, "I fell and..."

her lips clamped together as she tried to swallow another shriek.

"I remember that," Fin murmured, "their squad came back after fighting a pack of *Messenger* demons. Char was unconscious after falling through a rotten floor. No one thought anything of it, but now that I think about it, a short fall like that wouldn't render a hybrid unconscious. They could have gotten to her then."

Another scream tore through the room.

"Can't you take the pain away?" Gren pleaded.

"I wish we could. It's taking all that we have just to keep her heart beating," Cassia panted through her teeth; the lines stretching from the mark inched further down Char's arms, and up her neck to her cheeks.

The doors banged open, and Niah stormed into the infirmary, her eyes dark. She surveyed the room, her eyes sliding to Char thrashing on the bed under Sai and Gren's grip. She looked at each person in the room, at Gren and Sai panting as they held Char, at Dea sobbing in Merida's arms. And finally, they fell on Fin.

The darkness of her eyes seemed to swallow the light as she turned her gaze to Vinaxx and Cassia.

"Can I do anything?" she murmured.

Cassia's eyes widened, "Of course, we have another spell weaver."

Vinaxx stiffened.

"Will it be enough?" Fin asked.

"There's only one way to find out. Place a hand on each of our shoulders; imagine your power flowing into us." Cassia breathed, her hands now shaking with the effort of keeping Char alive. Vinaxx looked like he'd barely broken a sweat, but he was much older than Cassia, and far more experienced.

Niah did as instructed, closing her eyes; the blue glow from within shined through her lids as her hands blazed with light where they rested on their shoulders.

"Good, good! Keep going, more if you can," Cassia encouraged. Niah's lips pressed together, the glow around her hands brightening.

"What the..." Sai trailed off; Fin followed his gaze.

The black lines receded slightly. It lasted only a second before they surged forward once again. Char thrashed against the bed, her mouth hanging open in a silent scream.

The lines were spreading faster, despite the efforts from Cassia, Vinaxx, and Niah. They all squeezed their eyes closed, mouths twisting into firm lines as they concentrated. Niah's eyes flew open, blazing with velocity blue fire.

The blue swallowed the entirety of her eyes, blazing as she took a sharp breath, and light exploded around the room. Fin shielded his eyes. A terrible scream ripped through Char's body at the exact moment Cassia cried out as if in pain.

The sheer power radiating throughout the room ground against his bones, his veins, pulsing through his body as if it were trying to soothe some burning ache inside him. A power that spoke of protection and safety, and yet darkness lingered beneath the surface of it, a prowling shadow lying in wait.

The light dimmed, and that pulsing power vanished.

Char flopped onto the bed, the black lines had vanished. Sai checked the back of her neck, the mark was gone too. He and Gren rolled Char onto her back and stepped away, watching her chest rise and fall steadily.

She was alive.

Cassia's hands fell to her sides, Vinaxx and Niah steadied her, helping her to the bed next to Char's.

"What just happened?" Dea muttered. Fin shook his head; he didn't have an answer. How could he? Char was dying; they had all resigned themselves to the fact there was nothing they could do. Yet there she was, unconscious, but alive.

"Cassia, I'm so sorry," Niah panted, sweat shining on her skin. Her hands were trembling, her entire body was trembling. Sai and Gren came to stand at Fin's side, both staring, unable to take their eyes off Niah. She swayed on her feet, but Vinaxx was there to steady her, his eyes wary as he watched her.

"My child...you saved her life," Cassia whispered.

Fin wanted to go to her, to carry her away, but he stopped himself. Niah was not someone he needed to take care of, to rush to whenever she was weakened. She was the strongest person he knew. Gone was the vengeful girl he brought back from England; a warrior had taken her place.

She didn't need protection.

His chest tingled slightly. He didn't care if she never felt anything for him. It didn't matter if all he ever got from her was friendship. It was enough. All he wanted was to stand at her side, to fight beside her, to have her back when she needed it, and be there when she fell.

It would be enough.

Fin may not understand the feelings that kept him awake at night, wondering whether she was okay. Or the feelings that had the memories of their kiss replaying in his mind on loop, but it didn't matter. It didn't matter that he didn't understand it, because there was nothing to understand. He felt something for her, felt it in every fibre of his being, and he didn't care if she never felt the same.

As long as he got to walk whatever path she chose beside her, then it would be enough.

Hybrids didn't feel love.

But he didn't care.

NIAH

36

A wave of exhaustion crashed through her.
Her lids grew heavy, her muscles ached, even her bones ached.
Her legs trembled as they struggled to support her weight, but by some miracle, she stayed upright.

She'd heard Cassia's cry, but was unable to stop the flow of magic. It poured from her without a second thought, as if it had a mind of its own. From what she knew of magic, it was something that you had to use regularly, exercise like a muscle to be able to use more and more of it.

Niah had only received two lessons, but Cassia had explained that magic in itself is infinite. It will never run out and will constantly flow through their veins; only the wielder stops the flow when their mind and bodies cannot handle the output of that power.

"Stop fretting; I'm fine," Cassia murmured, waving away Niah's concern.

"I will take care of her," Vinaxx assured her, leading Cassia down the long line of beds and out of the infirmary.

"All of you go and rest. I'll stay with Char," Merida said.

Fin moved to her side, "I'll stay with you."

She opened her mouth as if to protest, but one silencing glare from

Fin had her closing it again and sitting down on the edge of the bed next to Char's.

Dea moved around the bed and took hold of Niah's hand, leading her from the infirmary. Niah didn't have the strength nor energy to protest.

The base of her skull throbbed. Her nerve endings felt as though they were sizzling from overuse. Her vision turned blurry, her mind swimming as she stumbled, and Dea lunged to catch her.

"Here, lean on me," she said gently. Niah did just that, unable to shake the dizziness from her head as Dea helped her up the stairs. She had overexerted herself before and passed out immediately in the bunker, but this time was different; she had a goal to make sure Char was okay. Now that she knew she was, her body wanted a rest.

Her vision blackened before they reached her room.

Her room was dark when she finally opened her eyes. How long had it been?

The thin curtains blew in the gentle breeze floating in through the open balcony door. Niah's head pounded, and she winced when she tried to sit up, desperately wanting a drink to soothe the burning in her throat.

"Are you okay?" a familiar voice whispered; she turned to see Dea gazing up at her sleepily.

"Thirsty," she choked out. Dea was on her feet in an instant, Niah hadn't meant for Dea to get her a drink, but there was no stopping her. She returned from the bathroom a moment later with a glass of water, and Niah didn't hesitate to drain the whole thing. Dea refilled the glass another two times before her throat was wetted enough to talk properly.

"How long was I out?"

Dea shrugged, "Couple of hours." Not as bad as she feared then.

"Char and Cassia?"

"They're both asleep. I went to check on them after putting you to bed."

Niah gawped, "You carried me up here alone?"

"I can lift a car; you're no problem," she said pointedly.

"Will Char be okay?" Niah asked. Dea huffed a sigh and dragged a hand through her hair.

"I don't know."

"I can't imagine what it was like," Niah whispered, "waking up and being told you were the reason the second half of your heart was dead, that you killed them."

Dea's face fell solemn, "It's not just losing someone you care for most in the world, it's like losing your heart. You saw how Char reacted to Tyson's death; that was real, you literally want to claw your heart out."

"Have you ever felt it?" Niah asked.

She shook her head, "No. It's extremely rare, and many hybrids don't even want to find their one. It's beyond horrific to lose that person. We all enjoy our way of life without that rare occurrence, we do what we want with who we want, and there's no weirdness about it," she shrugged.

Niah remembered what Fin had said about the bond, that it was both a blessing and a curse. After witnessing how Char acted when she found Tyson, she could see why people would think that way.

"I've read so many books humans have written, they describe love as this amazing thing, they also describe things like jealousy, relationships, insecurities, cheating, and other things like that. So I was...relieved, when Fin told me hybrids don't love the way humans do. But we do feel *something*, don't we?" she chewed on her lip. Dea gave her a knowing look but smiled and twisted a lock of her snowy hair around her finger.

"It may not be love, or maybe it is, who's to say? We feel what we feel; who cares about labels?" there was a gleam in her bright blue eyes as if she could see the very feelings she spoke about buried deep inside Niah. The feelings she hadn't acknowledged since the night Fin had kissed her.

"Is there a reason why we don't feel as humans do?"

Dea smiled, "Because we're not human. We may look human, but it only runs skin deep. Love is a human concept. Emotions themselves aren't exclusive to humanity, but love?" she shrugged, "Don't get too hung up on it. Humans can say they've loved someone for years, and still not know the meaning of the word."

Niah leaned back against the pillows and stared up at the ceiling. So, love was just a word? A label for whatever someone felt inside? If anything, it helped her understand a little more.

"I hope I find the second half of my heart," Dea whispered wistfully; Niah turned to her then.

"Why?"

Dea was quiet for a moment, a smile curving her lips, "I think it would be magical."

"What about the risks?"

"We take risks every day. I like to think I will find that one day. I hope for it all the time," she whispered. Niah leant forward and hugged her. Dea stiffened a little before her arms went around Niah. After the night, the last few days, Niah needed a hug. And unlike Fin, she didn't feel guilty for seeking comfort in Dea's arms.

"I believe you will find it one day too," her friend whispered into her hair. Niah pulled back and looked at her curiously.

"What makes you say that?"

"I just have a feeling," she smiled. Niah was quiet for a long moment.

"How do you know when you've found it?"

"I asked Char that once; she said it was like the world was suddenly full of vibrant colours. Almost like she was seeing everything through new eyes, like she hadn't realised she was missing something. She said she knew his name before he even uttered a word to her, like every nerve came alive when he looked at her, and that was that." Dea explained with a tentative smile, her eyes drifting into the memory.

"I don't think I could handle it if I lost that person."

"Maybe not, but I know you would keep fighting to the end," she smiled gently, Niah said nothing.

The feeling she had shoved down hummed as if sensing her will weakening.

The following morning was madness.

Benjamin arrived before dawn after spending the first night after the Summit making sure his other warriors were settled in the Paris facility and, no doubt, to remind them which leader they reported to. Helena had remained in Perth with most of Benjamin's warriors, who offered no help the night before when searching for the intruder.

Of course, it turned out there never *was* an intruder, but she wouldn't have known that.

Tensions were running high.

People were worried about further attacks, and everyone in the facility had been checked for marks. Thankfully, there were none. However, Char was still being kept under scrutiny, mainly by Benjamin. She had awoken during the night and was on her feet, but that didn't stop Benjamin from having his warriors follow her.

Niah and Dea made their way down the corridor, meeting Gren and Sai along the way, who had also received Merida's summons. Already, muffled, raised voices wafted down the hall, and both leaders barked their permission to enter when Sai knocked on the door.

Dea closed the door behind them. Fin stood at Merida's side, shoulders squared, hands behind his back with his chin raised, looking down his nose at Benjamin. The four of them took the same stance and bowed their heads to Merida out of respect.

"Why have you summoned these people?" Benjamin snapped, sparing only a glance in their direction before turning his beady eyes back on Merida.

"Because I would like their opinions."

"You already have an advisor, though I do question his *advice*." Fin remained unaffected, but all four of them stiffened, a growl slipping from between Sai and Niah's lips. Helena glared at them; Sai merely bared his elongated canines.

"Keep your snarky remarks to yourself." Merida snapped, her eyes blazing with venom.

"Fine. But it doesn't matter how many opinions you get; the vote has been cast."

"What vote?" Gren demanded.

Merida sighed and pinched the bridge of her nose, "Benjamin called a vote with the other facility leaders this morning to launch an attack on the compound in England."

"The compound is empty." Niah ground out through her teeth.

Benjamin didn't so much as glance at her as he said, "Not anymore." she paused at that.

Her blood turned to ice in her veins.

"My scouts sent a report an hour ago detecting movement within the walls."

"It could be kids that have snuck inside," Sai suggested.

"No, the compound is cloaked," Niah muttered. In all her years there, she'd never once heard of a human getting close.

"It could be a trap." Fin warned, not bothering to check his tone.

"Watch your mouth when you speak_" Helena spat.

"Enough." Merida cut her off with a glare.

"The other facility leaders approved this?" Dea questioned.

Merida sighed, "The majority did, but there is a catch." No one spoke as they waited for her to continue, "It is only to be the warriors in *this* facility to go."

"Why?" the three beside her spoke at once.

"Because the warriors here are more than enough. My scouts reported barely a hundred people within the compound."

"The plan is to capture a dozen prisoners for information, and kill the rest." Helena clarified.

There was nothing but roaring in Niah's head.

It was a chance.

A slim one, but a chance nonetheless that Nolan and Karliah might be there, maybe even Jeremiah and Katarina. It was a chance she couldn't pass up.

"I think we should do it." the words were out before she could stop them. All eyes turned to her. Merida closed her eyes briefly, and when she opened them, there was nothing but understanding there.

"At least one of your warriors has some sense," Benjamin smirked.

"This is not for you," Niah growled, his eyes snapped to her at the tone, the insult, "This is for Logan, for Tyson and Char. This is for all those bodies dumped on our doorstep. This is for *me*."

His eyes narrowed, and he whirled on Merida, "What is this?" Merida drummed her fingers on the desk and met his hateful gaze.

"Niah is a survivor of the Shadows."

"Oh?"

"That is all you need to know." Fin's words were laced with warning, low and dangerous.

"I think not, *boy*. What do you mean a survivor?"

Merida met Niah's gaze and gave a subtle nod, "The Shadows raised me." Benjamin's head swivelled to her, "They trained me and used me. They lied so I would bend to their will."

He whirled on Merida once again, "And you let her into your facility? For all we know, she could be the one behind the attack last night; she could have marked that poor girl as a cover-up."

A series of growls rumbled through the room.

Merida let out an icy laugh, "Enough, Benjamin. Niah's a kitten when you get to know her." the words were a taunt, Benjamin bristled and opened his mouth to throw more insults, but Fin stepped forward.

"You have your army, Benjamin. When do we leave?"

The leader turned a brilliant shade of red, his hands curling into fists at his sides, "Fifteen minutes." With that, he and Helena stalked from the room.

It was happening, finally.

"All of you, be careful today. Unfortunately, I have to stay here and watch over the facility, but please, come back alive. And if anything goes wrong, get as many as you can back safely." There was no denying the fear that laced her voice. No shaking the terror in her eyes as her hands trembled.

"We'll be okay," Niah assured her, already feeling her blood soaring from the anticipation of the impending battle. Merida held her gaze.

"I know this is personal for you, but whatever you do, use your head. Do not lose yourself to revenge." The words struck too close to home. She knew, they all knew why she wanted to go, and were all prepared to follow her into that battle without an argument. Guilt roiled in the pit of her stomach.

If anything happened to any of them because of her, she didn't know what she'd do with herself.

"Dea, take her to the armoury for her armour. Be safe, everyone."

"Until my last breath." They all muttered back.

NIAH

37

The leathers fit like a glove.

A full suit zipped up the back with extra padding down the front, hips, thighs, shoulders, and upper arms; it moulded to her body, having been slightly too big when she put it on, now felt as though it were made for her. It was as black as night, made from *Shiasium*, which Cassia had explained was demon hide.

Niah laced her boots up the front of her shins to her knees and fixed *Ruclite* plates to various parts of her body. A breastplate across her torso hung over her shoulders and spread down her spine, shoulder plates, and vambraces around her forearms.

Ruclite was the metal they used for their weapons, gleaming and black with a slight purple tint. The plates moulded to her body as the suit had. Apparently, the metal had to be treated a different way to get it to do that.

A demon-killing metal, three times as strong as tungsten.

With her swords strapped across her back, a pistol around each thigh, and an assortment of knives hidden on her person, Niah was practically glowing with adrenaline.

The others were ready. There wasn't an ounce of fear in any of their eyes, a wariness in Fin's, but not fear.

By the time they emerged from the armoury, the portals were open, and warriors were already filing through. Cassia and Vinaxx held open the portals, hurrying people through. Cassia wore leathers as she would come through with them to open a portal when the battle was done and tend to the wounded.

"I'm sorry," Niah murmured as they waited in the foyer for their turn to go through the portals. They all turned to her, "I shouldn't have forced this on you."

"You didn't," Fin said sharply, "Benjamin did. Whether you had said anything or not, the decision had been made."

"Why were we brought in then?" Sai questioned.

Fin sighed, "Because Merida wanted to see how we all felt about it, and to give us that final order at the end. As soon as things go wrong, which they will, we're to pull back."

"Benjamin's leading the assault, he won't let us," Gren countered.

"Maybe not, but our warriors will come with us."

"We can't just leave our people there," Dea shook her head.

"No, and we'll try to get as many of them as we can back through the portal, but if they want to stay, then we can't stop them. So we'll leave a portal open for anyone who changes their mind." He explained.

A sound plan.

Niah only had to glimpse at the determination in their eyes to know it would be pointless in trying to convince them to stay. But when things went wrong, she could slip away during the chaos while they tried to get everyone to safety. Maybe it would work, maybe it wouldn't, but she had to try.

They stepped through the portal when it was their turn, colours exploding around them, quickly dissipating as they stepped out onto the large grass fields surrounding the compound with the forest at their backs.

It was dusk. The sky washed of colour, everything bathed in the same blue-grey before the moon rose. Dense clouds rolled overhead as a thick fog crawled in from the woods that skirted the open space.

The compound loomed up in front of them. It was exactly how it appeared in her nightmares; the high stone and iron walls and the thin glass windows. The coldness surrounding the entire building, not physical cold, but something sinister, seeped into her bones and sent a shiver crawling up her spine.

Fingers brushed her own, and she looked up to see Fin at her side, his eyes wild, but gentle. Her body warmed, electricity sparking where his skin grazed hers. At least she would be able to fight beside him, even if only for a short while.

Benjamin stood with Helena at his side, both in armour. Except Benjamin wore a black helmet with curling horns sprouting from the top, the face was mostly open apart from a nose guard running down the middle and cheek pieces at the sides. He cast a look toward Fin, a slow smirk spreading across his lips.

"Warriors! Today we get revenge on those who have harmed us. Are you with me?" the leader bellowed, followed by hoots and cries as warriors raised their weapons to the skies.

Niah looked to the compound. She had expected to see some form of life, but there was nothing. The windows were dark, no light emanating from within.

Everyone fell silent.

There was no sound. Not even the wind rustling the trees. She shifted on her feet and glanced at Fin, but he was watching the skies as if he could see something in the clouds.

"We march!" Benjamin roared; his warriors surged after him.

Fin raised his arm, halting his warriors, they glanced at one another in confusion, but no one dared move. Benjamin's warriors followed him at a sprint across the field toward the compound.

"Benjamin, stop!" Fin's shout was swallowed by an ear-splitting howl that tore through the sky as something bright and burning shot through the clouds, leaving a trail of amethyst smoke.

No one moved or spoke for the longest of times. Benjamin was kneeling, holding his hands over his ears. He staggered to his feet, searching the sky, and when he found nothing, he urged his warriors to continue.

Niah searched the trees where the thing that slashed through the sky had fallen. She heard nothing but the thundering of her heart. Until their world fell apart.

A loud crack sliced through the air, the ground rumbled, groaning as it tore apart. Trees from the direction of where the mysterious meteor fell, began to fall over, no, not over, but down.

The ground opened into an enormous rift that worked its way across the field in front of them, splitting it into two halves, Benjamin's warriors on one side, Fin's on the other. Benjamin froze as he watched the ground fall away, before spurring his warriors through the compound gates.

"It's a trap. We have to stop_" Niah was cut off by a loud shriek radiating from the rift separating them from the compound.

No one dared get too close as shrieks, growls, clicks, and roars echoed up from deep within that rift.

A black, taloned hand with three grotesquely long fingers and inflamed joints gripped the edge of the rift. It hissed as it hauled itself over the lip of the crack.

A *Sarata* demon.

Its body was long and painfully thin, bones sticking out at odd angles, its head audibly snapping as it glanced around the field at the warriors standing before it, except there were no eyes for it to see. Only a gaping mouth filled with rows upon rows of teeth. Its skin sagged and hung loosely like black leather as it raised its ugly head and sniffed at the air.

The beast reared back, holding its thin arms out to the side, and let out a scream. Niah winced, resisting the urge to cover her ears as her blood hammered with adrenaline, and her canines lengthened.

More screams resonated from the crack as demons poured out one after another. *Tachra* demons took to the skies, long scaly creatures with beady red eyes and leathery, bat-like wings, with a long, slashing tail with a bone blade at the end.

They were creatures born straight out of a nightmare.

They would swoop down and snatch up a warrior before dropping them from a great height. Yet, even with the threat of the demons before them, no one baulked, no one flinched. Instead, growls tore from the throats of the warriors around her as they readied their blades, and then they were moving.

On the other side of the crack, Benjamin's warriors were being attacked from both sides. Shadows had begun pouring out from the compound, dressed in shining silver and gold armour, glittering swords in hand.

Within seconds, it was a massacre.

"We have to get everyone back!" Dea shouted, slamming her spear into the side of a demon.

"We can't leave these demons here, or they'll spread and attack humans," Fin argued. If they knew they would be facing an entire horde of demons, they would have brought more warriors. But this, no one expected this.

A loud screech cut through the air from behind her. A *Tachra* demon swooped down and clutched Dea in its talons, lashing out with its sharp tail that prevented anyone from getting close.

Niah sprinted after it, firing bullets aimed for its wings.

Dea thrashed in its grip but managed to pull a pistol from her thigh and shot it multiple times in the chest. The beast hissed and dropped her, and she plummeted toward the earth, landing neatly on her feet in a crouch; the demon fell a few feet away, and did not get up.

Dea turned to them with a smile. Niah's heart slammed, but she grinned at the snowy-haired warrior, and they took off, slashing their way through the demons one after another.

The sound of battle rose into the air, swords clanging, screams of dying demons and hybrids, the smell of blood and rot hung around them, making it difficult to rely on their senses.

"They're going to keep coming, we have to close the rift!" Sai shouted as he dispatched a *Tachra* demon as it tried to grab him off his feet.

"How?" Dea snapped, twirling on the balls of her feet, striking multiple demons as she went.

Benjamin's warriors had managed to push the Shadows back and were now inside the compound grounds. Bodies lay on the ground both in front and behind them; many were his own warriors.

It wouldn't be long before they were all dead.

"Where the first demon landed that opened it, through the trees," Fin breathed, slashing his sword through a *Sarata* demon. It collapsed in a heap, bones sticking out at unnatural angles. "Gren, you're in command. Niah, with me," he shouted before darting through the chaos.

Niah and Fin raced across the grass, quickly dispatching any demons that crossed their path.

They broke through the line of trees, following the rift as it grew narrower until the gap was too small for demons to crawl through.

At the end of the rift, where it narrowed into a fine point, sat a short blade buried in the ground. The whole sword was bright and vibrant, the colour of amethyst. A dragon decorated the guard, and purple flames licked up the blade.

It wasn't a demon that opened the rift at all.

Niah scanned the trees, the sword must have been put there by *someone,* but there wasn't so much as a whisper of movement. The hairs on the back of her neck rose. Something must be out there.

Niah reached out to grasp the hilt of the sword, but Fin grabbed her arm, stopping her, "It's too easy," he muttered as he too searched the trees for signs of life.

Hesitantly, he reached for the sword. His fingers barely grazed the hilt when a roar cut through the trees, followed by the boom of footsteps quickly approaching. Trees swayed violently, some collapsing under the force.

Niah and Fin readied themselves as a horse and rider emerged from the shadows.

The horse was as black as ebony with shining amethyst eyes, and purple fire rising from its nostrils. Its skin was ripped away in some places, exposing the muscle and bone beneath.

Its rider was huge, easily two feet taller than Fin, and wearing flaming purple armour the same colour as the sword, his eyes raging black through the narrow slit in his helmet. He swung himself down from his horse, landing with an earth-shaking thud on the moss-covered ground. He reached back and pulled out a long, thick sword.

Niah had never seen such a blade.

It was huge, as long as she was tall, and about as wide as she was too. It, too, had a dragon decorating the guard, except this sword didn't dance with flames.

She glanced at Fin, who gave her a single nod. Niah sheathed her swords and drew her pistols from each thigh, leaping into the air as she fired at the behemoth rider. He roared and swung that enormous sword straight for her.

Her feet connected with a tree, and she managed to push herself away just before the tree splintered into a million pieces as the sword shattered it. Niah gritted her teeth, reloading and emptying two more magazines into the rider.

The bullets did nothing.

While the rider was focused on Niah, Fin darted around behind him and thrust his sword upward through his back. It sliced cleanly through the thick armour. The rider bellowed and fell forward onto his knees as Fin yanked his blade free. The horse charged at him, and Fin barely had time to roll out of the way as it ran straight past.

Niah helped Fin to his feet, both panting as they watched the rider shake. It took a moment to realise he was laughing. Neither of them could move as they watched him throw his head back and roar with laughter.

"Stupid little hybrids," the rider bellowed, "You cannot kill me, I am one of the five."

Time slowed down around her as a quiver settled in her stomach. What *was* he?

Despite their opponent, Niah's blood was singing, her power pleading to come out. *Not yet,* she told it, *Soon.*

She had no idea how they would beat him if he could survive a sword through the chest, but they couldn't give up. Niah glanced at Fin, he gave her a subtle dip of his chin, and then they were moving. Fin pulled the shotgun from his back and started firing shot after shot as Niah holstered her pistols.

The rider barely noticed the shots, his eyes remaining on Niah. His head tilted to the side, as if wondering why she was stupid enough to stand before him without a weapon. He sneered. His armour clanged as he ran forward, his sword whistling through the air as he swung it at her. Niah could faintly hear Fin roaring at her to move, and then he was running.

Everything slowed.

Her power swirled and pulsed with hunger as she spread it down her arms and into her hands, focusing it on one point at the centre of each palm. It wouldn't be much, but she could make the blast as hot as possible.

Heat spread through her arms, into her shoulders and chest, the power hammering through her veins, begging to be released.

Niah released it.

The power shot from her palms in the form of the hottest blue flames she could muster. The rider screamed and staggered back, the sword falling from his grip and burying itself in the ground. It was only a small burst, but the heat she had achieved was enough to scorch the rider.

He fell to the ground, limp and still.

Niah dropped to her knees, breathing hard with sweat covering her brow. Fin knelt next to her, his eyes wide and worried. She shook her head, unable to speak, letting him know she wasn't hurt.

She could hear the battle raging on through the trees. Fin stood and yanked the smaller sword from the ground. In the next moment, the earth shook, loud groans and the screams of demons being crushed let them know the rift was closing.

It dawned on her then, she'd seen a similar rift.

While they were fighting demons in Perth.

"Nice sword," Fin muttered, turning it over in his hands. The flames died, turning to a rippling pattern on the surface of the metal. He slid the sword through his belt and helped her to her feet.

They turned to head back to the battlefield after Niah took a few moments to gather herself. As they did, a high-pitched wail, like a kettle boiling over, sounded behind them. Slowly, they turned to see the enormous sword vibrating, working its way free of the ground in which it was stuck.

Once free, it flew through the air and into the waiting hand of the rider.

"That's my sword, boy."

FIN

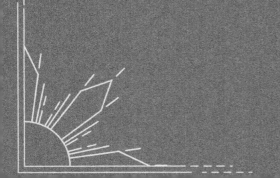

38

It was a losing battle.

They dodged the rider's attacks as best they could, but he was unnaturally fast, despite his mass. Fin's attacks barely scratched the armour, and Niah was slower. Having used a lot of strength with the fire, she had nothing left. It was all she could do not to be hit.

Fin grabbed a throwing knife from his boot and let it fly; it ricocheted off the rider's helmet just above his eye, and he let out a booming laugh.

All his plans to slow the rider and kill him had failed.

He was quickly running out of ideas.

Niah rolled in front of him and threw a handful of leaves into the riders face, blinding him momentarily. She slashed at his thighs and chest, but his armour was too thick to make any impact. He kicked her in the side, sending her sprawling to the ground, and brought his sword down, but Fin was there, blocking.

The blades clanged together, sending painful vibrations shooting up his arms and shoulders. The rider staggered back as Niah scrambled to her feet, clutching her ribs.

She darted to the side while Fin lunged for the rider. He had driven his blade through the huge man before, and he could do it again. He took a knife from his belt and ran toward the mountain of a man. He threw it. There was a wet noise as the blade buried itself in the rider's eye.

He howled, yanking his helmet off and taking the blade with it. The rider went down on one knee, raising his sword to slash at Fin. He cried out again as the sword fell to the dirt, his hand still clasped around the hilt.

Niah stood on the riders back, her blades still raised, slick with unnaturally dark red blood. The rider twisted and brought his elbow back, knocking Niah into a tree.

He had only a second to deliver a fatal blow, but his great sword would be too slow, so Fin took the dragon decorated sword from his belt, and drove it through the breastplate of the rider.

Metal scraped against metal, then flesh and bone before it burst out the other side. The rider opened his mouth in a silent scream, his eyes turning completely black as they rolled into the back of his head.

His veins blackened, visible from the surface of his skin, spreading until his skin crumpled and fluttered away like ash, leaving only the armour behind. The horse cried out, but it too dissolved until the remnants floated away on the wind.

Fin shoved the sword through his belt and ran to Niah's side. She struggled to her feet, her blades once again across her back. He checked her over quickly; her face was bruised along her jaw and brow, her lip split and bleeding, but he knew the worst of it was her ribs.

"Can you still fight?" he murmured as he stood holding her arm gently at the elbow. Her eyes were shining black and silver, her hair had come loose and hung freely around her shoulders to her waist. Her lips quirked up at the corners.

It took a second for him to realise how close they were.

Their breath mingled between them.

They almost hadn't made it.

"Of course," she breathed; they were both panting hard. Neither had ever faced such an enemy. With the adrenaline still surging through his veins, he leaned forward, but stopped himself, knowing it wasn't what she wanted.

Except, she closed the gap between them.

His arms went around her instantly, a low groan burning through his throat at the softness of her lips, despite the coppery tang of blood coating his tongue.

He savoured the sweetness of the moment, the warmth and softness of her lips, the urgency in which she pulled him to her, the way her fingers tangled in his hair.

He wished the moment didn't have to end.

But...

They pulled away breathlessly, his heart pounding as she gazed at him with wild, bright eyes.

"Well, I'm not sure we have time for *that*," he grinned. Her cheeks flushed with colour, the smile fading from her lips.

"I just needed to do that," she muttered, not meeting his gaze. He didn't care why she had done it; if it was just from the high of the fight and the fact that they had survived it, then so be it. Fin took her hand in his, and she finally met his gaze.

"We should get back." She nodded, and they left the forest, leaving behind that ridiculously mammoth sword.

The sounds of battle hadn't eased, which meant there were still demons to take care of. They sprinted through the trees, Niah slower than before as she favoured her right side, occasionally clutching at her ribs.

As they broke free of the treeline, they found the field was whole once again. There were few demons left that were quickly being dispatched as they ran to where Dea was fighting with Gren and Sai.

"What the hell took so long?" Sai shouted over the chaos.

"I'll explain later," Fin shot back, driving his sword through the skull of a demon.

There were no cheers when the demons were all dead—only

deafening silence. Fin turned his attention to the compound, to where Benjamin had disappeared with his warriors.

There should be sounds of battle coming from the building, but there was nothing.

"You lot," Fin said to a group of a dozen warriors, "Help Cassia tend to any wounded and get them back to the facility. Everyone else, with me."

He and the others crept toward the compound, Niah with her swords in hand, and a darkness in her eyes he hadn't seen since he'd taken her from this place. What was it like for her? To be back in the place where she'd known nothing but lies and loneliness?

They left Cassia with the dozen warriors to gather their fallen and tend to the wounded, as they entered the compound's gates. A shiver slithered up his spine as they approached the large doors.

Fin gripped one of the iron handles, while Sai grabbed the other, the doors squealed in protest as they yanked them open; Niah and Gren were the first ones through the doorway.

Inside, the walls were covered with tapestries; images of demons being slain by golden armoured knights on horseback, vampires being tortured, fairies having their wings ripped from their backs, lycanthropes tied down in wolf form and whipped. It wasn't just hybrids they despised, but all supernatural creatures.

His stomach churned as they wandered through the long corridors. It was as hard to stomach as the first time he'd seen them. The further into the building they ventured, the colder it became. The tapestries turned to paintings, following the same patterns as the ones before. Torture and cruelty.

"Where is everyone?" Dea whispered as they crept through the maze of corridors.

They should be hearing swords clanging, screams and shouts, but there was nothing. Instead, the only sounds were the soft scrape of the warriors' boots against the floor, and his heart hammering in his ears.

Fin let Niah lead the way, she knew the compound better than anyone, and he had a feeling she wouldn't hang back even if he did ask her to. A line of tension ran through her, her eyes now cold and empty.

"Can you hear that?" Sai muttered.

Everyone froze, listening until Fin heard the faint sound of sobbing.

"It could be a trap," Niah warned, but continued to creep down the hall, slightly faster than before. The sobs grew louder, familiar; Niah must have heard it too, because then she was sprinting. Fin cursed through his teeth but followed, not daring to tell her to slow down.

They came to a large room with stained glass windows and lined with wooden pillars. Bodies lay scattered around the room, wearing the black armour of the Furies. At the centre of the room was a girl on her knees, also dressed in black, her head low as she leaned over something, no, *someone*; a body.

At the head of the room were more bodies, but they weren't dressed in armour. Instead, they wore jeans and t-shirts, everyday clothes. They weren't fighters, yet their hands were bound behind their backs, unable to defend themselves.

Children.

Fin's stomach lurched, several warriors threw up behind him as he advanced further into the room. Dea rushed to the girl kneeling on the floor and pulled her into her arms.

Fin froze. Char.

She wasn't supposed to be here. She was supposed to be resting at the facility. Why was she here? And with Benjamin's warriors?

"What happened here?" Gren demanded.

Tears streamed down her face, making track marks in the grime, and blood dried on her skin, "Kill me," she whimpered in between sobs.

"Char... did you do this?" Dea murmured; Char said nothing, only nodded her head.

"How could you have killed all these people?" Fin breathed. The other Furies made their way around the room, checking the bodies for anyone that might be alive.

"Not all of them. The Shadows...they led us in here; they had our children, the ones we left behind in the bunker, for their safety. They were bound, the Shadows stood behind them and began butchering them, we tried to stop them, but they came out of the walls...the *walls*, who can do such a thing? It was a slaughter, and I was trying to defend myself, killing them one by one. And then everything melted away, and I was left in the room alone, with only bodies surrounding me, fresh blood on my blade and hands. This child, before he died, said there were never any Shadows here. We all turned on each other; they made us kill our own," she sobbed. Everyone was silent.

Fin choked down the bile rising in his throat.

"How could they have the power to do such a thing?" a male warrior asked.

"Be on guard, everyone," Gren barked.

"We can't find Benjamin's body," Sai said when he finished searching.

"Kill me, please," Char muttered.

No one spoke or moved.

Dea turned to gaze around the room. As she did, Char reached up and pulled a dagger from Dea's belt, she turned to stop her, but Char had already plunged it into her chest.

Black blood sprayed from the wound and spilt over her lips as she twisted the blade in her chest. Dea fell to her knees at her side, her fingers trembling as she pried Char's hands away.

"Why did you do that?" Dea pleaded as she lay Char back and pressed her hands over the wound, the blade still protruding from her chest.

"I was dead already," she whispered, her voice catching in her throat as a tear slipped down her cheek. Fin thought she would say something else, but her body went limp, her hand falling to the ground. Dea looked up at Fin with pleading eyes, tears rolling down her cheeks, and shook her head.

Char was dead.

Fin crashed to his knees, his strength suddenly leaving him. A chill seeped down to his bones as he stared at the massacre around him.

An unbearable weight settled in the pit of his stomach. He was second in command, and so many of their warriors were dead. Their *children* were dead.

He lifted his eyes to Niah, her canines had slid free of her gums, sharp and glinting in the dim light filtering in through the windows. Her eyes were dark, haunting, unfeeling.

Dea gently lay Char on the ground and straightened up, as did Fin.

"We have to find Benjamin," as much as he wanted to get the warriors away from the compound, Benjamin was still a leader, and they couldn't leave without at least retrieving his body.

Yet, it wasn't Benjamin he was worried about.

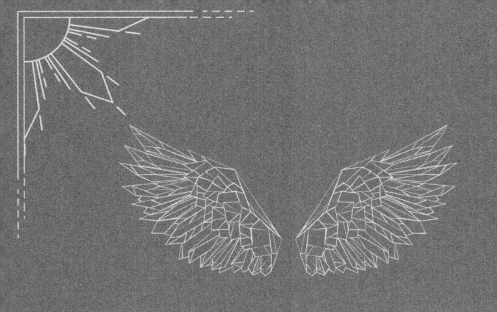

NIAH

39

She was going to make sure they all suffered.

Niah marched through the halls, the others close behind. They were exactly how she remembered them, except now they were littered with the bodies of her comrades.

Her heart raced, her breaths coming fast and shallow as she gripped her swords hard enough that the metal groaned beneath her palms. The scene in which she and Fin had walked into was printed on the backs of her lids.

She had turned and stormed out of the room before anyone could stop her.

Fin was at her side as he spoke with Merida on the phone. She told him that the spell weavers and warriors left with the children had managed to get the majority to safety. Though how the Shadows had found out they were there, or even where the bunker was located, was a mystery.

Niah was glad that it wasn't all of their children that had fallen, but it was enough of them. There shouldn't have been *any* children dead.

"You should get everyone else to safety." She said through her teeth.

"And what about you?" Fin demanded.

She ignored him.

They were making their way down a corridor which she remembered as being one of the dormitory wings. Doors lined the hall on either side. There was a creak, and the doors flew open; armour-clad Shadows poured into the hall, brandishing weapons whilst slashing at the Furies.

She was torn from the others as she had been leading the way. A group of Shadows stood before her, snarling.

One lunged for her, she ducked below the blade and ran her own along the length of it, plunging her sword through the soldiers' golden breastplate, through their ribs and heart and out the other side. The lifeless Shadow fell to the floor with a thud when she yanked her blade free.

She thought she would feel something the way as when she had killed Logan.

But this was very different.

Niah heard nothing over the pounding in her ears. She felt nothing but the glorious burn of adrenaline flooding her veins, and the slight sting as her canines sliced her lip.

The other Shadows glanced at each other before lunging all at once. She spun on the balls of her feet, slashing as she went, kicking, dodging, lunging with her blades, and parrying blows.

They were dead in a matter of seconds.

Yet, there was no satisfaction. They had been attacking with the flat of their blades. Their only goal was to incapacitate her, not to kill. If she hadn't killed them, they would have dragged her back to hell knows where.

There was a wrongness to killing people that were marked, but without knowing what marks they possessed, there was no way to tell whether they were acting of their own will or not.

If Niah hesitated for even a second, that would be the difference between getting what she came for or becoming a prisoner once again.

She stared at the bodies at her feet, scarlet blood dripping from the black of her swords, her breaths coming as feral rasps between her teeth.

No. It wasn't what she thought it would be, but once again, these soldiers weren't who she wanted to kill. They were simply in her way.

Niah turned to see Fin and the others staring at her.

"Go back." Was all she said before turning and continuing down the corridor. Dea caught up and fell in step beside her.

"Niah, I know this is personal to you_"

Niah whirled on her, "I said *leave.*" Dea didn't so much as flinch.

"No. Not without you."

The two glared off against each other. Niah knew she could manipulate them into leaving; she could say something unforgivable, do something even worse, but as she stared into her friend's blue eyes, she couldn't do it.

"You'll only get in my way." Was all she said before turning on her heel and taking off down the corridor, hoping she could lose them in the maze of halls. But as she rounded a corner, a large set of metal doors loomed up in front of her. Doors that hadn't been there when she had left.

Her eyes narrowed as she reached out and pulled the doors open. A bright white light filled the hallway. On the other side of the door was a set of stairs going deep underground.

"Go back." She said again, letting a plea seep into her voice. How could she protect them if they followed her?

One way or another, she would get answers, she would get her revenge, and try to keep the others safe. Whether that meant she made it out or not.

Before she could stop him, Fin descended the stairs.

A thick chemical smell hung in the air. The walls were white tile, as were the floors, the ceilings lined with bright fluorescent lights.

Despite her best efforts to push her way in front of them, Sai and Fin led the way. She made a point to ignore the gazes burning into her back. She had to do this. There was no turning back, not after all they had done.

They passed through another set of doors into a large room. Tables with various lab equipment lined one wall, test tubes filled with different coloured liquids, microscopes, and medical equipment. On the other side of the room were large glass containers with technical boards outside them.

To Niah's horror, they held lycanthropes, fey, vampires, and spell weavers, all with multiple tubes sticking out of their bodies and going up into the chamber at the top.

Further along, strapped to a nearly upright table, was an ordinary-looking man. His eyes were wide open, blue with a very dull grey ring around the iris. His hands were curled unnaturally at odd angles, his mouth hanging open, head tilted to the side. Dead. Niah's stomach churned.

Niah's throat went dry, her stomach wrenching as she stared at the experiments. She knew the Shadows were cruel, but this? It was monstrous.

She tore her eyes away, finding another set of doors at the far end of the room. She marched toward them, but before she could reach them, they swung open, and Shadow soldiers poured into the room, carrying strange, white guns with curving lines.

Fin tried to push her behind him, as did Sai and Gren, Dea clung to her arm, and she realised they had formed a protective barrier between her and the Shadows.

Her heart swelled. But she couldn't allow them to die for her. She loosed a growl, putting enough force behind it that they all stiffened.

"Niah," Fin warned.

Knowing they wouldn't move, she shoved her way to the front. They were safer behind her, if the Shadows were ordered not to kill her, then they wouldn't risk opening fire, but she didn't doubt that they wouldn't hesitate to shoot the others to get to her.

"Stay back." She hissed.

Last out of the door were two figures dressed in pristine, white suits. The very people she was looking forward to seeing.

Karliah and Nolan Springtower.

Karliah wore a wicked smirk, while Nolan stood with his hands behind his back, his expression unreadable.

Niah narrowed her eyes, a growl tearing through her throat as her knuckles turned white from gripping her swords. The sound of Karliah's heels on the tiles echoed through the room as she stepped closer, her eyes gleaming.

All that rage and hatred came flooding back in an instant, and Niah could think of nothing else. These were the people she trusted. These were the people who were supposed to keep her safe, and they had betrayed her.

Whether she was an experiment, a weapon, an ordinary girl, it didn't matter.

"Niah," Fin said again. Niah could feel the tension rolling off of the others behind her.

She didn't care.

These people had killed so many.

Logic abandoned her. She wanted their blood.

"Well, well, hello, Niah," Karliah offered a dazzling grin, Niah's mouth pressed into a firm line, her eyes narrowing. Fin stiffened.

The woman chuckled, "Nothing to say?"

An involuntary growl escaped through her teeth, which only seemed to delight Karliah further, but Nolan shifted on his feet, a crease forming between his brows.

Niah reined in her rising temper, forcing her mind to focus as she straightened her spine and tilted her chin, "I have nothing to say to you."

"Oh? No questions? You always did ask a lot of questions. Tell me, did you learn anything from your time with the Furies?" she asked melodically. A murmur ran through the warriors behind her; they must think she was working with Karliah the whole time.

"I want to know where my mother is," she said, keeping all emotion from her voice.

Karliah's expression turned unreadable, Nolan flicked his gaze to his sister before sliding his eyes back to Niah.

"Poor little Niah, you've always been gullible. What else did they tell you? What other stories did they weave to make you do their bidding?" she said, her teeth dazzlingly white as she smiled an awful smile.

"They told me what I needed to know. More than you ever did, but

I'm not sure I understand why you kept me around, why you didn't just kill me, perhaps you could enlighten me?"

The more she spoke, the more she could learn, and the longer Fin had to assess the situation and formulate a plan.

"Call it a whim," Karliah shrugged. There was so much she wasn't saying, yet so much she said just in those words.

"I don't think that was your decision, was it?" Niah smirked; something dark flashed across Karliah's features, but it was gone faster than she could read it. Niah didn't think the siblings were the leaders of the Shadows by any means, but Karliah, with her ego being as it was, would want Niah to believe she was.

"Whatever do you mean?"

"It wasn't your decision to leave me alive. You're nothing more than a minion, are you?" Niah taunted. Karliah's lips pressed together, her fingers twitching at her side.

"We've taken many of your soldiers, your children abominations. Do not think to assume our plans or ideals," she snapped, "We found you once before; do you think we could not do it again? No matter where you run to, Niah, we *will* find you."

Niah took a step forward, the Shadow soldiers raised their guns. She dared another step, ignoring Fin and the others' warnings.

"You won't kill me," Niah smirked.

Karliah bristled, "You think we care about a single hybrid that much?" a bitter laugh, "Don't be naïve. Look at you; you're weak. You formed attachments, and they can be used against you. Did you learn nothing all these years?"

Niah dared another step, "Careful, Karliah, your emotions are showing. You're getting all worked up over nothing." Karliah's hands balled into fists at her sides, her face turning red as she pressed her lips together.

"Niah," Nolan's voice cut through the silence, "Come with us, and we'll let your friends go."

"And what makes you think these people mean anything to me? After all, you taught me to lie, to manipulate to get what I want," she shrugged, "They got me here, that's all. They were a means to an end."

Karliah scoffed, "You think we don't see how they try to protect you?"

"More fool them. I guess I played my part well." The words turned bitter on her tongue. But if there were some way she could get them out of this without them having to fight their way out, she would do it.

She just needed to calm down and think logically.

Karliah flicked her eyes to Nolan, and there, in that one look, was a flicker of doubt.

"Enough. Come with us."

"Or what?" Niah growled.

Karliah gave Nolan a brief nod; he turned and disappeared through the doors, only to emerge a moment later, leading a tall man with dark hair in black armour. His mouth was gagged, and his hands were bound behind his back. Nolan shoved him forward onto his knees, Benjamin.

"This is one of your so-called *leaders,* is it not?" Karliah grinned, her eyes dancing with venom. Fin didn't say anything. "We will let you have him back, but you need to give us something in return."

Niah snorted, "Me?"

"No." Fin snarled; Niah stepped forward, and he made to grab her arm, but she turned her glare on him, hoping he read the message she was trying to convey. He searched her eyes, and his hand fell from her arm.

"Well, if you really don't care," Karliah shrugged. Nolan cocked a pistol and pressed it to the back of Benjamin's head. The leader whimpered but didn't flinch.

"Fine," Niah called out. A murmur ran through the room, and Karliah grinned; she wasn't expecting it to be so easy.

Niah handed her weapons to Dea and walked toward Karliah as Benjamin staggered to his feet and stumbled toward the Furies. The blade kissed her palm, hidden in the vambrace around her forearm.

She stood in front of Karliah and Nolan, smirks spread over their faces. She glanced over her shoulder, Benjamin had arrived and was being ushered into the group of warriors protectively.

Karliah stood in front of her and leaned forward, close enough so that her lips grazed Niah's ear.

"Now, you will watch them die," she whispered.

Niah jerked her arm, palming the blade. She grabbed Karliah by the shoulder and pushed her down to her knees, positioning herself behind the woman so that she was facing the Shadows with the blade kissing Karliah's throat.

"Shoot her! Now!" Karliah screamed.

"No! Hold your fire! We need her alive!" Nolan bellowed, Niah eyed him quizzically.

"Oh? Why would that be?" she purred.

Nolan pressed his lips into a firm line as the Shadows inched closer. Niah slid her eyes over them, "One more step, and she dies." She pressed the knife harder against Karliah's skin, blood welled on the blade, dribbling down her neck to stain her perfectly white suit. The woman went utterly still.

"If you won't come with us willingly, then we'll retrieve your body from the rubble." Nolan threatened, and before Niah could ask what he meant, he held up a black remote, and pressed the single button.

Explosions sounded beneath their feet.

Rumbling and groaning came from below as the ground began to shake. The tiles on the walls rattled free and crashed to the ground along with the lights, plunging the room into darkness. The guards started pushing Nolan back through the doors, and Karliah started laughing.

Niah could only stare as the floor began to crumble and the ceiling caved in.

"Run!" she screamed at Fin and the others. The Furies were already moving, except Fin, who looked like he was about to run to her, as did the others. Thankfully, the other Furies grabbed them and dragged them back the way they'd come.

She had to make a choice.

The others would make it out.

That's all that mattered.

She dragged the blade across Karliah's throat, deep and savage. But before she could make it even an inch, white-hot pain lanced through her shoulder. The knife clattered across the floor, and Karliah scrambled to her feet, clutching at her neck. Niah looked up to see Nolan holding a pistol aimed at her, his eyes wide.

He shot her.

The ceiling was coming down around them, but the Shadows surged for her. Unable to use her right arm, it was a struggle to just dodge them as they tried to grab her.

Huge pieces of rock fell through the ceiling, a wave of debris rained down on the Shadows that advanced on her. She looked up at the doorway, seeing a shimmering green portal open, and Nolan dragging Karliah through.

The portal vanished.

The Shadows lay either dead or unconscious at her feet.

Niah turned and fled.

Running back through the labs as rocks fell from the ceiling, landing on her as she ran. Ignoring the burning agony in her shoulder, she pumped her arms faster, sprinting back through the lab and corridors.

The front doors loomed in front of her, but the floors gave way and fell into darkness. Then, just as she thought about jumping over the gaping hole, the ceiling fell through, and she was forced to run in the other direction.

Each time she got close to a window, the floor would give way, or the ceiling would collapse. She was on the top floor now, the whole building swayed beneath her feet.

At the head of the building, overlooking the courtyard, was a large stained-glass window. With no other options, she backed up to the wall as far from the window as possible.

If her timing was off, if the floor gave way beneath her feet, she would plunge into that black pit that swallowed the rest of the compound.

She took a deep, trembling breath, and pushed off with every ounce of strength she possessed. The floor gave way beneath the force of her stride, but the rest of it held.

The floor below the window cracked and splintered as it fell away. Niah leapt, sooner than she would have liked, but there were no other options. She shielded her face from the glass as she smashed through it.

The ground rushed up to meet her as she sailed through the air. She lost her balance on impact and fell; pain shot through her side and shoulder, but the building was leaning. And falling. She scrambled to her feet and was running.

A whimper broke through her throat.

There, in the distance, was a shimmering pink portal.

They waited.

Stone fell from the top of the building around her. And to make matters worse, the ground leading to the gates was beginning to crumble and fall. Rocks flew past her mere inches away, and the earth was falling away quicker than she could run.

A rock struck her shoulder; she stumbled but stayed upright, a scream escaping her gritted teeth as she pushed herself harder.

They were there, all of them.

Standing by the portal, shouting at her to run faster.

They ran forward, Cassia included, to the gate surrounding the compound, where the ground stopped falling away. A shimmering pink portal rippled into existence once again.

There was no other choice. The building was coming down behind her, nipping at her heels as the ground fell away before her.

She called on her power. It leapt and danced in answer and spread down her arms, to her palms, concentrating into that one spot.

The jump was too far for her to make alone, but she had to try.

Niah pushed off with everything she had and soared through the air. While still ascending, the power in her veins surged, and two jets of fire shot from her hands. It lasted only a second or two before it sputtered and died. But it was enough.

She free fell the rest of the way as the others reached for her.

And then they were falling.

NIAH

40

They made it.

They were all sprawled on the floor next to the wall, a significant dent visible on the surface where they had all skidded across the floor after falling backwards through the portal and had hit the wall.

Her right shoulder was dislocated as well as a bullet hole straight through it, broken ribs and nose, and bruises covering her jaw and eye. But none of that mattered because the others were okay, they were alive.

They had waited for her.

She looked to them now, relieved that they had fared slightly better with only bruises and a few cuts here and there, Fin had a fractured arm.

The backs of her eyes burned, a sob escaping her throat as she hauled herself up and wrapped her arms around each of them, pulling them all together.

"You idiots," she sobbed, "You utter, utter morons."

No one moved or spoke, they just held her as tightly as she held them. She barely felt the barking protests of her injuries. She didn't care, she just wanted to feel they were okay.

"You should have left," she whimpered, "Why didn't you go?"

"I told you," Dea whispered into her ear, "Not without you."

Niah sobbed harder. There was no stopping the tears as her heart swelled with warmth and love.

They waited.

Her friends.

When the tears finally stopped falling, Niah flopped onto her back and stared up at the ceiling, not caring that Nolan and Karliah had escaped. She was just relieved the others had.

All around, warriors were panting. They had lost a significant number of their warriors during the battle. Spell weavers and casters were fluttering around administering first aid to the injured, sent by The Cross, it seemed.

"We didn't think you were getting out of there," Dea murmured as she struggled to sit up.

"Me either," Niah said. As the elation wore off, and the pain returned, her vision started to blacken at the edges, and sound became muffled as she tried to take deep breaths, only to have sharp pains shoot through her ribs.

"You, to the infirmary, now," Cassia ordered; Fin hesitated before slowly getting to his feet and was led away by Gren. Cassia's hands began to glow their usual pink as she pressed one to Niah's ribs, the other to her shoulder.

Warmth spread through her chest for a second before searing pain. She gritted her teeth together, squeezing her eyes closed before the darkness consumed her.

Niah woke to a dimly lit room. A gentle, salty breeze wafted in through the open doors that carried in the fresh scent of the sea air. She glanced around and winced, clutching her head. The pain in her ribs was gone, but her muscles and bones ached beyond measure.

Someone shifted by the desk; Sai rose to his feet and stepped toward the bed, handing her a glass of water as he perched on the edge. She gulped it greedily and discarded the empty glass on the nightstand.

"Is everyone okay?" she asked, her voice hoarse and weak.

"We lost many, but those of us who came back are fine, some more injured than others, but they'll live," he explained with a frown.

Her heart fell heavy at the memory of bodies strewn across the ground, the ones they were unable to give a proper goodbye to because the building and surrounding fields collapsed into rubble.

"Fin? Dea? Gren?" she asked one after another; something crossed his eyes, but it was gone before she could read it.

"Fin and Gren have been in meetings with Merida. Dea is in the infirmary helping with those who were injured worse," he answered with a small smile, "how do *you* feel?"

She was quiet for a moment. Physically, sore. Mentally? She wasn't so sure.

Trying to explain it all would take more energy than she cared to use. Nolan and Karliah had both managed to escape. It was a bloodbath. Their warriors were slaughtered, *children* were killed.

Fin was right when he said it was a trap. The Shadows knew there were scouts in the forests. They knew an attack was coming. Hell, they even knew the Furies left the children in the bunker, and where to find them.

It wasn't a coincidence.

And it was time to start looking inward.

There was a traitor among them.

"I feel fine," she said finally. Sai raised a brow.

"Bullshit," he scoffed, "We were unprepared, forced into making rash decisions, and it backfired," she swung her legs over the edge of the bed to sit next to him.

"What happens now?"

He sighed, "I guess we pick ourselves up and keep going."

"Is that it? Sai, you know as well as I do the Shadows aren't going to stop coming_"

"I know," he said sharply, "If I had my way, if we could even *find* where they're hiding, I'd be leading the entire Alliance army straight to their front door."

"So what has Merida said?"

"I don't know. We've been left out of the meetings. Fin and Gren aren't allowed to say anything. Whatever's going on, it's a secret." He frowned, dragging a hand through his hair.

A gentle knock sounded at the door, and Dea popped her head around, "Oh, good, you're awake. We've been summoned to a meeting," Niah and Sai exchanged a glance as Dea came into the room and shut the door behind her.

"Is it bad?" Sai asked.

Dea shrugged, "I have no idea." Niah sighed and dressed in comfortable clothes.

"Guys," she muttered, "You know I didn't mean what I said in there? To Nolan and Karliah, right?"

Dea grinned, "Of course, we know you were trying to protect us."

"I'm sorry."

"Shut it," Sai chuckled, squeezing her to his side before dropping a kiss on her head.

"Oh," he said, "Check your weapons."

Niah cocked her head to one side in question but opened the weapons cupboard. Her swords had been replaced, mounted on the back wall, oiled, and gleaming beautifully. At the bottom was a large wooden trunk with a piece of folded paper on top.

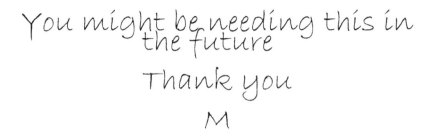

You might be needing this in the future

Thank you

M

She folded the note into her pocket and lifted the lid of the trunk. The armour she had worn only hours ago. Only this looked slightly different. The leathers had cyan stitching and piping through the lines of it. The neckline was slightly higher and squared, and there was more padding over the thighs and arms.

The *Ruclite* plates were as black as onyx, only now there was a slight blue tint rather than purple as the light shined on them. It was beautiful. Blue, the colour of her magic.

The only reason she even knew she had spell weaver blood, angel blood, was because of Merida. Her heart swelled with warmth as she smiled and folded it back into the trunk.

Raised voices emanated from the inside of Merida's office as they walked the hallway. Dea knocked gently and was told to go in. Merida was sitting in her usual space behind the desk, Fin stood next to the window with his arms folded across his chest, Gren was seated on the couch with Benjamin, who threw a glare in her direction before the door closed.

"You three, we're glad you could join us," Merida said stiffly; she looked a little fuller, her cheeks not as gaunt, but something haunted lingered beneath the surface of her ocean eyes.

"I guess we're here to talk about what happened at the compound?" Niah suggested, leaning against the door, folding her arms while Sai and Dea took the seats opposite Merida.

"Yes. How the Shadows want *you*. Of all things, I wonder if you can tell us why that is?" Benjamin spat, glowering through his lashes. Niah cocked her head to one side.

"Would you believe me if I said it was for my charms?" she asked in a sickly-sweet voice. Benjamin's nostrils flared, but she didn't miss the way Fin covered his mouth to hide his smile, or the way Sai's shoulders shook slightly.

"Don't play stupid; why do they want you?" Benjamin snarled.

"How would I possibly know that?"

"You seem very, close? Shall we say."

Niah shrugged, "You could say that…I was their prisoner for eighteen years."

"So, you admit it? That you are close with them?" he regarded her coldly as he rose to his feet abruptly.

"She saved your life. Show some gratitude." Merida snapped; Benjamin turned on her.

"She could be a spy. She could be the reason why they have had so many victories," he barked.

"The reason the last battle was such a defeat, is because *you* rushed into it without a second thought," Niah warned, glowering at him.

"It was a vote_"

"One that *you* pushed. *You* are the reason we lost so many. How dare you stand there and blame me when you are the one that cost us this fight." She yelled, straightening her spine as she took a single step forward. He flinched, filling her with satisfaction.

He bristled, "You will show me respect,"

"Respect is earned, and you have not earned mine." She muttered, his face flushed red as he pressed his lips into a firm line, his knuckles turning white where he balled his hands into fists. He opened his mouth to say something, but at that moment, the door flung open, narrowly missing Niah as she stepped out of the way.

Guardians dressed in pristine grey strode into the room. Behind them walked Amarah and Ragnar, the hybrid Elders. Those who were sat, stood. And everyone bowed their heads in respect as the Elders entered the room. Amarah's golden eyes scanned the faces before her.

"We are not safe here," she spoke calmly, "we are not safe in the bunker either, it seems. Tell me, where should we go?" she asked, her voice was chiming, clear, and as sweet as honey.

"We have not thought of that yet," Merida spoke with a smaller, yet equally clear voice.

"No matter. Nowhere on this Earth will be safe for us. Therefore, we must enact the Code of Thamere," Amarah said. At that, everyone's heads jerked up. Apart from Niah's, who had no idea what they were talking about.

Amarah glanced at her, her gaze lingering for longer than Niah felt comfortable with. Her eyes sparkled, a small smile tugging at the corners of her mouth.

"Child, you are young, yet I hear you were fierce in battle," Amarah said gently; Niah held the Overseers gaze.

"No more so than anyone else," she said, Amarah's eyes narrowed slightly, but her smile grew wider.

"Quite. You've joined us at an interesting time, young one." She said, "In light of what has happened, we have no choice but to call on the other Elders, and enact the Code of Thamere." she said, addressing the room before turning on her heel and stalking from the office, Ragnar and the Guardians following on her heels. Niah glanced to Merida, who merely followed the others as they hurried after the Elders.

"Did you know they were coming?" Niah muttered.

Merida shook her head.

FIN

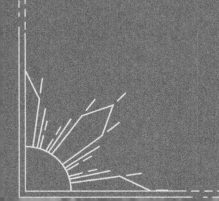

41

He never thought he would see the rise of Thamere.

The Code of Thamere was an ancient spell that had never been used before. There was never a need *to* use it.

Fin knew what it meant, that everything would be changing. They would no longer have the facilities around the world. Instead, the entire Fury Alliance would live on one island.

Because it was the largest room in the facility, the spell would be performed in the training room. All windows had been sealed to protect the vampires that would be attending the meeting. The warriors had gathered outside the doors waiting, watching, along with a small contingent from each of the five orders.

Inside the room, already waiting, were the four Elders. The Cross housed all spell casters and weavers. The Order of Nocturnal was the vampires, The Guild of Bones held lycanthropes and werewolves, and The Iron Union belonged to the fey.

All six Elders bowed to each other out of respect. Merida and Fin had been invited to watch from inside the room, including Benjamin. He peered over his shoulder to see Gren, Sai, Dea, and Niah standing near the doors. Whereas the others were mostly excited about witnessing the rise of a new era, Niah was somewhat more sceptical.

It was expected.

They hadn't spoken since the raid, Fin hadn't been able to get out of the meetings that kept him from her, but maybe that was okay. It gave her time to process everything that had happened.

Fin wasn't sure even he had come to terms with how many they'd lost, Char's death, the children.

And how Niah was willing to sacrifice herself to save them. He wasn't naïve enough to think that was the only reason she did what she did. Niah was consistent, and whether her feelings for them were a factor or not, her primary goal, above all others, was revenge.

A thought that made his chest ache, but he understood.

What Niah had done had given them the time to get out of the building. They may have been unable to collect their dead, but they would have lost many more if they hadn't had those extra seconds.

Yet, despite what she'd done to save them, to save Benjamin, she was watched with contempt and scepticism. It reminded him of the compound, and it set his teeth on edge.

That battle was for another day.

"We come here today under dire circumstances," Amarah began, "It is time we enact the Code of Thamere."

"I have been saying for centuries we needed to enact the spell, why now?" said an ashen man with carroty red hair and green eyes, Lord Keir of the Nocturnal Order.

"Lord Keir, we have always had threats, but they have never warranted this before. The Shadows have truly outdone themselves. Not only do we battle demons and rogues hellbent on pushing our generosity, but we're now made to turn on each other. A spell was cast during the last battle, making our warriors think they were fighting Shadows, but they were actually fighting each other. The Shadows found their way into the bunker, which, until now, only the Alliance has entered. I believe now is the right time," Ragnar explained, his tone considerably less icy than whenever he had addressed the leaders during the Summit.

The room was silent for a beat. Finally, the Elders of the guilds glanced to one another, a low murmur passing between them.

"Very well, we accept your proposal and agree to the Code being enacted." a slight woman with thick silver hair said, Morena White, High Sorceress of The Cross.

She clapped her hands together once, and the building trembled, the slate floors cracking as a large stone table rose through it. The table itself was a huge map of the world which appeared to be alive, a light layer of clouds passed over mountain tops. Whales came up for air in the ocean as cargo ships went by. A gasp of wonder ran through the crowd; Morena smiled to herself.

The weaver turned to a child with dancing red eyes and gestured for her to come forward. The girl carried a wooden box in her arms, decorated with vines and flowers; carved on the lid was the emblems for each Order.

The hybrids had their sword with wings and demon horns, the fairies had a set of butterfly wings, the nocturnal order had an eye, the lycanthropes had the silhouette of a wolf howling at the moon, and the spell weavers had a staff with a sparking orb at the top.

The girl popped the clasp on the box and opened the lid to reveal a glowing, moss green orb, shimmering as the contents swirled inside it. Morena waved her hand, and the ball floated into the centre of the map.

Each of the leaders put their hand forward. A spark of what looked like white electricity shot into each of their palms as another speared into the ocean of the map.

The orb glowed brighter as the leaders chanted a pattern of words in a language Fin didn't know. The light engulfed the room, and he was forced to shield his eyes. Power roared through the room, potent and demanding as it ground against his bones. He'd felt it before, when Niah helped Cassia and Vinaxx, but this was different. Whereas a darkness lingered beneath the surface of Niah's magic, Morena's was pure light.

There was a low hum as the light dimmed; the map had changed. In the centre of the South Pacific Ocean was now a small island. Not huge, but more than big enough for the Alliance. Morena snapped her fingers, and the map zoomed in on the island. It had sandy beaches, vast grassy plains, forests, and mountains.

"Thamere," Morena breathed as she gazed in wonder at the creation.

"Will this now be the home to all supernatural creatures?" a voice asked from the crowd.

Amarah answered with a dazzling smile, "It will be the home of all of us. However, there will always be clans, covens, and packs that wish to remain independent from the Alliance. They will always have the option to join us, but they will be on their own," she explained, "there is much to discuss. It would be best to do it there. Please, pack your things, we will leave as soon as possible. Fellow Elders, please prep your Guilds."

Fin's heart was racing.

A new home.

A second chance.

He only hoped it didn't hold as many nightmares as the facility had.

NIAH

42

Everyone was excited about Thamere.

But Niah only felt a numbness in her chest. The relief that her friends had made it after the raid had eased since she regained consciousness, and she was finally able to think about the things Nolan and Karliah said.

Not that she could make heads nor tails of it.

They wanted her alive, but were willing to bury her under tonnes of rubble to get her. Even for a hybrid, she doubted she could have survived that.

It didn't make sense, and try as she might, Niah could find no logical explanation for any of it.

Still, despite herself, she had been in awe watching the island of Thamere come to life. It would be a new beginning for all of them, only with the same threat hanging over their heads.

She couldn't help wondering if it was just going to be another failure. The Shadows had found the Alliance wherever they went. What made them think this place would be any different? Granted, she didn't know much about the spell, but she'd felt the sheer power radiating from that orb, and her own had stirred in response.

There was much that needed to be explained and discussed amongst the Elders, leaders, and advisors. There was no time for even a quick word in with Fin before he was whisked away into yet another meeting.

There were things she wanted to tell him. Something she had realised during the battle when she saw them all waiting for her as the compound crumbled around her.

There were things she still needed to deal with, but she wasn't ready. Not yet. But the one thing she *could* face, were the feelings she had shoved down so completely.

Something had clicked during the battle. After their fight with the rider, she was so happy that Fin was alive, that they were both alive after things looked so bleak, that she hadn't been able to stop herself from kissing him.

It was at that moment that she realised she'd been an idiot. That she'd pushed him away because of her hunger for revenge, and she needn't have bothered. It was what she still wanted, more so than anything else, but after years of focusing on that one goal, Niah decided that maybe she deserved a little happiness while she hunted for it.

For the first time in her life, she had friends.

She had love. Whether it was in the human sense or not, Niah couldn't deny the warmth in her heart.

She wanted to experience life and everything it had to offer while she worked for her ultimate goal. The Shadows would fall, and she would be the one to do it. But the journey leading up to it didn't have to be one of solitude.

If the raid had shown her anything, it was that any one of them could die at any time, if that happened, she didn't want to regret the time she hadn't spent with them.

They were warriors, each of them understood what that meant, what their duty demanded. But none of the others stopped living because of what might happen during a fight, instead, it was the opposite. They'd taught her what it meant to smile, to laugh, to love, to *live*.

And she was done running from it.

Her hand went to the locket around her throat. The jewel winked in the light. She tried to remember when Jeremiah and Katarina had given it to her; it wasn't a birthday, they never celebrated it. Niah closed her eyes, willing herself to remember. She fought past the itch in her mind, and grabbed the ribbon of thought that tried to swim away.

An image rippled into her mind.

She was young, six or so.

The woman she thought was her mother sat on the grass as Niah trained with swords against the man who claimed to be her father. He knocked her down, standing over her with his blade kissing her throat—a blunted edge, but a metal sword nonetheless.

Niah scrambled to her feet, and he knocked her back down again. Her mother, Katarina, called her to her. Jeremiah protested, but Katarina fixed him with a stern look, he silenced immediately.

Young Niah sat next to the woman, twirling a lock of her hair between her fingers. Katarina pulled out a small wooden box decorated with roses and handed it to her. For a moment, Niah didn't know what to do with it. It was too beautiful and delicate to be held in her hands destined to slay demons.

"It's okay, go ahead," Katarina encouraged.

Niah opened it to see the locket inside, the topaz glinting in the afternoon sunlight.

"For me?" she questioned, grazing her fingers over the intricate detailing.

"For you," Katarina murmured.

It was the first pretty thing she'd ever received, but her heart soared in her chest as she beamed at her mother. Katarina fixed the necklace around her neck, and it dangled down her chest.

"What's it for?" Niah had asked in her small voice, keeping her eyes low out of respect.

"Do I need a reason to bestow gifts upon you?" Katarina questioned.

Niah shifted where she sat, she didn't mean offence; she only wondered what she would have to do to earn such a lovely thing.

"It is so that we can always find you. No matter what, whenever you are in trouble, we will come to you." Katarina said with a small smile,

though something darker, sinister lay within her eyes that Niah hadn't noticed at the time.

Her eyes widened, and she fled the room, sprinting down the corridor, bumping into people along the way until she burst through the doors to Merida's office. She was gathering books into a trunk, Fin was helping her. They both dropped what they were doing and turned to her, their eyes tracking the locket as she slammed it onto the desk.

"This. This is how the Shadows knew, it's a tracker. They've been watching me," she panted. Fin and Merida exchanged a look. Fin picked up the locket, examined it, and smashed it down on the desk; the jewel shattered, nothing more than a glass bead. Behind it was a small chip. He gritted his teeth together, the muscle flexing in his jaw.

"I'm sorry, I didn't know," Niah breathed; Merida was staring at the locket in Fin's hand. She took it from him, and crossed the room to Niah, she thought she might hit her, but the leader placed the locket in Niah's hand, and closed her fingers around it.

"You should be the one to destroy it," she murmured, her gaze steady, not so much as a flicker of anger within her eyes. Niah held the necklace in her palm. Betrayal and deceit crept into her veins. It was by that locket that they were able to find the bunker and murder children.

Her throat turned dry as her breaths came faster, and the locket burst into bright blue flames. She held it in her palm, the metal melting, the picture inside bubbling before turning to ash. The flame grew hotter until there was nothing but a silver pool.

The locket may have been destroyed, but it did nothing to soothe the rage, the guilt roiling in the pit of her stomach. Niah dropped her hand, still stained silver as the flames died, and raised her chin, her eyes still blazing. Merida regarded her thoughtfully, a small smile at the corners of her mouth.

"All the anger you feel right now, use it. Train harder, be stronger. I promise you will get your revenge. I will make sure of that," she said firmly, gripping Niah's arm as she spoke. Niah nodded once, her eyes hardening to onyx. Fin was gazing at her, so much pain in his silver eyes, for her, she realised. Because he knew she would be in pain.

And she was.

Pain because she had been too stupid to realise what was right in front of her.

Pain because there were so many lives taken because she hadn't thought the locket could be a tracking device.

And because Nolan and Karliah had gotten away.

But they wouldn't again.

NIAH

43

The pounding in her ears had eased.

Her blood cooled the moment she left the office, but it had taken far longer for her mind to stop reeling, for her to stop fantasising about the day she finally got hold of Jeremiah and Katarina.

Niah hauled the trunk from the wardrobe and packed her weapons into it, laying them on top of her armour, along with books and anything else that didn't fit in her bag. She glanced at the leather-bound book on the desk and removed the key from her neck.

This time, when she flicked through the pages, it didn't hurt quite as much. For what reason, she couldn't say, and it didn't matter. Katarina and Jeremiah were out there somewhere, and now they knew that Niah would come for them; Nolan and Karliah would have told them enough, no doubt.

Good.

Let them know she was coming for them.

Niah went to the balcony, book in hand, and tossed it as hard as she could. It sailed through the air and landed in the ocean, bobbing for a few seconds before sinking to the depths.

She inhaled deeply, relishing being able to breathe a little easier.

She wheeled her trunk downstairs and found Dea standing in the foyer, her expression solemn.

"Are you nervous?" Niah asked; Dea jumped as if she hadn't heard her approach, and smiled.

"Aren't you?"

The warriors were funnelling through shimmering portals; some were excited, others nervous and wary. Benjamin stood on the far side, talking to a small group of warriors that nodded in agreement. Niah might not have thought much of it, had they not kept glancing in her direction.

It appeared there would be yet more battles to face.

"Not really, it's different," Niah shrugged.

"I just have this strange feeling, like it's not the end, only the beginning," Dea frowned as she glanced down at her shoes.

"That's because it is."

Dea said nothing as they walked toward Sai and Gren stood near a portal.

"You guys ready?" Sai asked with a dazzling smile. Dea hugged him tightly, and he kissed the top of her head. Gren offered Niah a slight smile, and together, they stepped through the portal.

The sun was warm on her skin.

Thick grass covered the expanse before her. From where they stood, Niah could see the faint outline of trees, and mountains beyond that. The ocean wasn't visible from where they were, but she swore she could feel it out there—tugging slightly as if some tether lingered between her and the sea.

She shook her head; no such things existed.

Tents were being set up along the grass, and fires were being built. Already, people had dumped their bags and gone to get firewood and various other things, though really, they wanted an excuse to explore.

Niah and Dea set up their tent after deciding to share one, while Sai, Gren, and Fin's were right next door. Their tents were set further back from the others, set in a circle around a large fire they had yet to light.

The sun was setting, but everyone gathered around. The vampires had yet to arrive, though it wouldn't be long before they could join them. Niah glanced around at the vast crowds, thousands of hybrid warriors, lycanthropes, spell weavers and fairies, all united together.

Amarah, Ragnar, Morena, Lyra of the lycanthropes, and Shade Rainrock of the fey stood before everyone with their heads held high.

"Welcome all," Amarah shouted for all to hear, "This is a difficult time for us all. As most of you will know, the Code of Thamere is not just about a safe place for us to live. It is the formation of a new way of life. The leaders of the former facilities will become Counsellors of the Oracle Conclave, the council of the Fury Alliance. All decisions will be filtered through them. The other Elders and I will be the overall decision-makers as we always have. The once advisors will now be Commanders of the various branches of warriors, as there are too many to be commanded by just one," she explained.

A murmur ran through the crowd, some in approval, others in annoyance. What Amarah said made sense, many of the warriors weren't equipped to make big decisions, and many of them had only ever been led by others anyway; it made sense for a council to be put in place.

Someone brushed against her arm, and she looked up to see Fin.

"Commander Fin, eh?" she grinned, nudging him in the ribs.

He chuckled, "It's got a good ring to it, hasn't it?"

"Watch it, don't let it go to your head; I can still kick your arse," she smirked. He gave her a wicked grin as if he was all too eager to meet the challenge.

"Don't push it," She smiled, turning to face Amarah.

"From now on, there is a lot more danger. We need to be prepared, which means working harder. We still have demons and rogues to deal with, and now we will do it with the Shadows looming over us. We are united, and we must stay that way," the crowd erupted into applause and whoops.

It was a nice speech, but how long would the people of Thamere remain united?

The vampires arrived when night fell around Thamere. Already the spell weavers and casters had created a temporary underground haven for them during the day. The lycanthropes and fey took to the forests and mountains, while the hybrids and spell weavers remained in the grasslands.

That night, everyone was silent. There were no celebrations. There was nothing to celebrate. They lost the battle and lost many during it. They were no better off and still had no answers.

The rites were chanted, and fires were lit in memory of the fallen warriors. Niah sat with a group of warriors from the Perth facility around a fire, and listened to them exchanging stories of the fallen.

All the while, she could only think about all those left behind, and wouldn't receive a proper farewell. The evening was sombre, but it could be far worse.

Niah found Merida sitting on a fallen log on the outskirts of the camp and sat down next to her, looking up at the stars.

"Thank you for the armour," she muttered as Merida followed her gaze to the heavens.

"Don't thank me yet. It only gets harder from here."

Niah lowered her eyes to her hands dangling between her knees, "Isn't that always what happens?" Merida eyed her for a moment, a small smile playing at the corners of her mouth. She still looked tired, her skin still grey, her eyes still dull, but there was a sense of ease about her, a strange kind of focus.

"Maybe."

"You're not well."

Merida sighed, "It's not that I'm not well. When hybrids live as long as I have, sometimes, our demonic nature takes over. I'm a long way from that yet, but it is getting harder. I won't say any more on the matter."

"You can always talk to me," Niah whispered.

Merida's eyes shimmered in the moonlight, "I'm so glad you're here with us. What happened at the compound?"

"Fin already told you, I'm sure."

"He did," Merida agreed, "but I'd like to hear it from you."

Niah shrugged, "There isn't much to tell."

"Bottling everything up only makes things worse_"

"I *can't* talk about it yet," Niah met Merida's gaze, "I have no idea how I feel about it, angry? Obviously. Everything else? I don't know."

Merida sighed and tilted her face to the sky, "It's to be expected, I suppose."

"How so?"

"From what Fin told me what Karliah said, I gathered that you were taught emotions and attachments were a weakness. So it's to be expected that you don't know how to process them."

"Merida," Niah sighed, "I don't want to talk about it."

"I know, and that's fine. I just wanted you to know that you can talk to me if you ever feel up to it."

Not knowing what else to say, and wanting to change the subject, Niah simply said, "Thank you," and got to her feet.

Merida smiled, "Enjoy the night, Niah. The building starts tomorrow."

FIN

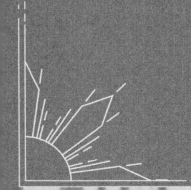

44

Thamere was everything he hoped for and more.

He sat gazing into the flames. Oranges, yellows, and reds dancing together as they licked toward the sky. He sat on the grass, leaning back on his hands, his legs stretched out in front of him, letting the gentle crackle of the fire soothe him.

He was a Commander now, which meant more responsibility. Fin had looked around the mass of people during the speech and was overwhelmed to see how many lives he would be responsible for.

They all knew it was only the beginning, and it was only going to get worse. Battle was all they knew, and they were ready for it. But no one could prepare them for what lay ahead, because no one knew.

The Shadows had exceeded their fears and expectations more times than he cared to count. And with the threat of the riders burning in the back of his mind, Fin hated to think what other atrocities they had cooked up in those labs of theirs.

Time would tell.

Fin wasn't too proud to admit he was terrified.

He sighed and raked his hands through his hair. Familiar footsteps approached; he'd know them anywhere. Niah sat down next to him, her warmth radiated through him for a second before his body adjusted.

He glanced at her, the flames reflected in her dark eyes, the silver shimmering as it contrasted with the amber of the fire.

"I thought tonight would be full of laughing and celebrations. A new beginning," she said, still gazing into the flames, "but it's not. We've achieved nothing," a spark of electricity passed through him when her arm brushed against his.

"Okay there, pessimist," he snorted, trying to break the darkness in her mood. She scowled into the flames. "Look, nothing is perfect. We were unprepared, but we won't let that happen again," he said as convincingly as he could, but even he couldn't deny the unease weighing heavily in his chest.

"I keep thinking about Karliah wanting me in exchange for Benjamin. I keep replaying it over and over in my mind, but I can't come up with any logical reason why they want me," she murmured as she ran a hand through her long, raven hair.

Fin shifted and brought his knees up, letting his arms drape loosely around them. "Trying to figure out what they're thinking is pointless; they're very different to us."

"We need to know what they're thinking, though," she finally turned to him, "trying to guess is only going to end with more of our warriors dying."

"We can talk about it tomorrow; I'm sure it's going to be all the new council can talk about for a while," he sighed.

"What happened to the purple sword?" she asked. The purple dragon sword had been used to open a rift and let hundreds of demons through.

"Amarah and Ragnar are examining it."

"It didn't suit you anyway," she said, a small smile on her lips; his heart began to race. "You're blushing."

"Can't help it when you're being so charming and not throwing swords at my head."

She chuckled and rested her head on his shoulder; it was an effort not to pull her closer.

"I was speaking to Dea the other day. She said she hopes she finds the second half of her heart," Niah murmured. He looked down at her.

"Some hybrids do," he found it difficult just getting the words out; it felt as though every nerve in his body was firing all at once.

"Do you?"

"No," he said truthfully.

Fin had never wanted to be that attached to someone. Though, he'd grown attached to Niah. In a way that was unfamiliar, yet comfortable. "I think I'm happy as I am," he grinned. She sat up then and gazed at him, she was so close that her breath brushed his face.

He longed to close the distance between them, to feel her lips beneath hers once more, and it took every ounce of willpower to stay completely still.

"Being able to sleep with anyone you choose? Shocker," she smirked.

He shrugged, "That's just the hybrid way."

"I've never...you know," her cheeks flushed.

"Shocker," he answered; Niah punched him in the arm playfully. "Do you want to?" he asked after a long moment.

She was silent, her cheeks burning brighter, "I do. Just not yet, not with just anyone."

"You're blushing." He grinned at the rosy flush across her cheeks.

"Shut up." He smiled and waited for her to continue, "I didn't mean what I said before, about not feeling anything for you."

His heart damn near stopped.

"Oh?"

She fiddled with a loose thread on her shirt, refusing to meet his gaze. Only Niah could stare down a massive rider without a weapon and still not be able to look *Fin* in the eye when trying to tell him something, "I do have feelings for you."

He wasn't sure he knew what true happiness was until the words fell from her mouth. He hooked a finger under her chin and tugged it so that she was looking up at him.

"Say it again."

She blinked and then smiled, "I have feelings for you." warmth spread through his entire body; his heart was about to explode, and his brain had stopped working altogether.

He brushed his lips against hers, a gentle touch. He'd leave it up to Niah to decide how far she wanted to go. She deepened the kiss, pulling him closer, a growl built in his throat; there was no holding back now.

He encircled her in his arms and pulled her into his lap as she tangled her fingers in his hair.

He could have died perfectly happy right there.

Fin pulled away just enough to whisper, "I don't want to do this with just anyone, not anymore."

"But I thought hybrids were polyamorous or non-monogamous?" Niah breathed against his lips.

"We are. We can't love like humans, but we still care deeply for some more than others. It might not be the same as the whole second half of my heart thing, but I feel something I never have before. So if you want to do all this with me, I want you to know I won't be doing anything with anyone else," he explained; his heart was racing, hammering so loud he could hear it pounding in his ears.

Fin had never been nervous about someone saying 'no' before. Niah searched his face, probably looking for a sign that he was joking.

"This sounds like you're proposing a very human relationship, except you know...without love," she grinned; he rolled his eyes, maybe she read too many human books.

"If that's what it sounds like, then I guess so," he trailed his fingers along her cheekbone, relishing when she leaned into the touch.

Niah leaned forward and pressed her lips to his once again, but pulled back, too quickly for Fin's liking.

"Why me?"

"You're brave and smart, the fiercest fighter I've ever seen, you're beautiful," he whispered against her jaw, "and I'm hoping that one day, not today or tomorrow or even the next day, just, one day, you'll tell me everything that goes on inside that pretty head of yours."

Her eyes guttered slightly, and he thought he'd said the wrong thing. "I want to," she whispered, "eventually, I will tell you."

It was all he could ask for, all he *would* ask for.

A grin spread across his face as he folded her into his arms, kissing her again, and again, and again.

She smiled against his lips, and he lost himself in the kiss. It wasn't love, not in the human sense. Yet he felt a warmth spread through his chest as she spoke the words he hadn't realised just how much he wanted to hear.

He thought he'd be fine if she said she didn't feel the same way, that it would be enough just to be her friend, and it would have been, if that's what she chose. But the feeling that bloomed in his chest when she said she felt the same way, was beyond his comprehension.

It might not last forever, but at that moment, forever would never be enough.

THE STORY CONTINUES
IN

CRIMSON DAWN

OUT NOW

Thank you so much for reading Until My Last Breath; if you want to stay updated with other projects I'm working on, then please follow me on TikTok @thatauthorsue

If you enjoyed this book, then please leave an honest review on Amazon/Goodreads/or any social media platform, and don't forget to tag me @thatauthorsue

Coming Soon:

The Demonic Convergence, Book Four:
Until The Ash Settles

The Forgotten Chronicles, Book One:
The Crucible